the AWAKENING ONES

ANGELICA CHRISTI

This book is published by Asherah Publishng

Copyright ©2018 by Angelica Christi

All rights reserved. Published in the United States. Registration Number TX 8-633-408. No part of this book may be reproduced or utilized in any form or by any means, electronic or mechanical, including photocopying, recording, or by any information storage and retrieval system, without permission in writing from the Publisher and author Angelica Christi.

ISBN: 9781794306813

Inquiries should be addressed through angelicachristi.com/contact or angelicachristicontact@gmail.com.

This book is a work of fiction. Names, characters, places, events, and incidents are the product of the Author's imagination or events that happened in Angelica Christi's life. Any resemblance to actual persons, living or dead, events, or locales are coincidental.

Revision 3-A

ACKNOWLEDGMENTS

Thank you to my dear friend Germaine Akin who was there for me when I most needed an Earth Angel.

To

The Awakening Ones

&

My Mom, who repeatedly encouraged
me to finish this book.

PREFACE

When I resumed writing *The Awakening Ones* for the final time on Christmas Eve 2017, planning to finish the manuscript I'd begun eighteen years prior, I did so through divine will and not my own. In the beginning, my objective, and prompting from the Divine, was to awaken humanity to their light and reveal the hidden truths and divine power each held within their own being, without the manipulation of society and religion. I believed I should write what I was witnessing through the pulse of creation and warn others of the chaotic and dangerous path humanity was taking that could lead to their demise, and that of the planet as we know it.

Almost every night since Christmas Eve 2017, the messages filled my mind in the early-morning hours and I immediately rose to capture whatever I could remember on my computer. I felt that if there were enough people like me, we could make others aware and change the outcome for millions of people. My mission was to assist those who had the ears to hear and the dedication to personal and spiritual transformation. This mission was not about saving the world "out there"; it was about understanding the soul through the inner world of possibilities.

But none of this could be done without my willingness to experience firsthand the highs, as well as the trials and tribulations, of human existence. Passing through the tests of initiation was important. The mind works diligently to deviate every soul from their journey into oneness. I fell into darkness many times during those eighteen years, yet each time, I discovered a deeper connection to my core self.

My writing was initially more detailed and factual. I predicted many events that came to pass during those years. But I deleted over three hundred pages because in this fast-paced, instant-gratification world, the language was too detailed, heady, and too many undisclosed events I felt our governments would have revealed to the public by now, were not. The facts became fiction.

I hope that as a novel infused with truth, my story will reach far more people—at least those who are ready to receive this information and dare to challenge their beliefs and break out of the powerful grip of fear and the obsession with materialism that causes the very stress most people want freedom from. Join me. This journey of awakening is a path anyone can embark on, and I would love your radiant light to reveal itself and bless the entire universe.

CHAPTER 1

The shadow of a man appeared. He stepped from the cave along a rocky path deep within the Himalayan Mountains. The snow loomed across the horizon, in stark contrast with the deep-azure sky. He paused to watch a majestic clouded snow leopard observing him from the entrance of a nearby cave. Their eyes locked. *What an exquisite creature*, he thought, watching her as she lay down on the rocks, unaffected by his presence.

His features looked different than in the past, and his unadorned clothes gave him the appearance of an ordinary man, which would prevent him from being sought out or recognized by those who couldn't see from the eyes of the soul. His presence, the energy that surrounded him, would be apparent to those filled with goodness.

He was tall and handsome, but not one who would attract undue attention. His skin bore witness to a life that involved a great deal of time in the outdoors. Although the sun and the elements had weathered his hands, children reached for them, desiring to be touched, and wild creatures did not scatter in his presence but grazed peacefully next to him as he sat in prayer.

It was difficult to tell his nationality, allowing him the ability to fit in, melting unnoticed into a multitude of countries like a chameleon. He had hoped that humanity would have arrived at the point of acceptance that would allow far more intermixed relationships, as they were all from the same source. Far too many people defined and judged others by their appearance, yet the diversity was what gave this planet its character and beauty.

With well-defined arms outstretched towards the vastness of the snow-covered peaks, the man filled his lungs with the crisp air and called out, *"It is time."*

It was time. How long this earth venture would continue to last was left up to his Beloved Creator. He came only as a humble servant to assist those who would be the new leaders, those who had contributed to protecting the earth and, most importantly, the commandment "Love your neighbor as thyself." This commandment included all of creation: humans, beasts, birds in the sky, all creatures were the breath of God, and the blessed Earth herself.

These were the ones who would be able to move with divine guidance and grace into the new world without the dark turmoil that likely would destroy the possibility of human life on the planet for eight hundred thousand years. Even those high officials, and those of extreme wealth, who built the underground cities, for the elite out of their greed and disregard for those they were meant to serve, would not survive.

Breathing deeply, he drank in the crisp air. He stood in awe at God's creative genius. Standing in the shadow of Mount Everest, between Pumori and Ama Dablam, his eyes sparkled as he took in the splendor of the Himalaya-Karakoram mountain ranges.

"Amazing. This beauty is God's Grace. This *is* God."

He was aware that the best time to trek was either pre-monsoon or post-monsoon. And that time was now. The journey down the mountains to Kathmandu would be the simple part. It was the trek from Kathmandu to Cairo that would take some time. He knew that the journey was also a part of the adventure.

He would visit places that he loved, meet with the Council of Nine, and touch people who had led lives of kindness, and those who had not. He loved them all regardless of their beliefs—Christian, Buddhist, Jewish, Hindu, Islamic, atheist, it didn't matter. All were brothers and sisters; all were cut from the same cloth from the Creator. Even those living in greed's dark shadow still had a chance if they took immediate and dramatic actions to alter their lives.

His thoughts focused on many who had walked with him over twenty centuries before. This reunion would be the first time since that unprecedented moment in history that they would be together on the earth all at the same time. At present, many of their lives were coming undone—or so they thought.

A gentle smile filled his face, and his eyes shone like sparks of sunlight off water.

"Don't be troubled. All is well. You will find me."

He had a great deal of territory to cover before meeting his beloved friends. Although he knew that none of them distinctly remembered, he was confident they would be there when he arrived.

Their dreams had already begun.

CHAPTER 2

"Come! We need to get him out of Jerusalem, now!" his companion urgently yelled.

But Jake knew there was nothing he could do or say to convince his determined friend to leave. "Stand quietly with me until he finishes. Don't draw more attention to the situation."

Jake's eyes were intensely focused on the commanding figure below, standing in the center of the mosaic stone floor, speaking to those who had gathered, as rays of light pierced through the opening between two columns and lit the floor below his feet. Jake's gaze broke and wandered to a small group of women who sat on the massive stone steps to the right of the speaker and who were intently focused on his every word.

One woman caught his eye; her posture and grace were that of royalty, yet the simplicity of her white garments revealed she was otherwise. Jake noted that the plain, simple cloth hung from her body as if it were liquid silk. He watched as her slender fingers tucked long strands of hair under the side of her semitransparent veil. Suddenly her eyes turned towards him as if she sensed the intrusion of his intense gaze. He was sure she blushed, and he could see her chest expand as she caught her breath. There was a flash of recognition as their eyes locked, but just as quickly, both looked away. Jake was embarrassed that she had noticed he had been staring at her, but at the same time, he realized that on some level, a brief yet familiar dialogue had passed between them.

His thoughts were interrupted when his companion yelled, "Let us go. He has angered the high priests. We must leave now!"

Jake took one last look at the graceful and striking woman before following quickly behind his companion's footsteps. Yes, he could feel the tension; the room felt as if it was about to emotionally explode. He sighed; this wasn't the first time.

"What the heck!" Jake yelled as he sat up and looked at the illuminated clock beside his bed: 4:44, the same time a similar vision had come to completion two nights before. "What's going on?" he demanded to the darkened room. "These dreams feel more like memories than just random dreams, so lucid, so real. *Too* real."

He listened for an answer. Silence. Dead silence.

CHAPTER 3

His eyes were red, intently focusing on her, and although she tried to scream, her voice produced no sound. He was just steps away from her, but he didn't move. Lisa froze with terror. His long, scale-like body was a hideous shade of green and red. His thornlike horns, forked tail, and clawed fingers were just like her Sunday school teacher had described.

At four years old, she had been warned of his presence in the world, and although Lisa prayed every night for protection, there he was, standing before her.

She had just woken in the night, frightened by another dream—a dream so real, and so recurrent, she felt like it was part of her waking life.

Lisa was on her way down the long, narrow flight of stairs to the kitchen for the comfort of a cup of tea when Satan blocked her passage. He stood on the landing, with only five steps between them. Never had she been so frightened. Again, she tried to scream, to no avail.

Suddenly, in her terror, she paused. There was something about his eyes—something that didn't equate to the rest of its terrifying form. The eyes were red and intense, but not evil or devious or frightening; they were moist and filled with great sorrow and a pleading to be understood.

Great kindness poured from them, telling her not to be afraid, that he wasn't evil but was only playing a part in the human drama. She stopped trying to scream. At that moment, Veronica walked down the hall and turned on the light. He was gone.

"Everything okay, friend?" Veronica asked. Veronica had crashed on Lisa's sofa. It was late when they finished studying, and she was too tired to head home.

"Yeah, just a bad dream," Lisa said, passing her encounter off as nothing, but she knew it wasn't a dream. It wasn't like other dreams she suffered through. Lisa had never told Veronica, or anyone, about the content of her dreams in more than a decade. She hadn't forgotten the look of disbelief on her mother's face when she told her about a visitation from Jesus when she was seven years old.

"I was just going to get a cup of tea," Lisa said. She steadied her breathing. *Not a word*, she thought. *I don't need her giving me the same look of disbelief my mother did.*

"Well, it's 5:00 a.m.," Veronica said. "Might as well make some strong coffee and start the day. We've got Professor Reynolds at 8:30." Veronica winked, but Lisa hardly even noticed.

"I don't drink coffee," Lisa replied as she sat at the small table.

"Still going to make you coffee. You look like you could use it," Veronica said as she grabbed the French press. If she hadn't been lost in her own thoughts, Lisa would have noticed that Veronica put double the grounds into the carafe.

She could not shake the image, nor the love pouring from Satan's sorrowful eyes—the one who had been manifested out of the human need to blame someone for their sorrows and ill choices.

Satan as evil was the last remnant of her childhood faith that clung on. Now she understood that everything was God in disguise, just as the compassionate eyes had told her on the stairwell.

"Earth to Lisa!" Veronica plopped a cup of extra-dark coffee in front of Lisa.

"Oh, sorry," Lisa said, grabbing the cup and breathing in the dark aroma. "And sorry I woke you up."

"You could repay me by telling me what your dreams are about— I'd take that. Like, are you being chased by some vampire or horrid monster?" Veronica shivered.

"I can't ever remember them," Lisa lied. She could remember every detail. "It's just the feeling when I wake up. Hard to shake, ya know."

"Dang, I was hoping for some juicy stories!" Veronica gulped her coffee down, which was more cream and sugar than coffee. "I'll make us another pot and maybe some eggs for breakfast?"

Lisa nodded.

After her second cup of coffee, she ate a well-intentioned but questionable breakfast. Despite Veronica's Italian heritage, she couldn't cook anything, except for the best vegetable lasagna Lisa had ever eaten. Still, her lack of ability didn't keep Veronica from cooking.

"Thanks for the eggs." Lisa picked up their plates and washed them, still unable to get the sad eyes out of her head. "I think I'll just head over to the university a little early today."

"Hey, mind if I hang out here until 8:00?" Veronica asked, followed by a yawn.

"Of course not, friend."

Lisa headed upstairs to get ready for school. She grabbed a fresh sweater and threw on the same pair of jeans she wore yesterday. She rushed downstairs, thinking, *I just need alone time to clear my head.*

Veronica was still in the kitchen, drinking coffee.

"Hey, Veronica," Lisa said, "make yourself at home. Feel free to raid the fridge. I'll catch you in class."

"Well, just remember, if you want to talk about it, I'm here." Veronica gave Lisa a smile. "But seriously, if not me, someone else, okay? You seem like you've had a lot on your mind. You've been quieter and more . . . distant than usual."

"Just school stress. Professor Reynold's class is really pushing me."

"Well, maybe you should stop by and talk to him then." Veronica winked at the mention of his name.

Lisa rolled her eyes and grabbed her bag.

Walking across campus to the library, Lisa was thinking about Professor Reynolds. Something about him told her he knew a lot more about the mysteries of life and creation than he was willing to reveal. Lisa's bewildering dreams were becoming more vivid.

And now she was being visited by the kindly devil himself.

"I know I need to talk to someone, but not Veronica. I can't risk my best friend thinking I'm crazy. Perhaps Professor Reynolds would be safe to share my experiences with," Lisa said, talking to herself, followed by a sigh. "But how do I broach the subject? Maybe the opportunity for private dialogue will come in the future. Until then, I will have to be content with discussions within the classroom."

Something stirred within her. "No," Lisa said quietly to herself, "I do not have a crush on Professor Reynolds as Veronica insists. That is so far from the truth!"

But the small voice within inquired, *Really?*

CHAPTER 4

Professor Reynolds threw down the newspaper he had been quoting from, concerning another political narrative creating distractions and pointing blame upon others, onto the podium. Putting his hands deep into his pockets, he strolled towards his students with a slight questioning shrug of his left shoulder. Monday mornings always presented a new question that would intrigue and sometimes haunt his students for the entire week, and often far beyond.

"So what is different?" He picked up the folded newspaper once again and shook it. "Aren't these the same headlines you have read your entire lives? Do they not resemble those of your parents' and grandparents'? Sure, they usually involve different people, different groups or situations, but isn't the core always the same? So why is that? Why do we spend so much time dwelling on our differences? Or past tragedies that we don't want, yet whose power of that negative energy manifests the same reality once again?"

Silence filled the space between his students and him. Jake realized it was a lot of information to digest on a Monday morning, so he allowed the silence to linger before repeating his question.

Several more moments passed before a throat cleared and a tentative voice from the back of the lecture hall replied.

"I'm guessing, regarding religion and politics," Mark said, "is because most people don't want to see beyond their own views. They don't want to confront their indoctrinated beliefs, so they protect themselves by hating those unlike themselves."

"Great observations, Mark, but . . . why do you believe that is so?" Professor Reynolds asked.

"Maybe they are scared of what they think they could lose, even if that struggle could bring about understanding or peace in the end." Mark shrugged.

He went silent for a moment before he continued. "This may be off subject, but the refusal to change seems to be linked to unfounded fears programmed in early childhood, such as religion. Or even the essential human need to survive by copying or blending in with family or peers. It doesn't help that we are living in a country that ceaselessly promotes obtaining endless stuff. And the only things people truly want, they can't seem to acquire, at least for long."

"And what do people want?" Jake raised his left brow as he posed the question to Mark.

Mark shifted his lean body in his chair and began tapping out an unrecognizable rhythm punctuating each word with his pencil. "Happiness, peace, and love."

Professor Reynolds' hands rested upon his hips but remained silent to give Mark the space to continue, as he sensed Mark had something more stirring within. Mark was a very reserved young man who stood about six foot three, with dark-brown wavy hair and thoughtful, hazel eyes. Ordinarily, he was reluctant to join the discussions, especially once the dialogue became passionate or intense.

Mark began speaking softly once again, causing his classmates to listen intently. "Well, my mum explained it this way. If you are not satisfied and grateful with what you have right now and you don't understand your connection to all humanity, you will always desire more in an attempt to fill that internal emptiness. Desire in itself is a merry-go-round that most people can't get off. It's such a temporary fix, yet they continue the same circular pattern of behavior, never realizing the metaphorical lessons."

Mark's comments lit a match in the room. As his students' expressions changed, Professor Reynolds could see the cogs turning in their heads.

"Yes!" Tony excitedly interjected. Tony was in his early thirties, having traveled the world before heading to college. He saw no reason to waste money on trying to figure it out at eighteen, so he used the cash to discover his passions through travel. Tony's wavy red hair was his trademark, and he wore it like a prized crown tilted to one side. His good nature and humor kept him on almost everyone's top-ten list.

Tony continued with his thought before any of the other students could interject. "Most people don't understand that happiness can't be satisfied out there. It's internal, and one can only feel it in the present moment. Being content in this moment is the secret, as well as not always wanting more and forgetting to be appreciative of what they already have."

"Seems you've experienced enough of life to get this. I'm impressed," said Professor Reynolds.

Then he turned his attention to Scott, a few seats over from Mark, who was mumbling under his breath. "Scott, is there something you want to add?"

Firing an accusing look towards Tony, Scott's posture was on the defensive. Raising his bulky body from his seat to make a point, he knocked his binder off his desk, which made him even more agitated. "Yeah, why not. Tony makes everything sound so easy when it isn't. It's damn hard. Being happy and appreciative in each moment when your life is not going great is almost impossible in a world that has made it clear that our value comes from what we achieve by comparing our abilities to the Kardashians. There is always one more bar to reach for."

"Hey, dude, Kardashians? Seriously? I didn't say it was easy. I just know how it works. No need to be all up in my face. The real issue at hand—you're not discussing. Why do we keep attempting to keep up with the Kardashians or whoever, when we know it doesn't make us happy or fix things?" Tony nonchalantly commented with a trace of disdain.

"This is a conversation, not personal accusations," Jake quickly cut them off, "so save your feud for after class."

"Professor Reynolds, Professor Reynolds," shot out the voice of Veronica, who possessed no concept of the word *timid* and was by far the most outspoken of his students.

"Veronica," Professor Reynolds responded, looking in her direction.

"Our beliefs are what we need to change," Veronica passionately proposed, "but most of us don't want to or just don't know how. Most people are stuck on the merry-go-round, as Mark put it, and they don't even realize they are repeating their same patterns over and over, no differently than a record stuck in a groove."

Veronica sat upright as she continued to speak. If she went on long, Professor Reynolds knew she would leap up and start pacing.

"What I can't understand is why people blame God for their misfortunes. I recently listened to a radio talk show where the woman declared, 'Why does a loving god allow these terrible wars to take place and these innocent women and children to be hurt or killed?' Can you believe it? Let us not forget that man created these wars, not God!"

Ben's broad smile filled his tan and freckled face. He slid slightly down in his chair as he turned and whispered to Veronica. "You don't suffer fools gladly, do ya? But don't worry, Veronica, karma is going to get them!"

Veronica whispered to Lisa, "If he weren't so damn spicy cute, I'd punch him."

"You never could resist those rugged outdoorsy ones." Lisa's sapphire-blue eyes flashed a knowing look at Veronica as she twisted her long platinum ponytail around her slender fingers.

"So are you saying, professor, that humankind has essentially stood emotionally stuck for two thousand years?" Mark surmised.

"Depends on how we look at it," Professor Reynolds said and then took a sip of water and placed it on a nearby desk. "If we compare our behavioral or spiritual growth to the lightning speed of technology of the last one hundred years, we are still infants and have progressed very little. If we view it from the 13.7 billion years when the universe began, the 'Big Bang,' and the 10.5 million years humankind has been on this planet in the form of a human, our process of behavioral learning is accelerating."

"Yeah, but don't you find it weird that our advanced technology, and *extensively* more than the public is aware of, didn't materialize until the Roswell ET crash in the 50's? Then . . . bam!" Ben threw out, mischievously squinting his eyes and raising his brow.

"Ben, I'm not dismissing what you are saying, but let's keep this as a theology class, okay?" Professor Reynolds was not ready to dive into those waters.

"Dang, I know you're familiar with a lot of what's going on behind the scenes, but sure, okay." Ben continued in a low voice, not wanting to give up on the possibility of a discussion. "Although, you know the Vatican is involved and behind a lot of the cover-ups, right?" Ben slouched down and sighed.

"Perhaps, and I am not opposed to discussing your suspicions outside of this room, but there is something far more important right now, and secret programs will only take us further from the urgency of what needs to be addressed at this moment." Professor Reynolds responded before pointing his finger towards Mark.

Mark pressed. "Professor Reynolds, I realize you are an optimist, but how can you be so certain when people behave so terribly with each other?"

"Honestly, I am not certain. We may not make it at the rate of destruction to our planet that we have created in the last one hundred years, and the earth may simply toss us off at some point. We may be progressing, but not as rapidly as the earth may need us to in order to keep sustaining us.

But what we do know is that one hundred thousand years ago, we entered the age of reason in the form of Neanderthal man and we progressed quite rapidly compared to our previous evolutionary patterns that took hundreds of thousands, and even millions upon millions, of years of progress from one phase of development to the next."

"Does that excuse man's inability to stop himself from throwing us into continual war?" Veronica's voice was demanding.

"No," Jake stated, "but we must remember that humankind has been at war for well over ten million years. The inherent nature to survive is the primordial law that flows through us. When we think of hatred, jealousy, and anger, these all stem from fundamental laws—herds fight for territory, and they fight for their mates, food, and shelter.

"We can't expect to throw away the very tools that helped us survive and evolve. As much as we would like to, we don't go suddenly from human to divine without going through a complete transformation. It shouldn't be too hard if we learn to live in present-moment awareness as the observer and not the person defending its egocentric fears invented by the mind.

"The issue of grave concern is that we are not spiritually growing at the same rate we are technically, and that spells disaster. I honestly don't believe we have much time left to turn our actions around."

The room was silent. Even Veronica, with her furrowed brow, was quiet.

"Let's get back to my question from last week. Would we crucify Jesus once again if he returned to rectify his original teachings?" Jake asked, reining in the off-topic conversation. "How would humanity treat him? If Jesus were here today, why would any Christian believe that he would ascend from a white cloud or desire to be recognized as anyone other than an ordinary man? Would Jesus not want to witness his followers 'walking their talk' and demonstrating his original teachings to all of humanity?"

Jake did not move, but his voice intensified. "My question to over a billion Catholics and Christians is, for what reason would Jesus come back if we don't honor or live the two fundamental truths he repeated over and over in story, in metaphor, and by example his entire life? Was his message not delivered in utter simplicity, not unlike the Tao Te Ching? Do those who exclude or denounce others unlike themselves believe that is the message Jesus came to convey?"

Professor Reynolds absently ran his fingers through the waves of his sandy-brown hair before continuing. "The law of evolution is desire. Although, identification with desire creates separation, and as long as we believe we are separate beings, we will suffer. According to Lao Tzu's teachings, if you see through your individual existence and recognize you are oneness, then you can contemplate the wonder of creation and not the limitations and boundaries that material desires create."

Lisa didn't hear a word he said until Veronica passed her a note: *Yep, like he said, <u>desire</u>. I caught that wistful Romeo and Juliet look in your eyes! "Oh, that I were a glove upon that hand that I might run my fingers through that gorgeous hair!"*

Lisa's pale skin couldn't hide the rush of blood filling her cheeks. Taking a deep breath, she crumpled Veronica's note and refocused on Professor Reynolds' dialogue.

"The world is being lacerated and dismantled by these personal and planetary wars, and at the same time, we are quite metaphysically alive, so how does humanity right its course to avoid imminent destruction?"

Professor Reynolds stopped and allowed the question to hang in the silence for a few moments before glancing at his watch. He had a few minutes left in class, but he was exhausted from wrestling with this question both in class and on his own. Professor Reynolds grabbed a piece of chalk and wrote a question on the board.

"We will continue this discussion next time. My query to you is," Jake said and pointed to the board, "how long are you willing to wait before taking responsibility for your thoughts and actions? Perhaps putting it off until tomorrow will be too late. Be the creator of your life, be the observer, observe yourself, and notice the patterns that play out in your everyday lives. You might be amazed at what you find. Take notes and report back. Until then, good day."

Professor Reynolds walked to his desk, wondering if he was pushing beyond acceptable teaching doctrine. The clarity and intensity of his dreams had alarmingly increased, reminding him of the importance of no longer treading lightly, so as not to offend parents, religious leaders, or religious groups.

His students sat in silence, and slowly they began gathering up their belongings.

Veronica turned towards Lisa as she placed her books in her knapsack and whispered, "Yo, didn't see that coming. Prof is getting more outspoken."

Lisa nodded in agreement. "I think it's good. We all need to start understanding how we are creating the lives we are living."

Ben chimed in. "He's right, you know, most people spend more time criticizing others than critiquing themselves and living a conscious life that reflects the power of their own words—heck, even when I realize what I am doing, I often do it anyway."

Scott interjected. "Are we not criticizing others for criticizing? Just saying."

They all looked at each other, knowing what he said was true.

Professor Reynolds pulled himself back into the present moment and wiped the sweat from his brow. The sunlit day was penetrating the lecture hall, and Jake felt that same urgency he experienced in his dream.

The core truth, the original teachings of Jesus, along with the hidden gospels needed to be exposed and made accessible to all people searching for answers, and Jake felt they had a right to know. It was time to reveal the deceptions that religious leaders had masterfully put in place to serve themselves.

He spoke to the empty room. "How much can I expose, and how far can I push and still have a job?" He took a deep breath, realizing he no longer had the luxury of caring about what the church or state thought of his teaching style. Time had run out, and humankind was on the brink of its destruction brought about not by a vengeful god—nor the influence of Satan, the Antichrist, or any other supposed outside source—but by humankind.

Jake opened his briefcase and placed a rare copy of the forbidden, unknown, and controversial manuscript from the archives of the Roman Vatican inside; he reflected upon his students, hoping he could reach them before his time as their professor ran out.

Hope surged as Jake's voice filled the hall with a low growl. "You religious leaders can no longer hide the secret teachings of humanity's true potential behind your cloaks, closed meetings, and locked rooms. You shouldn't be the only ones with documentation of the Creator's original plan. Karma, dear friends, is knocking on your door and demanding payment long overdue."

Grabbing his briefcase, he hastily left the hall.

CHAPTER 5

"This is ridiculous!" Jazz muttered to herself. "How many times is it going to take me to get this elixir correct?"

The morning was too crisp for her liking, and although she grumbled, she was determined to get the ratio right. The tincture was designed to ward off the increasing number of people getting Alzheimer's and to correctly feed the bodies' deficiencies due to a world full of vaccines, EMFs, pharmaceuticals, and pollution.

"How long can you taunt me? We have enough crazy people on this planet, and we don't need more running around forgetting things and getting lost!" Grabbing her wrap off an old iron chair, Jazz crossed the cold stone pavers of the solarium floor.

She took her fingers and swept back the sides of her long, wavy red hair and piled it up on the back of her head, sticking a twig through it to keep it in place. After the twig fell out for the second time, she quickly braided it instead.

The solarium was one of the two reasons she had initially bought the home. With its all-glass walls, except for the one wall constructed from old stone recycled from a farmhouse built in the 1400s, it was surrounded by beautiful fertile soil never farmed with chemicals. And of course, a well pumping pristine water—for what was the point of having an organic farm if watering it with city water and the multitude of toxic substances?

In the last few months, frustration presented itself more frequently for Jazz. Where had her peaceful, grounded, and confident demeanor gone? It was as though the more she tried to regain it, the more it eluded her.

In the dim morning light, Jazz thought about the shelves and cupboards extending to the top of the eleven-foot ceiling of the potion room filled with God's greatest gifts for self-healing; even Merlin would be in awe, but so few were interested.

People came to her for two reasons: love potions and desperation because their Western medicine wasn't working and it was a matter of life and death. Jazz would hold the antidote before them with strict instructions about how they had created the diseases in the first place and the importance of changing their lifestyle.

Each promised, but the minute they got well, they went back to their old ways, rarely following through with the balanced organic nutritional plan and lifestyle she had carefully outlined for them.

Jazz was not entirely against Western medicine. She felt they were exceptional at surgical procedures such as putting things back together after an accident, but as far as the human body and nutrition were concerned, forget it.

In frustration, Jazz tossed some herbs she had dried four days prior into a large mortar-stone bowl and began crushing the mixture with a matching pestle. "All I do is make excuses for why I should deal with sleeping mortals." Jazz sighed as she slumped down in a nearby chair.

Light filled the conservatory, shooting prismed rays across the worn wooden-planked table. *"Peace, dear one."*

"'Peace, dear one' is your answer to everything!" Jazz retorted. Suddenly she began sobbing and slid onto the cold stone ground. "I can't believe I agreed to help some of these folks. Why can't they see what the pharmaceutical companies are doing to them?"

A recent client's death had fueled her outburst. Together they had healed her of stage 4 colon cancer after doctors had given up on her.

They said Fay had tumors the size of grapefruits, and with not enough white blood T cells, she couldn't do chemo, and she wouldn't last more than a few months.

Jazz had changed this lovely woman with two young children to a wholly alkaline diet which included, organic therapeutic essential oils, herbs, and pure alkaline water, with strict orders of no sugar or animal products. Fay's "three months to live" became "no trace of cancer" when she visited her astonished medical doctor four months later.

Jazz had warned her not to go back to her old ways, which included excess sugar and negative or violent shows or news, including newspapers, which created anger and stress in her life. Her old ways fostered disease through over acidity in the body.

Jazz's warnings were unheeded, and four years later, the woman faced cancer again. This time, her husband suggested she should try "a new procedure" Western medicine was experimenting with. The woman died, and Jazz couldn't get over the loss even though she knew everyone had the freedom to choose.

The call from Fay's husband informing her of his wife's death came two days ago. He was crying.

There was nothing for Jazz to say to him besides expressing her sorrow; then she hung up the phone and wept. Surrender had been a harsh lesson for her this lifetime, and every time she thought she had mastered it, life demonstrated that she had not.

The light returned.

"Their 'stupidity,' as you so fondly put it, is what drives you, dear one."

"Drives me? It just makes me crazy!" she responded through her sobs.

"There is an herb in your garden for that," the light suggested.

Jazz stopped crying, stood up, and continued to crush the herbs. "Fine, I'll add some chamomile too!"

"*That would be lovely, dear.*"

"Lovely, right."

"*Dear one, do you always have to have the last word?*"

"Do you?"

Silence filled the room, but the light remained.

Jazz groaned. She knew she was acting childish. Her jade-green eyes flashed in the direction of her noble gray-and-white longhaired cat that often had twigs and herbs stuck to his fur. Smokey was lying on a stainless table among pots of catnip, lavender, and Helichrysum. He could always be found there in the early morning, as it was the first place that caught the morning sun.

Smokey looked up without emotion and stared unflinchingly at Jazz.

"Cats are so arrogant." Jazz winked at Smokey. "You have everything figured out, don't you?" Smokey's large green-and-yellow tinged eyes held fast.

"Don't look at me like that or I will take this blend of oils and add . . . I don't know, something that will make you disappear! I'm looking for a little comfort here. I don't need another critic!"

Jazz eyed Smokey once again, as his eyes were glued to her, and continued. "Really, Smokey, if they would only search their hearts, they would discover all the rare gifts this earth has to offer."

"Well, it's a lovely day, and I need to enjoy it," Jazz exclaimed as she threw open the glass doors to her garden and was greeted by a profusion of flowers and colors. She tossed back her long, loosely braided hair and looked back at Smokey as he rolled over on his back.

Smokey's marble eyes flashed a knowing look, and as the rays of sunlight hit the table, he rolled back onto his stomach and yawned as though he was bored with her discourse.

"Thanks for your support. No supper for you, now go catch some mice!"

Jazz came from Jasmine, which was the name given to her at the moment of birth, as her mother swore that the room immediately smelled of jasmine flowers. As a child, whenever her mother asked what she was doing, she always answered, "Merlin is teaching me how to make a new potion." Jazz wondered what kind of catastrophe it was going to take for people to wake up.

Smokey trailed closely behind, trying to be supportive; mice were not his favorite meal.

CHAPTER 6

Professor Jake Reynolds almost stumbled as he reached the last step that took him into the inner courtyard. He had caught sight of Lisa's long elegant strides as she hurried from the library across the campus lawns.

The early-morning sun played with the streaks of gold woven throughout her pale flaxen hair, rays bouncing with her every step. Instead of the simple ponytail she commonly wore, her hair hung loose, spilling across her shoulders to her mid-back. Her body moved in perfect rhythm, seemingly weightless like a cat gliding along the top rail of a wooden fence.

Jake nodded in response to Lisa's casual wave, noting the silver chains on her tiny wrists that contrasted with her long, slender fingers and the dimpled smile that lit her face. Dr. Reynolds' heart skipped more than one beat. "For God's sake, Jake, get a grip."

But he was secretly pleased; it was his class she was hurrying to attend.

Veronica, who was walking just steps behind Professor Reynolds, was the one Lisa had been waving to. Lisa blushed slightly at the mistake but went along with the pretense so as not to embarrass her theology professor. She also blushed because even though he was old, probably late thirties, she found him stimulating and attractive, and she had a strange sense of knowing him. None of it made sense to her, but it was there, some mystifying bond between them.

Veronica caught up with Lisa, giving her a playful poke. She raised one eyebrow and nodded her head in the direction of Professor Reynolds.

"Cut it out, Veronica," Lisa whispered.

"Oh, come on, Lisa, I've caught you staring at him many times. Anyway, he might be older, but he isn't ancient, and he *is* cute."

Lisa hoped the stern look she sent Veronica would put an end to her teasing. Veronica, on the other hand, wasn't in the mood to let it go. "Well you know what they say about older men."

"No, Veronica, I don't!"

Veronica laughed, tossing her heavy, dark Italian hair behind her tanned shoulders, which contrasted dramatically with Lisa's porcelain skin. "Well, for one, they have a lot more money than the guys we hang with! Two, they have much better manners. Three—"

"Stop!" Lisa replied wearily. "He's my professor, and he's wonderful. Don't ruin that for me."

Veronica gave Lisa another gentle nudge along with a flash of a smile. The glint in her eyes told Lisa it wasn't over; Veronica was just on pause.

CHAPTER 7

How far has humankind evolved in the last twenty centuries?

Professor Reynolds wrote the question across the board. Brushing his hands, he placed them on his hips and waited for answers.

"Jason," Jake pointed to the boy he knew was much more comfortable in a science lab.

"Well, Professor Reynolds, as far as man's love of war, greed, and killing, not much has changed. Society still hungers for the primordial need to conquer, dominate, and control. But as we previously discussed, technology, medicine, and science, has progressed quite far, I'm afraid."

"Why does that alarm you, Jason?"

"Because of our discussion a couple of weeks ago. You spoke of the need for humanity to find balance, to find the center, instead of swinging from one side of the pendulum to the other. Which, as you mentioned, keeps every generation repeating the mistakes of their grandparents.

"After your class, I talked with both my parents and grandparents. Both sets believed that by not repeating the mistakes of their parents, it would automatically make them better parents." Jason was hesitant but took a deep breath to speak again, but instead he suddenly paused.

Jake waited, to allow him to go on; he could see his peers were permitting Jason to continue. It wasn't so much what he was saying; it was that he was speaking—and this was the first time they had heard anything from the quiet figure in the far corner.

Jake felt that Jason's best friends were probably his microscope, test tubes, and a science lab. "Jason, please continue."

Jason looked down and thoughtfully studied both sides of his hands before continuing. "I guess I was curious because I realized I had planned to do the same with my own children—the opposite of what my parents did." Jason looked down again, as if he'd revealed more about himself than he had intended, and quickly murmured, "That is, if I have children."

Professor Reynolds noticed Jason's discomfort and diverted the attention from Jason to himself to break the spell.

"Class, how many of you did research into your family patterns?"

Dozens of hands shot up.

"Ben." Jake pointed dead center, "What example can you give us that made you realize you had the potential of copying an undesirable pattern of your parents'?"

Ben's deep voice was solemn. "Professor, I always hated how my dad was so hands-off, never giving me the direction I saw other dads giving their sons. Even when it came to college, he took the back seat. 'Take it or leave it, just go after what you love,' he'd say, and my mom was no better.

"I was angry, as I craved their direction, and all they ever said was, 'Just go after what you love.' I didn't know what that meant. I needed them to put me on the right path, and they refused. I thought that they honestly didn't care about me. Or worse, they thought I had no potential and wanted to spare my feelings."

Jake observed Ben's body language and realized there was more to share. The parenting style and a child's story around it was not an uncommon situation. "Ben, this is one of two predominate styles. Care to go on?"

Ben took a deep breath as he straightened his back and shoulders; power and certainty filled his voice. "I questioned my dad after your class. I will say it was difficult to approach him, as I had put up so many walls between us, but I needed to know, no matter the consequences, why he had refused to give me concrete guidance.

"First thing I questioned him about was how his father had felt about college. Suddenly my dad was filled with anger, not at me but at the memories. He told me that his dad tried to control every aspect of his life, what sports to compete in, what position he should strive for, what classes to take. My grandpa even told him who he needed to become." Ben paused.

Jake nodded, encouraging Ben to continue, as even Veronica was silent. He was moved that he and his students had created a deep, respectful bond with each other and were willing to put themselves out on a limb.

Ben continued. His voice became more profound and more serious, mimicking his father. "Your grandfather forced me into medicine. He would say, 'People will look up to you. You will make lots of money and be able to provide a better living than I could give you.' And putting his hand on my shoulder, he would say over and over, 'Make me proud, son, make me proud.'"

Ben's voice softened as he continued. "My dad said more, but heck, it was difficult to hear because I had never experienced that much emotion from him. He said that he realized his father would only be proud of him, and possibly love him, if he became a surgeon. Otherwise, he was destined to be a failure in his father's eyes. So he followed my grandpa's dream for him, secretly hating his profession his entire career."

"Wow," slipped out of Cole's mouth unexpectedly, and he softly whispered to Tony beside him, "He's talking my story!"

Ben continued as Jake's silence, as well as the eyes of his peers, encouraged him. "It blew my mind. I had no idea that being a surgeon wasn't my dad's chosen profession—he sure fooled me!

And then he said to me," Ben's voice broke slightly, "'Son, I wanted to make sure I never did to you what my father did to me. I promised myself in my third year of medical school that if I ever had a son, I would let him fly his own plane. I would let him soar the skies until he found his dream, and then and only then would I give him whatever it took to help him succeed, and I would be proud of him no matter what profession he chose.'"

By the time Ben's recollection came to an emotional halt, half the class was trying to contain their emotions. Somewhere in their souls, they could relate, to either the situation or the pain, or both.

Lisa had tears in her eyes, which she quietly and discreetly wiped away. But Veronica was audibly weeping, holding her heart with one hand and wiping her eyes with the other.

She turned to Lisa and said, "That could have been MY story!"

Lisa looked at her in disbelief. Lisa knew for a fact that it wasn't even close to Veronica's story.

Veronica saw the look on Lisa's face and replied, "Well if I had different parents, it could have been my story."

Veronica never bothered to worry about what others thought about her; she wore her feelings like a bright piece of clothing. Lisa admired that, as she was embarrassed when her emotions became the focus.

Thinking he would pull the class back together, Professor Reynolds asked the wrong question: "Ben, what did your father want to become?"

"He wanted to fly, Professor Reynolds. He wanted to be a pilot."

Veronica threw her head down in her arms and cried, loudly. "Fly," she kept repeating, "he wanted to fly. Instead, he was confined to the inside of a hospital. That is the saddest thing I have ever heard!"

Lisa's eyes widened at Veronica's theatrics, and she seriously doubted it was the saddest thing Veronica had ever heard, but that didn't stop Lisa from respecting how Veronica could express her emotions as she did.

Suddenly Veronica shot straight up. "Wait! There is still hope. He could become a flying doctor. You know, like doctors without borders!"

The entire class burst out laughing. Veronica's optimism turned the class from sadness to joy.

"O . . . K, now," Jake softly spoke to his class, "can we pull ourselves together?"

Professor Reynolds shook his head, and with a soft smile catching the corner of his lips, he said, "OK, it might be best to continue this discussion next time. In the meantime, work on your research project!" One thing Jake was sure of: teaching college students was never dull!

Jake did not notice the young mystery man with the piercing blue eyes slipping out from the back of his class; however, Veronica had.

CHAPTER 8

Veronica was Italian, and she was fire. Her pot called "life" was always boiling. She loved not only Italian opera but full moons and no moons, cathedrals filled with works of the renowned artists and philosophers, churches filled with candles, incense, statues of the saints, ancient architecture, Andrea Bocelli, Led Zeppelin, Beyoncé, the Stones, Hendrix—anything larger than life. Veronica was very intense. There were very few pauses in Veronica's life, making it difficult for others to keep up with her.

Veronica saw herself as the sleuth of humanity. She believed it was her job to dig up every injustice and every crime against society and expose it, just like her favorite writer, Oriana Fallaci. She didn't agree with everything Oriana wrote, but she was still her hero.

Besides, they were both Italian. And like Oriana, there was much more to Veronica than one would suspect.

Lisa and Veronica had met in Verona, Italy, at eighteen, right out of high school. Lisa, being uncertain of her life's direction, went to the place that had called to her heart for as long as she could remember. On a train from Verona to Rome, Lisa opened a first-class compartment door and asked the young man if any of the seats were available.

"This one is unoccupied!" He patted the seat right next to him, speaking in almost perfect English and flashing a big smile.

"How about this one?" Lisa managed to ask, pointing to the seat across from him.

"Sure, if you would rather gaze into my eyes."

Just then, a pretty Italian girl about Lisa's age barged into the compartment. "I apologize for anything my cousin Mario may have said. He's a moron when it comes to beautiful women. Actually, he's a moron when it comes to women in general!"

"'Ehi cugina, uncool!" Mario protested.

Extending her hand to Lisa, in her heavy Italian accent and without taking a breath, she continued. "Hi, I'm Veronica Valerio, and this is my cousin Mario Zeffirelli. Don't worry, he may be Italian, but he's harmless."

Lisa noted that had he been born hundreds of years earlier, he could have been one of the statues in the Vatican, carved in stone; he was that beautiful. Perhaps he had been. She realized she was staring and quickly looked away from his gorgeous and intense eyes with the long, slightly curled lashes.

The three became inseparable; they loved the same cities and the same food, art, architecture, famous people, and subjects. Veronica dragged a hesitant Lisa to Italian operas every chance she got.

It didn't take long for Lisa to become an enthusiastic fan. They sang down the streets of Rome, Milan, Venice, Naples, and Florence, and although Lisa made up half the words, she just followed along as Veronica belted out her version down Italy's cobblestone streets, where ancient walls gobbled it up.

Lisa loved that she could discuss religion, spirituality, and politics without having to be careful about what she said to her new Italian friends. Anything went—even her ideas about creation and "the plane between worlds," where each soul decides what they want to accomplish in their next lifetime and with whom they want to do it.

Veronica loved Lisa's perspective regarding this gap between lifetimes, and the choices and agreements one makes with other souls before coming into a human body.

"You know, Lisa, I never thought of life that way before, and it did seem strange to me, but the minute I saw you standing in the train compartment, I felt like I already knew you. I love the idea that we made agreements with our friends to meet again on earth as aides and companions before we were reborn!"

Although Veronica was Catholic, she believed in reincarnation and birth control, and didn't buy into telling a priest her "sins," or that ten Hail Marys after confession would erase her misdeeds.

"Reincarnation, it's the only thing that makes sense." Veronica exclaimed, "What a ridiculous thought that some people are more privileged than others, that some were born to drug addicts or into poverty and others into wealth. The 'one chance' thing makes no sense! Anyway, there are several references to reincarnation in the Bible, at least five. I figure those who altered the Bible to suit their motives couldn't figure out how to remove the references without messing up the entire context.

"Even Voltaire, the French philosopher, said, 'I don't find it any more surprising to have been born many times than being born once.' No kidding, right! I once read that the early church didn't think it was wise to allow people to believe they had more than one chance to get it right, so they removed all the references in the early writings after the third century. But karma and reincarnation make perfect sense, especially if you believe in a loving and fair God—which I do! I mean, think about it, if you were someone horrid in a past life, like a Hitler, you can't expect to come back living an idyllic life! There is a price to pay for that behavior! Right!"

Lisa's eyes were wide in disbelief, not because of what Veronica said but because of her ability to talk without taking a breath.

"Exactly," Lisa replied, inhaling deeply on Veronica's behalf.

When Lisa's four months came to a teary end, the two made a pact not to lose track of each other—ever.

To stop the flood of tears, Veronica responded, "Well since we were able to find each other this lifetime on planet earth, I think I can find you in the United States. Don't worry, I think it will be sooner than we know!"

Even Mario was having trouble keeping his composure. He had fallen head over heels for Lisa, and if it hadn't been for Veronica's protectiveness of her new friend and warning Lisa to beware of Italian men, he would have made a move to win her heart.

Mario hoped that someday he would have another chance to get to know Lisa on more intimate terms, but after she had shared stories of some of her experiences with Italian men before the three had met, he was not so confident.

"Damn Italian men, why do we have to flirt as we do?" had been his reply when Lisa recounted the stories of men pinching her all through Rome and the man who had dropped his trousers on the street just blocks from the Spanish Steps. Of course, he and Veronica had laughed so hard they literally fell off the coping surrounding the fountain where the three had been seated, eating gelato, and rolled on the ground with both tourists and locals looking on in amusement.

Having licked the dripping ice cream off her fingers, Lisa described her story to them. "I had been walking down the streets of Rome with a woman I met in Paris. We were heading to the Spanish Steps when an Italian man a short distance behind us yelled.

"When we turned around, he dropped his pants. He wasn't wearing any underwear. My new friend Pam stood with her mouth hanging open, but for whatever reason, I found it ridiculously funny and began to laugh, holding my thumb and index finger just an inch apart, repeatedly yelling, 'Petit! Petit!' With this, the man turned a deep shade of red and quickly pulled up his pants as he ran in the opposite direction!"

When my friend Pam regained her speech, she asked, "Was he small?"

"'I don't know' was my response," Lisa stated. "It's the first thing that came to mind! Thank God we'd just come from Paris!"

Pam and Lisa had laughed the rest of the way to the Spanish Steps, and every time either one of them saw an Italian man even touch the top of his trousers, they looked at each other and burst out laughing.

Mario knew that Lisa had permanently scarred the guy's fragile ego, but then, he had deserved it.

CHAPTER 9

Angelina could hear the church bells ringing in the distance as some ancient memory stirred and called to her soul. London's early-morning fog wove its way across the sleeping city as she slipped on her silk-brocade robe and walked towards the panels of antique glass and iron doors that extended across the entire east wall. Pushing back the sheer drapes, Angelina grabbed both levers and pulled them open.

"Still bloody cold," she mumbled as she stepped onto the small balcony with pink and white geraniums cascading over the eighteenth-century hand-forged iron railing attached to the limestone façade.

Angelina looked at the park below and thought back to the quote from Henry David Thoreau she had read the night before: "Go confidently in the direction of your dreams. Live the life you have imagined." That was precisely what she had yearned to do for years, but somehow the distractions of everyday life had gotten in the way.

Angelina was a woman of extraordinary vision and healing powers, and she faced life and her fears with considerable courage and determination. She knew truth when spoken and had a unique internal monitor to decipher fact from fiction in an instant—except when it came to her husband.

Still, she held herself with such grace and displayed deep compassion for others, reminding them of their oneness with their Creator and not the separateness the church tried to instill in them.

Even as a small child, she had pledged to serve God, serve truth, regardless of what others said or the obstacles she encountered. She often felt life was tugging at her as if she'd forgotten something significant that she came to do, and this troubled her greatly.

As she stepped back inside, she did not close the doors, although the morning air was still crisp and damp. Lost in thought, she crossed the room and picked up the notes lying on the bedside table before sitting cross-legged in the heavily carved baroque chair covered in ice-blue mohair mimicking the color of her soft, wide eyes that balanced the fullness of her lips.

Pushing back the silky waves of her golden-brown hair that cascaded down to her waist, Angelina absently glanced at the notebook upon her lap.

As she lifted the pages, she caught sight of her reflection in a stately ornate mirror leaning against the wall. She sighed as she examined the face that was pale and drawn from too little sleep. She had been unaware of the weight she had lost until she noticed her wedding ring hanging loosely on her finger.

Was it a metaphor for her marriage, which also no longer fit? She put the notebook down and stroked her arms, just to be touched; it had been so long since there had been any real affection within her marriage. He always had excuses or had fallen asleep before she got into bed, and finally, she got up the courage to ask him straight away if he was shagging his assistant.

Angelina had noticed, on more than one company holiday, how Diana had watched him when she wasn't aware Angelina was observing her. Her husband acted shocked that she would suggest such a thing, even when she got back to the hotel early and almost ran into Diana leaving their suite. Diana was quick to recover: "Cheerio, Angelina, I just popped by for a quick visit and to see your lovely suite, but now I've got to dash." Angelina felt sick, realizing that she no longer trusted her husband.

She sighed and looked into the mirror once again. Absent was the charismatic and self-assured woman she remembered; there was now a frailness that reminded her of her mother.

"Are you truly only forty-six?" Angelina whispered to the bewildered image staring back at her. "How is it I feel so old? And when will I know what is going on with all these dreams that feel so familiar? Perhaps my husband is right—could I be going crazy?"

Angelina was not ready to read what she had written regarding last night's dream, for she knew that soon enough she would be forced to make a choice that would shatter the luxurious life she now lived. It wasn't about the wealth; it was the unknown that haunted her, this missing piece yet to be discovered. She flipped to the front of her journal and began rereading the first of many dreams that started several months prior.

Her hands spread across her chest as the energy of the words resurfaced, and the swell of stinging tears gripped and tore at her heart.

The woman in the dream was trying to hold on to the hand of the man she loved dearly. Her heart was breaking as she glanced down at the dusty, dry dirt upon the road, so as not to look into the eyes that were shredding her heart. Her grip tightened on his hand as she tried to keep up with him, but the man would not be detained and continued to walk briskly to his destination.

He stopped only for a brief moment, and with his gray-blue eyes piercing her soul, he said, "Beloved, do not try to convince me otherwise. It has been written. It is 'The Agreement,' an integral piece of the Original Design."

The woman put her head in her hands and cried. And when she looked up, the man in the scarlet robe was gone.

CHAPTER 10

All of Andrew's worldly acquisitions and accomplishments were worn like badges across his chest. He was never even remotely affected by those who labeled him negatively.

One of his secretaries had read him a line written by a notable journalist: "At what price to others does Andrew Turner's extreme greed, an outright insatiable mental addiction to power, come?"

He brushed it off with a laugh. His secretary quit the next day. Without a blink, he called HR to get another. At the moment, he had seven, and one bleeding heart was one more than he wanted. He believed his victories to be proof of his worthiness and justification for his extreme wealth, the praise of others, the ability to call anyone in power—including the president of the United States—at a whim, and the affections of any woman he desired. Andrew knew he was envied by most, for he had it all, including being a handsome man of six two who was fit with hazel eyes and dark-brown hair.

With each new triumph, his ego was fed and deliciously satisfied, at least for the moment. He smiled, knowing that even his wealthiest friends envied his success—his multiple estates all over the world, private luxury planes, yachts, and limos. Each estate consisted of wardrobes the size of the average person's home, filled with the finest handmade garments, shoes, and accessories, which was further proof to him that he was a remarkably accomplished man.

He ignored panhandlers and those lying on the streets in the early morning. "Not my problem, get a job, you bum," he would remark if they reached towards him, asking for money or food, as he walked from his chauffeured limo to grab a coffee and a newspaper. Glancing at his Patek Philippe platinum watch, which he felt was a wardrobe essential, he quickened his step. "Big merger today, it's going to be a great day—again," he gloated.

This was not a necessity, Andrew getting his own coffee and paper, as all could be easily arranged by his staff, but it was a simple morning pleasure. He also loved to stride the half block to view the top ten floors of the glass-and-steel skyscraper that belonged to his company, and the floor at the top consisting of his private office and personal staff.

The shattering of Andrew's ego came not from a life-threatening disease, a colossal crash of the stock market, loss of his possessions through indictment, or some other financial catastrophe but from something far more terrifying to him, something he could not control.

He had been visiting one of his homes, located on a private island, just casually sitting on some rocks overlooking the ocean glimmering like diamonds from the rays of the sunlight, with his morning coffee, when suddenly the diamond sparks gathered like a great bird hovering just a few feet above the water and turned towards him.

Stunned, he dropped his mug as he heard the words: *"Why are you destroying my majestic and precious earth? For in the end, although she will barely survive, you will die a long and tragic death from the very chemicals you have so richly profited from. Do you not remember who you are?"*

Deep inside, something ancient broke open and a deafening explosion erupted within his mind. Sitting transfixed, Andrew watched a movie playing upon a screen, yet it was not outside himself; it was within his being. Moments later, a crippling and overwhelming soul remembrance took him to his knees; sweat began exuding from his pores, and he begged through his tears and sobs of gratitude to be reunited with this light.

"Please, I beg you, Lord, take whatever you want, even my life. It no longer matters. I now recognize the obsession with wealth and power has been only a pacifier to this deeper yearning that had been locked securely inside me!"

Within moments, the bird flew above him and ignited every cell of his being with a golden diamond light before vanishing into the rays of the sun's morning light.

Andrew woke hours later, lying below the same spot the bird had hovered, feeling a profound sense of deep rest and peace he had never experienced before. He knew precisely what he needed to do with his life and was confident that whatever questions might arise, the answers would be provided.

Andrew began reciting broken pieces of a song as he walked towards the house. "When you love someone…you take them into your heart…and that is surely why it hurts so much when we lose someone we love, because we lose a part of ourselves."

Andrew's grief had been so profound at the loss of his Lord that, lifetime after lifetime, he had searched for his teacher. Finally, in his darkest hour, he had abandoned his soul but now, again, was united through the grace of God.

CHAPTER 11

The next morning, Jake stood in his sunlit kitchen and poured himself a cup of coffee. His daily limit was two, both consumed in the morning. It wasn't so much that he needed it; it was the alluring aroma that hooked him.

He loved the morning light filling his kitchen, and thoughts of yesterday's conversations and the response of the woman Veronica heard on the radio talk show concerning why a loving God would allow humankind to suffer filled his mind.

As he glanced out of the French doors leading to his lush gardens, he watched in amazement as a tiny blue, green, and pink hummingbird hovered above a bright-pink daylily in the Italian terra cotta urn beside his door.

Neither Veronica's conversation nor the distraction of the hummingbird was what had been on his mind; he had been troubled by another dream he had during the night. Once again, it was playing out in the same time period of history as the others, thousands of years ago. He realized he couldn't avoid it, as it wasn't going to be readily forgotten. Grabbing his coffee, he strolled into his garden. It was his sanctuary, and he went there often to sort life out or to feel nurtured.

Sitting peacefully between two majestic maple trees, he allowed the night's lucid dream to fill his thoughts. With a deep breath, he closed his eyes and could see it vividly playing out as precisely as if on auto rewind.

The sky was suddenly filled with dark, forbidding clouds, whipping up the waters beneath them.

They were rowing against the wind towards Capernaum, and a furious squall arose quickly without warning. Jake knew they were all tired, and it had already been a long and eventful day among thousands who had followed his friend from surrounding towns to hear him speak.

The waves were getting stronger, and as the waves broke over the boat, Jake could feel the deafening wind and spray against his face making it difficult to stand or see. He became frightened and began calling out the name Peter, but his words dissipated in the wind. Their boat was being tossed about with such violent furry. He could feel the apprehension and see the fear in his companions' eyes and realized that he was not the only one frightened; this was not reassuring.

Suddenly, out of nowhere, came a great light upon the water, and he could hear a voice clearly over the stormy winds: "Do not be afraid." And just as suddenly as the winds had come up, the winds ceased and the sea calmed.

Once again, Jake awoke confused and anxious, wiping off seawater from his face, which wasn't there.

As Jake walked back to his newspaper with his newly filled cup, he couldn't comprehend the message of the dream, only that it was another of what was becoming a more frequent occurrence. "What did it all mean?" was the only question he knew to ask.

When no answer came, he changed his focus to the earlier discussion, asking out loud to the empty room, "Why did humankind believe that a loving God wouldn't allow atrocities to happen? Was free will not a part of the gift of our life? Did we not have to take responsibility for our transgressions?"

Jake raised one brow as he took another sip of the rich blend of coffee cradled in his hands. Humanity always became defensive and hardened their hearts when they didn't want the real answers to their many questions. Perhaps they just weren't ready, for the answer always pointed to their particular failures, not God's.

He announced to his dog, Zoe, lying on his forbidden chair, who wasn't paying attention except for the occasional one-eyed glance, "If God is all good, how come evil exists in the world at all?"

The sun's light intensified, or perhaps it was the light within, but the words were laser cut into Jake's memory. *"It's that way because you choose to believe it's that way. It's that simple."*

The light faded, and Jake looked at his mug. Choices. Life is all about our unique options. "God, I love when you do that!" Jake spoke out loud with more of a sigh than an affirmation, and this time, Zoe didn't even raise an eye.

"You too will do these things and even greater," the voice of his master teacher, Jesus, had echoed throughout his life. It was a promise, not an unobtainable or remote possibility but a guarantee in which Jake believed to the core of his being.

Jake thought about the topic of spiritual leaders and gurus he had enjoyed the week before. Rose had mentioned that Jesus never intended to be, nor did he ever want to be, considered a guru.

"Jesus saw all of humanity as equals, each a divine reflection of God, and resisted any title that suggested he was to be bowed to or treated as superior. Jesus demonstrated this often, including washing the feet of others, which normally was performed by a servant. He would find the role of guru, as well as the churches' pompous hierarchy, unequivocally appalling," Rose had offered with absolute conviction as if she had heard the words spoken directly from the master's mouth.

Rose was one of the gentlest ladies Jake had ever met. A graceful and slender woman with compassionate brown eyes and ebony skin that glowed with light. She didn't speak much, but when she did, it was with calm clarity and certainty, and with such sweetness that no one contradicted her.

Jake wholeheartedly agreed with her; Jesus did not need any decorations, such as spiritual labels or titles. There was nothing in him that felt inadequate, and everything he did was with great humility.

Briefly contemplating whether his role as a teacher was enough, and how he would find the mysterious nun who unknowingly in her rush to catch the awaiting taxi, had dropped the manuscript that now rested in his briefcase titled, *'The Lost Gospels of John'* written in ancient Aramaic. He had called out to her, as he raised the sheep-skin bound manuscript and was taken back by the look of terror on her face as she quickly shut the taxicab door.

That night Jake skimmed the manuscript until 3:00 a.m. He was blown away. Not knowing if he should laugh or cry at the wealth of information that was mysteriously bestow upon him. He wanted to know more about Yeshua's training with the Essenes, his missing years, and the chapters on the healing powers of the elements, called Angels. As he turned the last page of the section written in Aramaic, the first person he thought of to discuss the manuscript with was Rose. He also questioned why Rose was taking his class; she certainly didn't appear to need his direction and at times he felt she was the one that should be the teacher.

Jake shook his head and suddenly hit the newspaper with the back side of his hand and spoke out loud, "I wonder what percentage of our energy is lost each day by buying into blame, shame, hatred, anger, fear, and other people's stuff?"

Locating his keys in his blazer and then checking his watch, Jake picked up his step with the slam of the front door. His heartbeat jumped as he eyed the new deep-silver Mercedes convertible pulling out of his neighbor's driveway. An audible sigh escaped before he turned his attention to the ecology-conscious Prius parked in front of his home.

Jake shrugged. "Choices. It's all about choices."

As he listened to the Mercedes purr down the street, an image came to his mind. "Lisa," Jake said out loud before he could stop himself. Anger welled inside him.

"Don't be a jerk, Jake—don't even go there!"

CHAPTER 12

At the same instant Jake posed his question regarding wasted energy, a young man was running for his life through a dilapidated war-torn alley. Makeen had just witnessed the brutal murder of his older brother Ra'ed. His hardened face produced no tears as his lean but powerful body swiftly ran to the home of his mother.

His desire for retaliation blocked all rationale from his mind. Pain's bitter taste filled his throat. He swallowed hard, trying to remove it and, at the same time, forcing down any feelings that were trying to surface other than those screaming for justice. His need to protect his family, those who were left, was what fueled every muscle in his twenty-year-old body as he ran from one war-torn street to the next.

Makeen's rage at life's injustices saturated every fiber within. When he slammed his body through the back door of his family home, his wild dark eyes told his mother everything she needed to know. Najwa was standing there holding a knife she'd been using to cut vegetables for her family's evening meal. For a moment, they stood staring at each other in silence. Horror filled the air between them. Then, without a word, she slumped to the floor and wept.

Najwa's heart knew there was still more personal tragedy she had to undergo. Her pain of another child lost—another son, one she had lovingly named Ra'ed. *Ra'ed* meant "leader." Hope had filled her long ago as she held the tiny infant in her arms. And now he had been taken away. She wasn't sure how much more pain she could endure.

Bitterness erupted from her grief. "If women ruled the world, there would be fewer wars or no wars," she wailed. "A good woman would never send her child out to be slaughtered!" She believed a woman, or a man fully in his heart, would find solutions. Just like when her children fought—she strived to teach her beloveds how to work out their differences.

"Why don't women rule the world?" she repeated, pounding the floor with her fist. "Would any of this be happening?" Abruptly Najwa's sobs stopped. Now she feared for her daughter, Alea, and her only living son, the one who stood before her with death's shadow filling his eyes.

"Makeen, please," she begged, quickly coming to her feet and throwing her hands towards him. "Retaliation will only buy you a grave!" But Makeen was already heading towards the place his brother had directed him, in the event anything should happen to him.

Najwa stood helplessly in the doorway. It didn't seem that long ago she had held such hopes for her family's future. She had longed for a life that would include freedom, not their demise by a sadistic dictator who had choked the life from her country since 1979, when Saddam Hussein declared himself the actual ruler of Iraq.

Saddam was the same dictator who had taken the life of her husband. She had begged him to be silent, hearing whispered stories of the violence this dictator performed to those who challenged or opposed him. She also knew her husband was right: if their sons, and especially their daughter, were to have a chance at freedom, Iraq's leader must be eliminated to create justice.

Once, the hope for liberty briefly filled the air, freedom that Najwa and her daughter Alea had once spoken secretly about, with America coming to their aid. But one horrific incident after another had taken place.

Thousands of civilians were killed, not only by Hussein's militant group and other opposing groups but by U.S.-led military intervention, including misdirected drones. Terror and torture filled their world. When America killed Hussein in 2006, it was not the end of needless killing; one militant group after another continued the bloodshed.

The secret hope that Najwa and Alea had shared for America to free them had instead turned into a death warrant for her son Ra'ed. Ra'ed was only twenty-five. Holding her stomach and her heart, she wept in confusion, grief, and bitterness.

She called to her god and to the great prophet Muhammad. "Allah, Muhammad, help us! What should I do?"

If God or Muhammad had answered her, she was unaware, for just then, a powerful blast shook her home.

If Makeen could tear his heart out with his own hands, he gladly would—anything to stop the excruciating pain. As he stood in shock, staring at the rubble before him, his grief crippled him, and he fell upon his knees onto the bloody ground littered with debris from the home he'd lived in since birth.

"Muhammad, Muhammad, take me, take me!"

Only moments before, he had run from his mother's kitchen to the outbuilding that housed their few remaining livestock. Pushing back the boxes covering a hidden door below, he yanked it open and grabbed three rifles and a box of grenades. Blinded by his rage and fury for his brother's death, Makeen ran from the building, bent on retaliation.

"Ra'ed, I will make them pay!" he yelled as he tore into the center courtyard. "I will avenge you!"

As Makeen ran, one of the rifles began to slip, and then another. He swiftly reached down to grab them and tripped, but as he did, the box of grenades began to fall. He wildly grabbed out. Something caught on his middle finger.

The next seconds played out in slow motion; there was nothing he could do to stop the chain of events but watch in horror.

It was then that he realized a grenade was rolling quickly towards the open doorway where his mother was standing. He looked down in shock at the pin hanging from his finger.

"Mama, run!"

For one fraction of a second, their astonished eyes met. Then it was over.

"Muhammad, take me, take me, and let me be done with this life!" he yelled, wailing in pain, to an unresponsive God.

As he crawled on his knees to his mother, his torturous sobs increased. He gathered up her remains and wept into her warm and bloody bosom. He could not bear to live a moment longer with this torment.

"Forgive me! Forgive me!" he wept.

In the void of Makeen's sobs came a soft and gentle voice:

"Then you must forgive all others."

CHAPTER 13

José crossed himself with the crucifix at the end of his rosary and whispered, "Madonna, la Madre más Hermosa, ayúdame." Father José Cruz stood before the time-worn statue of Mary, mother of Jesus, and rested his hand on her feet, stained and polished by the thousands of hands that had prayed to her for over three hundred years. At times, her eyes felt alive as she gazed upon him with a sweet smile on her lips. She was the adoring mother, the mother who could see only the goodness in her children.

"Forgive me, dear mother, I am not worthy to stand at your feet." Father José Cruz crossed himself once again before he abruptly turned and left the cathedral. As he passed the central courtyard, his pace quickened, so as not to give himself a chance to reconsider.

Sweat was accumulating across his brow, but José paid no attention. It was now or never. He would have preferred never, but the dreams would not allow him any peace, of this he was sure. With his core beliefs shaken, all he knew and lived for began to come apart like a giant ball of string unraveling as it rolled down a steep mountainside, and no matter how fast he tried to run to stop it, he could not.

Last night's dream was still playing vividly in his mind, and a shudder raced through him.

"José, José, why do you not trust me? I have never led you astray."

The voice was becoming louder since its first emergence many months before, when just a faint whisper had interrupted his sleep. At first, José thought it was the devil that was tempting him to question his beliefs, but as the dreams progressed, his soul recognized the sound of truth, and he began to examine the ways of the church for the first time in his life.

The rules, the rituals, the restrictions of the Catholic Church had once comforted him, providing him with a sense of security he had never felt as a child. As a boy, he had witnessed poverty, cruelty, and a father who prayed only to the bottle of tequila permanently at his side.

And now he was being asked to take an enormous leap of faith for this mysterious journey and give up the security of monastery living. It was the first time since he was a young man that he was frightened, frightened like the seven-year-old boy who saw his father push his mother down a flight of stairs in a fit of drunken rage. Their eyes had met, and the message was clear: what he witnessed was never to be spoken of to another soul. He knew that his demise would be the price for a breach of silence.

José grabbed his small leather suitcase, looked briefly back without stopping, and began to run. He cleared the abbey grounds and was just beyond its walls when a lifetime of suppressed emotions snapped like a taut rubber band. José fell to his knees and sobbed like a wailing animal caught in an iron trap—it was the first time he had shed a tear since the moments before he had witnessed his mother's death.

He fell into a deep sleep, and when he awoke, his hair and cloaks were damp—either by his tears or from the dampness of the ground he found himself lying upon. But this time, it didn't matter, for as he spilled the pain of all those troubling years upon the earth, a great light had come to sit beside him and stroked his brow.

"*José, José, the light of God is upon you. Peace be with you, dearest friend.*"

José picked himself up, dusted off his garments, gathered his bag, and began to walk with fresh hope filling his heart, and at that moment, the past was swept away like morning ashes from a night's fire.

"I am coming, dear friend. Wait for me."

That night, José found a stable to rest in. He had intended to travel to a small town a few miles farther away and get a room, but he knew he would never make it. Exhaustion had caught up with him. Looking to the heavens, he whispered, "Dear Lord, please help me find a spot to rest." It seemed to appear out of nowhere—a lantern hung off the side of a small building in the near distance. José knew it was a sign from God and followed the light.

Although the wind had been sharp, the stable was warm and the straw fresh. He gratefully kneeled and prayed of his profound gratitude and his unyielding trust of God. He no sooner had put his head down on his blanket than he fell asleep.

"*Beloved, what is your wish? What thoughts rest so heavy upon you?*" José said with deep love and concern.

"*Those very humans who say they love and honor me also resent and fear me. It is time for the old structures to fall apart, for all churches and religious leaders to reveal my true teachings. They cannot hold my people captive much longer, or severe events will plunge the world into darkness.*"

José could no longer hear the sound of the ocean as it churned. All he could hear was the dire warning of his Lord.

"*Humanity says they fight for peace, yet one cannot fight for peace. Humanity says they love me, but all the while, they are intolerant of another. Humankind stands on the hallowed ground of the blessed feminine, yet they poison her daily, as they defile their sacred bodies. They cannot love what they so despise—themselves.*"

The wave now crashed against the shore as if punctuating the statement.

"*My brothers and sisters are afraid of themselves, and this reflects in how they fear each other and the world they have created. This greatly* saddens me, as it is my teaching they do not trust, set by example by how I lived my life.

"Continue to be loving and strong, José. Teach others what you know to be right in your heart, and walk your talk without trepidation. We will be together soon, my friend."

Just then, an unsuspecting wave threw itself against the shore, nearly knocking José to his knees. He went to grab the arm of the one beside him, but he was gone.

The dream shattered and José awoke with a jolt.

He felt newly born and filled with peaceful joy.

José had one crucial stop before continuing his journey. All his life, he had wanted to stand before the miraculous image of Our Lady of Guadalupe in Mexico City. Over and over, José would repeat the words: "Virgen de Guadalupe, please allow me to stand in the glory of your blessed presence." Father Miguel had told him it was unlike any other apparition of the Blessed Mother. Not only was it not made by human hands, but the image showed that she was with child. Father Miguel said he wept and saw the Blessed Mother filling him with a golden-pink light that had never left him.

More than life, José wanted that same experience, and he would do whatever it took to pay his respects. Perhaps he would be blessed as Father Miguel was. He also knew, even if the rest of his journey didn't go well, he would die a happy man.

There was also the matter of a scroll that appeared in his dream. He must trust that the location of the scripture would be revealed and tell him the next step of his journey.

CHAPTER 14

Professor Reynolds began writing on the board the moment he entered his classroom. Finding his sports jacket confining, he quickly pulled it off and threw it on the back of his chair. His students shot glances at each other—they had seen this behavior before. Their posture straightened, and they were suddenly awake, when only moments before, some were still half asleep.

Jake was trying to distract himself by focusing on a previous discussion that he had no intention of presenting until the reality of the letter Dean Mitchell presented to him rested in his hand.

He had received a call from Mitchell to stop by his office before heading to class. When he arrived, he was handed an envelope sealed with the coat of arms of Vatican City. Dean Mitchell looked questioningly at Jake.

"Haven't a clue," Jake responded as he took the envelope and quickly left the office. The dread in the pit of his stomach told him that he did know and that the letter had something to do with the extracted chapters of Angels, Mary of Magdalena, the lost years, and both Marys training in healing and sacred oils, from the *Gospel of John*.

Jake opened the letter in the hallway before entering his classroom. He didn't appreciate the tone and spoke out loud in a soft voice. "I certainly have no intention of accepting an audience with this group of cardinals. It is apparent that they only want to retrieve the manuscript and silence me, and I don't take kindly to their threats."

"Hey, professor, you okay?" Tony said seeing the scowl on Jake's face as he walked up behind him.

"Yes, thanks." Jake slipped the letter into his inside jacket pocket and followed Tony into the room.

There was nothing he could do at the moment, so there was no reason to cloud his mind. Keeping humanity in the dark was the intention of church and state, but Jake did not share their views. He reflected on a recent debate between his students two weeks prior, when they had displayed vastly different opinions and reminded him that diversity is what makes this an exciting world. By observing what we don't like or want, we begin forming beliefs about what we do want.

"And right now," Jake said to himself in a whisper, "what I want is to focus on shaking up as many beliefs as possible to wake up my students before I no longer have a platform to teach."

"Listen up. Pay attention." Jake wrote in big letters across the board:

Would Jesus be "crucified" today because of dogma and personal gain or convictions? Would a religion or a person's image of what they believe Jesus should look and act like blind them to his core essence and message?

"This is not a question that I am going to stop asking until it is contemplated from many different angles. Therefore, let's explore the possibilities."

Would we repeat history and condemn Jesus to death, once again, if he returned to earth today?

Professor Reynolds began reading each project out loud as he wrote.

"Project 1. What if Jesus were already here? What would his followers do differently in their lives if he showed himself? What if he refused to perform miracles—would they still recognize him?

"What if Jesus informed the Catholic Church or any other Christian Church that his words were misinterpreted or falsified, and he requested that the Bible be amended—would they? Why? Why not?

"Project 2. Share examples of how Jesus demonstrated women's equality to humanity. Why didn't Jesus pick women as disciples? Or did he?

"What other men besides Jesus demonstrated equality for women?

"Where was it said that Jesus didn't want women to become heads of his church? Was it males who formulated this situation?

"Was Mary Magdalene more knowledgeable and adept at understanding Jesus's teachings than his male disciples? Explain in detail through examples.

"Project 3. Both Catholic and Protestant governments promoted witch hunts. How and why could these churches get so far from the teachings of Jesus? What were the 'holy wars' and 'witch hunts' really regarding?

"Project 4. What do you believe were Jesus's three most essential teachings? Explain how they are being applied in the world today.

"What has the Roman Vatican done to help facilitate the teachings of these critical works?

"Project 5. Why do religions exclude people of different beliefs or behaviors, if the basis of Jesus's teachings was regarding love and oneness?

"Many religions are still waiting for a 'savior.' How will they know when their savior arrives?

"Project 6. How did the rulership of Constantine in Constantinople change the face of the Christian religion?

"If religions continue to try to convert others to their beliefs by presenting themselves as 'superior' or the 'only passage to salvation,' will the earth ever find peace?

"Church and state are supposed to be separate—when and where have we succeeded in this?

"Project 7. Excluding science and technology, what has humanity done in two thousand years to better themselves and the world?"

Professor Reynolds stopped and rubbed his hands together. "Dig deeply for the clearest, purest truth!" He returned to his desk and viewed his speechless students. *Hmm*, he grunted. *That's a first*, he thought.

"Oh, by the way, I suppose you are wondering how much weight I put on this assignment?"

A unanimous "Yes!" resounded from his students.

"Let's put it this way," his eyes bore into them, each believing he was directly focused on them, "this research project will represent fifty percent of your grade. It is up to you to decide which assignment you want to complete, and you are allowed to pick only one question, but it better be compelling!

"Remember the words of the fifteenth-century philosopher René Descartes—'If you would be a real seeker after truth, it is necessary that at least once in your life you doubt, as far as possible, all things.' Descartes is also responsible for the familiar Latin phrase '*cogito, ergo sum*,' or 'I think, therefore I am.'"

The class erupted into both groans and loud, excited conversation. Lisa and Veronica just looked at each other with wide eyes. Finally, Lisa commented. "This should be interesting!"

Veronica looked very seriously at Lisa, "This could start something that could rock the world, and we could be responsible for kicking people's butts out of the Dark Ages."

Professor Reynolds sat back. Looking at his students, he thought with satisfaction, *these students could be responsible for moving the acceleration curve of mankind's consciousness.*

More than two thousand years had passed since the time of the great prophet called Jesus, and people were still trying to control others with their beliefs—it was time for a significant change.

The age of brainwashing controlled by greed, and power that only sprang from deep fears and insecurities, was coming to an end, and Jake was willing to do whatever it took to facilitate that change, even lose his job or die.

CHAPTER 15

Angelina took a deep breath in an attempt to push back the tears. The dreams had become so tangible that she was convinced these events might have actually taken place; she shivered at the absurdity of her thoughts. But right now, her heart ached for a remembrance of either what was or the cruel timing of a joke. "Love existed for me once, real love, long ago. I am certain of this." She spoke to an invisible audience as she blankly gazed out the open French doors into her gardens. "And somehow it was crushed, never again to be granted.

"Can a heart bleed for so long there is nothing left? Why has every intimate relationship I've experienced turned into nothing but shallow words to woo me with no intention of fulfilling any number of promises? Was I only there to fill a void, a man's need to have someone by his side, so as not to be lonely or empty-armed at a dinner party or official event, someone to plan and make meals and look after the mundane day-to-day household obligations. Just someone's trophy, showing the world what he had won?"

But Angelina's conscience tugged at her. She knew this was not entirely the truth. Somewhere deep within was a knowing that no ordinary man would ever satisfy her. He had to be extraordinary, and she flushed as this realization crossed her mind. But the pain of loneliness and the desire to be deeply loved was still very present.

She shivered in remembrance of the vividness of last night's dream. "Who was he?" she softly whispered, "and is the woman me?" Even though Angelina was witnessing the visions, she also felt she was that woman. If so, it suggested that she was intimate with this beloved prophet. She couldn't allow herself to think beyond that point, as it felt sacrilegious.

She watched him as he stood near the river's edge, his eyes absently gazing at the water that rippled in the wind. She called to him gently, "What troubles have you?"

He turned towards her, and she saw his eyes soften, his shoulders drop. "Beloved one, do not concern yourself with my thoughts. The day brings forth much beauty."

She slowly rose from the edge of the well where she had been sitting, shook off the dirt that gathered at the hem of her garment, and walked towards him, careful not to knock over the earthenware water jug that rested beside her. "Please, share your worries with me so I may help you carry the burden."

He smiled at her with his eyes and pulled her towards him, whispering as he kissed her hair and lips. "Just your being here with me helps me shoulder my troubles."

She knew now was not the time to push for answers, as he had only recently had words with one of the men. One man, in particular, could be overbearing and unwilling to listen or grasp the fullness of the teachings from the one she called Beloved, and he became angered when she had been acknowledged for her wisdom and her favored relationship with the prophet.

She glanced over at her opposer, who was scowling in her direction as he sat near the other men in the shade of the tree. Their eyes locked for a brief moment—long enough to see the jealousy and disdain in his eyes. She quickly looked away.

Witnessing this envy had not been the first time, and her heart ached as she fostered no ill will towards him, and she knew how it troubled her Beloved. She was well aware that more than one of these men had a difficult time in accepting her as an equal, as did society, and this had caused harsh words. Trying her best to ignore him, she quickly focused on her Beloved.

Angelina flushed at the memory of the vision; a part of her tried to push the event from her thoughts, and another wanted the dreams to be real and never end. At least she knew that once, long ago, she was dearly loved.

CHAPTER 16

"Each of you has a design." Professor Reynolds started speaking before allowing the class to settle. "Our purpose on this planet is to put the pieces of all of the disciplines together so that what we present to the world is the experience of truth. Without a label or a thought process attached to it, and without a way for the world to take it apart and find fault with it."

Professor Reynolds had intended to allow time for questions and discussion regarding his assignment two days before, but instead, he felt powerful energy intensifying within him, and he began to speak in a voice uncharacteristically serious, with no trace of his usual casualness or ease interjected. Lisa and Veronica had glanced at each other and quickly stopped their conversation mid-sentence, directing their full attention to Professor Reynolds.

"What we are here to do is take all of the ages, all points, all capabilities, all gifts, all knowings, and the wisdom of all time, and put them together and synthesize them. So what is occurring is a way that the world can digest the information. They can relate to it and qualify and quantify what needs to be done regarding actualization so that the experience of the truth becomes the form in this dimension.

"What begins to happen is that these pieces or points of truth begin to affect reality, through our energy field, so that we have the capability to assist in transformation, literally, and not only in ourselves but in those around us."

As he paced, he continued. "We are here to distill the knowledge of all time so that it becomes basic truth. When we hear the truth, we recognize it, just like we recognize love or sorrow or laughter. The person who has to ask, 'Is that truth?' has yet to meet or know truth, as they have not tapped into their inner being, or intuition."

Jake paused only long enough to take a deep breath before continuing. "Know that we can organize consciousness. That we are capable of putting it into formulations and frameworks so that it will make sense—can be taught, can be integrated, and can be remembered by others because it is very simple, very accurate.

"We are here right now, in this time of humankind's existence, because we have reached a pivotal point—a point where we can come together as a human race—one race, one people, one Earth, united. We have the opportunity to shape-shift reality based on truth."

There were no breaks in his speech, just a continuous uninterrupted flow of dialogue with its unique melody and energy that penetrated their souls. The entire class sat silent and transfixed.

"So what we are going to do is dissect humanity, look at it under a microscope, and put together the pieces of the puzzle and create a story based on what is real in the universe. We are going to bring together these pieces in such a way that the story is not only understandable but also accurate so that the truth can replace the longing, humanity's longing to know itself and its Creator.

"We have come to bring forth a very authentic and practical way that this body of truth can sustain itself and magnify, and expand, in a way that brings that level of truth into this dimension.

"And we are putting out a call to all those who want to assist us in revealing humanity's true potential, where we ask people where they want to go, instead of where they have been, for that method has gotten them nowhere. We ask the mind of logic to stay out of the equation, without the religious or personal baggage that holds us to a world of limitation instead of the world we are seeking, one of pure potentiality and oneness.

"We are going to teach others how the *hologram* works—and that, I will explain in detail when you are ready. But until then, understand this, that all creation is a manifestation of what you believe to be true, nothing more. We are the co-creators of our own lives, and we create through our clear intentions, energy—i.e., feeling passionate, fully trusting, flowing with creation, and the most important, surrender."

Lisa was aware of the transformation that had come over Professor Reynolds. His facial expressions had softened, and he began radiating a light she had never witnessed before. It was as if this light was coming from deep within him; a chill ran through her.

He left no room for interruption as he continued his lecture. After several minutes, he became silent as he walked back and forth. With each step, the sun's light flickered across him, looking as if the window frames interfered with the sun's game of tag. When he began to speak again, his voice deepened, and a controlled urgency resounded throughout the room.

"If you want the world to change, *NOW* is your chance—your only chance before the world of illusion swallows you up, and with it, your dreams of true peace of mind and freedom."

Lisa realized that both she and Veronica gulped as their eyes locked.

Professor Reynolds had not finished with his discourse. After the room settled once again, he looked intently into the eyes of each student. "All of us, every one of us feels similar emotions as we first step upon the grounds of any great university. We are overwhelmed by a sense of history, beauty, potential, genius, and hope."

Jake paced down the aisles as if momentarily lost in reflection and then continued. "Lost are many along the way. Their original purpose slowly passes them by, taking one path while another distracts them.

"Often in life, we never get back on that intended journey, succumbing to each distraction. And then one day, you wake up from your 'fantasy of life' and ask, 'What happened to my greatness? When was it that I became separated from my original purpose?'"

Veronica quickly looked around the hall. Every person was motionless except for their eyes, which followed Professor Reynolds' every move.

"When you first gazed upon this campus, you were filled with that same hope—those hopes and goals that greatness shared." Jake paused again. Strength and intensity filled his voice.

"Hope for yourself and hope for humanity. You knew you were standing at the threshold of your potential. Your dreams for the future were worn on the cuff of your sleeve, just like your emotions when you were a child. You didn't care what anyone else thought or said. You were determined to voice your feelings, to let it be known to all who you were, what you wanted, and where you wanted to go."

As morning's sunlight threw prism rays across the room, caught and condensed by the edges of the beveled glass, Jake walked towards the bank of windows and pushed one open.

"Time elapses," he began again. "And you start to forget your original purpose, the purpose for your existence that was influenced by your soul before money and time intervened—a time before you cultivated the belief that both of these commodities were in short supply."

Professor Jake Reynolds stood before them, with his hands in his trouser pockets. He spoke to each one of them with urgency. Veronica was convinced that he was addressing her directly.

"I ask you once again," Jake's voice was explicit. "Why are you here? What is your purpose? What are your dreams and your aspirations for the planet? What is your potential?

"What legacy do you want to leave? Why? Who are you?

"What if we could take the wisdom of all the ages, which includes various cultures, philosophy, and organizations, and bring them together? That is my mission, to bring those people together and assist humanity in seeing their similarities instead of their differences. I am here to facilitate the uniting of humanity." He stopped and looked deeply into the eyes of his students as if he were penetrating their souls.

"Now why are you here? Dream. Remember. Wake up. Explore the deepest recesses of your soul. Do whatever it takes, just figure it out!"

With that, he retrieved his sports jacket from the back of his chair and walked out of the room, leaving the door open behind him—and a class full of astonished students.

The lecture hall exploded in conversation. Veronica had been holding her breath almost the entire time Professor Reynolds was speaking and now let out a deluge of air. "Were you ready for that?"

Lisa stared at Veronica, trying to make sense of the words Professor Reynolds had just spoken.

"No," she replied to Veronica's question, "I wasn't expecting anything remotely like that."

"Did you notice, well, of course, you did, how powerful prof became with each word he spoke? It was like he was in a trance, like something or someone stepped into his body and took over. That was intense!"

"I'm still stuck on Professor Reynolds' project list from the other day. What he wants all his students to do may not be possible without attracting fanatics from a multitude of religions and cultures," Ken Usher, who was sitting next to Lisa, piped in. "Some might not take kindly to this investigation."

"Look at where worrying about being silent or tactful has gotten us—not far enough," Veronica threw back at him. "Maybe it's time to stir up some energy around these subjects that people want to avoid or tiptoe around!" The force and sincerity of her voice softened. "Anyway, what he is attempting to do is get people to find their commonality, not just with each other but each culture and religion. That is what Professor Reynolds has always been about, and if people want to take it wrong, that's their problem."

Lisa knew that was true; Professor Reynolds had always stressed the importance of people looking at what they had in common instead of where their beliefs differed. That was one of the reasons she had waited so long to get into his class. His reputation was about making people think, to find answers. "Stay focused on the solution. No problem could exist if the solution wasn't already available" was his motto. Instead of looking to blame, find understanding and commonalities. He believed the answer to any problem already existed, and it was just waiting to be remembered, waiting for the right question to be asked.

Lisa had liked that concept; it made her look at the world as a place of discovery instead of impossible problems.

She reflected back on the first day in his class. Professor Reynolds stood before them and waited until there was silence. He removed his arm from the podium it was resting on and said, "See that?" pointing to the completed jigsaw puzzle on the desk next to him. "That's our design. That's the completed picture of creation, consisting of every answer, every solution, and each of our parts in it. Each of us is an important piece of that puzzle.

"When you first begin to put a puzzle together, a single piece doesn't seem to be that important, but in the end, it is the most important piece." He bent over and removed one piece and held it up. "Now look at the puzzle. It is incomplete—unfinished. Only one little piece is missing, but it is disconcerting. That one missing piece becomes the entire focus. Each of you is one of those pieces, and if you think your one life doesn't matter in the huge scope of life, think again."

Then suddenly, with one mighty swipe of his arm, he wiped the desk clean. The puzzle pieces scattered everywhere.

"Now," he said to an astonished class, "our job is to put the puzzle back together, to recreate the masterpiece. Our assignment is to remember that the puzzle was already whole, the picture of our creation and destiny completed before we allowed the mind to rule instead of the sacred heart. Each one of us is a piece of that puzzle. Each one of us contributes to the whole of the Creator's original design."

Professor Reynolds strolled back to the podium and grabbed both sides like he was going to shake it. "To refuse to allow all pieces of the puzzle to come together—although each piece is different—creates an incomplete picture. The masterpiece, the portrait that our Creator painted, will not be complete because we have not understood that our differences are what makes the painting unique and original. Our diversity is what makes us exceptional. Our diversity, not our sameness!"

Sliding his hands into his front pockets, he took a deep breath and continued. "Now is that time in history to pick up the pieces and put them back together. No matter how different each one may look, each one is of utmost importance to complete the Creator's masterpiece.

"Differences in religion and culture should not be viewed any differently than the clothing a person decides to wear. We are the only species that is so unique. Why shouldn't our beliefs be? The questions and answers that humanity has been asking since the beginning of time are as varied as the cultural and intellectual diversity of each one, as well as each individual's interpretation within that group."

Scanning each student as if he was looking for clues, he continued. "One's views, how they behave and relate to others, represent their level of evolution and the degree of mastery their soul has obtained."

Professor Reynolds stepped from the podium to the center of the lecture hall and, with eyes piercing into each one of them, said in no uncertain terms, "Never enter my classroom with prejudices of any type. It won't be tolerated. We are here to find solutions and to put the masterpiece back together. Do I make myself clear?"

Silence. Stunned silence.

"Well do I make myself clear?" his voice demanded.

By then, the class had regained their voices and a deafening "YES!" reverberated throughout the hall.

Veronica had raised her fist, punching the air, looking at Lisa with her big brown eyes she yelled, "EXTREME!"

Lisa had smiled and said with a sigh, "This is going to be a most unusual class."

And now, once again, the professor who just walked out of the room without another word left them awestruck—and hungry for more.

CHAPTER 17

Lisa and Veronica walked across campus unusually silent, lost in their thoughts. Stopping in the middle of a grove of ancient elm trees, Lisa glanced at Veronica and said, "I'll catch you later. There are a few things we both need to think about, and we have to do it alone."

Veronica understood the look in Lisa's eyes and the tone of her voice. She had seen and heard it before: "Don't ask me questions that I'm not ready to answer"—the message was clear. Veronica was not insulted. She knew, when her friend was ready to share, she would be the first to know. Besides, if Lisa hadn't said it, she soon would have.

Professor Reynolds' words were still echoing within: "Now, why are you here? Who are you? Figure it out."

Lisa headed towards her car, clenching her teeth as the tears pressed hard against her eyes; she took several deep breaths and blinked them back. She recognized her life was moving quickly in the direction she had begged for since childhood, and now Lisa knew time was on fast forward as events played out in rapid succession. She was overwhelmed with emotions of excitement and fear, besides the endless string of inquiries remaining.

It was just yesterday she had asked herself the same questions that were just presented by Professor Reynolds. Now she would be forced to take a closer look at her life and her intentions.

In the last six months, there was no more waiting for weeks, months, or even years at times, to get answers to her questions for the missing pieces to the mysteries of creation, evolution, and her life purpose in the grand master plan. Clarity had begun to resound throughout her being, and a feeling of peace had started to quietly settle in, noticed by her friends even before she had labeled it herself.

As Lisa climbed the steps to her apartment, she realized it was no accident that Professor Reynolds was her teacher. Somehow they were connected, and she hoped before long that too would be revealed. In the meantime, she had an assignment that left the indelible mark of great urgency.

She grabbed her stack of journals and began scanning them for clues to when her correspondence with God had taken a drastic and accelerated turn from the frightened but fierce little girl, to the person she had become.

Her finger rested upon a poem she had been moved to write to her Creator some years before. The energy still rested between the pages, immediately transporting her back to the night of its origination. It had started before she went to bed; she had felt as if she were walking in a trance all evening. By the time she slipped between her sheets, she had been overcome by a higher power she could not explain.

And when she awoke in the middle of the night, she did not hesitate to rise and walk in the darkness to the small loft lit only by the light of the half-moon streaming through the skylight above. Slipping into her chair, she picked up her laptop and began to type without thought or hesitation.

Lisa ran her fingers over the title, *In the Morn of the Half Moon, Poem to My Beloved Creator*, and reread the last eight stanzas':

> Upon that magical morn, when the moonlit half, high in the still dark sky, not quite yet turned by the kiss of morning's light,

I felt You.

I felt Your arms wrapped around me, like a warm blanket, so lightly, so sweetly.

I stopped and listened.

Someone was knocking on my door. Someone so patiently, so loving, so persistently.

I opened the door—the door right within my heart.

And I wept.

I wept for the centuries lost. I wept for my lack of realization, that all the while I had searched and searched for my Beloved, He stood patiently knocking at my door, the door right within my heart.

When Lisa finished, she realized tears of gratitude had been streaming down her face. She brushed back several loose strands of hair but did not bother to wipe away the tears. Something in her heart had pierced, new information penetrated every cell within, and although she did not know precisely how much of the information was strictly on a cellular level, she realized she had changed.

Now again, Lisa whispered, "I can feel you, thank you. I am so humbled." Lisa closed her blue eyes and felt a renewed love for all humanity fill her heart, for she knew God resided within every man, woman, and child—without exception. Some had closed so many doors within their hearts that it was just more difficult for them to find the divine, but the Creator waited patiently for them, as time was only a concept of human reality.

Lisa knew by her dreams that what was being requested of her was about to present itself soon, very soon. She just hoped she was ready. Suddenly feeling exhausted, she rested her head back on the soft plush fabric of her chair and became lost in some vortex in time.

Her white linen garments were flowing freely behind her as she rushed to the temple to join her friends. He had returned, the one they had called the awaited one, the savior, and this time, she would not miss him. She had not seen him since meeting him in Egypt many years before, and even then, she had known that he was bound for greatness. He had taken on the most learned priests and scholars, undaunted by their probing questions in an attempt to discredit such a young but wise man. She had smiled as his calmness grew, as their emotions boiled in an unsuccessful attempt to trap him and prove their superiority.

She ran up the massive stone steps, and when she reached the top, she rested her hand against a marble column and took a deep breath before entering the temple. In the distance, she could hear his familiar voice, and she again picked up her pace. Turning the corner and passing through rows of columns, she spotted the crowd. There he stood, upon the mosaic floor, with rays of light illuminating him; his beauty took her breath away. Quietly she slipped among her friends and smoothed her garments as she fixed her attention on his every word.

Some time had passed before she realized, in her rush to arrive, strands of hair had escaped her veil. As she tucked them back into place, she felt eyes upon her. As she turned her head, her heart skipped a beat as her eyes locked with those of an unknown man for a brief moment before she embarrassingly turned away. Who was he? Something had just happened, some connection between them, but what? She could still feel the heat upon her face.

Moments later, she spotted the same man rushing across the mosaic floors as he and several others surrounded the one called Yeshua and quickly departed from the temple. "Who was that with Yeshua?" *she whispered to her friend beside her.*

"They call him John."

Lisa woke with a start. She must have dozed off in her chair. Another dream she could not explain. But her racing heart told her it was not just a dream—it was a memory.

CHAPTER 18

Tyler had played on the dark side for as long as he could remember. He bought into the world's echoing voice of "unworthy," "a punk," "worthless," and just a general loser, and with no further expectations from life, that is who he believed himself to be.

Thrown out of school at sixteen, Tyler convinced himself that he didn't care. "It was lame anyway" is what he told his friends. Pushing drugs was the only time he felt important—people wanted something he had. Otherwise, he was a throwaway.

With dealing came money, more money than he had ever seen. And with money came friends; they seemed to be synonymous. He pushed away from the thoughts of the green-eyed fourteen-year-old girl who OD'd because of drugs she bought from him at a party. "Hey, it's not my fault. I didn't make her take them" was his explanation to himself.

And he dismissed the dark dreams of being endlessly chased and cornered in dismal alleys by "Doctor Death," who refused to let him walk away, which was just a part of the package. Anyway, the money was his drug of choice, enticing him to keep acquiring more, as it allowed him to live a life he otherwise would never be able to afford. He was well aware that he hadn't obtained skills to do anything else, as of this he was frequently reminded.

Before his mother had thrown him out of the house, she sat in the kitchen, sobbing, trying to reach him, trying to understand him, questioning him. He just coldly stared at her, tapping his finger on the table. Finally, she couldn't take it anymore and told him to get out and not come back.

Tyler's night sweats had forced his mother to question his damp sheets. He yelled at her and told her to stay out of his room and that he knew how to do his laundry.

He questioned it himself, just for a second. "I'm not afraid of anyone or anything," he confirmed to himself. But something dark and unseen lurked, and Tyler couldn't shake it.

Two days later, he slid into the back seat in a lecture hall to escape the old white-haired geezer who had begun following and questioning him about his business on campus as if he didn't fit in. He had been looking to expand his client base, and his friends bragged about the easy scores at colleges and universities. They assured him they were full of druggies and not to limit his business ventures to elementary and high schools.

He was about to slip back out of the class when some sexy Italian girl began to speak. She was so concise and fired up, and appeared confident of her world. He decided to stay for just a few more minutes; anyway, she was funny and hot.

Without forewarning, something within him ruptured, like a door stuck for so long he hadn't even realized there was something beyond the darkness in which he lived. A laser beam of golden light shot forth, almost blinding him, stopping him in his tracks. He had just turned twenty-three.

He found himself cleaning up his appearance, just a little, to improve his chances of a successful "job search" for new clients—that was the rationalization he gave as the excuse to the questioning voice within him. And somehow, almost every day since then, he found himself slipping into the far back corner of that class. He had never been exposed to such theories, conviction, or possibilities. "Hey, Jake's pretty cool, for a teacher," he would tell himself.

"So I ask you once again," Jake's voice was intense and explicit. "Why are you here? What is your purpose? What are your dreams and your dreams for the planet? What is your potential? What legacy do you want to leave? Who are you? Do you intend to be that rare person who does not allow their dreams to slip away but instead holds their purpose and passion in front of themselves on a continual basis and never forgets where they are going? Someone who enjoys the journey along the way but never lets the journey take them off the main road?"

Ordinarily, Tyler was the first to slip out when the class was winding up, but on this day, Tyler was one of the last to leave the hall; he was stunned. He had heard those words before; he didn't remember when or where, just that he had.

"Never lets the journey take them off the main road." Tyler repeated the words over and over. "Is it the words, or is it the energy behind the words I somehow recognize? Whoa, what the heck am I saying?"

Suddenly he realized that with only a few students remaining, he could be found out, and bolted from the room.

Blindly racing across columned courtyards and tree-lined lawns, feeling as though any moment he could be sick, Tyler found himself in a forested area adjoining the east side of campus. Still, he did not stop, as if trying to run from an unfamiliar and unyielding ache within that was bombarding him. Nothing had ever felt like this; this bizarre intruder was turning his heart inside out. He tried desperately to outrun the pain, as these unfamiliar emotions were far more terrifying to him than his nightmares of being chased by Doctor Death—at least he knew from whom he was running.

Somewhere buried within time, he heard the words more clearly than ever before: *Traitor, traitor, traitor!* The words pounded in his chest and his mind burned, but this time, he realized he was running from his past, some karmic history that could no longer be outwitted or postponed.

Tripping across protruding roots, he found himself sprawled across the ground beside the pebble-strewn edge of a stream. Tears overtook him, and he no longer had the strength to get up. He doubled over, kneeling with his arms wrapped around his chest. He held himself as he wailed, as if in excruciating pain. The ache in his heart was blinding and unrelenting until gratefully he lay upon the ground and fell into a deep sleep.

The dreams were different this time, and although they were dark, somewhere beyond the darkness, he saw a speck of light.

Many guests filled the seats behind the long wooden table set for a simple meal. He could barely look upon the man who sat so majestically in the center, fearing he would reveal himself for what he was about to do. Thirty pieces of silver rested in the treasury bag in payment for this treachery—coins that traded life for death.

The man's eyes fell upon him, and he said with great love and sorrow, "Truly, I say to you that one of you will betray me."

Those around questioned in disbelief, to which the man replied, "It is he to whom I shall give a sop after I have dipped it." Usually this was an honor, but in this case, it was evident that it was the sign of betrayal.

As his master dipped the bread and presented it to him, his heart raced and fear ignited his desire to escape. He stayed put as all eyes were on him.

The bread, representing the physical body, was being dipped into the wine, to fulfill the ancient rite symbolizing the death of the mortal nature. The master was foretelling his demise.

The others in the room were confused, and his eyes could not meet their questioning faces. Finally, no longer could he bear to stay, and he slipped silently into the evening to inform his relatives of his master's whereabouts. His fingers once again wrapped themselves around the bag of silver, and although a wave of doubt assailed him, it did not stop him.

Later that night, his heart raced as he led a small band of Sanhedrin guards to the sanctuary of Gethsemane, their burning torches lighting the way, the shadows cast from firelight and evening's call playing eerily across their faces. He could see his master waiting in quiet fortitude as they closed in on him, making no attempt to run.

"Why did I not foresee the cost of this betrayal, not only for the life of my master but also my own? How could I have been so weak and foolish?"

He saw himself running down darkened roads when he found out that a death warrant had been issued against Yeshua, yelling to those who now ignored him. "Take back your silver. I have made a terrible error!"

But it was too late, for he saw the looks on their faces. Even Annas and Caiaphas knew that a betrayer to one man would betray another. He threw the silver at their feet and ran with the echo of their mockery still filling his ears.

He wept when he realized his betrayal, for the priests and those of the Sanhedrim Council had told him his master would not be harmed, but this was to prove to the people that he was not the son of God, nor the awaited savior.

On returning to his home without the silver, he said to his wife, "Rise up, wife, and provide me with a rope, for I will hang myself as I deserve."

He could see her scorn in her eyes. "Why do you say such things?"

"The truth is, I have wickedly betrayed my master and allowed the evildoers to take him before Pilate and put him to death."

Although still in a trance-like sleep, Tyler relived those memories. The words and visions continued to fill his mind, reverberating through every cell of his being—words that had haunted him for thousands of years.

"Traitor, traitor, traitor!" they yelled, coming closer and closer.

As they closed in on him, he quickly slipped the noose around his neck and jumped.

As he watched the visions, he viewed as each lifetime sped across his memory in warp speed until he came to the light just beyond the darkness. A voice so full of empathy and love began to speak. "*You, my dear friend, were forgiven long before the act, as there was really nothing to forgive.*" The eyes before him spoke honesty; they were eyes that could only speak the truth.

"*My experience on earth was no different than yours. I did not conquer pain. I surrendered to it. I did not overcome death. I went willingly through it. I did not glorify the body, nor did I condemn it. I did not call this world heaven or hell but taught that both are of your making.*

"*I entered the dance of life as you have entered it, to grow in understanding and acceptance, to move from conditional love to the experience of divine love without conditions. There is nothing that you have ever felt or experienced, dear brother, that I have not tasted. I know every desire and every fear, for I have lived through them all, and my release from them came through no special dispensation.*

"*You see, I am no better a dancer than you. I purely offered my willingness to participate and to learn, and that is all that I ask of you. You were part of a design that was agreed upon by all before your life known as the 'traitor.' You fulfilled your role, our plan. You must forgive and let go of the past.*

"*Participate. Feel life and allow yourself to be touched. Open your arms to living truth. That is why you are here now.*"

When Tyler became fully conscious, he began wiping the tears from his face and suddenly noticed two big, startled brown eyes staring down at him.

"Holy crap!" the sweet familiar voice exclaimed.

CHAPTER 19

Veronica grabbed her teal sweater and, in a half sprint, rushed down the hall towards an exquisitely carved armoire dating back hundreds of years that her grandpa told her was copied from a cabinet belonging to the goddess Isis. The carvings were meticulously replicated from the walls of the Isis temple.

She had visited the temple when she was eleven years old, with her beloved grandmother. She would never forget the thrill of feeling transported in time as if she was there walking with the goddess upon the sacred stone beneath her feet. She often felt the same sensations when stroking the armoire that stood before her.

Veronica believed Isis to be the most powerful deity of ancient Egypt. She was a loving wife and mother who was considered to be a magical healer of the sick, goddess of protection, and had the ability to bring those she loved back to life. As far as Veronica was concerned, Isis was the ultimate woman, as even with all her talents and power, she was able to sit back and allow others to run things as long as all was going well, and she only stepped in when her assistance and wisdom were needed.

She recalled the countless times she had reached out and outlined the carving of the beautiful woman in the elegant sheath who sat majestically on a jewel-embedded throne with her elaborate headdress of a solar disk and cow's horns, with one hand holding an ankh and her other hand resting effortlessly on her staff. Some areas of the armoire had smoothed to a patina by hands like hers stroking the wooden doors for centuries, perhaps, longing to pick up some of the original essence.

Growing up, she was awed by the cabinet's beauty and the sense of magic that surrounded it as well as those few who were allowed to unlock the impressive doors with the old iron key that dangled from a worn golden-silk cord.

When her great-grandmother had discarded her old body in order for her spirit to enter into waiting realms, the key passed to her grandmother Julia. The ceremony had taken place just as the sun slipped beneath the western sky. And although she was merely five, she remembered in microscopic detail a room filled with candlelight and sacred incense smelling as old as time itself. This was the smell of groundedness in which she had been born. Frankincense, myrrh, rose, sandalwood, lavender, and fir filled every corner of the family's home that consisted of three generations of the Valerio family.

From a room just beyond came the muffled sounds of women chanting and the steady hum of crystal bowls made of precious stones, accompanied by a lone flute sweetly resounding across the four-hundred-year-old limestone floors. Only whispers were heard from Grandmother Julia and Grandmother Maria as they prayed with touching palms, just to be opened when Grandmother Maria passed the key from its satin box into the waiting hands of her grandmother Julia. Henceforth, rituals had become an integral part of Veronica's life. The transferring of responsibility occurred again when she was eighteen, this time to Veronica. Indeed, an honor beyond her dreams.

The armoire now occupied her new residence. It had not been easy, but miraculously Veronica's family had granted permission for the armoire to temporarily leave their home in Italy, where it had resided for hundreds of years. It was the only piece of furniture she insisted on taking with her, and she fully understood the responsibility that came with this decision.

"Grandpa, please," Veronica had pleaded, knowing his decision would be the final word. He sat with her for a long time as he held her hand in his. His words had always been few when contemplating a serious matter, as his silence brought forth a much deeper understanding of what was taking place.

He looked deeply into her eyes and saw the excitement of going away to college and the determination to be an adult, and beneath it, he saw his granddaughter already aching for the loss of family and home. The armoire represented the familiar and would keep them energetically connected across the many miles.

For reasons not clearly understood by Veronica, the armoire and its contents bypassed her mother upon her grandmother's wish to transfer the responsibility. "Why" was not explained, but Veronica sensed that her mother knew she lacked the same clairvoyance and spiritual gifts that her daughter held, as well as her mother and grandmother before her, so there was no internal struggle or need for discussion.

Tears streamed down Veronica's face when her mother had passed her the key. She had not even heard the sweet chanting; she focused on the pride and love in her mother's eyes.

Now Veronica stood before the cabinet, whispering, "You have held the contents of magic and miracles for lifetimes, and I shall always cherish you." Once again, her hands gently stroked the doors before turning the key in its lock and tenderly touching the sizable embossed-leather book that rested on a thick wooden shelf. She slowly brushed the dust from its cover and began scanning its papyrus pages. She did not know what she was looking for; perhaps it was just for the soothing effect it had upon her spirit or the connection to those before her.

The pages of the book fell open, revealing a single powerful blend. On the opposite page, she recognized her Grandma Julia's beautiful calligraphy, and her heart ached. The page simply read,

~Ultimate Clarity~

Add the following to the original Clarity blend. Remember, a tiny bit goes a long way: Frankincense, Sandalwood, Melissa, Cedarwood, Blue Cypress, Lavender, Helichrysum italicum

"Well if that won't do it, I don't know what will!"

When Veronica finished lining up the amber bottles upon the stone table, she removed a small stone mortar and pestle from the cabinet and placed them beside the oils. Lighting two tall beeswax candles in antique cathedral-style holders, she turned to a small drawer to extract a moss-green velvet bag and carefully removed one small packet of incense before returning the rest to the drawer. Cautiously unfolding the creamy paper, she removed yellow and brown translucent resins before reaching for the sandalwood in an elegant opaque bottle with a ruby stopper and set them beside the oils.

Veronica softly chanted as she lit the bed of charcoal housed in a Tibetan hammered-copper bowl and watched as the coal sizzled and spat before finally turning bright red. Carefully, she placed the frankincense, sandalwood, and myrrh upon it and continued to chant prayers of gratitude. She lifted the matching Tibetan bell from the table and rang it four times—in the directions of north, east, south, and west.

Soon the heat of the charcoal distributed the fragrance throughout the room. Slowly and deeply, Veronica inhaled the familiar scent—she was transported home—on a physical as well as a spiritual level. Veronica liked the ritual for another reason; by tapping into this energy flow, she became filled with the frequency of light, love, bliss, and ecstasy in its purest form.

This ritual was one that had been carried out for hundreds of years before her, one she understood to be essential to establish peacefulness and clear intentions, and be very grounded before beginning any potion. One needed to connect to the vibration of the universe, to be one with all things.

Veronica reached up and pulled down one of a dozen glowing yellow onyx jars that lined the top shelf of the armoire and then placed her focus on the amber bottles of essential oils that lined the stone table.

"Here we go," she whispered. "Om shanti om."

Bottle after bottle was set aside after selected amounts were poured into the vessel. Then dried rose petals, as well as dried chamomile, were removed from glass-etched jars and placed in the mortar, where she ground them into a fine powder with the pestle and added them to the container. Putting her hands together in prayer, she then turned them outward, right above the onyx jar. With this, Veronica bowed her head, took several deep breaths, and rang the bell three more times.

Sometimes the psyche of God was transparent to Veronica, but lately, the dreams had her running in mental circles. Now, with Professor Reynolds asking the same questions she had been asking herself, it was time to refocus on the direction of her life.

She lifted the onyx jar, secured its lid, and put it into a leather bag. It was time to head to the river, where she had created a simple stone altar between two ancient oak trees. Within a chasm at the base of one majestic oak was an opening where she hid beeswax votive candles in small glass containers. She used them for ceremonies, or for giving thanks to mother earth.

Veronica had discovered the river before Grandfather insisted on purchasing the cottage for her, saying it was "a good investment." Veronica knew he didn't want her to share an apartment or house with others, nor did he want the armoire moved from place to place. Although she was very outgoing and social, her privacy was also essential. The backyard butted up against a hundred acres of protected land that stood between her and the property belonging to the university.

She rushed down the worn stone steps that crossed the lawns to a garden gate that led to the entry of the forest and then picked up her pace, running through the familiar path, where even in the darkness of night, she could find her way. As the river came into sight, she sensed something was different.

"What?" Veronica gasped, caught off guard by the young man lying near the water's edge, and cursed under her breath.

"Damn! I have never seen a single person here, and now this intruder has violated my space." As Veronica approached, she could see the figure of a contorted man with tears streaking his face. Realizing he looked somewhat familiar, she didn't retreat, "OMG, that's the guy who slithers in and out of prof's class believing himself to be unnoticed! Is he sleeping, or is he dead?" Chills ran down her spine as her imagination ran towards the outrageous. She leaned her face closer to his, looking for signs of life.

Suddenly his eyes opened, and Veronica almost screamed. "Holy crap! You scared the bejesus out of me! Who are you, and what the hell are you doing on the ground next to my river?"

"Your river?" Tyler shot back. Trying to hide his embarrassment, he lifted himself up and tried to ignore her as he washed his face in the stream and walked away. As he did so, he left behind the armor of a hundred lifetimes and the cloak of darkness that had permeated his dreams as long as he could remember.

Veronica was well aware of the physical effect he had on her. He was gorgeous, tall and well built, with a square jaw and a slight dimple, rugged but still revealing a softness, with intense blue eyes that she would recognize anywhere. She wanted to touch his face, just for a moment; instead, he was quickly walking away, almost running.

"I will tell you tomorrow," he yelled back to a mystified Veronica, whose mouth was still hanging open.

By the time she regained her voice, he was gone.

CHAPTER 20

The glass of wine Jake held in his hand was more for comfort than for need. "No, thanks, Antonio," Jake replied when asked by the owner of the quaint Italian restaurant located a few blocks from campus if there would be anything else.

Antonio glanced briefly back in Jake's direction. Professor Reynolds had dined in his restaurant countless times over the last several years and had never before ordered a glass of wine. He had always liked Mr. Reynolds; he was kind and thoughtful, always sincerely asking about the members of his family. Although concerned, Antonio knew it was none of his business.

Something had happened to Jake when he finished writing the questions on the board. It was as if the "original model" of creation was infused into him within seconds.

That is what took place as he stood before his class, as hours' worth of conversation and images were "downloaded" into him within minutes. He knew he had to go home and write whatever he could remember, in order not to lose the experience. He wanted it to be more than just a cellular knowing; he wanted to be able to share it with and explain it to others.

Jake understood that vibrations were difficult to explain, and more so without looking like a fool. No, he needed to remember the words. But Jake didn't move; he wasn't ready. Although it wasn't even noon, he just needed to be there with his glass of wine. Noon wasn't the issue; it was that he usually didn't drink alcohol except on rare occasions.

"I guess I could say this is a rare occasion." He sighed, realizing within every cell of his being that there was much more to come.

Jake began reflecting on his youth, how he had wanted to dedicate his life to helping humanity out of their darkness, out of their hunger and pain. He wanted to show them how to open the doors to God, universal creation, and consciousness. He had wanted to be a priest.

Often just before he dozed off to sleep, or in the moments before becoming fully conscious in the early morning, he had visions of ancient times. Sometimes he was walking beside the River Jordan or seeing his woven sandals kick up the dirt of the dusty, dry streets of Jerusalem or holding a torch as they walked to the gardens of Gethsemane.

Other times, he was roaming the hills of Palestine or buying fruit or oils from street vendors in Israel, with a veiled woman by his side as they laughed and talked. In these times, there was one constant: he mostly walked beside the one called Yeshua.

During these visions, profound peace and a satisfying sense of joy filled him, that is until night claimed him or morning's consciousness stole the images away. How often he had tried to pull the covers over his head and return to where he had been, although he was well aware that it never worked.

Jake realized he had many of the answers to the questions humanity had asked for centuries, but there were so few who could comprehend what he was saying on an intellectual and cellular level. Others said they understood what he meant, but he knew they didn't, validated by the demonstration and consequences of their words and daily actions.

Even though his colleagues knew him as an original thinker, many couldn't comprehend the depth in the simplicity of what he said, although that didn't stop them from being intrigued by some of his concepts. It wasn't what he said; it was how he lived his life. Things appeared to come naturally to Jake, but he knew it was just because he was clear on what he wanted. He understood and applied the fundamental principles or the laws of creation to every moment of his life.

It honestly wasn't a great mystery; it was more about paying attention to one's thoughts and the powerful effect they had on each moment of one's life. It hadn't always been this easy for Jake. He had worked hard to understand and apply this knowledge to his life, and there were still internal scars that proved it.

Sipping his wine, Jake thought of Lisa. She didn't seem to have the baggage or wounds of living a life filled with demons like he had when growing up. No issues of unworthiness like his, brought about by a family that considered him strange and different. She did not have a mind clouded with doubt to block her ability to manifest her dreams. He saw her as someone who believed the world was her work of art.

What had moved him deeply was that she trusted him, every word he said, as was apparent by brief conversations that they had shared. She had once remarked to him that her world was conditioned by what she painted on her canvas, and he could see how she created beauty every single day in the lives of others. Jake found himself almost wishing he could be Lisa's age again, with a teacher like him. From that thought came the realization that every experience was essential for some reason often only seen as hindsight, which created the person he now was.

His eyes clouded. The pain was still there. If he had understood the internal demons he was fighting, perhaps he might still be married to Tessa today. But even that parting, he knew, was a part of the divine plan.

Now Jake's students were his purpose for living. This time, when he thought of Lisa, a smile came to his lips. She was extremely bright, logical yet flexible, and curious, and a quick wit. At times, he couldn't tell whether she was being serious or pulling his leg. She could dish it out, but she could also good-naturedly take it. Although Lisa was a kind young woman, she didn't mince words; she would say precisely what she thought. Her clarity and ability to grasp the core of what he was saying pleased him enormously. There were only three problems with Lisa: she was extremely attractive; she was twenty-five; and she was his student.

So many times, he had wished she were none of these things, for it was her mind that had initially captivated him. Lisa was someone who not only understood what he was saying but also applied what he taught to her daily life. She demonstrated this each time she reported back to him, overcome with joy and wonder.

"Although, by looking at her, who would believe that her mind is my number-one interest? No one," Jake replied under his breath in answer to his own question. "Now, if she were older and unattractive, no one would question long discussions outside the classroom."

Antonio glanced in Jake's direction but quickly looked away when he realized Jake was talking to himself. Jake looked down and gently spun his glass of wine, noting its deep burgundy color. He also noted that he was lying. The electrical charge that went through him each time he unexpectedly saw Lisa told him otherwise. What confused him was the impulse to run to her and wrap his arms around her as if she were an old friend. But until he understood why, he needed to keep his distance.

One compelling thought replayed in his mind: how to share what he knew before it was too late.

He also wondered about the story of the young man with dark hair and intense blue eyes, who believed himself to be unnoticed, sitting in the back of his class.

CHAPTER 21

As Jake walked to his car, he pulled his cell phone from his pocket and flipped it open. "Richard, Jake here, any possible way you can take the rest of my classes today? Something has come up."

"Uh, sure, you OK?" Richard inquired.

"I'm fine, thanks. I just have something I need to take care of. I'll talk to you about it later—hey, thanks, Richard."

Although Jake knew several faculty members who could step in for him, he also knew Richard would ask the fewest questions. Jake wasn't ready for questions. He wanted to get home to his office and write down everything he could remember regarding the information that filled him only a short time ago. If he waited, the distractions of life would mix new thoughts with old, fading them from his conscious mind like a sheet of rice paper resting on the wet ground.

Driving up the street to his home, he barely noticed the majestic maples that lined the roadway. Ordinarily, he took time to acknowledge their magnificence. They not only had a sense of history, but they were also beauty itself, and a reminder from the Creator that this planet was humanity's gift. He liked to believe that those trees stood in a perfect line just waiting for his return.

Jake had chosen to buy an older home in an established neighborhood. He loved the broad streets, tree-lined sidewalks, and neighbors who knew and looked out for each other, often catching up on the latest news or an invitation to a gathering as they stood at their mailboxes retrieving their mail. He also chose his home because of its architecture—a mix of Italian Renaissance, Mediterranean, and Zen.

The original owner was someone who had a great eye and, unquestionably, a gratifying time creating everything he loved in one structure. When standing in the interior of the house, one was aware that the gardens were designed with equal importance to the interior of the home. Every focal point of the house took one's eye to either a niche with a statue, a painting, a fragmented ruin of ancient architecture, or a place in the garden.

"Even the gardens contain rooms," the owner's son had told him. "The gardens were designed like individual rooms, unique although in harmony with each other as well as with the interior of the home. Rooms without walls," he had stated.

Jake had intended to play hardball when his realtor told him about the house. His nonchalant "take it or leave it" attitude would allow him room to negotiate the price below asking, as it always had in the past.

There was only one problem with this theory: he was unprepared for the effect the house would have on him. He came back three times that same day.

Terri, his bouncy but tough-as-nails realtor, commented after leaving the property the first time, "Good job, Jake, the drooling was an effective part of the plan to get Mr. Rossi to reduce the price!"

They both had a good laugh. But Jake knew the house was worth every penny, and the owner deserved to get it. Jake made Terri sit in her car and write the offer then and there.

The next trip to the house was to present the offer as Jake sat in the car. When Terri was finished, the owner shook her hand and said, "Nice young man. There shouldn't be any problem with the 'subject to inspection' clause. This has been a well-loved home. Tell Mr. Reynolds, if he would like to stop by later, I would be happy to give him a more historical and detailed showing."

The third trip was the moment Terri had returned Jake to his car. Jake knew in his heart that the house on Oak Street, lined with maple trees, was "his house"—he could feel it. He stood before the house with absolute clarity and claimed it.

"This or something better," he spoke to the universe, reaching his arms to the sky. With that, a powerful surge of energy poured through him. He felt the power of heaven and earth colliding within his solar plexus.

He knew at that moment that this was the house he would call home.

But today, as Jake pulled into his driveway, his only focus was on getting to his computer as quickly as possible.

The computer keys beneath Jake Reynolds' fingertips made lively tapping sounds, quickly accelerating as Jake's fingers flew across the keypad. Jake had walked quickly through the kitchen, absently throwing down his briefcase, keys, and jacket as he passed the table on the way to his office.

He had taken several deep breaths with his eyes closed as he sat motionless in the leather chair before his computer. Taking three more deep breaths to align himself with the internal space where this wisdom originated, he willed his mind to step aside to reveal it just as it had in the hall earlier that day.

Intuitively, he began to type, allowing the flow of energy to speak through his fingertips. He had known that if he just started typing, it would be like a dream that he woke up from, where only small fragmented parts were remembered. He had discovered in his teens that if he wrote down even one small piece of his dream, suddenly more and more recollection came to mind. Using this simple process, he was able to remember the entire dream.

He had also learned that visions believed to be fragmented pieces of complex stories with no beginning or end were, in fact, each a complete story in themselves. Instead of five unrelated, disjointed fragments of the same dream, they were five separate and complete dreams, which spanned the entire night.

Jake typed quickly, as the words revealed themselves once again. He was blown away by the intensity and the responsibility of the information being given to him.

When he finished two hours later, he was emotionally wiped out. He was awed, mystified, humbled, and most of all, overwhelmed.

"There is no longer time to waste. The acceleration curve of humankind is rapidly approaching."

As the last lines came to a close, he sat back and closed his eyes, feeling the heaviness of this responsibility. He had intended to print out the information and reread it. But right now, the only thing he wanted to do was lie down.

Although it was only four o'clock in the afternoon, Jake grasped the cool, timeworn limestone railing and willed himself up the staircase. His bedroom was at the far end of the hall, and today the hallway seemed longer. Never noticing the sheer drapes fluttering in the breeze of the open French doors at the opposite end, he walked into his room, removed his clothes, and left them in a heap on the floor. He threw himself onto the unmade bed. There was no trace of insomnia; he was out cold.

Again, he dreamt of dusty streets, Roman columns, and the man called Yeshua of Nazareth. Yeshua, son of Joseph ben Jacob, and a respected member of the Sanhedrin Council, the supreme court of Israel, and the son of Mary, daughter of Anna and Joachim, direct descendants of King David ben Jesse, the most powerful king in the history of Israel.

Many had gathered to hear the messages that could only be inspired by the direct voice of God. Jake saw himself speaking intimately to a woman who was also a disciple, and even though a woman's status was limited and restricted by Jewish custom, Yeshua never recognized these laws and saw women as equals, calling them daughters of Abraham and disciples. He also referred to them as members of his inner circle. Women were also not to be educated, but Yeshua overthrew tradition and became a teacher to many women, throwing out centuries of rules regarding women that had been instituted by the three Jewish religious groups: Pharisees, Sadducees, and Essenes.

Yeshua was speaking to a crowd that had gathered on the dusty, dry sands of Egypt, but Jake could only see this woman of great beauty and wisdom, who sat beside him as they listened, and was overjoyed that today she was not with Mary Magdalene but here sitting with him. He briefly reflected on Mary, for he did admire her, and acknowledged her to be an influential disciple who always walked with Yeshua as his companion and with whom Yeshua entrusted his most advanced teachings. Their devotion and love for each other were beyond question.

The woman beside Jake was the same woman who had caught his eye in the temple years before. He was reaching for her outstretched hand when a voice shattered the unfolding dream.

"My old friend, when are you going to find me? Isn't two thousand years long enough to be parted?"

And once more, Jake awoke in a sweat, still grabbing for the hand that was no longer there. Sitting up, Jake cupped his face in his hands and emotionally broke down. "God, what are you doing? What are you trying to tell me? And who was that woman?" As far as he knew, she wasn't mentioned in the Bible, so why did the dream reveal her as a disciple?

Silence. Still no clarity, just fragments of dreams spilling across Jake's bewildered mind.

CHAPTER 22

"Breathe. Chill. Those one million things you have to do can wait."

Obsessed, Veronica could think of only one thing, and that was to return to the river and find the captivating, but bewildering, guy with the mysterious eyes. The weekend had prohibited her from seeing him in class today, and because of her numerous questions, she had no desire to wait until Monday.

What had brought him to Professor Reynolds' class the week before? Why had she discovered him coiled on the ground near her altar? And what the heck was he doing in her dream last night?

For some reason, she was not at all frightened about going alone and finding him in the forest. In some bizarre way, he seemed familiar. She didn't know where she knew him from, but she needed to know, and now. He was a link, a piece of the past, and she realized this because last night, she woke up startled, reaching for a hand, and the hand belonged to *him*!

Of this she was confident: their eyes had locked just before she reached out to him, just before he evaporated into the shadows cast by consciousness. Veronica shivered. They were the same eyes that made her scream out the day before. Her curiosity doubled. He was not typically the kind of guy she would pay too much attention to, and although he was knockdown gorgeous, there was a dark shadow that seemed to lurk around him.

She half expected to find him waiting for her, for he did say, "I'll tell you tomorrow." Momentarily disappointed, she began removing some foliage and the half-dozen votive candles in glass jars that were hidden in the base of the old oak tree and lined them up on the roughly chiseled stone slab between the two ancient oaks. Reaching behind her shoulder, she grabbed the center of the long chiffon scarf that was draped around her neck and placed it on her head, throwing one side back across her shoulder, and began chanting softly.

The woods became quiet. Three long oms came in succession, a sound that seemed to unlock the door between the two worlds. "A removing of the veil, the ability to move between the world of matter and the world of the divine," Veronica would declare to those who inquired.

She began anointing herself with her recent mixture of oils, careful not to get it in her eyes. She still remembered, as a child, finding a bottle of Grandmother's oil, knowing she shouldn't touch it but doing it anyway. She put it on her forehead just like she had seen Grandmother do, except in her nervous state, she applied too much, and some ran down her face and into her eye. Ouch! It stung her eye so badly that she ran to the sink and wiped it with a wet rag.

Little Veronica couldn't believe that the pain intensified, and she cried out. Grandmother came rushing into the room, saw the ruby stopper resting on the table, beside a bottle of her latest blend, *Sacred Heart,* and knew immediately what Veronica had done. Applying olive oil to a soft cloth, she gently wiped her eye. Tears had been uncontrollably running down her face, and finally the stinging began to subside.

Her grandmother was kneeling before her with loving eyes and said, "Now, now, don't you worry, the olive oil will neutralize it. You will feel better in no time. Next time, young lady, don't use water. It only makes it worse. It intensifies it and can burn your eyes. Water is good for certain applications, but never near your eyes or in your ears!"

Her grandmother had never punished her for not asking permission, nor did she tell anyone else. A soft stab prodded her heart, and her eyes welled. Veronica missed her grandmother's gentle and loving eyes and her reassuring embrace.

Raising her arms to the cloudless blue sky, she bowed her head and then brought her arms down in prayer as she continued to chant in front of her altar between the two majestic oaks. Soon the energy of the forest seemed to vibrate and quicken its pulse. All stress fell away, and the heaviness of her physical body evaporated.

A deep echo began to come back to her, and she soon became aware that someone else was mimicking her and heading her way. She was about to open her eyes when something within said, "Continue."

The chanting became louder, and she could feel its deep resonance piercing her soul. Her heart leaped—it was him. As he got closer, she could almost see her aura reach out to greet him.

His physical body now stood next to her, never breaking the energetic spell, as they continued to chant. Suddenly their energies began to soar, and at the speed of light, they became witness to the beginning and end of time. Somewhere in the process, their souls became one—someplace between heavenly particles, volcanic explosions, vegetation, fish climbing out of the oceans, and prehistoric demise. Then time became a blur, and suddenly the divine human stood before them.

Their future, the potential of all humans—and it was beyond beautiful, beyond glorious, beyond explanation that could only subsist by God's grace, a promise fulfilled when the human soul remembered who it was, and God and humanity became one.

As swiftly as it began, it was over. Neither moved for what seemed an eternity. Finally, they turned to look at each other and in unison whispered, "Oh my god."

With a veil of tears in her eyes and while still holding one hand on her heart, Veronica reached out her other hand, saying, "Veronica Valerio."

"Nice to formally meet you in this life. I am Tyler Erwin, and you were in my dreams the last two nights, in some hot, ancient, foreign place."

CHAPTER 23

Lisa's essay lay on the ground next to the chaise. Jake allowed the warm breeze to caress his face. It was a glorious day, and an underlying excitement filled his body with potential. Taking a deep breath, he picked up the papers off the stone patio. It was titled "The Experiment." He began reading it once again.

"The Experiment"—rough draft by Lisa Landen

The impact of the scattering of the jigsaw puzzle pieces across the room on the first day of the class set up a thought process of reflective possibilities, and these particular thoughts I would like to share with you.

Much of humanity looks to God for the answers to their prayers. But what if God can't help us? What if God is waiting for our assistance? For us to understand that our undiluted power comes through realizing that we are consciousness as form appearing as this body. How can God save what she already is? God doesn't view herself as needing to be protected but only the perfection of creation playing out to have an experience.

What if "time" as we know it began at the moment God decided to know and experience her potentiality in form? What if God wrote the finale before she went through with "The Experiment," thus assuring the outcome? That no matter what happened in between, or how long it took, God was assured of that one thing: In the end, ALL consciousness would merge as ONE.

Oneness became the first "absolute," the first truth. As even Adam and Eve were only metaphoric, creation desired to not only expand but to experience both energetic aspects of itself. The feminine and masculine, the light and the dark, as separate expressions to comprehend division and the power of balancing the feminine and the masculine energies to expand consciousness and at the same time, maintain harmony and order. Thus, instead of the duality, it is the balancing of light and dark that creates all aspects of creation.

The script to God's production revealed that love would prevail above all else, as the "solution" was already "in form." And forevermore, all solutions would exist before the questions were asked or even conceived. In the symbolic end, because of "The Experiment," God would be even more expanded and more powerful than before, if that were at all possible—God expanding God through humanity.

Undoubtedly, the infinite has no end; it is only when we each awaken from the dream of separation and realize that we are consciousness, the state of grace and loving perfection is understood. For who am I if not consciousness in human form?

And because God resides within us, the Creator could give us direction through the still, persistent, and soft voice within. God could never lose us, nor could we lose God. No matter how many costumes we dressed in, it would be impossible, as it is only the hologram's reflection.

Professor, I realize this is in a simplified form, and I am rambling, but I was curious about your thoughts on the purpose of creation.
—Lisa

"Well, why not?" Jake spoke to the sky as he looked at three angrily squawking crows chased by a large eagle. God was waiting for us to discover that solutions to every problem already existed. And these would be discovered as soon as we focused our attention on finding the solution through the wisdom of the heart.

If God is asking for our help, this may be a very long wait. And validation of God's unlimited patience! Jake explained to the bird looking at him from the top finial of the birdbath.

On a separate piece of paper, Lisa had written, *Additional information came as a result of a dream last night. Can I share it with you and perhaps discuss what it may mean—that is, when you have nothing better to do? —L.L.*

Jake found himself frowning, and only because it seemed so intense and deep for someone in their mid-twenties. He picked up the phone sitting on the end table next to him and dialed Lisa's number, which was in the footer on each page. Everything told him this was not something he should be doing, but he refused to listen. Heart, not mind was his reasoning.

"Lisa, this is Professor Reynolds, and I just read the papers you gave me and would be happy to discuss the direction of your thoughts. I should be home much of this weekend, so feel free to call or stop by."

He left his personal number, and as he hung up, he felt a stirring in his heart as well as his loins—and a healthy amount of guilt. He had just broken his code of ethics regarding his students, but something in his heart told him there was more to his attraction to Lisa than her being a striking—OK, gorgeous—woman.

Regrettably, he also knew he wasn't the only man who desired her.

CHAPTER 24

Lisa was home when Jake called. Veronica was recounting the story about the lecture hall's intriguing mystery guest, Tyler, and the witnessing of creation unfolding before their eyes. Lisa had been listening wide-eyed as she and Veronica curled up on her large cream overstuffed sofa.

"Lisa, I can't believe the rush I get every time I see him," Veronica said.

"Seriously? I can see that probably occurs every time you think of him." Lisa smiled as she raised her eyebrows.

Veronica replied as if she were mortified, "Crap, it shows?"

"Yeah, like a flashing red light." Lisa enjoyed teasing Veronica for once.

"I hardly know this guy, and I am coming out of my skin."

"Well he is one good-looking guy, mysterious but hot. Can't blame you."

Lisa ignored the ringing of the phone.

"Do you want to get that?" Veronica threw a sideways glance in the direction of the phone.

"No, the machine will pick it up."

When Lisa heard Professor Reynolds' voice, she froze, listening as Veronica stared at her in disbelief. She was too far from the phone to gracefully pick it up and had to endure the realization that Veronica would hear the entire message.

"You have been seeing him! I knew you had a thing for him, but I didn't honestly believe you and he . . . seriously? You have been holding out on me. I can't believe it!"

"That's not true," Lisa said, trying to hide her embarrassment by nervously pushing her hair back, something she did when she was uncomfortable. "I am not seeing him. He just called because of a paper I wrote that I wanted to talk to him about, that's all."

"Oh, right! That didn't sound like a 'sure, meet me after class on Monday' call. He wants you!"

"That's not true—stop."

"Oh my god, now you're blushing. Admit it. It's me, Veronica. Come clean!"

"What do you want me to say? Nothing is going on between us. I swear."

"Well, whether you admit it or not, something is going on between you two. Sexual energy exudes from your pores."

"No!"

"Yes!"

"Oh god."

"Lisa, talk to me. What are you going to do? I see the way you both look at each other and pretend you aren't. Are you going to call him back and go over to his house?"

"I don't know." Lisa felt shell-shocked. "What should I do?"

"Do you want to? Hey, it's me. Be honest, do you want to go see him?"

Lisa looked directly into Veronica's wide brown eyes and said, "Yes, yes I do."

For a moment, Veronica was quiet. She had not expected such an honest answer.

"Well then, call him—now!"

CHAPTER 25

"Professor Reynolds?"

"Yes, this is he." His heart raced as if he were sixteen again, and he sat upright in his lounge chair.

"Hi, this is Lisa. I just picked up your message. If you are serious about meeting . . ."

Veronica shrugged both shoulders, wildly gesturing with her hands as if saying "what was that supposed to mean?" and rolled her eyes as she mouthed "seriously?" Lisa looked away and repeated, "If it works for you, it would be great to stop by when you have time."

"Now is as good a time as any," Jake responded as casually as he could, "if that works with your schedule."

"Sure, sure, now is great. I will just need to know your address."

Veronica quickly grabbed a paper and pencil lying next to the answering machine, thrust them towards Lisa, and then, on second thought, put the pad on the counter in front of her and gestured to Lisa with her fingers to give her the info, fearing she would mess it up.

"Yes, I know the street. I will see you soon. Goodbye for now."

"Sweet, Oak Street, here you go." And as Veronica handed the paper to Lisa, she suddenly pulled it back as she saw the look in her eyes. "You already know where he lives. I don't believe this—you already know. You scoped him out!"

"Does anything get by you?"

"Not much. Get going. Don't do anything I wouldn't do."

"That won't be difficult."

"Hey—unfair!"

"Kidding, of course—sort of." Lisa winked as she grabbed her purse and said, "Make yourself at home. See you soon."

"Not too soon, I hope," Veronica teased.

CHAPTER 26

The drive to Professor Reynolds' seemed to take forever, although when Lisa arrived, she slowly parked and sat without moving for several minutes. Was she crazy? This kind of behavior happened in movies, not in real life. Or did it? Well, it didn't matter, because one thing Lisa was sure of was that she knew how to act like a lady, and she knew how to handle herself.

Nodding her head in realization of this, she gathered her confidence and crossed the tree-lined street to his door. It was a beautiful home, one she had driven by many times and admired. He had fabulous taste.

The bell echoed in the hallway; she could tell by the sound that it was a big home with open spaces. Moments later, he stood at the door. He honestly was handsome, Lisa noted. His sandy hair was casually tousled. She loved his eyes but quickly looked away when she realized she was openly staring.

"Come in, Lisa. I hope you didn't get lost."

"No, I am familiar with the area." Lisa stepped into the hall but scarcely noticed its beauty. Her heart was racing so fast she was concerned he would hear it.

He closed the large wooden door behind her and turned to lead the way along the long open hallway. "How about something to drink and then we can head outside. It's a beautiful day."

"Sure, sounds good, anything is fine."

They entered the spacious kitchen. It was a serious cook's kitchen, with a commercial stove and two ovens, stone countertops, and double Sub-Zero refrigerators. Lisa briefly wondered if he liked to cook or if the house had come that way. She also noticed the newspapers on the table, which must have been where he read his paper each morning. He appeared so casual and sounded like this was just a typical day, having a student in his home—maybe it was?

As if reading her mind, he said, "I don't usually have students over, but I just happened to have a chance to read your paper and thought it might be nice to talk without distractions."

"Ice tea, juice?"

"Ice tea would be great."

He poured two glasses, handed her one, grabbed the pitcher, and headed out through the back doors. She followed behind him, enchanted by the beauty of his gardens. She was impressed. For some reason, she hadn't expected this from a bachelor. Suddenly he stopped to point at an exotic flower in the garden, and in doing so, she almost bumped into him. She quickly put out her hand and momentarily rested it on his back. "Sorry," she said as she swiftly pulled her hand away as if she had touched fire. "I wasn't paying attention to where I was going."

"No problem." But it was. Jake had felt an electrical charge run through his entire body more intensely than anything he had ever experienced before, including with his former wife, and if Lisa had been five years older, he might not have hesitated to turn around and embrace her.

Lisa was thankful that Professor Reynolds could not see her, because that would have been embarrassing. She could feel the heat on her face; she must have turned scarlet with the intensity of energy that just shot through every nerve within her. That was—it had to be—the sexual energy of passion or lust that Veronica had mentioned.

What should she do? Should she make up an excuse that she needed to leave, pretend that the sudden invitation from Professor Reynolds had caused her to forget a previous engagement? She realized she couldn't, as then he would know for sure of her feelings for him. Lisa took a few slow, deep breaths and continued to follow him to the awaiting lawn chairs.

The next two hours were without incident. They talked, shared ideas, laughed, and finished off the entire pitcher of tea along with some baked goods that he had retrieved from the kitchen. She said she had to get going, and he graciously stood up and put out his hand to help her out of the deep chair. She took it without thinking, and once again, a charge of fiery energy rushed through her. She dropped her hand and quickly turned away. Jake walked her to the door and casually told her to call or stop by anytime.

Lisa thanked him and, as she stepped out of the front door, turned and waved. "Thanks again, see you Monday."

When he closed the door, he found himself speaking out loud. "Did that really happen? Again?" At first, he thought he was the only one feeling it, because what would a beautiful young woman want with a thirty-seven-year-old man? But he caught the flush of color on her face when she touched the hand he had reached out to her.

Whom does one discuss situations like this with? he wondered. No one—he couldn't mention this to anyone. He would need to be discreet and sort this out himself.

CHAPTER 27

"Oh god, Veronica will want to know the details, and I'm not ready to discuss anything. Anyway, I can honestly say nothing happened—well sort of." Lisa sat in her car and couldn't move because her whole body felt weak. She was trying to digest what took place beneath the disguise of an interesting conversation. He was unlike any guy she had ever known.

Nonetheless, she felt like she knew him, and always had. It was a strange sensation to believe that someone she looked up to and admired from afar, and with such an outstanding aboveboard reputation, could make her feel this way. Even if he felt anything for her at all, like Veronica insisted he did, he would never risk his reputation on her; she was just a student who was infatuated with her good-looking, wise, and engaging professor.

She had noticed how some of the other women, women of all ages, looked at him, and she was well aware that he treated each one with the utmost respect and in no way acted anything other than professional.

"I could be making this whole thing up, and it's just me. He didn't even notice or feel anything other than enjoying a casual conversation with an inquiring student," Lisa said aloud. She put her head back against the headrest and closed her eyes. She could feel the charge all over again just by thinking about her hand touching his.

Lisa felt flushed. She could feel the heat on her face spreading throughout her entire body. She wondered how she would act when she saw him again on Monday. Lisa knew she would have to pull herself together by then. The last thing she wanted was to have other students look at her and wonder if she had a crush on him, because that sounded so juvenile, and that is not what she wanted.

She found herself wrapping her arms gently around herself and imagined how his arms might feel. She touched her neck and then opened her eyes, removed the key from the ignition, and opened the door as if some invisible force was propelling her. The next moment, she found herself at his front door, ringing the bell.

Jake heard the bell just as he was heading back outside and contemplated not answering it. He wanted to be alone with his thoughts, and anyway, it was probably just a neighbor wanting to talk or someone selling something. Neither of these was something he wanted to engage in, but he found himself heading to the door to answer it regardless.

Lisa was embarrassed. The moment of impulsive craziness had passed, and she headed back to her car.

"Lisa, you're still here. Did you forget something?"

She turned and said, "No. Thought I left my keys—got them." She smiled and jingled them as she held them up.

Jake watched her return to her car. Then she turned once again and said, "By the way, there was one more thing that I wanted to ask you."

Jake stood on the porch, realizing that his heart was pounding as he watched her elegant strides and otherworldly beauty play out before him once again. Her hair looked silvery gold in the sunlight and fell straight down her back, softly bouncing as she walked. He closed his eyes just for a moment to center himself and took a deep breath to stop the image from consuming him.

She got close enough so as not to yell and softly said, "I forgot to ask you . . ." She looked into his confused yet kind eyes and then unexpectedly put her hand on his face. "Did you feel what I felt?"

On the opposite side of the globe, the tapestry was being woven. What appeared to be separate lives in separate worlds would soon be colliding.

CHAPTER 28

The heat sizzled, baking the midafternoon streets. He and his friends walked to the Ganges River to discuss the teachings of India's great Brahmans. They came upon a caravan that had traveled a great distance through the desert.

Akbar noted the man of about twenty-seven, who was not much older than he, speaking kindly and tending to his camel. His skin was dark, but it was his gray-blue eyes that set him apart from the dark-brown eyes of most from the Far East. It was apparent that the man's journey through the desert had altered the color of his skin. Akbar turned to his friends and said, "He is the one who comes into my dreams."

As Akbar approached him, he realized that the man was speaking to a companion in his native Hebrew. Although, when the young man turned to those who had journeyed with him, it was apparent that he had learned enough of the Indian language to communicate eloquently.

Akbar heard the young man speak to everyone, including servants and women, in Sanskrit. This was not normal; servants and women were considered lower castes and spoken to in Prakrits. Akbar noted this to Yeshua, thinking he wasn't aware of his mistake.

Yeshua turned to him and said, "I honor all. In my Father's eyes, all his children are equal." Akbar realized for the first time that perhaps one should question traditions.

Akbar told the man addressing himself as Yeshua that he had also journeyed to the Far East with his family three years earlier and would be honored to provide accommodations. Akbar realized that this was not only the man who appeared regularly in his dreams but also whom, one day, he would follow back to Nazareth.

Yeshua accepted Akbar's enthusiastic invitation as well as the scenic tour of the city along the way. Yeshua delighted in this glorious and exciting land alive with vivid colors, vibrant fabrics, the Indian wares, and rare spices. There were macaque monkeys, an Indian king cobra snake swaying to the tune of a man's flute, elephants, sacred cows adorned with flowers, and off in the far distance, a Bengal tiger sitting on a rock and watching.

The sunset saturated the sky with color, casting flaming orange, red, and saffron rays across the water, as well as the colorful birds that matched it. But what captivated him most was the number of those seeking mastery of their own lives. There were three dominant religious beliefs in the northern sectors of India at that time: Hinduism, Buddhism, and Jainism, and Yeshua yearned to immerse himself in each one.

Akbar, with the permission of his family, accompanied Yeshua on his journey. Together they became very devoted friends and joyously studied everything they were permitted.

One monastery, hidden high in the Himalayas, was only realized because of a miracle. Akbar was about to suggest they turn back because they could barely see fifteen feet ahead of them, as the snow conditions were getting worse, when Yeshua said, "Fear not, help will come."

Suddenly the storm parted, and out of nowhere, a sheepherder came towards them, motioning for them to follow. They had walked no more than two hundred feet when the snow seemed to mystically part, and they found themselves standing at an entrance to a well-concealed doorway. When they turned to thank their guide, he had mysteriously vanished. Akbar realized that this was the monastery of the holy man he had heard stories about since childhood—only those sanctioned would be led to it and allowed to enter.

Akbar was permitted into several rooms to examine documents written on a variety of materials, including papyrus, palm leaf, animal hide, and wood. Although, there was one room that only Yeshua was allowed in. This did not offend Akbar; he felt privileged to be there. Yeshua was called Isa; it was the Arabic name for Jesus.

Akbar marveled at the monks' ability to levitate and, one day, said to them, "I can't believe you can do that." They looked at him in wonder and remarked, "We can't believe you don't realize you can."

When they were together, Yeshua shared endless stories of his travel of the last twelve years, which also included Kashmir, Persia, Assyria, Greece, and Egypt, and what he discovered in the Tibetan monasteries through his studies of Buddhism. He also spoke of his intention to travel to Priddy and Glastonbury in Britain, where his father would meet him.

Then it was time for Yeshua to leave the company of Akbar and his family. Akbar felt deep sorrow.

"Do not despair, my friend, the years will pass quickly, and we shall meet again."

With that, the vision had come to an end, and Akbar awoke knowing that it would not be long before he met his friend once again. This would be their third lifetime together.

Akbar was aware of his good fortune to be born into a family in India that honored sages and saints as well as understanding the connection to all of creation. His mother had often told him of various images that came to her as he grew in her womb. He was a chosen one, and she had reminded him of this ever since he was a small child—a child born to become great. And this she repeated to anyone willing to listen.

His schooling focused on the divine plan for humanity, and the quickest path to get there.

There was one goal, and that was the ability to dwell in the infinite ocean of God's creative power and to serve humanity. Akbar was lovingly trained in the Hindu Four Paths to the Goal, the way to God through knowledge, love, work, and psychophysical exercises.

These were some of the practices that were part of Akbar's daily life. And because of his sincere commitment and genuine love of all people, sadhus and yogis were among those who found their way to his doorstep to consult him and ask for his blessing, even at a young age.

Akbar had never had a thirst for money. He was a witness to his parents' total devotion to serving God first and society second. With their love and dedication came a deep trust that they would always be provided for, and invariably, the perfect opportunity or item came at the precise time needed.

He had analyzed humankind's insatiable drive for materialism. Everything they desired, they seemed to feel they "needed." They did not understand that by placing their wants first in their lives, they could never be satisfied. There were always more "things" to desire when it was not God one found first.

One can't get enough of what one genuinely doesn't want. Akbar particularly liked a quote by Huston Smith, one of the most regarded authorities on the history of religions: *"To try to extinguish greed with money is like trying to quench fire by pouring butter over it."*

Although Akbar had been granted permission, and even encouraged to study other religions, he held Hinduism and Buddhism as the ones most suited to him. He loved the rituals, the saints, and the deities, such as Shiva and Ganesh. But it was not as though he worshiped them more than God, for they were aspects of God as well as reminders of what one must overcome to find enlightenment.

He understood that the infinite was right there within himself; all he needed to do was remove the barriers that blocked his undeniable connection to God from being realized. His only desire was to cleanse his mind of all that kept him in separation, eliminating thoughts and actions that were rooted in "fear," and allow the light to shine within. Once again, Akbar heard the words spoken so assuredly in his dream.

"Do not despair, my friend, the years will pass quickly, and we shall meet again."

CHAPTER 29

"Did you feel what I felt?" For a moment, Jake did not respond. His body was in a state of intense confusion over the euphoric feelings, as well as determining if he indeed did hear her correctly.

He had—he could see it in her eyes. His words stuck in his throat. He had assumed that he would have time to take a cold shower and rationally figure out how to deal with the affection and intensity of the energy he felt towards Lisa. Instead, she stood before him, posing a question he could not avoid nor dispute.

He looked deeply into the longing and intensity in her blue eyes and knew they matched his own. Suddenly his boundaries disintegrated. He did not care what would be considered proper. He took her face in his hands and pulled her to him as he kissed her lips. She did not resist; she reached out, resting both palms on his chest, and increased the pressure of her lips.

With one hand still on the side of her face, Jake grabbed her around the waist and pulled her into the hall, shutting the door with his foot. His tongue ran across the inside of her lips, and she grabbed him closer, with both hands positioned behind his head. They had been moving towards the living room sofa, but suddenly he regained his control and stopped.

He raised her head so she would look into his eyes. "I can't do this," he whispered. Lisa looked back at him, startled and confused. It *had* been all her, she realized.

"I am sorry and embarrassed," she stammered.

"Please, no," his voice intensified, "I want you more than I have ever wanted anyone."

"Then why?"

"Because I could not endure it if you realized it was a terrible mistake on your part and felt I took advantage of your age and my status as your professor."

He saw the relief in her eyes. "It is I who shamelessly pursued you," she whispered. "You have done nothing that I haven't dreamed of for months."

"Are you sure?"

"More than you can know."

Jake tenderly pushed her hair away from her face and held it gently, searching her questioning eyes for seconds and discovering eternity. He was biding his time. Jake needed to make sure he was not taking advantage of her, but all he saw was kindness and love. This mutual attraction was not a game for her; she was not that type. He outlined her face with his fingers and took her hands in his, kissing her fingertips before releasing them to lightly stroke her face. Her beauty awed Jake. Her eyes were pure love, and her skin was so radiant that a divine essence poured from her.

Lisa arched her neck back, and slowly he kissed every inch of it, continuing up her neck. The rush was beyond anything she had ever experienced. She could feel the lightness of his tongue in and around her ear, and she no longer knew if she could take the intensity of feelings, for she believed that her legs would collapse at any moment. He backed her into the sofa, gently forcing her to sit. He knelt before her and continued this provocative ritual. Lisa closed her eyes, allowing herself to feel his touch with every fiber of her being.

At some point, she grabbed his hair, pulling back his face from hers, looking into his hazel eyes. She spoke to him without words, and once again, her lips found his. She was so insatiably hungry for him, as if she had waited lifetimes for this moment.

As he stood before her, something told him he had done this before. An ancient memory locked away was unveiling itself.

He took her by the hand and led her to the staircase.

CHAPTER 30

Lisa opened her eyes to sunlight streaming through the slightly parted drapes. She knew well where she was, as she had awoken several times during the early-morning hours to see him peacefully lying next to her, breathing softly and rhythmically. Lisa yearned to pounce on this handsome man beside her, or at least touch his lips—they were so beautiful, but she didn't want to wake him. Instead, she would be content to watch him, feeling such profound joy, before once again falling asleep.

This time when she awoke, he wasn't there. She softly called his name, "Jake," and realized she had never called him that before. She heard his footsteps on the staircase, coming towards the bedroom. She began stretching like a cat after a long nap.

He entered the room with a tray of food. "Hungry?"

"Ravenous, for both you and the food!" She blushed when she realized how bold she sounded.

Something flashed across his eyes. For a second, she was alarmed but then realized relief was what she saw on his face. "You OK?" Lisa smiled.

"Yes. I was concerned that choices made last night might be viewed differently now that the light of day had arrived," Jake confessed.

"Come here," she murmured, grabbing for his hand.

Jake set the tray on the nightstand beside Lisa and sat next to her on the edge of the bed.

Lisa sat upright and ran her fingers through the soft waves in his hair. How she had longed to touch them every time the professor—she caught herself—*Jake* had run his hand through it when he was wrapped up in dialogue. He closed his eyes and pushed his head into her hands like her cat used to do. She continued to run her fingers and the palm of her hand across his cheekbones and dug into his hair, massaging his scalp. She sighed, feeling the contentment and naturalness of their connection.

He reached for her, and abruptly, she put up her hand to stop him. "Jake," she smiled, "I need food. I haven't eaten since yesterday morning. Cookies and iced tea don't count, and with it sitting there enticing me, it's hard to ignore that fact."

"Of course!" He jumped up, recovering from the pleasure of hearing her use his name, when only twenty-four hours ago, he could have never imagined this possible. He walked across the room and parted the drapes to reveal a beautiful balcony set with table and chairs overlooking the garden they had sat in the day before.

Jake threw open a set of tall glass-and-iron doors, grabbed his robe off the chair next to the bed, and held it up for her. She shyly dropped the sheet covering her, stood, and turned her back to him as he wrapped it around her. Catching sight of her took everything for him not to grab her and throw her back in his bed. Instead, he gently rubbed her shoulders, kissed the top of her head and the back of her neck, and grabbed the tray as she followed him to the balcony.

Holding the chair out for her, Jake tentatively asked Lisa, "Sure you're OK with what happened last night?" as he removed the contents of the tray, which consisted of a lovely selection of sliced fruit, yogurt, granola, eggs, and goblets of orange juice, onto the table before her. It felt similar to the events of one of his dreams that seemed so real, although each time, he woke up.

She waited until he sat before answering. "It felt natural—surreal but natural—and it still feels that way. I am just not sure how I am going to pretend there is nothing between us on campus. One part of me says, 'So what, I don't care what people think,' and the other knows that your position doesn't need to be questioned, scrutinized, or put under a microscope. I don't expect you to reveal your private life to those who will want to find fault with it, so I am not opposed to keeping it to ourselves and those we choose to share it with."

Jake wasn't expecting her to be so considerate of his position and would not have required that from her. He was not one to hide in shadows or ask another to for his sake, but the way she thought of his career and his feelings moved him deeply. "I am willing to do whatever allows us to hold on to the uniqueness of what we have. I will do whatever I must to protect you, the beauty of our passion, and the opportunity to understand what it means or represents, as long as I know we can still be together."

Jake surprised even himself. There had been other women after his divorce, but none had evoked these deep emotions within him. No woman ever heard him make a statement like "I will do whatever I must to protect you." That was not the Jake he knew; he was cautious about not being misunderstood or leading a woman to believe something he did not feel or even think he was capable of feeling. But here he was, speaking with Lisa as if they had spent passionate months or years together.

He stopped in surprise. Reaching his hand across the table, Jake touched the slight frown upon Lisa's face. "Let's do whatever feels right at the moment, heeding caution to what might interfere with our ability to be comfortable together. Let's take this moment by moment."

Lisa gently swept back her hair and responded, looking directly into his eyes. Her own eyes were appearing even bluer as the sun filtered across them. "That is all we can do right now, as you said, live our truth from moment to moment."

The rest of the conversation was a chance to get to know each other and the events of this lifetime. They laughed, toasted glasses of orange juice, spoke of the beauty of the garden, and shared stories of childhood.

Finally, Jake stood and began clearing the table. "Sometime soon I would like to share with you some interesting dreams I have been having."

Lisa looked at him in surprise. "That is something that I have wanted to do with you."

"Great, then it's a date."

"When?" Lisa asked, holding one hand over her heart.

"Can you make dinner tomorrow night?" Jake hopefully inquired.

"Tomorrow, I can do that. Where shall we meet?"

"Here, if that is OK. I am a great cook." Jake stopped for a moment and laughed. "Well, I should say, others have informed me that I am a great cook, but I will let you determine that. Seven o'clock?"

"OK, seven o'clock, but make it simple so we can talk." Lisa's smile lit her face, and her dimples were irresistible.

"Come here," Jake said as he placed the dishes back down. She stood before him, and as his hands slipped between the openings of his robe, which now adorned the curves of her body, it slid to the floor. Lisa unbuttoned his shirt and pushed it off his shoulders, allowing it to fall next to the robe. She loved his build. It was evident that he ate well and took care of himself.

Jake swept her up in his arms—his heart was pounding as it had the night before—and carried her back to his bed. She smiled that smile that had lit up his heart since the first day he laid eyes on her. He realized that he had never known this kind of joy.

It was two o'clock in the afternoon before Jake and Lisa rolled out of bed for the second time. "Hey, do you know where my clothes are?" Lisa inquired, lifting her brow.

"Follow me. I believe we left a trail," Jake said as he began walking down the front staircase, with Lisa close behind.

"Oh my gosh, that's right, a temporary lapse of memory." Lisa followed a trail of clothes from the staircase to the pool.

Last night, they had headed for the staircase, but Jake needed the memory with Lisa to be different from any other woman he had dated. He had scooped her up and headed in the direction of the pool, where now, once again, they found themselves standing. They looked at the water, and at each other, each one knowing they had to part in order to get things done before class tomorrow.

The clothes they had just retrieved were suddenly on the ground, and as they yelled, breaking into laughter, they pushed each other into the pool.

Late that afternoon, Lisa walked out the front door where, twenty-four hours before, she had done the same thing, although nothing could have prepared her for what had taken place in that short duration of time. She placed two fingers on her lips, kissed them, and turned them towards Jake.

Standing in the doorway, he duplicated the gesture, only closing the door after she was completely out of sight.

There was a high level of respect that hung in the air, and a love that was far greater than either one of them could imagine.

CHAPTER 31

Veronica was furious with Lisa. She had spent the night at her house, waiting for her to come home. "How could she do this to me? No phone call to tell me what happened at prof's house or to tell me she was OK? How hard was that?"

Veronica knew that it was none of her business and that Lisa would tell her when she was ready, but what if something had happened to her? She gestured to the air and made a face because she knew that was not the case. Nothing evil would happen with Professor Reynolds. Sooner or later, Lisa would have to call, but right now, Veronica was off to meet Tyler by her river—their river, as he now called it.

Some part of her was attracted to the fringe of darkness that he carried, although it had dramatically shifted since she first spotted him at school. Maybe it was her Catholic upbringing. Boys like Tyler were the ones the nuns had warned her to stay away from, but there was something more to him, and she knew there was indeed nothing dark about him at all.

Veronica was surprised to find him already there, sitting in the river on a large boulder, moving a long thin stick along the surface.

"Hey, Tyler."

"Hey, beautiful."

Veronica flushed and was momentarily speechless. "What are you doing?"

"Thinking about the dreams I have been having, thinking about you."

Veronica's voice dropped. "Oh. Did you want to talk about them with me?"

"Actually, you are the only one I can talk to about them. They are about you. They are about us." Tyler's eyes shot her a questioning look that was a mix of love and pleading.

"I could use someone to talk to about my dreams also," Veronica confessed as she walked to the boulder to join him.

Tyler grabbed her hand to steady her as she stepped onto the large rock. Veronica felt the charge. *This is extreme, so unlike me to behave this way*, she thought. Tyler did not let go. Instead, as Veronica sat beside him, he held her hand in his lap, rubbing it and playing with her fingers as he spoke. She did not attempt to pull away.

He couldn't look at her as he spoke, focusing on her hand. "It is as if my life has this glitch, like in *The Matrix*. It is playing out in two different dimensions, one past and one present, but now they are starting to collide. I can't explain it, but I think you and I have lived a life together long ago, and now we are here again to do something regarding the unfinished business of the past, but I don't know what it is or why." He stopped, allowing the silence to freeze the moment.

Chills raced through Veronica, and the hair on the back of her neck stood up on end. Before she could stop them, tears were spilling down her face. "I know precisely what you are saying." It was difficult to speak, as her heart was in her throat. She pulled her hand away from him and covered her head with her arms. Drawing her knees close to her body, she rested her forehead on them.

Tyler looked at her, startled, and then wrapped his arm around her shoulder and pulled her to him, allowing her to cry. They sat in silence for a long time, each trying to grasp the mystery unfolding before them. Finally, Veronica sat upright and questioned, "You were my lover thousands of years ago, weren't you? And I was extremely unkind in the end because of my fear for some preordained plan that seemed to be playing out."

"Yes."

Suddenly time evaporated and she was back in his arms as if she never left two thousand years earlier, the night before the tragic event. The gap from now to then stacked one memory upon another like chapters of a book. Longing and desperation replaced any hesitation or apprehension, and suddenly Veronica's heart expanded, revealing a hologram of light and the truth. She screamed as she remembered the pain from when she found his body hanging from the noose in the tree where he had hanged himself.

He was not yet dead, and as he looked at her tear-stained face, he mouthed, "I love you," his eyes pleading for forgiveness. "No, no!" she yelled, but he was gone. It had never been about greed, as the Bible stated. It was her fears for a man she dearly loved, what might happen to him if he stayed in the company of the prophet, and she didn't want him associated with the one who was stirring up so much discord.

As the memory took her, Veronica began to beat on Tyler's chest. "How could you? How could you?"

He didn't know what had happened, but he grabbed her and began to kiss her with such passion that she finally stopped, and her yelling turned to whimpers.

CHAPTER 32

Lisa, although exhausted, knew she needed to find Veronica. She tried her cell, and when she didn't answer, she went to her home. Her door was unlocked, so Lisa walked in, calling for her throughout the empty house. She noticed Veronica had left some of her treasured oils on a counter; it looked like she had been mixing something up.

Lisa decided to head to Veronica's special place next to the river and hoped Veronica would forgive the intrusion, but she had to talk to her. Lisa knew her friend would worry about her, and she realized she had not heard the end of the story regarding her encounter with this mystery guy Tyler.

It took her some time to find a path that looked familiar. Lisa loved the peacefulness of these woods and the smell of foliage and trees; it reminded her of her dad and the good times they spent hiking together. Thankfully it also seemed to recharge her, as the weekend was really catching up with her. She picked some wildflowers, and just as she was considering going back, she thought she heard Sanskrit chanting.

Puzzled, Lisa headed towards it and suddenly stopped. It was Veronica's voice, but there was also someone else, a man's voice. Was it Tyler? Lisa was uncertain what to do. What if she was interrupting something sacred between them or, worse, something she would prefer not to witness? She decided she should go back and leave Veronica a note telling her she stopped by. When she turned to leave, she stumbled on the exposed root of a tree and yelled "Ouch" louder than she thought. The chanting stopped, and she heard Veronica's voice yell out, "Lisa, is that you?"

"Yes," Lisa responded, somewhat embarrassed.

Veronica appeared with Tyler by her side. She was glowing. "Were you coming or going?"

"I was just leaving. I didn't want to intrude."

"Intrude on what?"

"I didn't know if I would be interrupting something private or a sacred ritual." Lisa flushed as she spoke.

"Well, actually, now that you mention it, we were looking for a beautiful virgin, but you will do," Veronica teased.

Lisa smiled at Veronica's humor.

"Hmm, by the look on your face, you probably wouldn't be a prime candidate! Is that the glow of love?"

"Veronica, please!" Lisa gestured towards Tyler.

"Tyler can be trusted. He is one of us. Come on, I am sorry I teased you. Come, join us. I want you two to meet. Multiple events have been unfolding, some heartbreaking and others that are very revealing. We need to all talk soon."

"I know." Lisa sighed. She realized that despite Veronica's humor, her eyes were a bit puffy. "Have you been crying, Veronica?" Lisa asked with concern and compassion.

"That was ages ago. I'm OK now. Really."

CHAPTER 33

When Lisa arrived home later that night, there were two dozen flawless and gorgeous white long-stem roses sitting on her porch. She smiled as she unlocked her door and reached inside to put her things down on a chair nearby. Lisa lifted the vase with both hands and brought it inside, placing it on her forged-iron and glass cocktail table. Her heart was racing as she sat down and reached for the attached card.

Lisa, I miss you already. How blessed I feel that you found your way into my life. Although these roses cannot touch your beauty, kindness, and grace, they were the closest resemblance I could find. Thank you for sharing your radiance with me. With love, Jake

Lisa recognized Jake's writing. He had not taken the easy way and called the florist to order the roses; he had gone himself to get them. She was sincerely touched. A smile hung on her lips as her fingers caressed his words, knowing his hand had been there a short time before. Her heart choked back tears of gratitude.

Lisa took her time washing up, quietly reflecting upon the last forty-eight hours and the unexpected events that took place. She brewed a cup of tea and curled up on her sofa for much-needed downtime, when she heard someone running up the pathway to her steps, taking them two by two.

"Veronica," she deemed. Although she just wanted to be alone with her thoughts and feelings, she knew Veronica would be hurt, and that would take more energy than sharing. Lisa took a deep breath and sighed. "I'm in here."

"Hey, Lisa, I imagine you must be mentally and physically worn out and, wow, beautiful roses. He's romantic! As I was saying, you can tell me if I just need to hold my horses for a while before asking you a thousand questions I couldn't with Tyler there. I'm OK if not."

"Hey, back at you. You're right, I'm wiped out." She saw the disappointment in Veronica's eyes. She hadn't honestly meant that she wanted to wait. "OK, fine," Lisa replied, "I will give you a quick overview."

Lisa gave Veronica the condensed version of the weekend events as Veronica sat wide-eyed, not saying a word.

"Wow" was all Veronica said when Lisa finished.

"Wow is right."

"Is this going to be a weekend affair?"

"Perhaps."

"Perhaps what?"

"He's making me dinner tomorrow night at his place."

"My god, you two don't waste any time! Are you concerned about your studies, as you well know tomorrow night's dinner will probably turn into tomorrow night's sleepover?"

"I realize that. But I can't imagine going back home when I am already there with Jake. I don't have that much discipline! Unless, of course, he is the one who ends the evening."

"Jake? Oh, I see, no more Professor Reynolds," Veronica said in a concerned, questioning tone. "How is that going to work if you slip in class?"

"I'm clueless. That just slipped out. I will have to be careful, at least for now."

Looking at the roses and the card sitting on the table next to them, Veronica crooked her head. "I don't think he will be the one to end the evening. I can't imagine he has the discipline either, after seeing some of the intimate words his message expressed."

Lisa blushed. "Hey, you weren't supposed to read that!"

"How could I not? It's right there in front of me." Veronica rolled her eyes.

"Well I am sure things will settle down. They always do once you date for a while," Lisa said, secretly hoping they never would. "Anyway, I want to talk to him about some things that have been on my mind that I know he can help me with."

"Like what, an 'experiment' on the pursuit of pure lust and pleasure at every conceivable opportunity?" Veronica teased.

"That is not true! And unfair, don't make me sorry I showed you my paper on the experiment. And I did send it to Jake, I mean, Professor Reynolds."

"Sorry about that. I was just getting caught up in the moment and playing, but you are right, it's probably a sensitive subject right now, and it wasn't the right time for that kind of comment. Hey, it's OK to call him Jake. I didn't expect you to sleep with the guy and then call him Professor Reynolds!"

Lisa let go of the need to be overly sensitive and defensive. "You don't need to apologize. I am embarrassed to say it hit a nerve. It was partially a true statement." She let out a soft sigh.

"You know I love you and wouldn't take it personally, for long anyway," Veronica reassured her. "Although, what are you going to do? How are you going to be around each other and not expose what's going on in your relationship? I could see it coming months ago. And now you, for one, glow when you just talk about him!"

"I have thought about that, but I think we can both treat this professionally on campus."

Veronica frowned but didn't say anything, although it was apparent by the subtle scrunching of her eyes and the small forward neck movement that she didn't believe Lisa for a second.

Lisa quickly changed the focus. "What about you and Tyler? That seemed to be an interesting, energetic connection."

"Yeah, wow, that was a total surprise. Seems like we have a lot more in common besides this lifetime."

"What does that mean?"

Veronica pulled herself out of the chair and said, "We will save this for next time. It's a long story, and you can barely keep your eyes open. Get some sleep."

Veronica reached over, gave Lisa a hug, and left.

CHAPTER 34

The woman in white stood at the end of his bed. Jake shook his head, trying to figure out if he was still embroiled in the vivid dream of the disciple John, with a woman who energetically reminded him of Lisa. John was referring to the church's rendition of his masterpiece known as Revelations.

"*They speak not the truth,*" John's voiced had boomed in indignation. "*The minds of those not illumined cannot possibly translate the real meaning of my great works, clearly delivered from my master. The more they attempt to understand it from a literal point, the more they alter it, and the further it gets from its original meaning.*

"*My writings of Revelations were written symbolically, through sacred symbols, as they do not change through time, as languages and interpretation do. Revelations is comprised and saturated with those symbols misunderstood by those who have not journeyed successfully through the dark night of the soul and passed through the gates of mastership into illumination.*"

Urgency filled John's eyes. "*You must find the woman in white. Humanity awaits. I have given her the keys to crack the coded symbols. Revelations has been misrepresented far too long. It is she who dropped the manuscript that you picked up. The Vatican will come to you and insist on its return. Do not allow that to happen!*"

Jake shot upright, although the image and dialogue between John and him had faded, replaced by a sudden light.

A semitransparent form now stood at the foot of his bed. The woman in white waited patiently for Jake to acknowledge her presence. She was holding a book. Was this the work his dream was referring to? But as soon as he reached for the oxblood-colored book, the figure evaporated.

"What is going on?" Jake, now wide awake, demanded to the empty predawn room. "Is she Sister Elizabeth?"

No answer came, only the memory of the image of the woman with short dark hair and a sweet smiling face, grasping the book embossed with gold and reaching out for something with her other hand. She seemed to be challenging him.

Jake knew he must find this woman and the book she clutched so tightly to her breast. Was she the nun who dropped the manuscript? Once again, he reflected upon the smile in her eyes that seemed to challenge him.

"We will see if you are worthy," the eyes had declared.

"Worthy of what?" Jake demanded.

He was answered only by the liquid movement of the sheer drapes dancing in the morning's breeze as they swept across the wood floor.

"This is crazy. Why should I care?" But he also knew the truth. He did care—deeply.

Jake realized that by not responding to either letter from the Vatican for the "immediate return of stolen documents," the Vatican police would soon come looking for him. He had already made copies of the manuscript that was handwritten in both old Latin and Sanskrit, as well as a translation in modern Latin. He guessed the modern translation was written on paper dating from mid-1800s and didn't hold the same value as the ancient papyrus.

Both the unfamiliar parchment, most likely an early papyrus, and the ragged sheepskin cover are what Jake couldn't bring himself to give up. He knew a photocopied replica held no proof of authenticity.

He also realized, the lady in white was the one he needed to find before the Vatican found him. "How?" was the question. All he had to go on was the cover of the oxblood book the vision held in her hands.

Jake rested his hand on the spot where Lisa had peacefully slept as he watched her breathe the morning before. His heart ached for her, and even though he would see her in class soon, he could not reach for her or touch her. He would barely be able to acknowledge her. He would have to wait until tonight, and that would not be easy.

CHAPTER 35

Within six hours, the oxblood book embossed with the golden dragon sat frozen in the palms of Jake's hands: *Odyssey of the Apocalypse*.

He had been lecturing, debating about how much of the information that had been "downloaded" into him the Friday before should share with his students.

Professor Reynolds was not one to stay put at the front of the class. He preferred to engage more personally with his students and often walked up and down the steps, looking them in the eyes. Today was such a day, and as he passed one young man, the sound of a fallen book stopped him. He knelt to return the book to the desk of his student, when he caught sight of its gold-embossed cover. His heart raced. He could not move. Narrowing his eyes, Jake looked up at the questioning face of the young man.

"Cal, where did you get this book?" Professor Reynolds softly inquired.

"It arrived yesterday from my mom, with no explanation." Cal looked concerned. "I was going to call her today and ask her why. Is there a problem?"

Jake stood up, regained his composure, and made a whispered request. "May I borrow it?"

"Yeah, sure, why not."

Jake skimmed the pages of the book and realized immediately that the book was a translation of St. John's Revelation. His heart raced even faster when the back page revealed a woman in white with short dark hair, challenging him with her hand on her hip.

There was no mistaking it: it was she, the woman who had stood at the foot of his bed the night before.

Jake turned and looked directly at Lisa. She had been intently watching him, and until that moment, he had successfully avoided eye contact, but now their eyes remained locked. Veronica whispered Lisa's name, and the spell broke. And both quickly looked away.

The stage was set; the battle between mortality and immortality was about to begin.

"The battle of Armageddon," Jake whispered. "It is time for the Vatican, governments, and all cults and religious orders to become accountable!"

Veronica's eyes widened. "I know her!" she whispered to Lisa.

"Who?" Lisa had no idea who Veronica was talking about.

"Sister Elizabeth, the woman who broke the symbols contained in Revelations!"

"What are you talking about?"

"You know I adore symbols and codes." Veronica's arms were waving wildly. "The woman who wrote the book prof just picked up off the ground! I studied with her last summer. She is incredible. She's the one I told you about. Mark was often there. He helped her out, mostly with digital stuff."

"Calm down, I remember you were telling me about her. I just hadn't linked all the pieces."

"Sister Elizabeth's knowledge, research, and experiences are captivating. She also was a friend of a professor and priest who had access to the archives of the Vatican for thirty-six years."

Lisa opened her mouth to speak but closed it. She calmly waited for Veronica to finish, half listening, as she still couldn't shake the image of Jake's eyes locked on hers. "Maybe we should see about bringing her here. Perhaps she would be willing to lecture in some of our classes."

Veronica looked at Lisa as if she were a genius. "Ultimate!"

"I thought so."

"By the way, why are you always so bloody calm?" Veronica questioned.

"I'm not, just in comparison to you," Lisa said with a wink and a smile.

"OK, it's settled. I'm on it. How could prof refuse? You saw the look on his face!" Veronica sat back, nodding in great satisfaction. "Time to rock the cradle!"

Why stir up a little trouble when she could stir up a lot?

Lisa barely heard another word that Jake or Veronica uttered the rest of the class. Her heart was still in her throat after their eyes met. What did that mean? Why had he looked at her like that? When class was over, she hung back, slowly putting her papers away. Veronica was already standing, ready to go, when she looked down at Lisa knowingly. "Hey, Lisa, I am going to run. Catch up with me later, OK?"

Lisa just looked up and nodded. Veronica flashed one last look at her and another at Professor Reynolds as she walked out the door.

Jake walked over to Lisa. "You OK?"

She looked up at him. "Are you?"

"Yes." He looked in the direction of the open door and then at her. "You were in my dreams again last night, and so was the woman who wrote this book. We can talk tonight." He reached out and touched her face. She closed her eyes to ground the rush of stampeding horses that suddenly took off within her. She was glad she hadn't stood up, as visions of her throwing herself against him kept her in her seat. She dared not touch him or respond. He kissed his finger and touched it to her lips. "Tonight?"

"Yes. Tonight."

Jake was glad she hadn't opened her eyes. She would have noticed, for the moment he touched her face, there would be no stopping him from going further.

A figure witnessing the interaction between teacher and student quickly vanished from the doorway.

CHAPTER 36

When Lisa arrived at Jake's that evening, the front door was slightly ajar. Pushing the beautiful, carved wooden door open, she was surprised to find the length of the hall bordered with candles in etched crystal containers throwing off beautiful patterns of light across the mirror-like finish on the ivory Venetian-plaster walls and cream-colored stone floors. "I would have never guessed he was such a romantic," Lisa whispered to herself.

There were also significant works of art by respected artists, and she admired his ability to mix old and new, and even though it was a big home, it was gracious and retained a relaxed and welcoming air.

Calling out "Hello," Lisa followed the candlelight into the kitchen, breathing in the delightful aromas. When he was not there, she continued following the candlelight through the open doors to the veranda. She took in the sweeping views of the lush gardens that ensured absolute privacy from the neighbors.

The candlelight outlined one end of the rectangular pool where a large stone Buddha sat, and the flames danced and flickered off the water. Her heart raced. There he was, feet up on a stone cocktail table, lounging in a deep, finely woven rattan chair with his back to her, gazing towards the pool. Her heart was in her throat, and she felt her cheeks flush. She had hoped her reaction to seeing him again would be that of a mature woman. Instead, she felt like a schoolgirl.

Taking several slow, even breaths, she came up from behind him and ran her fingers through his hair. Jake tilted his head back and said, "Come here," grabbing her arm and pulling her around him until she was sitting across his lap.

"I've missed you." He held her close to him as she buried her face in his arms and chest.

"I've missed you too," Lisa responded, looking into his eyes before kissing him passionately.

When Jake caught his breath, he said, "You're late. I was wondering if you changed your mind."

"My bad, of course not. Time got away as I was trying to catch up on homework I hadn't completed on the weekend, as I was mildly distracted," she said with a mischievous smile. "I should have called. I have missed you every moment since I have been away from you."

"You're forgiven. So have I—missed you, that is. Come on, dinner is ready, and I won't kiss your beautiful lips again or we will never eat," Jake said with a knowing smile.

Lisa stood up, and Jake rose to his feet right behind her, sliding his arm around her waist as they leisurely walked back to the house.

"Your home is a piece of heaven. I was so distracted last time I was here. I didn't pay attention to how amazing every detail is."

"Thank you, I admire it also, as I am captivated by good design, architecture, and antiquity. It definitely feels like home."

When they arrived in the kitchen, Jake inquired, "Would you like a glass of wine, or would you prefer something else?"

"A glass of wine would be great." Lisa was not much of a drinker, but she hoped it would take the edge off her nervousness.

"Red or white?"

"Red please."

He handed her a glass of wine and lowered the volume of an Italian opera with the sleek remote control lying on the counter. "I'd like to make a toast to life, us, and the absolute joy I find being with you. You look stunning, by the way."

As their glasses touched, Jake could see Lisa blush, and a timid smile appeared that accented one of her dimples as she lowered her eyes and pushed her hair back to one side. He loved that about her. She was so beautiful as well as humble.

Lisa toasted back, "To an amazing chef who not only is providing a culinary experience beyond anything I imagined but can evoke all my senses, not just the aroma but sound and sight as well. I'm sure this is a dinner I won't soon forget, as I am well aware that it is not easy to flawlessly blend all those things. Here's to you, Jake, and don't expect me to follow suit. That would be impossible!" Lisa giggled as she sipped the wine.

"Truth be told, it was easy." His eyes flashed. "The details came together effortlessly as I thought of you. And as long as I don't have to try to speak as eloquently as you, we are even. After that speech, I hope you honestly do like the simple meal I have prepared." He raised his glass again and escorted her to an awaiting table consisting of small silver restaurant-style covered buffet dishes with flames flickering below.

"Wow, you don't miss a thing."

"This approach to dining makes it easy to keep things warm, as I had no idea if we would be eating right away."

"I wanted to tell you how touched I was, not only by the gorgeous roses but by your handwritten note. Thank you."

Jake kissed her hand. "My honor."

Jake had prepared a table on a terrace filled with even more glowing candles overlooking the gardens. *He is definitely a romantic!* Lisa smiled remembering Veronica's comment. A fire was blazing in a large stone fireplace, creating a homey feeling as they small talked for almost an hour before Jake mentioned the dreams he had been having the last few months. This was the only time Jake had shared them with anyone, and although he was a bit tentative at first, Lisa didn't stop him, so he continued, one dream after another.

Lisa didn't say a word; she just watched him, intently drinking in every drop of what he said. Then suddenly there were tears streaming down her cheeks, and Jake stopped abruptly. He had scared her. Why hadn't he eased into all this information? What was he thinking?

"I'm sorry, Lisa. I didn't mean to overwhelm or upset you. Forgive me." He attempted to wipe the tears from her cheek.

Lisa put her hand up. "It's just—well, read this." Lisa pulled out two folded sheets of paper from her jeans' back pocket, which she had printed from her computer right before she came in case she got the nerve to share some of her dreams with him.

Jake took the pages from her and carefully unfolded them. As he began to read, Lisa could see that his face was ashen.

"This can't be." Jake pushed his plate back, put his elbows on the table, and rested his head in his hands before looking down at the pages once again.

Strands of hair had escaped her veil. As she tucked them back into place, she felt eyes upon her. Turning slightly, she felt her heart skip a beat. Her eyes locked with those of an unknown man for a brief moment before she embarrassingly turned away. Who was he? Something had just happened, but what?

Moments later, she spotted him rushing across the mosaic floor as he and several others surrounded the one called Yeshua and quickly departed from the temple. "Who was that with Yeshua?" she whispered to her friend beside her. "They call him John."

My dreams are always about this woman. I now believe I am the woman, as they are beginning to feel like I lived that life. That is not a symbolic dream but an actual memory. I wish I could talk to Professor Reynolds about them—perhaps someday.

Jake folded the pages back up and looked up at Lisa. "It's true, it did happen. It is more than just a dream, symbolic, or a metaphor. My god, it was you I saw in the temple!" Jake's eyes began to water, and neither said a word for several minutes.

Lisa finally whispered through the tears running down her cheeks, "What does this mean?"

"I don't know yet, but I have a feeling we will be finding out soon enough," Jake assured her as he reached for her hand.

CHAPTER 37

Two days went by before Jake finally had time to read the book he borrowed from Cal. Arriving home, he pushed open the French doors leading to the back loggia and sat quietly for a few moments before opening the book with the oxblood cover resting upon his lap: *Odyssey of the Apocalypse.*

Jake had tried to track Sister Elizabeth down, to no avail. The phone number Veronica gave him no longer worked, and Mark said he lost track of her six months prior when she gave notice to move out of her office.

As he began to read, his eyes could not be diverted as he grasped the importance of the information before him. Chills ran up his spine, his eyes welled, and he shook his head to clear the barrage of emotions.

St. John's Revelation finally made perfect sense. The dragons, horses, swords, battles, and darkness—every symbolic explanation—rang true in his heart. He did not need to spend weeks in research; his heart told him that what his eyes beheld was his truth.

He had always known that noble works written by the illumined were not to be taken literally. How many times had he told his students this? He was like a broken record, but now before him were the encrypted codes, the keys to understanding the fallacies that had been shoved down the throats of millions of Christians for two thousand years. Jake felt that this slender, unassuming book contained many important meanings of symbols within the numerous works of John the Beloved.

It was 2:00 a.m. when Jake finished and once again viewed the photo of the woman in white on the last page. "Thank you, Sister Elizabeth, it is apparent that you are also a mystic." He nodded as he spoke. Revelations was revealed. It was about time. Humankind need not be held captive by the fear of an outer Armageddon; it was the internal Armageddon that one must face and fight that battle instead of the endless external ones.

One's right to divinity did not come without a price, as those without awareness were easily seduced by the ego and lured back into a subservient role again, enslaved by the mind and trapped by desire's shallow enticements. How the ego laughed at humankind's superficial desire and continual chant for a world of peace!

Ah, if one could not even find harmony within themselves, how did they think they could create peace in the world through marches or demonstrations bound and fueled by blame and anger? What power the ego enjoyed knowing that as long as it could make one believe that another was to blame for their unhappiness, the longer the egocentric mind could keep them from looking within.

Ordinarily, it was when their suffering became far more oppressive than their joy that people were willing to question their lives and desire something higher, something beyond external desire. Grievously, so little bait was needed to lure humanity away from their good intentions. The only war in reality that existed was between the egocentric mind and the human, and thus far, the ego had triumphed. Such a minuscule percentage of humankind rooted in peace.

Jake knew he must find Sister Elizabeth. It was urgent that he discover why she dropped the manuscript, and since the vision of her a few nights ago, he was convinced it was on purpose, knowing he would be the one to pick it up. Why couldn't she just hand it to him? Was the black car that pulled out at the same time the taxi did following her? And how did she get it in the first place?

The Vatican letters were vague. Perhaps they didn't really know if he had them or not. They could be just fishing. He would ask Dean Mitchell if he was the only male to get a Vatican letter. Who else shared his physical description? He would start there.

He sighed with relief knowing it was possible that they didn't know he was the one who had the manuscript hidden under floorboards specifically designed with temperature control for rare documents. This wasn't the only Vatican-claimed manuscript resting in that safe.

His thoughts changed to Lisa. How blessed he felt that he and Lisa could travel together in this life. The written account of her visions last night proved his belief and yearning that she was the one appearing in his dreams.

CHAPTER 38

Lisa sat curled up on her sofa, reflecting on her dinner with Jake two nights before. She decided to share the experience and her visions with Veronica, but that was after Veronica had already begun to tell her about her dreams, and those that Tyler had been experiencing.

When they finished, they sat quietly for a long time before Lisa disclosed to her friend, "This is the same feeling I had the other night with Jake. I was so stunned by the realization that something significant that would change my life forever would be coming about soon, I could barely move.

"I asked him to hold me. I slept in his arms the entire night, and I dreamt that I was watching a glorious sunset with rays of light washing shades of glowing pinks and lavenders across a range of mountains, and below was a lower range in dark greens and browns with touches of light on the tips.

"I turned and saw Jake in long robes in a doorway that appeared to be a small stone structure built into or near a cliff. It was cave-like. I stepped onto the floor and noticed the baked-clay tiles before I reached for his extended hand. The walls were of whitewashed stucco. I remember we were getting ready for bed, and he lit two small oil lamps before rolling out mats, putting them right next to each other."

Veronica was staring at her in disbelief. "How did you remember all that detail?"

"I wrote it down the moment I awoke. It was still so vivid and fresh like it just happened," Lisa said. "But wait, there was more. It was as if we had done that very thing together thousands of years before, him holding me in his arms all night. And it was so lucid that I expected to wake up and find myself lying on a mat and wearing garments from twenty centuries ago. It was all so surreal—almost eerie."

"Do you have any idea where you were," Veronica inquired.

Lisa nodded her head. "The first thing I said when I woke up was 'Nazareth.'"

They both sighed at the same moment and then sat quietly for some time. Eventually, Veronica said, "I think it would be helpful for the four of us to get together and share this information. I find it very peculiar that all of us are having the same types of experiences during the same period of history—and how odd and timely was it that Tyler 'happened' to start appearing in prof's class?"

"I was thinking about that also," Lisa admitted.

"I noticed that you didn't see Jake tonight. Everything OK, or did you just need a break?" Veronica inquired.

"I think we both did. It has been pretty intense. I also know Jake has wanted to read the book on the apocalypses that he borrowed from Cal a couple of days ago. How about you and Tyler?"

"Same, needed time to digest."

The two of them spent the evening talking about the rest of their dreams, revisiting how they had met in the first place, and once again finding each other in the same college, and even more intriguing, taking the same course. "Nothing is by accident, is it? It is all a harmonious dance that appears to be predesigned," Veronica marveled.

Lisa nodded her head in agreement, shivering at the thought of it and questioning what the days and weeks ahead had in store for them.

High in the mountains, Sister Elizabeth had escaped the clutches of the Vatican police. She spoke out loud to herself, "Did they not understand that the truth was impossible to disprove?" She realized their unyielding beliefs would keep them and their followers imprisoned in unnecessary darkness for generations to come. By some means the cycle must be broken; somehow the light must prevail. She would prefer that her fellow humans not have to endure another two thousand years of darkness—but Elizabeth knew it was not up to her but each of them to choose.

In a distant recess of her mind, the woman in white could see the light seeping from beneath the doorway of death. A blissful smile crossed her face, knowing her time had come.

CHAPTER 39

Angelina's heart was breaking. She knew now without question that to expect her husband to meet her emotionally halfway was just a ridiculous fantasy that long ago blew away like particles of dust. His comment when she asked him to go to counseling with her was met with a shrug and no more emotion than if she told him she decided not to go to dinner and a show with her girlfriends.

How sad it felt that she had worked so hard at finding ways to create happiness with him. Even though her friends mentioned that he probably didn't know how to handle his feelings, she had no choice but to let go. There was nothing more she could give or do, nothing left to keep them connected.

Last night, their eighteen-year-old son, Edward, had summed up his parents' marriage in a few words, something she had been trying to understand for years, and suddenly it all made sense, so why was there still a dull ache in her heart?

Yes, logically she knew she deserved much more than James was willing to give her, and this was not on a materialistic level but on an emotional level. Edward had been describing his relationship with his dad: "Mum, I can't say I am surprised to hear that James has no interest in counseling. He is such a distant bloke. I wouldn't miss him if you were no longer together. My relationship with James has always been emotionally distant and exhausting, and I can honestly say, I seldom felt even an ounce of love from him."

It crushed Angelina's heart to hear that and, furthermore, troubled her that her son called his dad by his given name, but it was in that moment that Angelina understood what her marriage had been for her: emotionally exhausting, to an emotionally unavailable man. It had drained her of her life force. Trying to make something work that couldn't succeed if only one of the parties was willing to do what it took was not what she deserved. James did not want to honor his original promises to her, nor did he want to change. She did. It was as simple as that.

Her counselor had warned Angelina that he didn't feel James would do the internal work necessary to walk with her on a clearly defined spiritual path that was a part of who she was. But Angelina wanted the promises James made to be true, so she ignored the warnings, for this was the man she wanted to share the rest of her life with, or so she thought.

She saw the possibilities, and more than one psychic told James that he came to be a great teacher of the people—if he chose to speak his truth instead of avoiding feelings that might create discomfort or lead to differences of opinion. They warned him that he would have to make a sincere effort to heal childhood parental issues for this to occur.

She recognized his marvelous instinct for people, and if he chose to listen to his feelings, he would be truly inspiring. He had a quick and wonderful sense of humor, but Angelina found out too late that this was not just used to entertain or fit in; it was used to avoid discussing important issues between them.

They had so much potential as a couple, and that was what made it even more heartbreaking to Angelina. They were both physically striking and would have no problem commanding audiences for lectures or retreats together, or building communities of homes and shops designed around conscious living that was grounded in beauty, mentally and physically supporting the human and spiritual desires of those it attracted. She dreamed of their joy in creating high-vibrational properties together, something both of them had exceptional abilities to accomplish.

But these dreams turned out to be only hers, as with every attempt she made to team up on projects, he found excuses not to. Angelina remembered back to the early years, when she had danced for him, dressed up for him—surprised him and attempted to share her spiritual world. But it became so inequitable that her sadness turned to bitter moments, or desperate comments, hoping for some emotional contact from him.

Angelina sat next to the stream, and although it was cold, there was such beauty and sweetness in the fluid dance as the water swept around and over the rocks, collecting into its current whatever was light enough to accompany it on its journey. She watched a ruffled leaf passing by and wished she could be like that leaf, just riding along with no concern or thought about where the voyage would take it, and all with no emotional ties to the outcome.

Angelina sighed remembering their counselor Richard's words early on in their relationship: "James, if you don't show up in this relationship, and instead you continue to emotionally check out with your jokes or choose silence when you need to be Angelina's husband and partner, one day, she will no longer be there. When an adult discussion is required, especially regarding your folks, you cannot remain the silent child—heal your issues or lose her."

James just looked at their counselor blankly as the warning continued.

It was the only time Richard verbalized his opinion so concisely. Sadly, although James had listened to his words and said he understood, it seemed the request was beyond his willingness to execute.

Later, when she reminded James that she needed him to emotionally show up in their relationship, he was silent. It felt exhausting and ineffectual to try to communicate with him, like pulling water out of a dry, sunbaked stream.

It was getting dark, but Angelina continued to sit by the water, touching it gently as it moved beneath her fingers. Her heart felt so dense that she didn't feel she could make the walk back to the house. The memories kept coming, and the facts became more apparent and painful. She needed to understand why she had attracted James in the beginning, to never again recreate this same type of relationship by healing the unhealed within herself.

Angelina couldn't face going back home; instead, she took both shoes off and put her feet in the water, hoping to release her sadness, allowing it to flow away just as the leaf had. She knew she couldn't stay in their marriage much longer—it was killing her spirit.

Angelina swished the water. "Lord, I don't want to struggle anymore." The response in her mind surprised her: *"Then don't."*

Angelina knew she needed to heal the wounds below the surface and rid herself of the shame she had kept buried for so long, the humiliation of being unloved. The sadness that she could attract this level of non-commitment, this level of uncaring—that was the gravest wound.

Just as Angelina was removing her feet from the water and wiping them on the soft moss, she was struck hard by a profound realization. "My dad was emotionally unavailable. My husband is emotionally unavailable. Does that mean I am emotionally unavailable to myself since I have attracted these types of men?" And right then, she became aware of a voice within.

"Perhaps at times, as you have been waiting for another for so long."

She tried to push the thought aside, but something in her heart caught. Bursting into tears, she knew what she heard was accurate, and for once, Angelina didn't try to contain her emotions. She knew these feelings were older than this lifetime, considerably older.

Returning home, Angelina sat at her desk, ran her fingers over the silver-embossed leather cover of her journal, and began writing.

Gratitude.
I admit,
I am grasping at straws right now,
trying hard to remember authentic joy,
or genuine happiness.
Once again, there is nothing for me to offer to you, except for these tears I cry.
These tears that tear at my heart,
these tears that reveal a lifetime or lifetimes of loneliness,
and shred my heart to bits.
Even when the men in my life were there,
they were not there.
Am I?

Angelina gave up, put her pen down, went to her room, and slowly washed for bed. She was relieved James was away. Slipping between the luscious ivory sheets, Angelina closed her eyes, hoping to end the pain still heavy in her heart by quickly falling asleep. She pleaded to whatever divine energy was listening. "Divine Angels, please wrap your arms around me. Let me find some peace and comfort in the night."

Instead, it was her tears that finally exhausted her, and Angelina fell into a deep and troubled sleep.

"Run, my beloved, you don't need to do it this way! This will prove nothing! Please, there is still time to escape!" the woman desperately pleaded until her words turned to sobs. He stood looking at her with untold love, holding her hands between his.

"Mary, my beloved, you more than anyone knew this day would come. It is written."

"No, no! It is only written, tear the words, it doesn't mean it has to be so." Tears blinded her ability to clearly see his loving eyes. She was familiar with this look. No amount of persuading was going to talk him out of his decision.

"No, no, please, I beg you, I cannot bear to lose you!"

"Beloved Mary, it is you who needs to carry on with my teachings. It is you who has the understanding of the inner worlds of initiation and the wisdom the others do not share. I need you to take my place as teacher. It was our design before we came into this life."

"Do not ask me this when my heart is being torn from me. I cannot endure witnessing this untimely event. There is so much we can still accomplish together. I beseech you, not to betray my heart, my love for you." Her sobs were now choking her.

He kissed her eyes and her lips, smoothed her hair, and walked towards the approaching guards.

She fell to the ground and wept.

"Betrayal, is that all I have ever known?" Angelina woke from her dream, covered in perspiration. "What do you want from me?" she yelled desperately to the darkened room. "What do you want?"

This time, it wasn't from exhaustion that she fell back to sleep; comforting hands touched hers. And although she could not see them, she felt her hands between them. She closed her eyes and felt a light fill her heart. The feeling of complete and absolute peace poured into every cell within her being, joined by a love so exquisite it was beyond description.

"Thank you," she whispered.

Hundreds of miles away, only one baffled astronomer noted the peculiarities within the movement of the distant planets.

"What mayhem looms?" Luke's disheveled eyebrow rose as he

rubbed his salt-n-pepper beard as he meticulously charted the second discrepancy in two weeks. Luke had no intention of sharing this information with anyone—just yet. He knew there was more to come.

CHAPTER 40

Andrew cut his holiday short, not wanting to wait another moment before heading back to his London office. The image of the great dove and the remembrance of the words, *"Why are you destroying my majestic and precious earth? For in the end, although she will barely survive, you will die a long and tragic death from the very chemicals you have so richly profited from. Do you not remember who you are?"*

On this day, he did not ignore the beggars on the street but instead greeted each one like an old friend, shaking their hands and giving them words of encouragement such as "Be well, mate" as he pressed folded hundred-dollar bills into their hands. Many who had encountered him before and knew better than to approach him were dumbfounded and could barely utter a thank you. One just wept.

His chauffeur, Sam, followed him after witnessing his strange behavior since his return from the island. He could only nod at each person and shrug as Andrew pressed money into their hands. Finally, before Andrew stepped through his office building's front doors, he said goodbye to Sam and told him to have a great day.

"You all right, sir?" Sam inquired. Patting him on the back, Andrew remarked, "Great! Now go buy Erica something she has always wanted, and put it on the company account." "Well bee's knees!" Sam said under his breath.

Sam had worked for Andrew for twelve years, and he didn't realize Andrew even knew he had a wife, let alone her name. After Andrew was well on his way to the elevators, Sam chuckled. "If he only knew, what my lady has always wanted was for me to quit and get a new job! 'Just tell the bugger to sod off!' Erica had exclaimed more than once."

As Andrew stepped off the elevator and entered his tastefully decorated offices, he was unaware that he was humming a tune. Although, it didn't go unnoticed by those he passed.

"Morning, Meg, do me a favor. The first thing I need from you is to get me a list of the best, not top ten but the most ethical, spiritual activists on the planet."

Bewildered, Meg began to mumble. She was still stuck on his asking for a "favor." He had never asked her to do him a favor. Bark a command, yes, but he never asked for a favor.

"It's OK, Meg. I realize it's a tall order. If you need help, pull as many staff members as you need from the office, those who are environmentally conscious." Andrew thought a moment and realized he may have fired all the "bleeding hearts." "You might want to check the other nine floors. You might have better luck."

"Sir, I don't want to sound ignorant, but what is a spiritual activist?" Meg inquired.

"Not really sure, it's just a phrase that keeps running through my mind. I just know they do planetary good works and are not associated with religion, government, nor dogma." As an afterthought, he added, "One other thing, would you call a board of directors meeting for Thursday, late afternoon? That will give those overseas a chance to get here."

"Sir, all of them? From all your companies?" Meg had only seen Mr. Turner gather groups of fewer than twenty—never all of them.

"Yes, how many are there?"

"A lot. Honestly, sir, I don't know," Meg sheepishly responded.

"I guess we'll find out." Andrew winked as he headed to his private corner office with sweeping views of the city.

Thirty minutes later, Meg knocked on Andrew's door. "Come in," came Andrew's voice.

"Sir, I just did a quick search, and there are dozens of links to different groups, but I thought I would just give you a few to see if I am on the right track of what you are looking for."

"Who's this chap?" Andrew asked, pointing to the first name on Meg's list.

"His name is Andrew Harvey. His name may have been what caught my eye," Meg confessed. "He's raw, passionate, seems authentic—I listened to a video. A scholar, well traveled. And I am wondering if he could help us find the right groups. I just sent you a link to his website. It should be in your email."

Andrew found the link and clicked on it. Looking up at Meg, he pointed to a chair next to his desk. "Have a seat."

Meg didn't think he could surprise her any more than he had, but he just did. She had never been invited to sit in his office.

"Interesting gentleman, I feel I would like this chap. Anyway, he has a fine name," Andrew said with a wink. "Could you set up an appointment to see him?"

"Here? Or perhaps the club?" Meg inquired.

"No, I'll go to him," Andrew said with certainty.

"Africa, sir? I think his website said he's about to head to Timbavati, South Africa, on a white lion excursion, about bringing awareness to save them."

"Well that would be a first. See what you can find out. It would be the perfect setting for me to get to know this intriguing fellow." Andrew nodded with excitement. "Have you started notifying the board of directors?"

"I turned it over to Rachel," Meg answered.

"Tell her to get the list together, notify each of them, but tell them to wait until further notice. Who knows, I may be traveling to Africa," Andrew said, flashing a boyish grin.

"Right away. I'll get Andrew Harvey's personal number and call him," Meg assured him.

"Why don't you get the number and put me through when you contact him. I would like to speak with him directly," Andrew said with satisfaction.

When Meg left, Andrew put his Dami alligator slip-on shoes on the top of his desk, crossing his ankles. "Hmm, I wonder if I should open a shoe company using only non-animal natural planetary sustainable materials. Well, that's a mouth full! I don't want to be responsible for killing animals. I am sure I have enough blood on my hands."

CHAPTER 41

In her youth, the more Angelina had questioned the church, the more frustrated she had become. Her mother, Joan, being a devout Catholic, had a difficult time with Angelina's persistent questions that escalated at the age of four. Most of the time, she could not answer her daughter but realized her arguments often stirred something deep within her.

At the age of seven, Angelina had challenged the monsignor at her Catholic school, who had come to set the children straight about being sinners and how Jesus died because of those sins, and that he was the only son of God. After several additional false statements regarding Jesus and Mary Magdalene, Angelina couldn't stand one more lie, and her typically shy, silent self burst out, *"That's not true, nor what Jesus wants us to believe!"*

Angelina was silenced and shamed in front of her peers with a piercing glare and stern "Go to the office this instance, young lady!" Angelina was upset and heartbroken as she waited for her mother to pick her up and couldn't help but think, *Why doesn't anyone believe me?*

When her mother arrived because of her "outrageous" behavior, Joan said nothing, but Angelina could see from the look in her eyes that she was completely baffled about what to do or say, and this made Angelina's heart ache. She felt more alone than ever. Angelina stayed firm in her beliefs but felt bad that her mother had to walk the mile that it took to get to her school, as they only had one car.

Growing up, Joan had not questioned what she was told; she had just believed it must be correct. Now she had a daughter who challenged every belief she was taught. She prayed for Angelina, but her prayers were not prayers asking to turn Angelina into a believer of the Catholic Church or to silence her. Joan prayed that Angelina would find the truth, her truth, and realize that she would only be able to share her wisdom with the few who could hear and know the purity of her soul.

At eleven years old, she informed her mother that she refused to go to church ever again. "They think themselves infallible. But, the church is run by fallible men," Angelina would sigh in dismay at every misrepresentation or misquoted passage of her beloved Jesus. She saw him as her teacher and friend, and knew that what he had cried out for, his entire lifetime, was compassion, love, and the desire for every soul to be liberated and become Christed as he had.

Angelina knew how hurtful it was to be misquoted or misinterpreted. She often wondered how Yeshua must feel to be dishonored in this way, to have his words used to manipulate instead of empower people for over two thousand years.

Was his life in vain? she often questioned.

Angelina's early twenties had been spent directing her anger towards the Catholic Church for hiding what she considered the truth, withholding the information that she believed would take humanity out of the darkness and allow them to be self-empowered.

She thought about the suppressing and withholding of information regarding the Dead Sea Scrolls, the Gospel of Mary, and tens of thousands of illuminated works. She knew much had been transcribed by those who could not possibly decipher the meanings behind the words of those so enlightened. Even rarer was the correct translation from the ancient language, in which they were first written, into another.

Someday the truth would be revealed, for even if the church refused to share the information, she also knew the church would never destroy it. Or would they? Realizing they had burned and destroyed thousands of books, scriptures and teaching in the past was unsettling.

Angelina turned her back on the Catholic Church, although she never turned away from her love for Yeshua, Mary Magdalene or Mother Mary. She missed the rituals but could not support the adaptations to the words, nor the falsifying of God's pure joy and love for all humanity.

Angelina thrust herself into a journey that led her to explore numerous spiritual paths, and she treated each one as an archaeological exploration, carefully uncovering one hidden treasure after another. However, by the time Angelina was twenty-eight, she was frustrated and exhausted, and believed that it was time for the old structures to fall apart. Thankfully, people were waking up to these suppressive, fear-based models.

Angelina knew the majority of the men of the church were by no means evil, just unawakened souls who more often than not only held parts of the convoluted truth. Indeed, there were those who were young souls and misused their power and position consciously, driven by their idolization of control, money and power, but even those men had something to teach those who gravitated to them.

Those followers would eventually learn that it was their own divine heart and intuition they needed to listen to and not give their power away to someone they hoped would save them from their fears, suffering, and confusion. Jesus' messages on love, forgiveness, acceptance, and compassion were evident to Angelina. What else did one need to understand?

What tugged at her soul was the unease she felt each time she judged, but she didn't know how to support each beloved in God's sacred dance with all creation and not cry out about the injustices.

Angelina let out a great sigh. "It always comes back to me, doesn't it, God? To ignite the self-love so completely within that compassion seeps into every crevice of my being. God, I don't want to be a part of the problem. I do want to be the love you have shown us. Help me to see with your eyes and know how I may assist."

That night, the moon shone brightly through the skylight of her meditation room. She loved this beautiful and sacred space. It ignited such devotion for the Beloved, with its hand-painted fresco walls depicting a lovely ancient temple with olive trees and paths lined with wildflowers and birds in flight. The hand-blown crystal teardrops hanging from a clear fish wire from the ceiling were catching sparks of the moon's reflective evening light and scattering them like stars across the room.

She lit the three candles and watched them flicker in their golden mercury-lined containers. They danced on the walls and diffused a soft glow across the altar. She breathed in the intoxicating smell of the incense that had initially beckoned her to the room and fixed her gaze upon the eyes of her Beloved Master, whose portrait took the prominent center space on her altar. His presence in any form immediately calmed her, and she again filled her lungs with three deep, cleansing breaths.

Angelina grabbed an aqua silk floor pillow and sat cross-legged. She began pouring her heart out, begging Yeshua to prove to her what her heart whispered was accurate.

Two hours later, feeling peaceful but exhausted, she blew out the candles, bowed to the heavens, and went to bed.

Just as she was falling off to sleep, she experienced the most profound and vivid vision she had ever had. A soft golden-white light filled the room. She was not afraid because its energy was so magnificently loving.

Then she saw him: Yeshua, the Christed One, walked up to the side of her bed and reached for her hand, saying, *"Come. You no longer need to follow me. It is time, once again, you take my hand and walk beside and within me, as me."*

His eyes and form were profoundly luminous; no amount of human words could describe this vision. As Angelina reached for his hand, she felt the most profound love fill her being. Her heart exploded with pure joy. Then he was gone. Now fully awake, Angelina began weeping in gratitude for his affirmation that she was not crazy or disillusioned as the church had tried to persuade her to believe.

The remembrance still left Angelina with chills, and her heart leaped in gratitude whenever she thought back to that night.

It wasn't until Angelina was an adult that her mother revealed to her the admiration she felt for her as a child. Joan had laughed, "What great courage you had as a little girl going against a powerful group of men, and being considered a heretic without fear of the consequences was impressive!"

Angelina was shocked. "Mother, why did you never share that with me? All those years, I thought your silence meant you agreed with them and disapproved of my behavior?"

"I figured you knew," was Joan's baffled response.

It was then that Angelina had turned her attention to herself, and it was then that she embarked on a crusade to request that the universe make itself more available to humanity.

She thought back with a smile, back to the day when her anger and her mission to prove to the world every fault of the church came to a halt. Her frustration was replaced with a new awareness, and anger shifted to compassionate and gentle acceptance.

"Giving truth, and the power it contains, to those who have not diligently searched, nor are highly evolved, is like giving a sword to a child."

CHAPTER 42

Exhausted, hungry, and grateful, José thanked the driver of the old blue Ford for picking him up and arranging a room for eleven dollars a night in a hotel the drivers cousin worked at, which was less than a mile from Basílica de Nuestra Señora de Guadalupe.

Grabbing his belongings from the back of the old truck, José dusted off the remnants of hay and dirt as he thanked his new friend, Pedro, once again. Pedro had been kind enough to drive him past the Basilica so José would know his walking path in the morning. He was sad to learn that the old Basilica had been replaced by a new modern structure because the former church became dangerous due to the sinking of its foundations. José loved the energy of old architecture, but even this new insight didn't dampen his spirits for long.

The hotel was an unattractive mid-century, mustard-yellow building, but José paid it no mind. He was there to see Señora de Guadalupe, and nothing else mattered. All he wanted to do was eat from the modest rations he had packed and sleep.

The bed was no harder than his bed at the monastery, and within moments, José fell into a sound, dreamless sleep until just before 4:30 a.m.

"My son, I have come to console you. Do not be concerned by your choice to leave the monastery. It was at my request that you should come, and I will never leave you." Reaching out her hand that was

emanating rays of golden light towards José, her love penetrated his heart and ignited a passion within so profound that he tried to reach out to touch her otherworldly bluish-green-colored mantle to stop the penetration of any more rapture; thus, he would undoubtedly perish before his mysterious mission concluded.

The Blessed Mother spoke once again. "José, you will know where to meet the others when you find the alignment of the constellation Leo, upon the tilma of St. Juan Diego. Give the scroll you find to the two young Americans."

The light ceased, and unlike Father Miguel, José did not fall to his knees and weep. Blessed Mother's loving eyes and profound grace were unlike any other experience José had ever felt, including those times grace merged him in oneness with God and all of creation. Instead, he lay perfectly still, desiring to remember the pure sweetness of her voice and relive every ray of golden light that poured from her hands.

Although José had been fascinated by the stars and the heavenly sky since he was a young boy, and was given his first telescope at the age of five, he did not understand Blessed Mother's message regarding the constellation of Leo.

What he did know was that forever his heart would be ignited by the fire of Señora de Guadalupe, and she would always light his path.

CHAPTER 43

Luke had been tracking the movement and peculiarities of the planets for years but became obsessed with Our Lady after discovering that the stars on the tilma of Our Lady of Guadalupe aligned with the constellations in the Mexican sky the exact moment when the image first appeared.

Even though Luke questioned that the original mantle was not what was seen in the church today, that the Catholic Church altered it by adding accents to enhance their claim shortly after the image first appeared on Juan Diego's tilma in 1531, he was still mysteriously captivated and decided to visit Our Lady himself.

That day long ago would never be forgotten. The sky was blue. Luke's walk from his hotel was highlighted by the sounds of chirping birds, barking dogs, and chattering voices of people busy with their day.

He had respectfully entered the church and found a seat to pray before approaching the image of Our Lady. This behavior was not typical of Luke, as he was not Catholic and had resisted all forms of religion.

When Luke approached the cloak made of cactus fiber, which the Mother Mary's image was imprinted upon, he stood transfixed and time ceased. At first, he thought he was hallucinating; the image of Our Lady began to move. Her hands that were held in prayer now reached towards him, and a golden-pink light poured from her fingers.

He watched as the cherub at her feet and all gold adornments, including the rays and stars, fell away, and what was left was a miraculous image of a truly divine woman. Her cloak began to move as if a breeze caught it, and as it did, Luke saw a star map unlike that which had been shown in gold as depicted when he had first approached the image.

Luke fell to his knees and began to sob. What he witnessed was so pure: the indisputable image as it originally appeared on Juan Diego's tilma. No one in the church bothered him, as they believed his behavior was due to being profoundly moved by the image of Our Lady.

When Luke recovered, the benevolent energy was gone and Our Lady was again as she had been when he first approached. He quickly wiped his tears, pulled out a tablet, and began sketching the image of Our Lady, marking the exact positions of constellations she had shown him in the vision. Luke knew the star systems, although he was not familiar with what she was revealing to him.

There was one imposing brilliant star, unlike anything he had ever seen. Luke sensed it wasn't a comet, or Jupiter, or even a supernova—that perhaps it would depict a single event and he would have to wait for its appearance.

For the next forty years, the image of Our Lady stayed fresh in Luke's memory as he studied the heavens in hopes of witnessing what he was shown as well as dozens of past events in an attempt to see if there was a way to predict another significant event upon the earth.

Tonight was different. Luke watched in surprised wonder as the final star systems began to align. His heart raced, and he shook his head several times to convince himself he wasn't dreaming. According to his calculations, in a month's time, the formation would be complete.

Over 480 years had passed since St. Juan Diego stood in the presence of Our Lady of Guadalupe. Now Luke was witnessing a similar alignment of the constellations from the original "star map" Our Lady of Guadalupe had shown him forty years prior. Luke knew the initial occurrence was on the winter solstice in 1531 and realized this new event might well occur this new moon or winter solstice.

What puzzled Luke was that he thought the stars would align directly over Bethlehem, but his calculations showed the constellation was farther north. Would the final dazzling pulsar he witnessed from Our Lady still be another year or more off?

Had his theory been incorrect? For the first time, Luke wondered if he would live to see the prophecy of his celestial vision upon the night sky.

Exhausted from endless star calculations, celestial navigation, measurements with assorted instruments, and the wait for star and planet sights, Luke never made it to his bed. "Only for a moment, I will put my head down and then continue," he assured himself.

Resting his head in his arms upon his desk, Luke fell asleep and was transported somewhere beyond any known galaxy. There was no twilight, nor sun, moon, nor anything recognizable—only a void that was neither light nor dark. An unexplainable blissful peace began to fill his mind.

"My brother Luke, you may not have walked with me during my life, nor known me personally, but you were willing to give up your comfortable vocation as a physician to become a follower. It was said that you traveled with Paul, wrote, and studied the gospel.

"These stories were correct, but you explored so much more and were willing to gather information from all those who claimed to be witnesses. You may have written about the experiences of others, but you were a more learned man than most, and therefore there is distortion.

"Often, those who claimed to be eyewitnesses were not, and second- or third-hand information was shared and enhanced. The Gospel of Luke as well as the Book of Acts were altered by those of lesser wisdom.

And this is why humanity must learn to go within to discover their divinity beyond mind.

"It is in the silence that all is heard and all wisdom is gained. It is in the void that the word becomes wordless and, at the same time, contains all knowledge. In this wordless state of silence, all manifestation is born. It was you who shared my beloved stories, such as the Parable of the Prodigal Son, and the Parable of the Good Samaritan, filled with insights for those willing to look deeper into their lives.

"Dissolve into the silence. The mind has no place in discovering the final meeting place where we will speak as brothers. Watch the stars, but do not use logic. Do not measure. The answer is in the gap between time and no time."

"The answer is in the gap between time and no time. The answer is in the gap between time and no time. The answer is in the gap between—"

Luke had awoken with a jolt. "What does that mean?" he said as he continued to repeat the final words. "For Pete's sake, Luke, it means to get out of your head, chap! Just do it!"

CHAPTER 44

The dark night of the soul had once cast an unearthly shadow across the portals of Angelina's mind. She thought back to those days when clarity had no longer been a possibility, or so it seemed. She had lived for years feeling as if she were at the edge of an emotional cliff, barely hanging on.

Angelina was committed and determined to successfully pass through the resurrection of the dead—the journey from human to divine. But something new had penetrated her dreams three months prior.

Images of unrest caused a feeling that there was something she was supposed to remember but couldn't put her finger on—something important, something that had taken place long ago. At first, she retained only small pieces of the dreams and dismissed them as unimportant.

When the frequency increased and the visions became more explicit, she began awakening and jotting down notes on the pad of paper she kept on her nightstand, just enough information to jog her memory and piece the dreams together in the morning.

Now, three months after the dreams had begun, Angelina stood at water's edge, staring back at the pained and mystified eyes of her reflection. At times, the face of a lovely young woman also appeared. It should have been unsettling, but she felt only love for the mysterious image. The evening was rapidly approaching, and the fears of surrendering to the mysteries of the night were slowly seeping in.

The early morning had once again brought proof that the five consecutive repetitions of the same visions were not a coincidence. She could no longer blame the meal eaten the night before, nor could she deny the dream's seductive nature. It had left her unnerved and shaken once again.

What did it mean?

At first, she had been ashamed. It was not a dream she could call her loyal friend Fergie up and say, "What do you suppose this means?"

Its energy was so sensual. No, it was more than that. It was passionate and sexual—there, she said it: sexual.

Again, Angelina felt the heat of embarrassment envelop her. "How could this be? How could I have such shameful dreams?"

The dreams had taunted and mocked her, like those of a molested child holding the evil secret of a parent's shameful behavior—a child held captive only by their terror and humiliation as though their abusers conduct was a direct reflection. Such disgrace could not be shared.

Angelina thought of Father François, and although he was open-minded and more progressive than most Catholic priests she had come to know, he would be embarrassed and horrified.

This reality she could not bear. Father François had stepped into her life after her father passed on when she was twelve, and he was more like a father to her than a priest.

Reflection replayed the memories of the joyful times he had helped her unravel the mysterious symbols of her dreams. They both fancied themselves as "code breakers" and would laugh at the cleverness of the universe and its willingness to share its mysteries if one even attempted to understand the language of God—but not this time, positively not this time.

"God, forgive me. Yeshua, forgive me," she whispered to her reflection that bore witness to her disgrace.

"There must be another meaning than what appears on the surface, a symbolic meaning," Angelina said out loud in a feeble attempt to reassure the reflection in the pond. She had always dreamt in symbols, as long as she could remember.

But these dreams were so different than any she had ever remembered. They had been so alluring, the way "he" had awakened her skin when he touched her face—so utterly lost in the moment that her heart exploded in joy and her body had climaxed within the dream. She had never felt such bliss and connectedness before.

The fruitful discussions and the familiar touch of the man she knew as Yeshua seemed so innocent and natural during the night, but as soon as the spell of the dream was broken, her thoughts quickly turned to puzzlement and shame.

So successful the Christian religions and most others were at sadly destroying the beauty of the sacredness of sexuality that the connection to Source, the blessed and divine energy of creation itself, became twisted with humiliation and brutality, allowing the demonic forces to take control.

Once again, the vivid memory of last night's dream brought Angelina to tears. She silently watched as they fell and hit the surface of the pond, distorting the face peering from the water below.

She replayed the piece of the dream where she was anointing Yeshua. She witnessed her life as a priestess, through the teachings of Isis, anointing the receiver with sacred oils. It was for this reason that Yeshua requested she purify him to become Christed. *Christ* was the Greek word for "the anointed one."

Conflicted with uncertainty, Angelina walked up the moonlit cobbled pathway to her home, knowing her husband would soon question her whereabouts. She laughed at that thought; he no longer even asked where she was or what she was doing.

Entering through the atrium, she barely noticed the pots of roses lining the entry—rose of Sharon, her favorite, or the sweet smell of white lilac filling the room. Usually the beauty and delightful scents enticed Angelina to stop and breathe in their sweet aroma.

Entering the den, she found James asleep with his newspaper still clutched in one hand. She was relieved that she did not need to explain her whereabouts or her swollen eyes. There was no sense in trying to wake him; long ago, she had given up that feeble attempt. Sometime during the night, he would wander to bed.

Slowly and methodically, she undressed and prepared for bed. By now, daylight had already gathered itself into one blazing ball of light and slipped beneath the horizon's westerly sky.

Angelina sat slumped at the foot of her bed, silently fearing what sleep might bring. After nodding off three times, she finally peeled back the covers and slid between the soft linen sheets.

It was not long after Angelina's head hit the pillow that the ongoing dream of ancient time began.

The night had been dark with only a few stars when he came to her home. "My friend, my love—what brings you to lie beside me once again? Although I need no reason to delight in the sweetness of your gentle touch and drink your delicious words."

His eyes held hers and he tenderly smiled.

"Tell me, will we ever be able to display our affections to the world beyond the night?"

"Not in the same manner, dearest Miriam of Magdala. Night alone holds our secret."

"My friend, my love, which life can this be so? My heart weeps each time you leave, each moment that your touch can no longer be mine as you were so long ago. Is it only death that will allow a respite from my aching heart and human limitations?"

"Do not torment yourself with matters that do not serve this lifetime's divine plan, for we agreed to serve without question, twin souls appearing as two, but in reality, one. Let us not forget our agreement and be satisfied with our purpose."

"Then, my dearest teacher, friend, confidante, and love, let me be consumed by your words." Her playful laughter broke the seriousness of the moment.

"But for now, weave the pulse of your being through my hungry soul like braids in a child's hair. Let my heart cease knowing the cruel words of those who are jealous and dance again in joyful praise with thoughts of you.

"Let morning's first light know of no other kiss, nor a face 'cept yours. Dear one, beloved one, there is no other who can satisfy me—you, only you, hold the flame that lights my heart and soul."

Before her words finished, he held her cradled like a child in his arms. As he buried his face in her hair, he whispered, "Beware, dear one, that no one leads you astray. Be true to your own heart, for it will not betray you. Remember, I am always with you. We will be together again, beloved, soon, very soon."

Removing himself from her bed, he picked up his garments, slipped into them, and arranged the linen scarf upon his head just as he had two thousand years before. Turning towards the moonless night, he glanced back in her direction. She saw the sweetness of his smile, and all was well in her heart.

Angelina suddenly awoke. But this time, a soft smile formed on her lips. She turned to see her husband asleep next to her. "Miriam of Magdala?" It was the first time she had remembered a name upon awakening. She smiled. Peace filled her heart; confusion slipped away. Grabbing a pen and the notebook beside her bed, she began to write:

> Let the kiss from my lips
> be as sweet as yours.
> Let my heart accept and rejoice
> in the bounty of your love.
> Let me not turn away—
> in unworthiness or shame.

> Break open my heart,
> that I may find you dwelling there.
> Let your hands tenderly
> hold my face,
> so that I am aware just how far I have come—
> to believing
> in my deserving
> of You, and God's grace.

Something was unfolding that would change her entire world, and Angelina believed that it was swiftly approaching. Her spiritual practices had long ago ceased being her second or third priority and had become first.

Once again, she turned the pages of her journal and read another passage, God's response to a bedside request she had written two months after her poem, one that was deeply rooted in bliss, some innate knowing that lurked just beneath the surface in cellular memory.

"Take one step at a time, beloved child, don't try to run ahead before you are clear as to what direction you are to take. There is no sense running down roads and having to turn back.

"No more talk, dear one, just do it. You are loved beyond comprehension, as I am within you, and you are within me. I will watch and support your every move."—Your Beloved

"One step at a time," Angelina repeated out loud in an attempt to instill the words into her memory. "I have to remember that or I will not survive this life journey."

CHAPTER 45

Women and Men as Equals

When Professor Reynolds walked into the lecture hall, he could see his students were eagerly awaiting his arrival. He had predicted this might occur after the explosive news reports accusing film mogul Harvey Weinstein of sexual harassment.

"I suppose you want to address the sexual misconduct and growing allegations against Harvey Weinstein?" Jake said as he removed a book that he had grabbed before leaving the house from his briefcase.

The silence shattered, and everyone spoke at once.

"Thought so," Jake smiled. "But let's keep it in context with what we have been exploring."

Nods of agreement responded. Jake held up the book as he read the title. "*The Gospel of Mary Magdalene*, translated from the Coptic and commentary by Jean-Yves Leloup. Jean-Yves Leloup is a scholar, theologian, and mystic, and his interpretation is inspiring and thought-provoking.

"I feel it is the perfect time to discuss the role women have played during and since the time of Jesus, as well as the reasons for either man's blatant removal of them from the pages of the Bible or the false accusations against woman, especially regarding Miriam of Magdala, whom we know as Mary Magdalene."

Lisa and Veronica looked at each other, knowing this was a topic they were excited to explore.

"I want you to think about this. Two millennia ago, a man named Jesus took a radical path in demonstrating the union of the divine feminine and the divine masculine by honoring men and women as equals.

"He did this by engaging in practices considered to be against their scriptural laws. Although his actions elicited disapproving reactions from his contemporaries, he was not afraid to challenge the status quo.

"Jesus's dealings with women were dangerous to his reputation by publicly including women in his ministry, as well as teaching them to learn and study forbidden sacred text, which at that time, only men were allowed to do. These were just a few of the many examples of equality Jesus commonly demonstrated, thus shattering the prejudicial customs of the time."

Lisa watched Jake intently as he paced back and forth. She loved how his body moved, his strength, his posture, and how he tilted his head to the right side when deep in thought. She wanted to touch him, remembering just this morning, she lay in the safety of his arms, never wanting to leave.

Her head snapped to attention as he began to speak. "Many women in the church today still feel invisible and unheard. The gospels point us towards including women's voices, yet why are scores of nuns still fighting for the right to be equal to priests?

"Why, after two thousand years, has there never been a woman pope, or even cardinals? There is a legend of a woman who reigned as pope for two years during the Middle Ages, Pope Joan. Most versions of her story describe her as a talented and learned woman who disguised herself as a man, reigning as pope for those short years.

"The story was widely believed, but most modern scholars regard it as fictional. I hope it was a hoax, as it goes on to say she gave birth to a child and was stoned to death."

Jake paused long enough for Max to partially raise his hand. "Go ahead, Max, did you want to add something?"

"I do. This has brought my attention to how antiquated the Catholic Church is about gender."

Max continued, "If Jesus confided in and trusted women like Mary Magdalene, and as we previously discussed that Phoebe was a leader of the early church, then why can't women be priests or cardinals today? I believe the disrespect of the privileged good old boys' club is a big reason why every time I go back to Italy, there are more rows of benches missing from the cathedrals. Women are fed up, and women are the heart of the church."

"I agree, Max." Jake nodded in his direction. "While we live in a time and culture far different from that of the historical Jesus, his way of welcoming and responding to women has much to teach us. Two millennia have passed, and still, a woman is viewed as inferior to a man in the eyes of the church as well as in most cultures.

"Did Jesus himself not marry opposites—the light and the dark? To birth our divinity and restore our connection to humanity, as well as nature—every creature and element. How can religious groups claim to know the will of Jesus when they cannot honor the very words he spoke or demonstrated?"

Veronica leaned towards Lisa and whispered, "I was furious to hear that on several occasions, Pope Francis was asked about possibly admitting women to the positions of the clergy. Each time, he gave a firm no. I had such great hopes for him."

"Sorry to hear that," Lisa sincerely replied.

"It is deplorable. My mom and grandmothers in Italy were extremely upset about it."

Jake continued, "The striking thing is, that these accusations against Weinstein, of sexual harassment, have brought awareness to not only the deplorable behavior of particular men but also women realizing how they were programmed by the deceptive influence of a male-dominated world to turn against each other.

"I hope that women break this pattern and stand with each other, for it is indeed a time in history that the feminine energy is desperately needed. This balance is not just a feminist position. This goes for both men and women, the importance of balancing the divine masculine and feminine within, to become the divine human."

Jake walked to the whiteboard and, turning back to his students, he asked, "We touched on some of the differences between the lives of men and women at the time of Jesus a couple of months back. Give me some examples."

Tony spoke first. "A man's responsibility was to be out in the world, where a woman's life was confined largely to the family home."

"A woman could not engage in commerce, except for a woman who had been forced to be the breadwinner, and even then, she was prohibited from conversing with men. I can't even imagine," Veronica threw in, shaking her head in dismay.

"The sad thing about this is that any money a woman did earn belonged to her husband, and that left her in a very vulnerable position since a man could divorce his wife, but a woman could not divorce her husband," Lisa added.

Jake was condensing the points made on the board. "Anyone else want to add imbalances between the sexes?"

"At the temple in Jerusalem, women were restricted to an outer court and, in synagogues, separated from the men," Ben offered.

"A woman was stoned to death for adultery, whereas a man received no punishment for the same actions." Veronica spoke with such utter disdain that every man in the room shrank back in his chair.

Lisa shot Veronica a surprised look and shrugged both shoulders as if to say, "Did you need to be so harsh?" Shrugging back, Veronica mouthed, "Well?"

Rose decided to mend the discomfort and sweetly offered, "Jesus regularly addressed women directly while in public, which was unusual to do, but he also spoke to them with kindness and respect. There are records of Jesus addressing women tenderly as 'daughter,' 'daughter of Abraham,' or 'daughters of Abraham,' which gave them equal status to that of men."

Mark raised his hand. "Mark," Jake pointed.

"I have been reading the same book you brought today, *The Gospel of Mary Magdalene*, and have been inspired by the realizations that have occurred, which I never put together in the past. I heard the scholar Andrew Harvey call Jesus an 'evolutionary pioneer,' and he was!

"I never thought much of it because in this age, there is nothing unusual about it. Actually, I should clarify that—at least in the countries with equal rights. Wow, I just realized what I said. Maybe 'spouting' equal rights is a better way to put it after the many allegations in the United States that have come up in recent years, which include more than one president.

"Jesus was exceptionally bold and outrageously courageous to speak out against the norm. To go against the customs and religious leaders of his time—I can't imagine what strength that took, and belief in God and his mission. As much as I would like to say I would do the same, I don't believe I could."

"You are right, Mark. He was daringly courageous. It is interesting that Jesus's male apostles disappeared when he was sentenced to death, and it was the woman who stayed with him. Additionally, these same men wanted to claim leadership after his death, except one, although according to ancient gospels and scrolls discovered, it was the women to whom Jesus imparted the advanced knowledge.

"In particular, Mary Magdalene, she alone was given the highest secret teachings, for he realized his male apostles could not comprehend their true meaning, as they used the mind and not intuition.

If you spend time in sincere contemplation with the words and profound energy of Mary Magdalene as felt in the gospels, you realize that she was Jesus's equal, that she might have shown him how to love on a more intense level, thus marrying the divine masculine with the divine feminine within each of them.

"She was as much a gift to him as he was to her." Jake paused and looked back at Mark. "Since you are reading the Gospel of Mary . . . after the crucifixion, these same male apostles attempted to discredit Mary Magdalene as she repeated the words Jesus had spoken to her. After all, they were the ones who asked her, 'What is your view on these passages?'"

Mark straightened up, a bit uncomfortable by the attention, but spoke clearly. "I was moved by the realization that Mary Magdalene saw Jesus in either flesh or vision, and he gave her his secret teachings. She was able to repeat the words so accurately and with profound beauty to the male apostles.

"I believe it was Peter who initially invited her to tell him what Jesus had told her—*'tell us whatever you remember of words he told you which we have not heard.'* And when she did share his words, both Andrew and Peter challenged her. Andrew said he didn't believe her, and Peter said something along the lines of, 'How is it possible that the teacher talked to her, a woman, about secrets of which we were ignorant?'

"It seemed clear to me his concern was that these words were a threat to themselves as well as the customs of the time not permitting a woman to speak, let alone be a teacher or lead a church. Peter just couldn't get over the fact that she was Jesus's beloved, his favored disciple, and it seems to me, far more evolved than the others."

"Can you imagine," Veronica interjected, "what a different world we would have today if Mary Magdalene had headed the Christian movement bringing forth Jesus's purpose on earth? One of love, equality, honor, kindness, and compassion, instead of domination, control, and power!"

Rose sweetly replied, "It is true, she was far wiser than the rest and possessed no motivation to control, manipulate, or alter the true teachings. There was jealousy, and even Peter said to her, *'Mary of Magdalene, we know he loved you differently from other women.'* And they had asked Jesus, *'Why do you love her more than all of us?'*"

Jake looked at Rose in surprise. This lovely soft light of a woman spoke so assuredly, as if she knew firsthand. Jake flashed back on the first day he laid eyes on her, and his immediate reaction was the vision of the Black Madonna. "Rose, is there no question to the accuracy of these translations?"

Without hesitation, Rose answered, followed by a quote. "No, I dreamt it last night, and it is still fresh in my mind. Mary wept, and answered them, *'My brother Peter, what could you be thinking? Do you believe this is just my own imagination, that I invented this vision?'* It was Levi who spoke up after Peter's accusations and called him hot-tempered, scolding him for repudiating a woman just as their enemies did. Clearly, Jesus held her worthy, so who were they to reject her?"

Rose paused before continuing. "There are those of us who came to create a new world, not repeat the mistakes of the old paradigm. No one said it would be easy, yet we have forgotten our purpose, so instead it has become our burden. The most important teaching Jesus had left them was 'love one another,' and they had already forgotten." Rose sighed, she ceased speaking, and the room was silent.

Jake finally broke the silence. "Remember that silence often during your day, for it was in the silence that Mary claimed to have heard the words of Jesus. Each of us must take time for silent contemplation, or else an unsatisfied world will carry you away and you will not live your own centered and creative life.

"The question came up, was Mary Magdalene given teachings that the men were not ready to hear?" Jake began reading from the book resting in his hands, "*'For, in spite of her status as a mere woman, she has gone farther upon the path to becoming fully human, anthropos.'*

"What was this 'anthropos' that Jesus spoke of? Was it an attempt to assist in the birthing of a newly evolved divine human? I believe so, the marriage of the divine feminine and divine masculine to birth this new child within ourselves."

No one responded. The room remained silent and contemplative. Time had run out. Jake put his hands in his pockets and thoughtfully scanned the faces before him. He spoke with passion and sincerity. "Your assignment is to research our topic today, discover the similarities between the time of Jesus and the world we live in today.

"What cultures, religions, and groups of people still abide by this imbalance of equality between men and women? Question how male dominance still has such a firm hold after thousands of years? What are the underlying factors that do not allow the evolution and the balance of the masculine and the feminine? How does religion stagnate the progression of the human race?" Jake outlined the questions he felt were relevant.

Lisa had been intently watching Jake. She could see how deeply he cared about all humanity and how it troubled him to view a world still filled with jealousy and the tragic hunger for power and control. Jake caught her eyes. They locked, lost in another time.

The sound of Veronica's book hitting the ground broke the trance. "Good god, Lisa, what was that about? All eyes are on you two!" Veronica whispered.

Lisa reached down and handed Veronica her book without saying a word.

Just then, Tyler, having turned his head to examine the faces of Lisa's peers to see if they'd caught the interaction between prof and Lisa, noticed a woman quickly closing an exit door where she had been quietly peering in.

Tyler had spotted her a few minutes earlier and thought it was odd that she appeared to be watching them. He assumed she was waiting for prof's session to end to speak with him and didn't want to disturb the class, but her hasty retreat told him differently. He whispered to Veronica but told her to say nothing, yet.

Tyler just knew, whoever she was, something didn't feel right.

CHAPTER 46

After class, Lisa ordinarily hung back, waiting for Jake, but today Veronica and Tyler stayed put as well. "You guys don't need to stay. We will catch up with you," Lisa offered. "Sometimes it takes Jake a while to get everything together."

"We'll wait," Tyler offered.

"Hey, you two, what's going on? First, offering to stay back? And the tone of your voice, Tyler, is concerning. And Veronica, you're speechless and sheepish! Come on, what gives?" Lisa questioned.

Jake stopped placing papers in his briefcase and walked up to them. "What are you three whispering about?"

Veronica shot Tyler a quick look and nodded, saying, "Go ahead, Tyler, maybe it was nothing, but trust your instincts. They have always been right on."

Tyler repeated what he saw to Lisa and Jake, ending with, "As I said, it was probably nothing."

"What can you tell me about this woman?" Jake inquired, looking concerned.

"White woman, medium build, thirty-something, stylish dark-black hair, just past her chin, probably about Lisa's height, gauging by the door. But I'm not sure," Tyler offered.

Lisa saw the look on Jake's face, and chills ran across her skin. "Jake, what is it? Who is she?"

Taking a deep breath and then exhaling, Jake said, "Earlier in the school year, a woman named Nancy was pursuing me. I know that may sound like male bravado, but she would show up at my favorite Italian restaurant and made several attempts to join me even when I told her I was grading papers or just wanted to reflect on my thoughts.

"It didn't stop her. She told me on the third occurrence that this restaurant just happened to be her favorite and that she had been coming there for years, and it was just a coincidence that we happened to meet three times in a row.

"When I asked the owner, Antonio, if this was true, he said he had never seen her until a week ago, the same night I was there. Then the next day, in the faculty lunchroom, she asked to join me. I said sure and went back to what I was doing. She started talking, saying she would truly like it if I would come to her place for dinner that night and she wanted to get to know me. I tried to be kind and said I was not interested in a relationship with her outside the campus. With that, she picked up her things and huffed off.

"She went to the dean and told him that I was 'uncomfortably pursuing her' and that it could be considered sexual harassment! He asked her if she wanted to file a formal complaint, and she backed off, saying it wasn't necessary but she just wanted it to be known.

"I got a call to come in and discuss the matter, and I was so genuinely shocked that Dean Mitchell said, 'I didn't think so. Didn't sound like you, but I needed you to know. Avoid her when possible. She could cause trouble.'"

"I hate to mention this," Tyler spoke softly, hating to be the bearer of bad news, "but do you remember when I was first sliding into your class?"

"Yes," all three said in unison.

"On one of those days, I slipped out the back, side door, and there was the same woman who had to move out of the way as I brushed past her. I had only gone a few steps and felt like something was up—my street instincts, I suppose—so I turned back to watch."

Tyler stopped and took a breath, I could see through the crack she was looking through, and I saw you touching Lisa's face. It was obvious something intimate was going on between you two. She saw what I saw."

Both Jake and Lisa remembered that day vividly. It had been a sweet memory, until now.

"I remember touching Lisa's face. I kissed my finger and touched it to her lips. I believe I said, 'Tonight,' and Lisa replied, 'Yes, tonight.'" Jake sighed, resigned to the fact that there were witnesses.

"Sorry to say that is what I saw. The body language was pretty powerful. Only a fool could have missed it."

Veronica elbowed Tyler, sending him a stern look. "You didn't need to add that."

"Well isn't it better they know all the facts so if anything comes of this, they will know how to deal with it?" Tyler shot back at Veronica.

"He's right, Veronica, knowing this is important," Jake responded. Contemplating the situation for a moment, Jake added, "Dammit, I am sure she has been watching us since."

"And now Nancy shows up just when you were broaching the subject of Weinstein's sexual misconduct." Tyler looked at both Jake and Lisa, "whatever that frozen-moment interaction was about between you two, Veronica and I aren't the only ones who caught it."

"Well, at least that was all Nancy saw. It wasn't as if they were kissing," offered Veronica.

"Thank God is right," both Lisa and Jake replied, releasing a sigh of relief.

"What does this mean?" Lisa asked, fearing she might have jeopardized Jake's position.

"It means we don't worry about it unless something comes out of it, and then I will deal with it," Jake assured Lisa.

"I would like to be with you if that is the case," Lisa offered.

"Let's just let it be. We all know something is going to be requested of the four of us soon, so this may all be irrelevant."

As the four of them left the hall and went into the courtyard, Jake put his arm around Lisa's shoulders, pulling her close.

"What are you doing, Jake?" all asked at once.

"I figure the best ammo is not hiding anything. If it's in the open, Nancy can't accuse me of something that is now public domain."

With that, Lisa rubbed his back and slid her arm around him. Walking in the open for the first time, Lisa caught Veronica's smile, and she smiled back.

Just then, Tyler caught Nancy watching them as she stood by a courtyard column. "Jake, she's to your left."

Turning towards Nancy, Jake raised his free hand in a half wave. Tyler and Veronica followed suit as Nancy slid back into a shadow, pretending not to notice.

CHAPTER 47

The waters of the river Jordan were cooling his hot and dusty feet. He heard a voice. It appeared to come from both the river and the wind. When the brief dialogue was finished, he glanced to shore and saw a man in robes of white. The man gazed at him in silence. He knew this man. His hair fell across his shoulders in waves, and his eyes seemed to be penetrating his soul. The man waited. Something as ancient as time stirred within Jake, and he knew he must go to him without delay.

This time, Jake woke without the panic but with a knowing that he was soon to begin an unknown journey. He also knew there was nothing he could do but wait for each step to reveal itself. As he walked to the shower, he was filled with excitement, curiosity, and a sense of forlorn.

This last emotion disturbed Jake, but as he stepped into the warm water, he pushed the feeling away.

It was time to make plans. And no sooner than the thought came to Jake, he also heard a voice clearly in his mind.

"ROMA."

"Rome? Why are you giving me this information? What is the purpose of this?" Jake questioned thoughtfully.

A voice reverberated:

"You honor all aspects of I Am. You, my son, tread upon all of my creation with the utmost respect. Therefore, you are one of the chosen *whom I will entrust with my secrets, as I have done for others throughout the ages. Worry not, The One will lead you."*

"The One? Lead me where," Jake wondered aloud, "somewhere beyond Rome?"

Just then, his phone started ringing. Jake had just turned off the shower and didn't rush, knowing the answering machine would pick it up. "Jake, Dean Mitchell here. Hey, give me a call when you have a moment. You've got my home phone number."

Jake was sure Nancy had informed Mitchell of what she witnessed, plus a few exaggerated extras. Why else would he get a call on the weekend? The one thing he knew was that everything was divinely orchestrated, so he would not allow it to trouble him.

Once dressed, Jake picked up the phone and dialed Mitchell's number. "Mitchell, Jake here, what's up?" he asked, already knowing the nature of the call.

"Hey, Jake, sorry to call you on the weekend. I got a complaint, and it may prove serious to your career if we don't handle it right away. Can you stop by sometime today?"

"Sure, no problem, I am sure Nancy will be delighted that she may have disturbed my weekend," Jake said without malice.

"Oh, so you know it has to do with Professor Miller?"

"Yes, she has been spying on me for months. It seems it sent her over the top to see me with Lisa Landen yesterday."

"Oh, so you are pursuing her?" Mitchell asked, sounding a bit impressed.

"Pursuing her? No, not at all. It's quite mutual, but it may take time to explain. You don't mean to say Nancy suggested I pressured, as in pressuring or being inappropriate, with Lisa in any way?"

"Let's say there was an emphasis on that possibility and she slipped in a mention of the Weinstein situation."

"How convenient, she's trying to back up her claim about my stalking and harassing her earlier in the year." Jake was getting bored with Nancy's lies and childish behavior that could destroy another person's life. "So, Mitchell, what do you need me to do? What will make your life easier?"

"I wanted to talk to you in person, but since we seem to have everything on the table, we can decide the best way to handle this now. That is if Ms. Landen is in a relationship with you of her own free will, which I cannot imagine would be anything but true, having had many engaging conversations with her regarding her classes and goals. I do know Ms. Landen is a lovely and charming woman, but not a pushover.

"Therefore, perhaps you could take a leave of absence until this blows over? I realize that isn't ideal, as you have a lot of students who will be upset and final projects due, but I would hate to see you get caught in something instigated by a jealous woman. Although, I will have to speak to Ms. Landen."

"I am happy to take a leave of absence if you think that would help until this all resolves. And yes, please talk with Lisa to put your mind at ease." Jake was shaking his head in disbelief.

"I hope you can enjoy the rest of your weekend. Sorry, that was a slip. I will update you Monday. Take care, Jake, you know I wish you the best." Both Mitchell and Jake hung up.

Jake was a bit stunned. With all the events where men were undeniably abusing and exploiting women and getting away with it, he got accused of two situations—by the same woman—that were bald-faced lies.

There are always those willing to smear an innocent person for their twisted personal reasons, to create doubts. What Nancy had done was a crime against both women and men; both sexes suffered from these lies.

After making some breakfast, Jake called Lisa and left a message on her machine. "Good day, beautiful. Well, I guess I don't need to worry about requesting a leave of absence. I got my temporary walking papers. I am assuming that you are on the phone with Dean Mitchell now. Call me back when you have a moment.

"Don't worry about anything, as you know it's all playing out as the divine intends. I love you." Jake hung up the phone and realized it was the first time he had said he loved her. "Over the phone, good gosh, Jake, what were you thinking?" He was also aware that was the first time he had used those words since long before his former wife had left him.

CHAPTER 48

Lisa called Jake the moment she hung up the phone. Jake picked up on the first ring, knowing it had to be her. "You OK?" Jake asked when he heard her voice.

"Yes, thanks, the message you left me was correct. I was on the phone with Dean Mitchell, and he sounded relieved that it was a mutual attraction. I also informed him it was I who approached you—at your home, no less!" Lisa responded.

"You didn't need to do that. It must have taken Mitchell by surprise!" Jake chuckled.

"Actually, I thought I heard admiration in his voice. Although, I am not sure if it was for you or me." Lisa chuckled back. "And how are you doing?" This time, she spoke with concern in her voice.

"I'm good now that I hear you are fine. I am also confident everything is playing out as designed," Jake said with renewed assurance. "Would you mind calling Veronica and Tyler to ask them to come to my place as soon as they can? I had another dream last night, and the time has come to embark on this mysterious journey."

"Veronica and Tyler are both at my place. We'll come right over. Veronica and I have been sharing our dreams from last night. It turns out we both had the same visions about papyrus scrolls and where to find them, before heading to Rome." Lisa excitedly answered.

"Rome?" Jake asked.

"Yeah. You also?" Lisa inquired.

"Yes, but mine was about a young man I am supposed to meet," said Jake.

"We will be right over. By the way, did you ever get ahold of Sister Elizabeth?" Lisa questioned.

Jake spoke softly. "No. And even though I found out through Mitchell that I wasn't the only one that received the certified letters from the Vatican, I believe I am being followed. That's another reason to get out of town. Although Mitchell confided in me that three of the four others had similar builds and hair color as mine, I don't want to take a chance of having you involved.

"Wow" was all Lisa could say.

CHAPTER 49

Six nights passed, and Angelina sat upright and yelled three words: "Oh my god!" Her husband stirred only for a moment before his dreams dragged him back to sleep.

She grabbed her notepad and the robe lying at the foot of her bed and tiptoed out of the room. Sitting at the kitchen table, she began quickly writing her dream. But this time, she did not stop; more and more details filled her mind. Information was so transparent it could have happened yesterday. Her pen flew across the pages without pause.

When she finished writing, her notepad was full. She looked up at the clock when she heard the upstairs shower turn on. Three hours had passed, and she had written nonstop.

She looked down at the pad of paper as if she were still in a trance and flipped back to the first page. She distinctly remembered the lifetime with the man in the scarlet robe. They were not make-believe characters and situations for the benefit of night's mysterious ways. It was real. What took place in the dream had unmistakably happened long ago.

And she knew without question that she was the woman in the vision—she had been Mary of Magdalene. She had walked the earth with Jesus over two thousand years ago, and not only had she been his disciple, but she had also been his friend, confidante, and love.

This last piece of history was conveniently stricken from all writings because it did not fit in with the image the Catholic Church wanted to foster. He was human just like the rest of us, and they had turned him into the only son of God.

This claim had never been expressed nor supported by Jesus; he viewed everyone as a son or daughter of God. Angelina was well aware that she could never share this information without ridicule and disdain.

It no longer mattered, for at this moment she was filled with joy. She could feel his presence as if he were sitting right beside her, holding her hand, and she yearned for that which she had not understood until now.

Momentarily, Angelina felt sad; guilt rose from her heart. No wonder she felt something was missing in her marriage, as she had longed for something profoundly precious, something James could never give her no matter how he tried. Naturally, he looked to another to fill what she could not.

Angelina knew she had to find her beloved friend, no matter how long it took her—no matter at what cost. And something within informed her he was somewhere on this planet.

The shower turned off. She would have some explaining to do. She knew it was time to tell him they must part and he could be with his lover.

Angelina whispered, "It won't be long, my beloved husband." She caught herself in horror. "Oh my god, what have I said. I didn't mean that. I meant beloved friend."

Angelina's husband walked into the kitchen, smartly dressed and ready to head out the door.

"Sleep well?" he asked in a kind voice, although it was clear he honestly didn't want to know if it was anything different.

"Great," she replied as he kissed her cheek goodbye.

"We need to talk when you get home," Angelina informed him.

"Sure" was all he said before closing the door. The displeasure in his voice was apparent.

It was not until James left for the office that Angelina returned to her bedroom. Throwing herself across the rumpled unmade bed, she wept—tears of relief, fear, and anticipation of the unknown road she was about to travel.

She abruptly stopped. "I must make travel plans!" Realizing she had no idea as to where, she yelled, "Where am I going?"

"Egypt" reverberated through her body and mind as clearly as her husband's recently spoken words.

"Egypt," she repeated. And Angelina knew without question that was where her journey would begin.

"Wait for me," she spoke aloud. "I'm coming!"

CHAPTER 50

Dean Mitchell entered the lecture hall and stood before Professor Reynolds' students. Immediately there was silence, as this had never before occurred.

"Good morning," Mitchell boomed but did not wait for a response, "I will pass out a letter to each of you from Professor Reynolds. He informed me that you don't need another professor this late in the term but that you do need to take this last assignment seriously, and you can continue to use this hall to gather until the end of the term."

Dean Mitchell approached two students. "Please pass these out. I am sure, at some point, Professor Reynolds will contact each of you. He communicated the seriousness of these questions and believed you would also see the urgency, as shall I." With that, Dean Mitchell returned to the front of the room, looking perplexed and a bit unsettled.

Dear esteemed students,

I am taking what may seem an untimely sabbatical, but it is necessary. I am leaving you with one last assignment.

The events taking place on our planet may have crossed the point of no return. Because of the greed and disregard of humans, humanity plausibly hit the tipping point in favor of the dark energies. Do not allow this to be an assignment that is swept away once finished; make it your constant practice.

I suggest you look closely at your lives and anything you can do to assist humanity in the possibility of being saved from destruction. Serve to preserve the earth, and at the very least, redeem your soul. We discussed the proven power of meditation and present-moment awareness, and I would suggest you add it to your daily lives, as well as speaking and acting in integrity at all times.

Below is the new question:

"What are you doing as the world is burning? What are you giving of yourself outside of yourself?"

Go beyond the topic of "Would we crucify Jesus if he came to earth today?" Instead, please ask yourself, "Are we not crucifying God/Creator and each other every single day?"

Grievously, the answer is yes. It is our Creator we are crucifying daily, as we further destroy the water, the air, the soil, and the seeds, as well as contaminating and slaughtering millions of creatures because of our reckless, self-serving greed.

I believe our most significant crime is, we have also butchered each other through words, actions, or lack of action taken; therefore, we kill aspects of ourselves. What humanity does not understand is that the Creator is calling out for you to discover the truth, "Stop perpetuating a life of ignorance. Find Me, and you will find yourself. Love Me, and you will love yourself. The veil of ignorance will lift, and then you shall remain untouched." This is a quote from Mooji.

If you speak ill of another, your lips have blood upon them, and you have defied the commandment "thou shalt not kill." We have read the book, but you may want to listen to the audio of The Gospel of Mary Magdalene and allow it to penetrate your cells.

Ask yourself, "Is there blood upon my lips?" For the true meaning of the commandment "thou shalt not kill" is not just killing someone's physical body but also killing the spirit of another, through ill deeds, actions, or words. Each is deadly.

Please take this very seriously. There is no time to leave it for another to fix. It is yours to do.

It has been a profound honor to be your professor. I wish you all the best, and I hope to see you all next spring.

I will leave you with one last quote, which I shall attribute to Anne Louise Germaine de Staël's writings in 1813 instead of Friedrich Nietzsche, who penned it in the late 1800s. Madame de Staël envisioned herself watching a ballroom filled with dancers, and she imagined her reaction if she had been unable to hear the music. Below is the quote from Friedrich Nietzsche, whom I believe was inspired by Madame de Staël:

> *"And those who were seen dancing were thought to be insane by those who could not hear the music."*

Do not forget these words, and know, I believe in each of you. Follow your music, and when the world finds you insane, it is they who can't hear the voice of the universe calling out.

With sincere friendship,

Professor Jake Reynolds

Max whispered to Sandra, "Did you notice that Veronica, Lisa, Ben, Tony, and Tyler are also absent?"

"I noticed it right away when it was apparent that Professor Reynolds was late, as he has never been late," Sandra affirmed. "Veronica would have loved that last quote. Too bad she missed it!"

"I somehow don't believe she has." Max gave her a knowing glance.

"Oh, wow, you think they are all together?" responded a surprised Sandra.

"I do. Can't say why, but this is deadly serious. Prof doesn't exaggerate. He believes we may have hit the point of no return. We need to form a study group as well as a daily meditation group. You in?" Max inquired.

"Without question. We can stand up and ask our peers, once Dean Mitchell leaves, who wants to join us," Sandra replied with sorrow and hope.

"Prof has warned us about this. How many civilizations have been terminated and then tens of thousands of years, or even a million, must pass before human life can again exist upon the earth? Dang, when will we learn?" Max said in frustration and grief.

Returning to his office, Dean Mitchell told his secretary to hold his calls. As he closed and locked his door, he realized his longtime friend Jake had never sounded as urgent as he had when he requested him to present the papers to his students.

Mitchell wanted time to think about his life and what he had honestly done to contribute to the betterment of the world outside of his self-interests while the world was burning from its greed.

CHAPTER 51

Had Ben and Tony known about the announcement, they might not have skipped Professor Jake Reynolds' class that day.

It wasn't something either wanted to do; each felt they had no choice. The two friends had spent the weekend hiking, and it was around their campfire as they cooked the fish they had caught that each discovered they were both having unusual dreams the last four months. Tony had been the one to bring it up when Ben asked him what he wrote about in his time-worn journal.

"Thoughts, events, or things I am trying to figure out, as sooner or later the answers seem to appear on subsequent pages," Tony said lightly.

"I should have invested in a journal months ago. I have random notes on pieces of paper stuffed into my nightstand drawers. It would have been helpful to have them in chronological order, but I didn't think the dreams would keep occurring," Ben stated, wondering if he had shared too much.

"Dreams?" Tony inquired.

"Yeah, dreams of events a couple of thousand years ago," Ben replied cautiously.

"Same here," Tony said, deciding to be more forthright. "I have been having visions about what appears to be a lifetime with a great prophet and a group of people I may have known in that incarnation."

Ben looked startled. "Same here! I have wanted to ask Professor Reynolds about these events, but when I have the opportunity to ask him, I chicken out."

"Let's talk to him on Monday. We can set up an appointment with him and go together," Tony suggested.

"Let's do this!" Ben remarked.

The rest of the evening, the two friends stayed up well into the night sharing their dreams of the life they may have experienced centuries ago. The stars were far brighter, as the moon was too close to the sun in the sky to be visible.

Tony loved nights like this. A new moon meant that the moon set and rose with the sun and the night sky was dark, allowing him to view shooting stars and other celestial objects. In midsentence, both boys would shout out some descriptive phrase and point to the heavens each time something otherworldly shot across the winter sky.

"Smell that air, there is nothing like the fragrance of pure night air away from civilization!" Tony sighed.

"Too bad we polluted so much of our beautiful earth," Ben woefully added.

The next morning, when night had barely taken her final bows, both boys unzipped their tents, excitedly looked at the other, and began talking at the same time. "You first," Tony said, directing his arm towards Ben.

"I had a vision of a priest. He was praying in front of a large portrait of Mother Mary. I am almost certain he is in Mexico. We are supposed to find him and take him somewhere. He will know, but apparently, wherever it is, we are supposed to be there also."

"Almost the same," exclaimed Tony, "the vision showed me that he had a narrow piece of parchment with some writing on it unrolled on his lap and he was trying to figure out what the missing words could be. We are to take him money, but I am not sure if he is to go with us. Regardless, I feel we will know when we find him."

"First we need to get to where we have internet and search for prominent paintings of Mary in Mexico to see if I can identify where he is. Oh, and I will pick up my ATM card and credit card. Apparently, this priest doesn't have much money," Ben remarked.

On Monday morning, Tony and Ben completely forgot about calling Professor Reynolds until they were at the airport, heading to Mexico City.

Finding the painting of Mother Mary had been easy. On the first attempt, Ben typed in "famous painting of Mary in Mexico," and there it was, dozens of images staring back at him, just as he had witnessed in his dream. Now they knew her name, Our Lady of Guadalupe. "We will see you soon," Ben whispered to Our Lady, "and do not worry, we will get your priest to his destination."

Once they got through airport security, Tony called Professor Reynolds' extension to leave a message about their absence and shared the desire to speak with him when they returned. Instead of the normal recorded message, it said, "Professor Reynolds here, leave a message and I'll get back to you soon. I will be on sabbatical for an undisclosed amount of time. Please press pound fifty-eight to reach Dean Mitchell with any questions. I wish you well."

Tony had found a quiet corner to make the call and rushed back to the gate where Ben was waiting. "Something odd is going on," Tony apprehensively proclaimed. "Out of the blue, Professor Reynolds is on sabbatical!"

"What? This is crazy," Ben blurted out, scratching his head. "What the heck *is* going on?"

CHAPTER 52

Father José Cruz sat quietly on the wooden bench, staring at the worn parchment. He had been there since the doors opened at 6:00 a.m., reading and rereading the words written in English: "of my birth." Over and over, José repeated the words. Looking up at Our Lady of Guadalupe, he asked, "What do you want me to do?"

He could see that another word had preceded the first, and perhaps the end, but the papyrus was torn, and José had not been able to find any more pieces. Again, he looked sadly at Our Lady and spoke aloud. "Have I failed you? What did I forget? I found the scroll, but I do not know what it means." José began to cry silently. He had hardly slept the night before, and without notice, his head nodded forward in sleep.

"José, you will know where you are to meet the others when you find the alignment of the constellation Leo, upon the tilma of St. Juan Diego. But wait for the two young Americans and give them the scroll. They will also supply you with a ticket for your passage, but tell them no more, as they have others to meet."

Suddenly José's head snapped upright and he was wide awake. Carefully rolling the papyrus, he slipped it into his robe pocket and rushed up to the image of Our Lady. "Find the alignment of the constellation Leo," he repeated the words he had heard. Searching for familiar star patterns, he was delighted that he found several; he just could not see Leo.

Finally, José stopped looking. It was then that he discovered Ursa Major on the left and the Southern Cross on the right, and between them was a four-petaled flower on her garment, just below the black girdle around her waist. This sash was the symbol the Aztecs knew meant that Mary was pregnant.

José began to laugh and cry at the same time. "Blessed Lady, the constellation of Leo would be between Ursa Major and the Southern Cross! I know where you are leading me, but I will wait for the young Americans and give them the scroll."

CHAPTER 53

Akbar was not surprised when the dreams of two thousand years ago took over his meditations and nighttime rest. Nor was he surprised when the voice told him of the man he was to meet in Roma—an American man called Jake. But first, he was to meet a young man named Aaron, who would be getting on the same train he would be departing from, in India.

The vision informed him to stop this blond-haired chap Aaron and take him on the trip to meet the American in St. Peters Square after they recovered the papyrus that Aaron would find near Gurdwara Damdama Sahib.

The next morning, Akbar quietly informed his parents of his need to connect with those who were to come together for a great journey. His father bestowed his blessing and embraced him. Although his mother had talked about this day his entire life, now that it had arrived, she was unprepared. Running about flustered and in tears, she began to pack everything she thought he would need.

"Mother, please, I need but little. Parameshvar will take care of me." He looked into her eyes, telling her all she needed to know. And then he was gone.

Finding Aaron might not be easy in the crowded station, but this did not concern Akbar; he knew he was in the hands of the Creator. Upon arriving at the New Delhi railway station, Akbar quickly exited the train and saw a tall young American sporting a five-o'clock shadow about to board, who appeared to be looking for someone one final time. Akbar called, waving wildly, "Aaron! Aaron!"

Aaron turned in his direction, halted briefly, and pushed through the crowd towards Akbar. "I know you also. You have filled my dreams!" Aaron exclaimed in relief. The two hugged like brothers who had been apart for a long time.

"By the way, I'm Akbar."

"Good to know," Aaron said with a smile.

"Why were you getting on the train? Aren't you supposed to be headed to Gurdwara Damdama Sahib, which is only seven kilometers away?" Akbar inquired.

"Seriously? I am sure glad you found me. I was heading south to the Taj Mahal. I thought that was the image I was seeing. I almost took a 220-kilometer detour!" Aaron responded gratefully.

Akbar laughed. "That's presumably why I had the vision of Ganesh, and why I needed to meet you."

"The remover of obstacles?" Aaron responded.

"Yes," Akbar affirmed.

With that, Aaron pulled out a journal and pointed to a symbol he had written before getting off the plane: गणेश. "Does this mean anything?"

Akbar laughed again. "Ganesh, in Hindi. You might want to ask your guides to transcribe in your native language!"

The two young men chatted as they ran to catch the bus, Aaron in a mixture of English and broken Hindi, and Akbar in excellent English. Jumping aboard the coach, they made their way through the crowded aisle. There was only one seat left, and Aaron said, "Please take it, I have been sitting far too much."

Their dialogue came to a halt when Akbar said, "Next stop is ours."

After exiting the bus, as they headed to Gurdwara Damdama Sahib, Akbar asked, "Do you know who you are meeting?"

"Haven't a clue!" Aaron said, widening his eyes. "I am just assuming it will be evident when the moment arises, as everything else has been. At least I hope so!"

"We are both alike, brother," Akbar said. "We have great trust in the Creator to guide our way. Until directed differently, we will walk around and enjoy the beauty."

"This temple is truly magnificent," Aaron said, gazing up as the sunlight reflected off the white stone structure that appeared to be marble.

Just then, a white-and-black-faced bird flew over Aaron's head, almost touching his hair. "Yikes, did you see that?"

"Sure did, he has something in his mouth. Let's watch where he goes," Akbar suggested.

They watched as the bird rose higher and higher to a rooftop, where Aaron saw several white cylindrical columns. The white wagtail landed at the opening of one of the pinnacled canopies above them. "Come on!" Aaron excitedly shouted and then added, "How do we get up there?"

"Follow me," Akbar exclaimed. "We have a lot of steps to climb!"

When they arrived on the floor with the marble canopy, Aaron and Akbar walked across the mosaic tiles with care; they did not want to frighten the bird. They could see the nest, but as they approached, the bird flew off. They noticed that he carried nothing in his beak or claws. Aaron reached up and moved his hands about in search of anything resembling papyrus or paper. Finally, his fingers wrapped around a roll of woven paper. Excitedly, Aaron pulled it out as Akbar gathered around. "What is it?" Akbar questioned.

"Papyrus," Aaron said in awe.

As the young men unrolled it, they realized the scroll was torn. The beginning and end sections of the papyrus were missing, and only part of a message remained:

The eight of you will travel together. We will meet

"Eight? Meet where?" Aaron demanded. With that, he handed the papyrus to Akbar and once again attempted to find the remainder of the scroll, but there was nothing more.

"Now what?" Aaron asked.

"Trust, my brother. We will go to Roma as directed to meet an America man named Jake."

"You're kidding. I just came from there!" Aaron informed Akbar.

"What were you doing there?" Akbar asked, surprised.

"I missed my connection to India and ended up meeting a woman about my mom's age named Britt in Assisi. Don't ask," Aaron said when he saw the question in Akbar's eyes. "I will tell you on the plane. We will trust that what we have found will be enough. Perhaps this Jake will know more than we do."

"We don't have to be in Rome for a few days. Let's enjoy the sites and flavors of India," Akbar recommended.

"Sounds great!" Aaron was delighted they had time to tour and visit some sacred sites and temples, and enjoy the "flavors," as Akbar described. Perhaps the overwhelming smells and noise were more than Aaron liked, but he knew with Akbar as his guide, it would be a great adventure.

CHAPTER 54

Britt carefully strolled across the uneven cobblestone streets still shadowed by night and passed the only person in sight: a street sweeper with his exceedingly long, straw-bristle brooms attached with thick crisscrossed wire to equally long wooden handles. He appeared so peaceful in the silence of the predawn morn, as Britt heard just the gentle sound of *swish, swish, swish* as the straw swept across the ancient stone streets. It was a beautiful and magical sight in the silent early morn.

For unknown reasons, the moment she came to the massive stone steps of this goddess temple, her mood shifted. She became profoundly somber and felt overly emotional. Everything in her told her she once lived in this town 1,200 years ago, before the streets were built over the original square and covered most of the massive steps and public spaces and shops. In her mind, she could see herself walking the streets and climbing the massive stone steps over and over.

When Britt reached the Minerva Temple, she slipped through a side door she had been shown by a kindly monk two days prior, after sharing with him her desire of being silently alone in the temple before the tourists came gawking, with their disrespectful conversations and loud voices.

And now, at the crack of dawn, in the profound stillness of the temple, Britt fell to her knees, ignoring the cold, hard stone floor beneath her. She prayed to God and the statue of Divine Mother with her golden crown of stars, begging for help.

When there was no rest in her mind, she began sobbing into the soft kidskin gloves covering her hands. Her shoulder length dark hair fell across her eyes covering her shame for her lack of trust. She tried to stop the intense burning in her heart for some unknown desire, as it would surely shatter if she couldn't contain her longing. She had hated the Catholic Church and the misery it had brought her, as well as so many of her friends, growing up.

Britt had turned away from anything that had to do with the Church, even when her grandmother threatened her for not attending mass, "I will take you out of my will!"

"I never asked you to put me in it," had been Britt's reply, "I am not going to lie to you like the rest of the family. Anyway, you say the rosary every day and what good has it done you?"

Her remark plainly upset her grandmother, so Britt remained silent, and the subject never came up again. When her grandmother died, Britt found that she was still in her will.

Having spent many hours in the chapels and basilicas of Assisi, from large to tiny, asking for answers to her questions regarding her dreams with no answers, from whom, how, or where Britt could not comprehend, finally, she let go and did the only thing left—surrender. She could only trust that this bewildering ache rooted in her soul would reveal itself when the time was right.

As Britt reached for her coat to leave she head a soft voice, *"My beloved daughter, only when you become empty of personal beliefs do you become a vessel for the manifestation of the Supreme. You must once again discover the void within to gain access to what you have been asking. Life won't bring you what you want, but it will bring you everything you need.*

"Remember, the nature of fear is to try to suppress and control the events around you, but Love tries to control no one. Within Love, fear

cannot exist. Keep opening your heart, keep loving everything light or dark."

"Thank you," Britt said gratefully, and equally so for the tissue in her pocket as she wiped her eyes and sat in silence until the glow from the statue of Mary vanished and the Church bells down the road rang an additional three times, signifying it was quarter to the hour. Slowly she got up and headed back home. The town had awakened.

Upon reaching the apartment on the top floor, Britt decided to make herself brunch with the scrumptious food she purchased yesterday and eat it on the balcony overlooking the ancient town of Assisi. She added marzipan cookies for dessert, before trying to reflect on the meaning of the unsettling dream she had the night before.

It was not just the closing of the old doors that brought Britt to Assisi; it was the dreams and finding the young man, Aaron. She was being told very explicitly that it was the energy of her beloved St. Francis, Santa Chiara, the Blessed Mary, and even that of the original goddesses of the Temple of Minerva that would assist her. All of these beings carried the divine feminine energy, and she knew she needed to remove the hard-core defenses surrounding her heart, and it needed to happen now.

Britt knew Assisi was where that would take place before leading her to a still-obscure location that would be the pinnacle of her journey this lifetime. As mysterious as it was, as uncertain as it was, and as lonely as she felt, she knew on some level that her soul had agreed to embark on this journey. She merely had to trust, deep radical trust, something she had begun to master the last few years during the agony of her divorce.

It was early morning when Britt awoke, she found herself speaking these words: "They said he would be at the synagogue in Capernaum."

"Who? Capernaum?"

Britt shook her head, trying to clear her mind, although she could only remember fragmented pieces of the dream.

She had been frantically running across large stone pavers, with tears stinging her face and her cloak flying behind her in the cool morning air. She had been in some ancient time, trying to find the man who disappeared behind the walls of the temple only moments before. She was desperate, but she had no idea why. She knew him, but she could never see his face in the dreams, as she always awoke before the visions finished.

Britt didn't move; her heart was racing, as it did each time she awoke from these extraordinary events. It was as if her soul were trying to find its way back into the body that lay upon the bed she now occupied. She was relieved to discover herself in bed in Assisi in the twenty-first century.

She tried to go back to sleep, but all she could think about were the dreams that had brought her to Assisi and the production she saw of *Chiara di Dio*, the musical by Carlo Tedeschi. Both the dream and the performance of Santa Chiara and San Francesco's story had somehow touched her more profoundly than she expected. Britt knew Assisi drew her because of both of these saints, but until now, she hadn't realized how intensely that affection would grow on a daily basis.

She felt like she should remember something, although she had no clue as to what it was. Tears began spilling down her face. She was sure she had cried more in Assisi than in her entire life.

Falling back asleep, she dreamt.

She was praying next to Francesco and Chiara in a small church made of stone blocks from the beautiful pink and white stones from Mt. Subasio nearby.

She was shocked when she first arrived at the tiny church a few months back after not seeing her friend for some time. The Chiara she had remembered had strands of long golden curls flowing down her back, but they were gone, cut short and mostly covered by a veil. There were a dozen others in the tiny room, but she was still cold.

The floor was hard, and the garments they wore were more like rags made of coarse wool in browns and creams. They were tied around their waists with a cord or fabric to hold the garments closed, but it was not enough to keep the winter chill from seeping in.

The others said nothing about the snow outside the door, nor the wind blowing through as if unaffected by the walls of stone.

She felt unworthy to be in their company, secretly complaining, which made her feel insignificant, and so she prayed to overcome external conditions.

She had initially come to deliver a message to Chiara from her parents and never returned to town, finding such joy and inspiration in their love and devotion not only to God and Jesus but to all humanity.

She rearranged the folded wool blanket she was kneeling on, thinking back to her family and how displeased they were with her, as was the man she was betrothed to. But she knew she could never marry, for she still dreamed of the man she could not find but knew existed, somewhere or at some point in time.

She had many dreams of him, of his kindness, his compassion, of a time that was joyful that suddenly turned to terror. It made no sense, to chase a dream, but she had no other choice than to dedicate her life to Jesus to feel that safety and peace within. Her family had sent relatives to try to bring her back, to no avail, for the simplicity of her new life filled a deep void within her that none of the luxuries of her privileged childhood had given her.

This drafty humble structure was now home, and although there were many times she had secretly wished for more food, a warmer blanket or garments, she would not trade this life for the one she left behind.

She had felt such a deep connection to both Francesco and Chiara, and looked at them as brother and sister.

Britt woke up in the still dark of night with a startling realization. "I have known them before! I have walked with them in many lives! But why am I having these dreams, and what purpose do they serve?"

CHAPTER 55

Ruth had not been able to reach her son Aaron to notify him of her departure to Assisi, Italy, nor had she heard from him for several weeks. She was not alarmed, as Aaron had his own life and he would surface when he was ready. She was relieved that she no longer needed to worry about his survival as she had the last few years when this vibrant wise soul vanished, and was replaced by a dark and reckless young man she barely recognized. Thankfully, her wise son reemerged. She sent him an email just in case he was checking them, telling him she believed herself to be the same Ruth as Jesus's younger sister of biblical times.

Her dream had suggested an urgency, and as she rode the train from Florence to Assisi, all Ruth knew was that she was supposed to head to the Basilica of Santa Maria degli Angeli, where she would meet a woman in her early fifties with shoulder-length dark hair. The vision had also shown Ruth the woman would be praying in the Porziuncola, housed within the Basilica. That was all she knew, and it was enough.

Departing from the train, Ruth bought a bottle of water at the small shop and headed through the front door to catch a cab for the short ride to the Basilica. She had been given a name, description, and number of a taxi by her friend Annie, who traveled to Assisi often: "You must call Bruno. He is the best! And he speaks English." Ruth had called ahead, and sure enough, Bruno was calling her name and rushing to get her bags.

"How did you know it was me?" Ruth asked Bruno.

"Easy, our friend Annie told me you were tall, blonde, and beautiful," Bruno said with a big welcoming smile, which was appreciated after the long journey. Thankfully, he kept the small talk to a minimum, which on this day made Ruth feel grateful. When he pulled up to the front of the breathtaking Basilica of Santa Maria degli Angeli, Bruno notified Ruth he would wait for her.

"I don't know how long I will be," Ruth confessed.

"Do not worry. I will be here. Any friend of Annie's is a friend of mine!" Bruno reassured her, adding, "Leave your bag. It is safe here."

Once Ruth walked into the main square in front of the Basilica, she could not help but stop and gaze up at the statue of Mother Mary standing peacefully and lovingly, high above the entrance.

Ruth spoke aloud in the busy square. "Divine Mother, help me on this journey. Grant me your grace, clarity, and guidance."

Entering the smaller door just left of the massive center doors, Ruth almost choked as her heart expanded, and tears of gratitude flooded her eyes when she saw the Porziuncola. The energy was palpable. Prayers from millions of devotees filled the space. Breathing deeply, Ruth walked across the large diamond pattern of cream and deep-rose marble towards the spot her vision showed her the dark-haired woman with the porcelain skin would be.

Touching the stone around the entrance of the tiny church where St. Francis had first built his chapel, Ruth gazed in and discovered there was only one row of single-person prayer benches on each side of the chapel. There to the right was the only woman around fifty with shoulder-length straight, dark hair and pale skin, praying as though her life depended on it. Ruth was not sure what to do. It wasn't exactly like she could kneel behind her and tap her on the shoulder, but at some point, she might have to.

Just then, the prayer bench in front of the woman opened up, and as the bald German man walked out, she slipped in to take it. As she passed the woman, she discreetly glanced in her direction and was embarrassed to find the woman had turned to glance at her at the same instant. Ruth was about to look away when an arm reached out and the woman stopped her.

"Come," she said in a hushed voice as she rose and directed Ruth out of the Porziuncola and into the Basilica. Ruth followed her to a row of chairs off to the side, about twelve rows down.

"I'm Britt, and I have been waiting for you," the woman said as they sat down next to each other.

"Ruth, and I'm glad it wasn't difficult to find you Britt!"

Ruth let out a sigh and pressed the inner corners of her eyes to push back some tears. Suddenly both women reached towards each other and embraced.

Britt had been holding something in her left hand and opened it to show Ruth. "It's a scroll I was guided to find, but I don't know what to do, as part of it is missing." She passed it to Ruth, who unrolled the papyrus and gazed upon the words *on the December solstice.*

Ruth looked up at Britt, a bit troubled, and whispered, "Clearly there was something written before this."

"I know, but this is all I discovered," Britt explained. "I only know we have to believe the rest will be made clear. At least that is what I keep telling myself."

Ruth patted Britt's hand. "It will be. I am sure of it."

Britt hoped Ruth was as confident as she sounded. "Why don't we get a cab up the hill to Assisi, where I am staying? We can get some food, and I do hope you will stay with me. I have plenty of room!"

"Are you sure?" Ruth asked, not wanting to impose.

"Of course! I recently had a wonderful young man named Aaron stay for a nap and lunch—"

Before Britt could finish, Ruth grabbed Britt's arm and interjected, "Aaron? Not a tall young American, about six two, with blue eyes?"

"As a matter of fact, he was." Britt raised a brow, questioning, "You know him?"

"He's my son!" Ruth laughed. "No wonder I haven't been able to find him! He's been in Italy."

"Actually, he was on his way to India to meet someone and took an alternate route. I was told in a vision that he would be in the piazza across from my residence and I must meet with him." Britt smiled."

"India, oh my gosh. At some point, I do remember him saying he needed to go there to find someone. Did he say who this person was?" Ruth asked.

"No, sorry, I didn't ask," Britt said as she frowned.

"Incredible! How was he?" Ruth inquired.

"Cold, tired, and hungry. But no worries, all needs were taken care of. He was a great gift, and provided me with some beneficial information. These events taking place are getting stranger all the time!"

"No kidding!" Britt confirmed. "Let's grab a cab."

"I have one waiting for me outside with my bag." Ruth smiled.

That night, the women ate in the magical town of Assisi filled with the sparkle of Christmas lights and holiday music. They talked until well after midnight before heading to Britt's apartment. Ruth loved this about Italy, being able to dine until long into the night. Finally, Britt showed her to her room, and it was only minutes after her head hit the pillow that Ruth fell into a deep sleep. When she awoke, she jumped out of bed and rushed to Britt's room to find she was already up making espresso in the kitchen.

"I know where we are to go," exclaimed Ruth even before saying good morning. "I saw a young Indian man and an American talking in St. Peter's Square. They had a part of your papyrus—I am sure of it! We need to be there by noon today!"

Britt smiled. "Good, then we have time for coffee, conversation, and a lovely breakfast. Rome is a little over two hours away. And I am sure your driver Bruno will get us there in a lick!"

CHAPTER 56

Andrew awoke with a start. "Who on earth was the fiery redhead in my dream?" Andrew didn't move a muscle. He wanted to remember each part of the dream and piece it back together. "She had documents in her hand. She was trying to talk to me about them. I pushed her away. She had several vials. She begged me to listen. I had her escorted out of my building, threatening to have her arrested if she ever came near me again."

Jumping out of bed, Andrew rushed downstairs to his home office, repeating, "Oh bloody hell, I need to find her. Good lord, help me find her."

Andrew lifted his phone and called his secretary at home. Before she could say hello, he blurted out, "Meg, sorry for the early-morning intrusion, but do you remember the woman who came to my office several months ago, with the fiery red hair, posing as a medical doctor with vaccine information?"

"Yes, Mr. Turner, and she wasn't posing. She had extensive medical training," Meg answered cautiously.

"Do you have any information on her?" Andrew asked hopefully.

"I do, as she was leaving, she threw the documents on my desk with two of the ampoules attached in a bag and begged me to find a way to persuade you to examine them. She said it was life or death for the entire planet." I must say, her urgency frightened me.

"Did you keep them?" Andrew optimistically inquired.

"Yes. They are locked in a cabinet in the office. Would you like me to go to the office and put them on your desk so you can have a read of it?" Meg offered.

"I know it's early, but yes, please!" Andrew exclaimed, adding, "I will order breakfast to be sent up, and I will see you soon. And thank you, Meg!"

"Certainly, see you soon." Meg hung up the phone, held back a few tears, grabbed her dog Cooper, and as she gave him a big hug, said, "This is a miracle I never thought would happen."

When Andrew arrived at the office, Meg was already there, as was the breakfast he had ordered for the two of them. "Good morning, Meg. Did you find the documents?"

"Good morning, sir. They're on your desk," Meg said with a smile, "as well as your breakfast."

"Why don't we bring everything into the small conference room and we can both eat as we go through this information brought by the redhead?" Andrew suggested.

"Do you fancy cream with your coffee this morning, sir?" Meg inquired as they settled in.

"Black today, thank you. What else do you know about her?" Andrew asked.

"Her name is Dr. Jasmine O'Sullivan. I just looked her up online. She goes by Jazz, at least to her friends, and she is in England right now. I was able to get her hotel information and number, knowing you would want them," Meg offered.

Surprised, Andrew looked at Meg with deep respect and gratitude, and noticed she blushed. He realized that before his holiday, he had never genuinely thanked anyone unless it was someone fattening his pockets. For the first time in a long time, he felt shame.

"Thank you, Meg. Would you see if you can leave a message for us to meet? And then come in and join me so we know what this 'life or death for the planet' is about."

Fifteen minutes later, Meg walked into the conference room to join Andrew. "As luck will have it, sir, Dr. O'Sullivan was leaving for the airport and agreed to delay her flight to come here to meet with you. She was at the Harrogate International for a medical conference. She said it would take three hours by train to get to London, but I let her know you would be sending your private plane. I do hope I didn't overstep, sir?"

"No, not at all, you saved time by doing what I would have asked you to." Andrew nodded.

"I booked her a suite at the Four Seasons with views over Hyde Park, as a peace offering." Meg winced, hoping she wasn't pushing her luck.

"Great, let's get on this. I am finding the information from Dr. O'Sullivan very organized and easy to follow. Highlight anything important you read that you believe I should know," Andrew said, handing Meg a yellow highlighter.

After twenty minutes of pouring through the papers, Andrew looked up at Meg. "Perhaps you should stop highlighting, as I see every page you have read is yellow."

"Yes, I believe it is all equally informative and important, and you will want to read all of it even though the information may be very controversial," Meg said, nodding.

One and a half hours later, the office staff was bustling about, but no one dared to disturb them until Meg spotted an assistant trying to get her attention. Meg excused herself to see what was so urgent.

"Sorry to bother you, Meg, but a woman is insisting she has an appointment with Mr. Turner. A Dr. O'Sullivan."

"Oh dear, I didn't realize how late it was. Please bring her right in. No need to knock," Meg assured.

Within moments, Andrew was rushing to the door to greet their guest with the fiery red hair. Smiling and with sincerity, he said, "Dr.

O'Sullivan, it is an honor to have you. Thank you for coming, and I deeply apologize for my behavior in the past. Can we get you anything to eat or drink?"

"No, thank you, you have rather good food on your aircraft." Curiosity is what brought Jazz to the meeting with the man she thought she would never see again—that and the dream she had last night, which included Mr. Turner.

"Apology accepted. Now tell me what this is about."

"My assistant and I have been going through your compelling documents. I had the vials delivered to one of my top research labs, and we are awaiting results." Andrew was ashamed to mention that his scientists were surprised that he would be interested in a cure for Alzheimer's and dementia, knowing his companies made billions from pharmaceuticals and owned over a thousand health-care facilities for the elderly that further financially benefited him.

"We have poured over your research and test results, as well as the findings of one of my former scientists, turned informer, who I noticed came to you with relevant information about this as well as some speculation about a lab developed virus. I cannot change the past, but tell me what you propose for the future?" Andrew asked with earnestness.

"I happen to have an outline that I presented at the medical conference I just attended. To be honest, it was a catastrophe, I wasn't getting much support—too much money in pharmaceuticals, vaccines, disease, and elderly care. We could start by using your health-care facilities—all 1,700 of them that I am aware of. We can start by replacing the most dangerous drugs and vaccines with herbs, naturopathic remedies, and diet changes. I am aware that some of these drugs will gradually need to be substituted."

"That many?" Andrew knew advances in medicine had prolonged the average lifespans of most people, requiring more health-care treatments over longer terms. He also knew this was not about the quality of life; it was about keeping people drugged longer and paying to stay in his facilities.

The main objective of a pharmaceutical assemblage he had attended fifteen years ago was "Get people hooked on drugs early in life, the younger the better. Colored pills help to attract the young, and then they're held captive for life." One drug needed another, then another, as each organ or millions of brain cells were destroyed.

"The plan was, whatever inheritance was available would not pass on to the next generation. It would belong to the shareholders. The average consumption for the elderly was eighteen pills a day. There would be nothing left in their savings when they passed."

Jazz saw the deep sorrow that came over Andrew's entire being. "My rule is, forgive the past, focus on what we can do right now."

Andrew nodded at Jazz before turning to Meg. "First, Meg, would you get ahold of Dr. Allen and ask him to meet with us? We can go to him if he would prefer. Also, ask if he would be willing to contact as many of the other scientists that supplied information to him as possible. See if they are willing to speak." Andrew paused. "That is if Dr. O'Sullivan is amenable to stay a couple of days to assist us."

"Call me Jasmine," Jazz offered, "and I believe I should be the one to call the rest of the informers. I don't believe they would trust your radical transformation."

"Quite right, quite right," Andrew acknowledged.

Meg left the room to make the call to Dr. Allen. This was one whistleblower who would be shocked at the turnaround of Mr. Turner!

Jazz wondered if she should take the opportunity to broach the topic of her dream that involved Andrew. She knew it expressed urgency, although she decided to wait a while longer to make sure the unexpected events transpiring would occur.

CHAPTER 57

Lisa, Veronica, and Tyler arrived at Jake's home to find him waiting at the front door to greet them. Giving Lisa a kiss and a big hug, he ushered them into the family room connected to the kitchen. "Drinks, anyone?" Jake asked, pointing to glasses, a container each of iced tea, lemonade, orange juice, and alkaline water.

"Help yourself. We will keep this casual. And if you are hungry, grab anything you would like from the fridge. Don't be shy, it makes it easier for me. I'll make us dinner, in an hour or so."

"Thanks," they said in unison and began pouring drinks. No one was hungry. There was too much excitement to think about food. "Grab a seat." Jake pointed to two facing sofas and four club chairs in the spacious room looking out to the gardens.

"Fabulous home. Some of the details remind me of my ancestral home in Italy. The mix with open modern spaces is amazing. And I love, love, love what I can see of your gardens from every room," Veronica said with admiration.

"Thank you," Jake said with gratitude. "And I hope we have the opportunity to visit your family in Italy when we are there."

"I have already alerted them of our coming, so there will be no way out!" Veronica assured him.

With Dean Mitchell handling the class announcement, they could now focus on the core issues during Jake's sabbatical. Looking at Veronica, Jake said, "Lisa mentioned the two of you had similar dreams about the location of one or more papyrus scrolls that may be relevant to this mission we seem to have found ourselves a part of. What can you tell me about them?"

"In the vision, we both saw the scrolls in a church in Verona where Lisa and I first met. Oddly, we were on a train from Verona to Roma, but in our conversation, we realized we had most likely been at Cattedrale Santa Maria Matricolare, or Verona Cathedral, at the same time before boarding the train."

"Tell me about the scrolls." Jake wanted to get to the point.

"The dream was a bit strange. First, I saw a rolled paper in the left hand of a large bronze statue of an angel at the entry, and then I saw it moments later, in her other hand. Veronica saw a scroll, under the same angel's right foot. We think there might be only one scroll, but for some reason, its position keeps changing." Lisa recounted.

"That is mysterious," Jake said. "Veronica, how far is it from Verona to Rome?"

"By plane, just an hour," Veronica replied. "There is an international airport in Verona, so at times, you can get a direct flight from JFK, but usually I make one stop in Florence."

"Great." Jake sounded relieved. "We are running out of time. In a few days, I meet the young Indian man in St. Peter's Square. That means, if we fly into Verona, spend the night, and head to the church in the morning, we will have time to get a plane to Rome before my meeting."

"We can stay at my family's home. There are several guest rooms, and they would love to have us," Veronica informed Jake. She then turned to Lisa and said, "You don't need to pack much. I have tons of clothes in Italy, all geared to the weather."

"Excellent, thanks, Veronica. That is one thing I don't like about traveling, hauling clothes around," Lisa said with a smile. She then turned towards Tyler and asked, "Tyler, you haven't said a word. Are you OK?"

"Yes, thank you, it's all a bit crazy, and it's better for me to listen right now," Tyler admitted.

Nodding, Jake seconded Tyler's assessment and then looked at Lisa and said, "Why don't you give Veronica a tour of the house and gardens while Tyler and I make the final arrangements? And then we will start dinner."

"Yes!" Veronica answered for Lisa. When they were out of hearing range from Jake and Tyler, she whispered to Lisa, "I find it all very exciting!"

Dinner was informal. They all decided eating at the counter would be the easiest. The conversation ranged from the seriousness of the upcoming events to the joys of friendship and travel. Two hours later, they all began cleaning up the dishes. Jake said, "We got this. Veronica and Tyler, you need to get home to pack and sleep, we are leaving in two days."

"Lisa, do you need a ride, or are you staying here?" Tyler inquired.

"Thanks, Tyler," Lisa responded, "but I'll spend the night with Jake. I already have toiletries and several outfits, including two sweaters and a coat. Tomorrow morning, I will head to my place and pick up my passport and come back here."

"Convenient," Veronica smiled.

"I will pick you both up at Veronica's at 6:00 a.m. sharp in two days' time. Does that work for you, Tyler?" Jake asked.

"Works for me. I'm going to pack tonight and spend the night at Veronica's the next two nights. I want to make sure she doesn't run off to the river and forget about our flight," Tyler said with a wink.

Veronica didn't respond. Once, it had actually happened. "See you then, if not sooner, you two" was all she said as she blew them a kiss.

After closing the door behind Veronica and Tyler, Jake wrapped his arms around Lisa and embraced her lovingly as he kissed her.

They held each other a long time before Jake said, "Let's get to bed. And when I said on the phone that I loved you, I meant it."

"Thank you. I love you also. And honestly, I wasn't sure if you said it out of habit, so I didn't bring it up," Lisa confessed.

"That's just it. It isn't something I had said in a very long time," Jake stated as he grabbed her hand, kissed it, and gently led her up the stairs.

CHAPTER 58

"Hey, what's up? I thought I was meeting you back at your place." Lisa asked with concern when Jake showed up at her front door without a phone call. "And don't say nothing because I can see and feel it!"

Pushing his way in and closing the door quickly behind him, Jake said with urgency, "We have to get out of town now. Call Tyler and Veronica. Our timeline has moved up. Have them meet us at the airport ASAP."

"Jake, what is going on? You are scaring me! And why didn't you call them yourself" Lisa said with alarm. "I also noted your car isn't out front. Did you come by taxi?"

"Yes. Dean Mitchell called me this morning and told me two men were inquiring about me concerning some missing texts that belonged to the Vatican and demanded them back immediately. They wanted to know where I was. When he asked them why they believed it was me that had the texts, they said I matched the description of the man that witnesses said picked it up in the courtyard. Mitchell insisted that a dozen men could have matched my description. They responded by saying, 'perhaps, but he is the only one that is fluent in five languages including Sanskrit, Latin, and ancient Aramaic. Someone else would have turned them in."

"Jake, I'm scared. What do we do? Did Dean Mitchell suggest you return them?"

"No, quite the contrary. That was the surprising part. Mitchell told the men he believed I had left the city for a conference to buy us time. He told me to hide the manuscript and get out of town knowing they would come back when they couldn't find me elsewhere. I let him know where a copy was and told him that you, Veronica and Tyler knew where the original was in case anything should happen to me."

Jake saw the tears running down Lisa's face. He grabbed her and kissed her face, "Don't worry, we haven't come all this way for this ending. Have Tyler and…"

Lisa cut him off, "Jake, that car across the street went by once before. OMG, the two men are coming towards my place! Hide!"

"Lisa, stay calm. Go upstairs and call Tyler and Veronica now. Tell them to get to the airport and we will meet them. Get on any flight to Italy, and if I don't get there, go anyway. Promise me you will. I swear I will catch up with you guys."

Lisa couldn't speak, so she nodded.

Seeing the look of alarm on her face, Jake assured her, "Don't worry, I will find you, I promise. Now quickly grab your passport and a few things. Go out the back door to get to your car and wait for me two houses down the street facing away from the house with the engine running. Get in the passenger side and stay down. Don't ask questions, just do it," Jake kissed her and gave her a gentle push.

He headed to the kitchen to create distance. Moments later the doorbell rang and Jake called out, "Hold on, I'm on the phone. I'll be right there."

Jake slowly approached the front door. When he heard Lisa exit the back door, he called out, "Coming."

The moment Jake opened the door the two men pushed their way in and slammed the door behind them.

"Hey, what the hell is going on?" Jake yelled.

"You know why we are here, just turn over what is ours and there will be no further trouble!" Growled the man with the heavy Italian accent who looked more like a mafia character than a member of the church.

A wave of energy washed over Jake. And what came out of his mouth was completely unexpected, "Back off!" Jake growled back, "or that manuscript will see the light of day before the Vatican knows what hit them! I AM John the Beloved, and those are my writings. It is you who has stolen them from humanity and there is a karmic price to pay! Just so you are clear, if anything were to happen to me, there are four copies in safe hands that will be released to every form of media. Now get the hell out of here!"

Glaring at Jake and thrusting out his chest, the man responded with a menacing snarl, "You haven't seen the last of us. You better watch your back and also warn your pretty lady."

Jake waited until they drove off before he picked up his phone to text Lisa. "Slide into the driver's seat and get to the airport. They will be watching me, and I don't want you to be seen with me. I will meet the three of you in Italy. I promise. I love you. Go."

CHAPTER 59

Ben and Tony landed in Mexico City and were both relieved when they got the green light through customs, as the time was closely approaching to meet the priest at the Basilica of Our Lady of Guadalupe. They grabbed the first cab they were directed to after exchanging $200 U.S. into Mexican currency. "I don't know how much the priest needs, but I figure I can give him this for his stay in Mexico and then see if another $1,000 U.S. is enough for wherever he is going," Tony remarked.

Ben laughed. "You must have had the dream about the money part knowing you were a trust-fund baby. Thank God for that!"

"Do you understand where we are asking to go, Carlo?" Tony asked, seeing his name on the badge attached to the dashboard.

"*Sí, sí, no hay problema.*"

"I believe he would say yes regardless of whether he does or doesn't. At least it's a common tourist spot," Ben reassured Tony.

As they stood in front of Basilica of Our Lady of Guadalupe, Ben said, "It's mammoth! I had hoped for something more intimate and traditional. I feel like I could be in L.A. at a rock-and-roll or sports stadium."

"I saw the old Basilica online, but I believe it was sinking or some such thing," Tony revealed. "Come on, we aren't here to critique the architecture."

Once inside the Basilica, they were even more overwhelmed. There were hundreds of people occupying the benches and approaching the guard railing to the altar.

"Unbelievable, how many people do you think this place holds?" Ben asked in astonishment.

"I think I read ten thousand. Just be glad it's not full!" Tony motioned to Ben. "This way, the vision showed me he would be sitting on the right side and close to the front. Look for a priest who is holding a scroll or rolled piece of paper."

"Holy crap!" Ben blurted out. "See that?" He pointed down a row of benches where people had rolled or flat paper on their laps.

"No kidding, what are they holding? Looks like rolled-up songs or prayers. Must have been a mass," Tony said, "but let's start at the front, since the vision showed us he was close to the altar."

Ben was the first to see José, and his heart skipped several beats. *I'm too young for a heart attack, or at least I hope so*, he thought. Ben flagged Tony, who was in the opposite aisle, and asked the woman sitting next to the priest if he could sit next to his friend. She looked at him sternly, undoubtedly unhappy that he disturbed her rosary. Ben quickly said, "*Hermoso Rosario, debe ser muy especial.*" The woman softened and moved to the bench two rows behind them.

"Father, we have come to meet you, and I am enormously grateful to find you. I'm Ben."

"I have been expecting you. I am Father Cruz." José flushed. "I mean to say, call me José. Our Lady said two young Americans would arrive," José expressed in confusion.

"You are correct. There is my friend Tony," Ben said, pointing to the approaching young man.

Tony whispered to Ben, "What did you say to that woman? I didn't realize you were fluent in Spanish."

"I told her she had a beautiful rosary and it must be very special,"

Ben said with a smile. "And I'm not. I sold rosaries when I was a kid on the beach in Puerto Vallarta, so that's about all I know."

Both boys sat, and Ben turned to José and quietly introduced Tony to him. "Good to meet you, José," Tony whispered.

José took Tony's hands and clasped his over them. "The Divine Mother has a gift for you," José said with sincerity. "Somehow you will know where the remainder is and discover where you should be."

The scroll was now in Tony's hands, and he looked at Ben. "It's in my hand!" he whispered excitedly. "The papyrus scroll is in my hand."

"Well open it!" Ben said, not wishing to be tormented one moment longer.

Tony put it on his lap and unrolled the small woven paper and read, "Of my birth."

"That's it? Are you sure?" Ben asked as he picked up the thick paper and turned it over. "OMG, that's it. That's all it says."

Tony whispered to José, "Is there anything else you can tell us?"

"No, Our Lady said you would know and would help me get to where I need to go."

"Yes, of course, we are here to help you. We were shown that also," Ben assured José.

Once Tony had given José the money, he explained that if he needed more for his trip to please tell him, as he wasn't sure where José was going and what he needed. Tony realized as José stared at the money on his lap that he had no idea what to do with it.

"OK, I'll tell you what, let's get your ticket to . . . incidentally, where are you going?" Tony inquired.

"Tel Aviv," José responded.

"OK, so let me check my phone to get an idea of a ticket cost," Tony assured José. Seeing it was around $1,300, he realized $1,000 would not be getting him there but didn't want to make José feel bad about the money, so he did not relay this information.

"José, write all your information on this piece of paper. I will purchase your ticket right now, and we can print it out at our hotel. I also need your passport number. You do have one, don't you?"

"Yes," José said, pulling it out from a pouch under his cape.

Tony could see it was new. "Great, write the number down and put it back. Keep that passport safe!" Tony warned.

It only took Tony fifteen minutes to purchase José's airline ticket. "Done. Let's get to our hotel and print your ticket. If you would like, we could all have supper together and have a cab drop you off at your hotel after."

"I would like that," José said as he handed Tony back the envelope with $1,000 U.S. in it. "Thank you for purchasing my ticket. I wasn't sure how to do that."

Tony put his hand up. "No, keep the money, that's for you. You'll need spending money and a hotel when you get there unless you are going to a monastery."

"I'm not going to a monastery," José assured them. "I humbly thank you and don't know how I can repay you," José admitted.

"You don't owe me anything. It was my honor to do this. Don't worry, I have a trust fund, so I am happy to share," Tony assured José with a big smile. "Now let's go print your tickets and find some great Mexican food. I'm starved."

As they were leaving the church, Tony looked back at Our Lady of Guadalupe and swore he saw her turn her eyes towards him and smile. He shook his head to clear his vision.

"What was that about?" Ben asked. "Did you see something?"

"Nothing, I'm certain I'm clearly tired," Tony responded.

"By the way, you're a good man, Tony," Ben noted in a whisper.

That night before retiring, Ben looked at Tony and said, "I sure hope our next destination will reveal itself soon. I was certain the scroll would direct us, but it is all only more confusing."

"Remember when Professor Reynolds gave us the assignment to spend the entire week not planning anything but watching for each moment to unfold?" Tony inquired. "He said it was inspired by Paramahansa Yogananda's train journey as a boy."

"You're right, this is like that. I do know that I became very aware of how many opportunities I would have missed if I had been planning my days or the next thing to do," Ben reminisced.

"Let's try that now. Trust the wisdom of living in the present moment," Tony stated.

"Sound good, now let's get some sleep!" Ben said as he slid under the blankets.

CHAPTER 60

Andrew and Jazz arrived at Marcus just after 8:00 p.m. Andrew had picked a three-Michelin-star restaurant to dine with Jasmine but then thought better of it. Turning to Jazz, he'd said, "Why don't you take a look at the internet and see what restaurant you would like to dine at tonight."

Meg peeked in the door and asked if there was anything else they needed.

"Meg, if you had a choice of any restaurant in London, what would you pick?" Jazz inquired.

"Marcus or Hélène Darroze," Meg said without hesitation, "but I will quickly pull them both up, and you can see if you fancy either."

Moments later, Meg had both restaurants showing on a laptop and put it in front of Jazz.

"Marcus," Jazz said. "They had me at 'the lavish and indulgent ambiance is offset by a surprisingly laid-back menu that offers five courses of fresh and seasonal produce.' But to be clear, it wasn't the lavish and indulgent ambiance, although I like that it looks comfortable and not uptight. However, what was most important was 'five courses of fresh and seasonal produce.' How does that sound to you, Andrew?" Jazz smiled. "Just so you are clear, it is only a two-Michelin-star restaurant." She winked.

"It's quite good," Andrew acknowledged as he pulled out his phone to make the call.

"Sir, I can do that for you," Meg quickly responded. She was not used to Andrew making his reservations.

"Thank you, Meg, but I got this. And make sure you take a friend to each of these soon, on my account. You better get home to feed and walk your dog. You have been here since early morning."

"Have a great evening, sir, and thank you." Meg turned to Jazz and said, "It was an honor and pleasure to meet you."

As Meg grabbed her things to head home, she was still questioning how Mr. Turner knew she had a dog.

Not only was the meal delicious, but it was also pure art. Each course that was presented was more beautiful than the last. Of course, Andrew's notoriety helped, and the chef was delighted to prepare for Jazz an outstanding four-course vegetarian meal. She smiled to herself as this master of cuisine came to their table and Andrew made the request. In her mind, Jazz questioned whether she might have been thrown out if on her own.

"Why are you smiling?" Andrew asked Jazz.

"Almost everything on the menu consists of meat or poultry, and I have a feeling if it wasn't for you, I might have been asked to leave if I had suggested alterations," Jazz whispered.

Andrew laughed. "Not here, but perhaps if you were to go to Gordon Ramsay and ask to pull apart an existing dish, you might be met with such a request. He is known for his temper but excused because of his three Michelin stars. Although, I do believe he has a vegetarian selection."

Dinner was delightful, and after a long day of reviewing documents and statistics, and joining conference calls with a dozen leading scientists, Andrew began to give orders to do more research in wellness through natural remedies instead of synthetics. Jazz heard the shock as well as admiration for Andrew in several of the scientists' expressions and voices.

She could barely believe the change in this man who had thrown her out of his offices and was responsible for promoting destruction on the planet through his insatiable and reckless greed.

Getting up the courage, Jazz asked, "Andrew, would you be willing to share with me what transpired that created these dramatic changes in your life? Was it news of an illness?"

"No, it was not an illness. And only if I can call you Jazz," Andrew said with a smile.

"I believe you have earned the right of friendship." Jazz laughed.

Andrew continued, "I was at one of my homes, sitting near the water, when I heard words I will never forget. They are etched in my being: 'Why are you destroying my majestic and precious earth? For in the end, although she will barely survive, you will die a long and tragic death from the very chemicals you have so richly profited from. Do you not remember who you are?'"

Jazz could see that Andrew was shaken as he repeated the warning he had heard. She rested her hand on his arm and listened.

"This will sound like I lost it, but there was also a giant bird that hovered above me, and something in me broke open. That is the only way I can describe it. It revealed to me who I had been and what I had done before greed had darkened my mind and consumed my life. I 'remembered my true self'—that is the only way I can describe the event." Andrew dropped his shoulders as if the weight of his world was falling away.

"Thank you for sharing your profound and personal story. I would like to share something that I dreamt, if you are interested," Jazz said with compassion.

"Yes, please, I am interested. It can't get much more bizarre than mine," Andrew sincerely answered.

"We will see. I had a vision that in a past life, I was Brigid of Ireland, and although I knew you from that time as a brother, I also was shown that you had walked with Jesus as the disciple Andrew." Jazz stopped, wondering if she had gone too far and if Andrew would consider her crazy and retract what they had accomplished.

Andrew grabbed her hand. "Yes! You are correct, I did walk with Jesus two thousand years ago. I also dreamt that I lived in Ireland in the fifth and sixth centuries, as did you. I didn't realize it was you until now. You founded a monastery at Kildare as well as two monastic institutions, one for men and the other for women, and that is when you invited me to come help you. You also founded the school of arts that I oversaw."

"Conláed?" Jazz grabbed both Andrew's hands. "It is you! I saw you as my brother, but brother was not defined."

"Surely," Andrew said, nodding his head, "it is I you granted so many titles and privileges too. However, it was you who performed many miracles, including healing and feeding the poor. And it is no wonder why you have continued as a healer and protector of all people. As for me, I have no excuses."

"You were a good man in many lifetimes, I am certain. We both know that any hidden shadows from what could be thousands of lives gone by must rise from the unconscious to the conscious mind to be healed," Jazz said as she looked him in the eye. "We all must go through the fires of purification."

"Yes, but instead of healing them, I dove right in. Somewhere along the way, I forgot myself, my soul, and gave way to the darkness," Andrew confessed.

"Think about it. I was considered a saint or holy person during my life as St. Brigid of Kildare, and this life, I have been a disaster in intimate relationships with men. As Brigid, I was bound to chastity and viewed sexual relationships as unholy, or not in alignment with God. Yet is it not all God? I am not saying it is about random sex for instant gratification. It is about divine lovemaking, and one must know a person on the deepest levels to know loves true glory.

"When most don't know themselves, it is difficult for another to create that level of intimacy with them. All those shadows and the shame must come up to be healed through acceptance and love, as the real objective of a human is to become fully or divinely human. The divine human is the one who has successfully balanced the internal masculine and feminine qualities.

"It loves all aspects of the self. Believe me, you are making amends right now. Much can still be turned around. We cannot spend any more energy on what we have done wrong. Let's focus on what we can do to assist the planet. We can do this together as we did in the past, if you are willing," Jazz offered.

"Thank you. It would be an honor to work beside you." Andrew bowed his head.

Jazz looked down at their fingers that were holding each other's forearms, pulled one hand free, and tucked several fallen locks of hair behind her ear.

"Wow, not sure where all that came from, a bit much for first-time dinner conversation!" Jazz flushed.

"Remember, we have known each other from multiple lifetimes, I am sure. I also feel comfortable with you. It is like I am speaking with an old and dear friend," Andrew confessed.

"Yes, I agree," Jazz said with relief. Then looking up at Andrew, she asked, "There seems to be a nervous group of waiters lurking in the distance. What do you suppose that is about?"

Andrew pulled his hand away from Jazz's arm, sat upright, and looked around before laughing softly. "It's truly not funny. They are so used to me demanding continual service that they are unsure what to do with this other man who looks like me but doesn't act like me."

"Well, it is this man before me who is a joy to be with," Jazz confessed, "but it is late, and we are the last ones here. Besides, we certainly both need sleep!"

"You are right. I'll take you back to your hotel. Let's get some rest and meet tomorrow. I will have a car pick you up. Just call in the morning to let me know what time is best for you," Andrew said.

"I will walk—too much sitting today. It looks close. I noticed we passed it on our way here," Jazz replied.

"I will walk with you. You shouldn't walk alone this late at night. Anyway, I also need to stretch my legs. My driver will meet me at the Four Seasons," Andrew said with finality.

CHAPTER 61

Usually, Tyler would not answer a phone call from an unknown number, but these were not ordinary times. "Tyler, it's Jake," said the voice on the other end of the line.

"Thank God, man. Veronica and I were losing it when Lisa told us about Dean Mitchell's call and his visit from the dark visitors demanding information. You all right, dude?" Tyler asked with relief.

"I'm fine. However, listen, I'm heading to the airport, but I don't want to be on the same flight as you three. Once you are in Italy, head to Veronica's parents' home. About five kilometers from the family home, you can pick me up in front of a restaurant called Luigi's. I'll be waiting. Hey, and please reassure Lisa I'm fine."

"Got it. No worries, I will tell Lisa everything is great. Even if I'm not feeling it inside," Tyler confessed.

"Thanks, Tyler. And I will be dumping this burner phone in a garbage heap, so don't call back."

"All right, man, just make sure you get to Luigi's!" Tyler replied.

"I will. But, Tyler, if I'm not there, get to Rome after Lisa and Veronica find the scroll at the Basilica, and meet the young man I was to connect with. He will be near the fountain in St. Peter's Square at noon. Tell him what is going on. He won't recognize you, but if you are wearing tan slacks and a white button-down linen shirt, he will do a double take. You will find each other. And whatever you do, don't tell Lisa what I just said."

"Crap, Jake, just be there, man!"

The three barely spoke on the entire trip to Italy. The silence was painful. After customs, Tyler was trying to keep it light as he and Veronica picked up the rental car at the airport, but it wasn't working. "I'll drive," Tyler announced cheerfully.

"Like hell you will," Veronica said as she reached out for the keys.

"I guess you don't need me to navigate," Tyler stated.

"Bro, YGTI!" Veronica shot back. "Just buckle your seat belts and hold on."

Tyler looked at Lisa and, as he pointed to Veronica, said, "As always, TTP!"

Lisa managed a weak smile. She knew they were trying to distract her, but it wasn't working.

The drive to Luigi's felt like an eternity to Lisa. Keeping her face turned towards the window so she would not be found out, she tried to focus on the architecture and landscape. But as she sat in the back seat, tears silently ran down her cheeks.

"Oh My God, Oh My God, that's him! That's him!" Lisa was the first one to spot Jake in front of Luigi's. "Thank God!" she exclaimed.

Tyler hadn't even come to a full stop when Lisa threw open her door and jumped out.

Running towards Jake, Lisa threw herself into his arms and started sobbing. "It's okay. It's okay," Jake assured her as he wrapped her in his arms and repeatedly kissed the top of her head.

Tyler strolled up with Veronica and thrust out his hand. "Hey, man, I can't tell you how good it is to see you!"

Jake took it and then embraced Tyler, saying, "I knew you wouldn't let me down, my friend. Good to see you too."

Tyler parked the car on a side road near Luigi's while Jake pointed the ladies to the waiting cab. "I'm not taking any chances. I didn't want the same driver who dropped me off from the airport to take us to Veronica's."

Whatever dialogue hadn't taken place since the news from Tyler, regarding Jake taking another flight, was quickly made up for on the taxi ride to Veronica's family home.

CHAPTER 62

"*Bentornata a casa*, Veronica! *Bentornata a casa*, Veronica! *Benvenuto anche, gli amici di* Veronica!"

"Grandpa!" Veronica ran from the taxi, across the fine pea-gravel circular drive, and into the waiting arms of her grandfather.

"Wow, this place is right out of a movie!" Lisa whispered to Jake and Tyler.

"No kidding," Tyler said in awe, "if I knew my girlfriend's family was loaded, I might have been too intimidated to date her!"

Lisa laughed and glanced back at Jake.

"No words," Jake replied to her gaze, "no words. It's breathtaking!"

The home was gorgeous, everything Italian: fresco and stone walls, iron balconies with double patio doors upstairs, the range of mountains in the distance, the expansive grounds with paths to lush gardens, and groves of olive trees that lined the entry path. Huge pots were dripping with glazes reflecting the sun as well as terracotta pots that the lime had leached through and whitened from age, each holding dwarf fruit trees, including lemons, oranges, figs, and pears.

This land and the home had indeed been loved and honored for centuries.

Mario came out and greeted his cousin. "I couldn't stay away when I heard you would be visiting."

"Oh, come on, you don't fool me. You heard Lisa was also coming!" Veronica teased, giving him a big hug. "Too bad she's taken, not that you had a chance anyway."

Mario flushed when he saw Lisa smiling. "Thanks for always ratting me out, cuz!"

Lisa came forward with her arms out. "Great to see you again, Mario. We had such fun. I will never forget it." When she pulled back from his embrace, Lisa turned to Jake and said, "This is Jake. He is the one who stole my heart."

"Good to know he isn't some bum, and reasonably handsome for an American," Mario teased before graciously shaking Jake's hand. "Welcome to Italy, Jake," Mario said as he patted him on the back.

"Thank you, Mario, great to meet you also. I've heard wonderful stories about your travels with the ladies. I'm under a lot of pressure to match that." Jake laughed.

"I want you all to meet my beloved Grandpa Francesco. Grandpa, this is Jake, my best friend Lisa, and my boyfriend, Tyler," Veronica said with a big smile.

"Boyfriend? *Oh mio, oh mio, mia cara* Veronica, it is a good thing your parents are away on holiday, as you have not spoken about this young man, Tyler. You better stop on the way back or you will not hear the end of it!" Francesco said with a mischievous smile.

"My boy," Francesco reached out his arms to Tyler and embraced him. "I didn't think anyone could steal my granddaughter's heart. You must be a fine young man!"

"She makes me the best me, Francesco," Tyler admitted.

Francesco held Tyler by both shoulders, looked him intensely in the eyes, and said, "Call me Grandpa." Tyler sensed there was also a warning in Francesco's eyes.

Everyone hugged and exchanged pleasantries, and then Grandmothers Julia and Maria came rushing out, pulling off their aprons, and it started all over.

"Come in, come in, the meal is ready," Grandmother Maria exclaimed.

"You better get going," Grandpa teased. "Your grandmothers don't like food getting cold!"

"I will show them to their rooms and let them wash up, and we will join you," Veronica said.

"All right, but make it snappy!" Grandpa warned with a playful swat on Veronica's backside.

When Lisa and Jake had settled into their suite, Lisa came up behind Jake, who was looking out of the upstairs window that overlooked Lake Garda as well as snowcapped mountains in the distance. On the far side of the terrace below was a large rectangular swimming pool framed by lawn and more potted trees. She wrapped her arms around Jake as she looked over his shoulder and said, "Can you believe the beauty of this place?"

"No, it's hard to take in. The mix of Venetian plaster, light stone walls and floors, hand-sawn wood beams, and old wood-planked floors is perfectly balanced. It is gracious and beautifully orchestrated. Even the furnishing colors are understated but full of life, inviting, and how can you beat these extraordinary views?" Jake said in awe.

There was a tap at their doors. "Hey, you two, no time to linger, time to eat. You can rest later!" Veronica announced.

"Coming!" Jake and Lisa replied, walking through the double doors.

Rushing down the stairs, past a large formal living room, to a spacious embracing kitchen, they were greeted by a long wooden table laden with food and drink. There were several types of pasta, two large bowls of salads, cheeses, sliced tomatoes, fresh sliced mozzarella, olives, home-baked bread, and a variety of homemade and seasoned olive oils.

"Wow!" Tyler, Jake, and Lisa all exclaimed at once.

The meal lasted over two hours and two bottles of Grandpa's prized red wine from his small vineyard. Jake commented on how excellent the wine was, and Grandpa lit up with pride: "Indigenous Corvina, Molinara, and Rondinella grapes—the best! Some of the world's most famous wines are produced here in Verona."

Finally, Veronica said, "I want to give my friends a tour and stretch our bodies a bit after the long journey. We will have to leave tomorrow by 9:00 a.m. to stop at Cattedrale Santa Maria Matricolare, which Lisa and I want to visit, and then catch our plane to Roma. We want to get plenty of sleep tonight so we have time to join you for breakfast before we leave."

"Breakfast will be at 7:00 a.m. sharp. Don't be late!" Grandmother Maria warned them.

"We won't. Would you like to join us on our tour?" Veronica asked as she looked at both grandmothers and her grandpa.

Grandma Julia said, "Take your grandpa and go. He is useless cleaning a kitchen. Maria and I are happy to clean up."

Tyler, Lisa, and Jake stood and profusely thanked the family for the incredible meal and conversation as they began clearing the table. "No, no, we have this, go, enjoy!" Maria said as she shooed them off.

"Don't argue with Italian grandmothers. You will lose every time!" Veronica assured them with a laugh.

That evening as they all sat together in the living room, they were too tired for conversation. Instead they watched as final rays of light disappeared in the winter sky. Finally, Jake spoke. "I feel I need some rest before our journey continues, although the beauty and hospitality of your family make me wish we had more time to visit."

Grandmother Julia had retired for the evening, but Francesco and Maria nodded in agreement. "Please come back anytime. You are all welcome with or without my granddaughter. Now you are family!" Francesco expressed with sincerity.

"Thank you," Jake and Lisa said as Tyler nodded in gratitude.

CHAPTER 63

José went through customs without issue. He was awkward in his new attire and thought he would set off alarms, even though Luke had assured him he looked great and not to worry. It had been so long since José had worn anything but the traditional clerical clothing that he felt lost and naked without them. He also felt strangely confined, but he was grateful for Luke's help in assisting him with his selections.

José and Luke had met after an experience Luke could not explain with his logical mind. It occurred in his third week of learning to meditate and silence his mind. In frustration, he gave up, completely threw out any attempt at doing it "right" as taught in the dozen online videos he had watched. It was in that surrender that his thoughts fell away without effort.

With no agenda, Luke fell into a breathless state and witnessed a single brilliant star in his frontal lobe that exploded into light. No thought. No desire. No stress. Only profound peace. The blue glow turned to a pink light and began to fill the spaceless vacuum, and Our Lady of Guadalupe showed herself as she had forty years before in the church in Mexico City, pure and without adornments.

Her hand moved to her abdomen, revealing the final days of pregnancy before birth. The bright light she had shown him was indeed not in the heavens where he had been looking for it all these years; it was glowing from her womb.

She looked at him and spoke in a voice that sounded like an angelic choir: *"Come now. A priest will be there sitting on a bench, clutching a ticket. Go to him. Tell him the event will occur on the winter solstice. He knows where you are both going."* With that, Luke came back into his body and gasped for breath.

Luke did not try to make sense of the event; he now knew better. The winter solstice was quickly approaching, and he needed to get to the priest and discover where the "birth" was to take place.

His calculations of the sacred event did not align above Bethlehem, the birthplace of our Lord. He started to panic at the thought of not knowing where to go after waiting forty years for this event. "Breathe. Just breathe," he heard himself say, and he did.

The next day, Luke arrived in Mexico City and took a taxi to the Basilica of Our Lady of Guadalupe. He preferred the old church and was grateful his first experience took place there. He was as nervous as he had been on a first date as a teenager. "Why has it taken me so long to come back?" Luke wondered aloud before entering the Basilica's doors.

He walked up the far-right side, scanning the benches for a priest with a ticket on his lap. There were many priests, but not his. The building was immense, and it might take him some time. He had to trust that Our Lady knew when he would arrive and that the timing would be perfect.

Luke scanned every bench on the right side and was heading to the next aisle when he stopped to speak with Our Lady. He stood behind the rail that forced him to stay back much farther than he would have liked and spoke to her like a dear beloved friend, asking for nothing, only to express his gratitude.

That was when a beam of light from above reflected off the crown above her. Luke turned his head towards the benches and followed the ray; it touched the top of a dark-haired man's lowered head. Luke blew a loving kiss to Our Lady and came upon the man. He knew he had passed him but had not seen the ticket until now. His hand had been covering it, but now he was stroking its edges gently.

There were two empty seats beside the priest, and Luke asked if he could join him. José nodded. It was several minutes before Luke opened his mouth to speak, but José spoke first.

"I am José. Our Lady said you would be looking for me."

"I am Luke, and happy to meet you." Luke felt the stress he had been unaware of evaporating.

"Look at Our Lady's womb. Can you see it?" José inquired.

Luke looked at the image and saw nothing unusual. Instead, he decided to be the observer and let go of his mind. And it was then that he noticed a pregnant woman with a bright light shining from her abdomen.

"How did I not see that on her garment forty years ago?" Luke asked. "It wasn't until she spoke to me recently that I saw it."

"You searched trying to see with your eyes and could not see. Then you looked with your heart, and you could see," José clarified the situation and handed Luke his ticket.

"It says you are heading to Tel Aviv," Luke queried.

"Yes, and you are to get a ticket on the same flight. We are to go together," José informed him. "The two young men who purchased the ticket for me did it on their phone. Maybe you can do the same?"

"I will do it right now, but outside," Luke responded and questioned, "Tel Aviv? I have been tracing the stars for forty years and always felt Bethlehem would be the place they realigned, but they don't. It is showing some miles farther north."

"I am sure they are, but do not bother yourself with that. What we are to do is to be in Bethlehem. Although I am not sure by when, the rest will be made known," José answered.

"Oh, I was to tell you, we need to be there by the winter solstice!" Luke replied.

"Not much time left," José acknowledged.

"No, but as you mentioned, it is perfectly unfolding," Luke offered.

"I have one favor I would like to ask of you," José asked in all seriousness.

"Sure, anything," Luke answered, wondering what this favor could be.

"Would you help me to buy clothes so that I will fit in with others? I am at a loss," José confessed.

Luke wanted to laugh, but he saw the look of embarrassment on José's face and quietly answered, "Of course."

CHAPTER 64

Although Veronica, Lisa, Tyler, and Jake would have loved to stay longer to chat after breakfast the next morning, they felt the urgency to reach the cathedral before too many people had arrived. Besides, they did not want to miss their flight to Rome. After repeated hugs, kisses, and tears from Grandpa as well as requests to return before heading back to America, the four were off to Cattedrale Santa Maria Matricolare.

Lisa and Veronica both knew the location of the larger-than-life angel they saw in their dreams, so they were not concerned about having to search for an obscure relic or other perplexing puzzle piece but instead chatted away excitedly about what the message on the scroll would tell them.

"Nervous?" Veronica asked Lisa, realizing she was talking more than usual.

"No. Well, perhaps a little. The dreams have been going on for months, and it was so intense when each of us thought we were alone. Now we are getting close to discovering where this mystery will lead us and what it is regarding. I can't wait to discover what the scroll will tell us," Lisa admitted.

"Same here," Tyler revealed, "I get excited and nervous at the same time. Then I wonder if it is all nothing and we will be so let down." He quickly added, when he saw the looks on everyone's faces, "Sorry, I guess my dark side came out. I still feel unworthy to be a part of this.

And not only to be forgiven but to discover it was all preordained is hard for me to grasp."

"You agreed to a tough assignment, Tyler! Not many would have consented to such a task. To know you would be despised for centuries by humanity, at least Christians, is hard on the ego. You must have deeply loved him," Jake said with respect.

"That I did, and still do," Tyler said in a whisper as if talking to himself while Veronica lovingly rubbed his back.

The taxi pulled up to the cathedral as close as possible before dropping them off. Jake paid the driver but asked him to wait. The driver agreed, mainly because of the generous tip.

The moment Lisa spotted the statue of the angel in front of the Duomo, her heart began racing. Veronica grabbed Lisa's hand and said, "Come on, I can see something in its left hand, and there is a bus of children unloading!"

They were too late, as the children swarmed around the angel, grabbing its outstretched left hand. As they got closer to the statue, they realized the scroll was no longer there. Lisa pointed. "I think I see it. It's in his right hand!" But by the time they pushed through the children, it was in neither hand.

Veronica rushed around to the back side, and there it was, just like in her dream, under the raised ball of the statue's right foot. She pulled off her right glove and exclaimed to Lisa, "Got it!" A young boy came up behind her and tried to grab it out of her raised hand. "Oh no you don't." Veronica's stern warning surprised the child enough that he backed away.

"Let's get back to Jake and Tyler before we open it," whispered Lisa.

When they joined the guys, Veronica carefully unrolled the small scroll made out of a beautiful paper with long, tightly woven reeds of grass still visible. The text appeared to be written using a broad-tipped calligraphy pen. Veronica looked at the words and a frown shaped her mouth.

"What?" Lisa asked, rubbing her arms in the cold winter air. "What does it say?"

Veronica passed it to her.

"'At the actual place,'" Lisa read aloud several times before asking, "What actual place?"

Lisa passed it to Jake's extended hand. "There is undoubtedly more, and hopefully the scroll wasn't accidentally torn, as it appears that another word preceded this, by the ink at the tear. Let's get going, and perhaps we will know more after my meeting in St. Peter's Square."

After carefully rolling the scroll, Jake handed it to Veronica, who passed it to Lisa, saying, "You are better at keeping things safe."

The children had moved on, and Lisa walked back to the angel, examining his hands and feet to make sure there was nothing more to find, and whispered, "Thank you. I bet you have known since your construction almost a thousand years ago that one day you would be a part of something far bigger than any of us could imagine."

And for one brief moment, Lisa saw the wise and compassionate eyes wink, and a cluster of wavy hairs blew in the winter wind before once again being suspended in time.

"Did you see that? Did something just happen?" Veronica turned to Jake, wondering if she was seeing things. "Perhaps" was all Jake said before reaching out for the approaching Lisa, tucking her under his arm and guiding her back to the waiting cab.

The flight to Rome was uneventful, and there was barely time to have a cold drink before landing. Flagging a taxi, Lisa told the driver, "Hotel Columbus," and read off the address on Via della Conciliazione.

Jake had booked everyone into an elegant hotel, but Lisa had asked if she could book one that was more moderate because she loved all the frescos, saying, "It feels old Italian, except for the name." They were both equally close to St. Peter's, so Jake figured if the beds weren't as comfortable, so be it. He loved how happy simple things made Lisa.

After checking in, Jake informed Veronica and Tyler that he would be going up and taking a quick shower before heading to the fountain in St. Peter's Square. With his arm around Lisa, he asked if she wanted to eat something in the hotel restaurant or to have something sent up.

"Veronica and Tyler, what are your plans? I am hungry. None of us ate much at breakfast to the disappointment of your grandma's. Too excited for food. Did you guys want to get something?" Lisa inquired.

"We passed a few inviting restaurants on the way. Should we try one?" Tyler asked.

"Let Veronica pick. She knows all the best ones!" Lisa smiled, adding, "Veronica, are you OK?"

"Oh, yeah, still stuck on why we were led to the scroll when the information was useless," Veronica responded.

"We have to assume we will know when it is necessary," Jake offered.

"You're right. At least I hope so," Veronica replied.

Tyler put his arms around her and said, "Don't worry, Jake is right. Everything is as it should be."

Lisa looked at Jake and said, "Would you make sure our luggage gets to the room? I have my room key, so I will meet you back there after we eat, or you can call me if it's sooner and you can join us."

Jake gave Lisa a big hug and said, "Take this jacket, and bundle up. It's cold outside." Turning to Tyler and Veronica, he nodded and said, "Have fun. See you guys soon."

"Wait, stop," Lisa said as Jake was heading to their room, "I'm too nervous to eat. I know it may sound silly, but I would rather stay here and wait for you." She turned to Tyler and Veronica to apologize, but Tyler put up his hand up and said, "Same here, we feel the same. Lisa, do you want to hang out in our room and order something light to eat and get some tea sent up?"

"Yes, thanks." With that, she kissed Jake and got one last hug before heading to Veronica and Tyler's room.

CHAPTER 65

Andrew and Jazz awoke to sunlight streaming in through the open drapes and birds in song. Jazz grabbed the sheet and tucked it around her in a panic. *What have I done?* was the first thought that came to her mind, and she unintentionally spoke them in a whisper. Without opening his eyes, Andrew reached up and took her arm, pulled it towards him, and kissed it. Instead of bolting out of bed as she intended, she asked, "What exactly happened last night?"

"Nothing you would regret," Andrew said with a smile, opening his eyes to look up at Jazz. "Wow, your eyes are stunning with the light hitting them. They look emerald."

"Don't change the subject," Jazz insisted. "I remember we decided to walk through the park, and then we ended up at the pub for one quick nightcap."

"Yep, sure did. And we danced until we couldn't drink or stand anymore," Andrew smiled. "It was a great night."

"We did, didn't we? Dance and drink, I mean," Jazz said, putting her hands over her face.

"Not to worry, I was a gentleman, as I promised you I would be. Quite unusual for me, I must say. I did not allow you to take off your panties or bra when I discovered that you sleep in the raw." Andrew's smile turned into a broad grin. "Although, I wouldn't mind at some point exploring the possibilities of 'divine lovemaking and its true glory' that you mentioned at dinner last night!"

"I never sleep with a work associate. I don't know what got into me!" Jazz confessed.

"Not me, unfortunately, but it would have been nice." Andrew pushed his limits.

Jazz grabbed the pillow and hit him. "I'm serious, that was extremely unprofessional."

"How many lifetimes did you say you have known me?" Andrew inquired in all seriousness.

"We agreed to take it slowly and discover what we weren't able to when I was a priest and you were a saint. If you do not remember last night and choose not to pursue the possibilities, I will be disappointed, but I will survive. Please tell me you meant what you said even if you don't remember."

"How can I mean something I don't remember?" Jazz wanted to know.

"You said that the first time you set eyes on me, even though I was horrible to you and had you thrown out, you knew some part of you loved me," Andrew recounted.

"I told you that?" Jazz stammered.

"Yes, you did! Honest," Andrew swore.

Jazz groaned. "It is true, some part of me did know I knew you. Did I really tell you that some part of me loved you?" Jazz was dying from embarrassment.

"Yep. Come here, and wrap those graceful Irish arms around me and hug me like you did last night," Andrew pleaded as he reached for her.

Reluctantly, Jazz dropped the sheet and allowed him to gather her in his arms, not because she didn't want to but because she questioned the repercussions if things went awry. Admitting that her entire life had been a series of well-planned and controlled decisions, she decided it was time to allow something different and new to rock her world.

"I have never felt so happy holding a woman in my arms," Andrew confided as he kissed the top of her head and ran his fingers through her red hair. "And then again, I have never enjoyed a woman as much as I enjoy you."

"I admit, I feel the same. You have surprised me, and I am not easy to surprise," Jazz confessed as she wrapped her arm around his toned body and ran her index finger gently across his abdomen. She felt his body quiver and pulled her hand away.

"Careful, I promised to be a gentleman, but I am not a saint." Andrew laughed.

"Sorry, you have such an inviting body, I got carried away. Should we get back to your office? It's already 9:00."

"We didn't go to bed until after 3:00 a.m. The office can wait. Meg will cover for us. Anyway, I rarely have a woman overnight. I simply want to enjoy you," Andrew divulged.

With that remark, Jazz sat up and looked him in the eyes. "I find that hard to believe. I understood you to be quite the playboy."

"Don't believe everything you hear," Andrew warned, "but the truth is, I may date a lot of women, but you won't find them in my bed in the morning. Most are pretty, or fun, and fill a void, but not much more. It is unusual to find a woman who is all the things you are. You are stunning, free thinking, fiery like your hair, open minded, intellectual, funny, challenging, and hardworking. You pursue what you believe in, are a great pool player, hold your alcohol, and are a great kisser, to name a few.

"So I thank you for marching into my office and then being willing to come back after I had you escorted out. And mostly, I thank you for taking me up on my offer of dinner and inviting me to your suite. Now let's order breakfast, and while we wait, let me feel this gorgeous woman in my arms."

Without speaking, Jazz lowered herself back onto his chest and pulled his arm around her. Breakfast could wait.

After several minutes, Jazz spoke. "You know I am going to ask Meg if you give that speech to all the women you ask out."

"I can't wait to see her face. She will turn twenty shades of red!" Andrew laughed, as he rolled her over and kissed her lips. "Great lips!"

CHAPTER 66

At the same moment that Angelina was packing her bags a thousand miles away, Jake stood before the steps of the Vatican, near the fountain in St. Peter's Square. There was a young man he was supposed to meet. He was glad it wasn't raining, and the sky was mostly blue with a few fluffy clouds.

He heard the fountain splashing from its three tiers but hardly noticed the birds singing and flapping in the water as they bathed, nor the beauty that surrounded him.

Lisa, Veronica, and Tyler waited anxiously back at the hotel as agreed. To the casual observer, Jake appeared calm, but internally he was anxious with anticipation.

The man in his vision was of Far Eastern descent. He knew the young man would find him waiting in this very spot. Of this he was confident. So far, nothing that had taken place was coincidental. In his dream, he had called him Akbar, an East Indian name that meant "powerful."

He did not understand their connection, but Jake knew it would become clear as they traveled together. The dream had also shown him that Akbar would hold a piece of the puzzle to unravel the last of the clues that would lead them to the final meeting place.

CHAPTER 67

José showed Luke the map he had drawn from his vision the night before he met Luke in the Basilica. The only information José had was that they would recognize this man of Middle Eastern descent when they saw him at the airport and that he would take them to the designated meeting place.

José had relinquished all doubts about what his dreams were showing or telling him, having experienced continual examples of events based on trust and divine timing.

By the time José and Luke arrived at the Tel Aviv airport, they had covered the events that led them to find each other, and pondered the possibilities of what lay ahead. Both believed that Bethlehem would be the final destination, although no discussion could prepare either of them for this Middle Eastern man.

The airport was busy, but the energy was magnetic the moment they collected their luggage and headed to the doors that led them to transportation. It was there they found the displaced Iraqi man with half his face concealed. José was confident that he was the man he saw in his vision days before.

He appeared uncomfortable as he stood next to a post, trying to mask his underlying fear. The coarse black cloak also covered the top of his slightly lowered head, with one dark eye visible, peering straight ahead. His face was a testimony to the fact that he had not shaven in several days.

José walked towards him and reached his hand out in greeting, but the man pulled back, startled, and appeared about to bolt.

"Sir, please, Our Lady of Guadalupe sent me to you," José whispered convincingly. "My name is José, and this is my friend Luke. You were waiting for us, is that not correct?"

Makeen's face relaxed, and he reached his hand out towards José and then to Luke. "I'm Makeen. Apologies for the introduction. I have had a difficult journey."

"Understandable. I have followed the events recently and realize there is still a lot of unrest. I can't even imagine what you have gone through for the last decade," Luke offered sympathetically. It was evident to Luke that Makeen was from Iraq.

"It is true. I was fortunate enough to be taken into a monastery in the desert years ago. It was truly a miracle that led me there after the death of my family members."

José shook his head. "What crimes we humans cast upon each other. It is truly heartbreaking."

Makeen closed his eyes for a few moments and then began to speak. "Yes, it is. I lost my father and brother, killed by others, but it was I who was responsible for the death of my mother and sister. If God did not interfere, I would not be aboveground myself."

Luke and José were taken by surprise by this confession and said nothing. After an awkward silence, Luke put his hand on Makeen's shoulder and said, "Let's go. If you wish to say more, we will listen, but we have no judgments of those God sent us to."

They were able to hire a private driver with an off-road vehicle, who would take them to the monastery twenty kilometers into the desert, where Makeen had been a monk since the death of his mother and sister. When the journey became void of structures, Makeen began to speak of his stop in Bethlehem, along the Wall of Separation filled with graffiti created by artists from all over the world.

"It is apparent how the wall affects the lives of the locals and those who have been cut off from their own land that had been passed down for generations. I could feel the anger, frustration, hopelessness, and shame of those who could no longer appropriately house or feed their families.

"Israel continues to build without consideration for the lands of others, and this is only creating more resentment, violence, and unrest. When you take away a man's dignity, you will never have peace nor protection.

"I was fortunate to meet an Israeli man who speaks up regularly on behalf of the Palestinians. He is a part of a movement of Israeli activists against the wall, but it goes on deaf ears. Even according to the International Court of Justice, it is in clear violation of international law. The wall is better known as 'The Wall of Shame.'"

"Regrettably," Luke confessed, "America is a censored country with only a few powerful families owning the majority of the media. Although most Americans don't believe this, it is true.

"We don't get the information about the rest of the world that I get from other countries I visit, especially if it doesn't align with the wishes of the one percent, the powers that own these media sources. I did find a source on the internet that said, despite condemnation from the UN and the EU, the wall continues to expand."

There was silence for some time before Makeen began to speak about the events that had transpired since Hussein had killed his father over twenty years before. He spoke with great sadness and ended with, "Through years of prayer, I have been able to forgive others, but I have never succeeded at forgiving myself."

"Thank you for sharing your tragic story with us, Makeen. I can't even begin to imagine your pain and sorrow from such events. And I am sure it was not easy to tell," Luke compassionately responded. It was a story that brought tears to José's and Luke's eyes.

"Honestly, this is the first time I have shared it with anyone. It has been a crushing burden to carry, I confess. A great weight has been removed," Makeen acknowledged.

Luke and José silently nodded in understanding.

Twenty kilometers east of Bethlehem did not seem like a long distance, but this remote location through the desert proved differently. The land was bleak and barren in parts but spectacular through the Judean wilderness as well as having vistas of unbelievable beauty. At times, they passed tents and animals. It was a place inhabited by nomads and Bedouin tribes.

Luke wondered how a monastery could survive in such a remote place. Makeen informed him that once, more than three hundred monks had lived there, but now fewer than twenty remained. They did have their own business center as well as donations from male tourists who were allowed in restricted areas.

Finally, they drove down a steep road, and Luke spotted the monastery which resembled a small village surrounded by a wall. Visible was a complex composed of various metal-domed churches and other buildings, all in the stone colors of the desert. A short distance outside of the monastery was a tower.

"What is that tower?" Luke inquired.

"It is called the Women's Tower. Women are not allowed in the complex and haven't been for over 1,500 years. It's for women visitors. They may only look over the complex from that vantage point but cannot enter the monastery. Even St. Sabas's mother, who financed the monastery, was forbidden to enter."

"Wow, that would not go over well with most modern-day women!" Luke exclaimed.

"Can you tell us who we are meeting?" José asked, changing the subject and speaking for the first time since the airport.

"I don't know. I was informed that when we returned, an honored guest would meet us at supper. Very hush, and as a rule, we do not question. We mind our own business, so there has been no discussion nor inquiry."

"I'm not sure whether this makes me feel comforted or question my sanity for making a long trip with no clue to what is about to transpire," Luke confessed.

"For all of us, it certainly has been a journey of trust without knowing," Makeen calmly offered. For him, nothing could be more horrific than what he had already experienced during his life, so whatever was being asked of him now was accepted without resistance.

José's heart began to race, he assumed that he would never enter a monastery again, and he wasn't sure whether it was from the excitement, as Luke mentioned, or dread. His life had been an even-paced ritual, and he knew from one day to the next exactly what to expect and what was required of him. That was where José was comfortable, but now life had been moving much too swiftly for him, and he realized it wasn't excitement but fear that consumed him. He could feel its grip as his face flushed with heat and his throat contracted.

José shook it off and quickly concealed his emotions by pointing out the stone wall that surrounded the monastery, to change the subject.

"I had no idea it would be this large," José spoke in the most casual voice he could muster.

"We are approaching our destination," Makeen informed them just as the sky was turning to shades of dark yellow and gold as the sun started setting in the west. They wound through a narrow road that split into three directions. All were silent as they approached the ancient monastery, for here, time stood still. It was a profound moment; soon, each man knew, the events that would be transpiring would forever radically change their lives.

As they approached the mysterious little door, the driver informed them, "Your destination, gentlemen."

Within minutes, the fortified door opened for them to enter and the driver assisted them with their belongings but went no farther, as he did not have permission to enter. The three men thanked him and tipped him generously.

Makeen had learned to cherish this place he had called home since his escape from life in Iraq. There was a silence that permeated the grounds, and therefore no one spoke as they walked through a courtyard, following closely behind Makeen and another monk who had greeted them at the entry. It was not just a monastery but a mini-city with its own laws, business center, industrial area, and two copper- or, perhaps, lead-domed churches. Makeen had explained that these areas were off limits to tourists, and only the monks and invited guests were allowed.

"It's beautiful," Luke said in a soft voice as they walked through the courtyard and marveled at the endless steps and mazes. He was astonished by the size as well as the beauty of the compound.

A captivating city built 1,500 years ago lay before him, waiting to be explored. He had heard rumors that this was where a Secret Gospel of St. Mark—a book that tells the secret love story of Jesus and the woman Mary Magdalene that the church wished to remain untold—was found.

Their welcoming monk bowed his head and silently parted as a monk in black robes, sporting a full dark beard and black hat worn by Greek Orthodox monks, appeared beneath an arched stone passageway.

All Luke could think of were the words of Mark Twain when he had come to visit the monastery in 1867: "They wear a coarse robe, an ugly, brimless stove-pipe of a hat"—an accurate description, Luke acknowledged, and told his mind to be silent. Instead, again came the words of Twain: "They eat nothing whatever but bread and salt; they drink nothing but water." *Oh dear,* Luke thought, *I hope not! Now, silence my mind!*

Makeen greeted the monk and introduced José and Luke, telling them he would be directing them to their rooms to freshen up before meeting for supper.

Luke awkwardly asked, "How will we know where to meet?"

"I will collect you in an hour," informed the monk.

"Thank you" was all Luke could manage. It was all too cryptic for him. Stars, solar systems, black holes, and such were simple, but this secrecy was too baffling.

He tried to meditate to calm his nerves, but his mind would not allow him that peace. Finally, he gave up and washed and changed into fresh clothes. Forty-five minutes later, Luke heard church bells ringing, followed by a knock at his door. The monk was early.

He was relieved to see his escort and José waiting in the hallway, because frankly, the suspense was genuinely taking its toll on his nerves. Both he and José remained silent as they followed their guide through a corridor and several large rooms before the guide nodded his head and disappeared.

CHAPTER 68

Just beyond the fountain in St. Peter's Square stood a man casually but classically dressed in tan slacks and a white button-down linen shirt in the exact spot that Akbar had seen him in a dream only nights before, when he and Aaron were staying in Amritapuri at Amma's ashram. It was apparent that the man was waiting for someone, and Akbar knew he was that someone. Aaron stayed back at the café as they had agreed until Akbar spoke with the American.

Akbar quickened his pace to the beat of his racing heart. He had waited for this moment his whole life, not just the four months since the beginning of the dreams. He had been born to take part in the pivotal work that would soon be coming into manifestation, a mission that would shift the consciousness of the planet into a new age.

This time in history was not just about the age of balance between male and female, nor the age of transparent, authentic communication of what had been held secret by churches and governments for thousands of years to control the masses.

Humanity was about to enter into the final phase of earth's creation and destruction, the age of purification and peace for those headed to a new world. A time when Satan—in other words, greed, fear, power, and control—was about to reveal its shadow self in every human to be healed fully. Now was humanity's opportunity to have the peace, joy, and unity their souls desired, if they were willing to plunge in and could pass the tests of initiation.

God had and always would lovingly assist humanity. But because of "free will," God could not interfere. Akbar knew well that a person does not listen when one has not asked for advice, so he often stayed silent, although he was very distressed knowing how many humans would not enter the frequency of the new world.

It would be easier for them to take the lazy path and succumb to the dark forces. Akbar had awakened in tears several nights since the visions began. The destruction of humanity upon the earth drove him to plead with the Creator for a different outcome, but it appeared to be too late.

Regaining control of his emotions, Akbar began to run towards the man his vision had referred to as Jake.

As he ran, Akbar thought back to the dream two nights prior, which because of its clarity, he could replay in his mind without effort. That is when he first became aware that John the Beloved was now known as Jake.

Yeshua was walking along the deep valley of the Jordan River, and just beyond the twists and turns, Akbar could see the hills of Galilee. Seven of Yeshua's disciples had joined him, and he felt honored to be included in the group, having traveled far. John had been the son of an influential fisherman named Zebedee. He had been mending nets in Capernaum with his father and brother James when Yeshua came to seek them out.

Although the surrounding hills were bare when Yeshua arrived, oleander flourished around the shore. At first, they did not recognize the man in the white robes. He had lived and studied with the Essenes before heading from Merom, Hazor, Kedesh, past Mt. Hermon to Damascus, Babylon, where Yeshua spent time mingling and studying with learned men.

He also studied with the Chaldean astrologers, who fascinated him considerably, before he headed to the Far East and India. Each held Yeshua enraptured. During this trip to India was when Akbar had first met Yeshua when he was twenty-seven. The same age he was now, but two thousand years earlier.

Yeshua stayed in Capernaum for several days, and it was not long before John and James knew they were to be associated with Yeshua and bid their families farewell. Since that day, John had never left Jesus's side and hung on every word of his cousin's discourse. On this day, as they walked along the muddy shores of the Jordan River, it moved slower than its normal rapid pace. Akbar was aware of John's concern over their Master's energy; it had been a long day of teaching and healing for those who had sought him out.

Yeshua had spoken passionately about the importance of one's connection to nature for healing. For the angels of the sun, air, water, life, health, and joy were all there to serve all humankind. But many would not listen to the teachings and only came for the miracles, returning soon after to their destructive ways.

They were the ones who claimed Yeshua to be a false prophet, for soon their illness would reverse, as the behavior that created the disease was unaltered. They were like young children who did not understand that their unwillingness to change their lifestyle was the cause of their unhealthy situation.

There was always some loss of energy after these healings, and Yeshua headed for the hills for rest and solitude, where he regained his strength through communion with the angels who restored his body and soul. His disciples stayed nearby in conversation and prayer but did not approach the Master; they knew when Yeshua was ready, he would come to them.

In the early morning, Yeshua again returned and continued to teach them the secret teachings; these were not given to the multitudes, for they were not ready. Although it was Mary Magdalene who was the most learned and beloved of Yeshua, neither Akbar nor John felt any jealousy, for they recognized her position, wisdom, authority, and purity.

When Yeshua concluded, Akbar looked at each of the disciples, knowing they were the privileged few, and although Akbar only traveled from

India infrequently to meet with the group, he and John had become like brothers.

When the remembrance of the dream had come to an end, he found himself in front of Jake. "Jake, I presume?" Akbar said, extending his hand.

Jake froze, looking a bit shaken. Akbar promptly saw the spark of recognition in Jake's eyes before Jake reached out his arms, ignoring Akbar's outstretched hand, and hugged him, exclaiming, "Yes, it is I, my brother!"

CHAPTER 69

Thankfully, Britt was correct: Bruno dropped them a block from St. Peter's Square in record time. They had been lost in their breakfast conversation when Ruth finally heard Bruno's third call to notify them of his arrival.

"Oh heavens, I can't believe the time!" Ruth rushed to her room, picked up her cell phone and said, "Bruno, I am so sorry, I didn't hear the phone. We lost track of time! We will be down in a few minutes." It was a marathon to throw clothes on and remember the scroll.

Bruno was patiently leaning against his cab and talking to another driver when they finally made it down the six flights of steps. He quickly opened the back door and ushered them in.

After twenty minutes of speed driving while weaving around cars, streets, signs, and motorbikes, Ruth whispered to Britt, "I sure hope we make it alive!"

"No worries," Britt assured her, "he's got this."

Ruth decided it was better for her to close her eyes and meditate than to watch the road. Close to an hour and a half later, she was elated to put her foot down on the solid pavement when arriving in Rome. They thanked Bruno for getting them there so quickly, as well as for his repeated calls.

The church bells chimed the quarter hour. "Run," Ruth said to Britt, "it's already 12:15."

As the women ran down the street towards the fountain in the square, Ruth heard a familiar voice: "Mom? Mom!"

Ruth looked back and saw her son sitting at an outdoor table at Pizza Zizza, holding a large piece of half-eaten pizza.

"Aaron! What are you doing here?" Ruth halted and exclaimed in dismay.

"I was going to ask you that question. I was thinking about you and how much you would have loved to be here. I'm sorry I haven't taken the time to get ahold of you, but life has been a bit fast paced," Aaron apologized. "So, why are you here, and with Britt?"

Britt waved to Aaron and smiled. "Small world!"

"We are here to meet a young Indian man with a saffron shirt near the fountain in St. Peter's Square. I'll explain later, but we are late!" Ruth said as she started to run and motioned for Aaron to follow them.

"Do you mean my friend Akbar?" Aaron asked in amusement.

"Your friend?" Ruth questioned as she came to a halt.

"Yes, he's meeting an American man named Jake. He's there right now." With that, Aaron put down the remainder of the pizza, left some euros, and said, "Follow me, I was waiting for him to come back, but they have had enough time to talk. I'll ask later how the two of you met!"

CHAPTER 70

Before them, a tall man of slender stature, wearing everyday work clothes, with penetrating gray-blue eyes, stood calmly observing them as they approached the entry to the dining hall. Luke's heart began racing. His footsteps ceased, and he turned to José for confirmation of whether his eyes were fooling him or not. Seeing the blood drained from Jose's face, he knew it had to be true. José fell to his knees, not aware of the impact of the hard stone floor beneath him.

"But how can this be?" Luke stammered. "Do our eyes and hearts deceive us, Master?"

There was silence. Finally, the man spoke. "Undoubtedly you know me. I would know you in any form, anywhere."

With that, tears sprang to Luke's eyes and he kneeled before his Master, beside José.

"Rise up. You are my brothers. There is no need to act otherwise," Yeshua said as he held out his hand.

The two men rose, and all three embraced like those who love each other dearly do after a long separation. For several minutes, the only sound was José quietly weeping.

"Yeshua, Yeshua," Luke repeated, pinching his arm, not believing he was awake but desperately hoping he was.

"How? Why now?" José asked, wiping his face with his shirttail.

Suddenly there was a gasp from twenty paces away. Makeen had just approached the dining hall and had been speechless from the shock of what he was witnessing. Gathering his voice, he repeated, "Yes, why now? How?"

"Come, brother," Yeshua said, reaching out his arms. "'How?' is not the question. 'Why now?' is."

As Makeen rushed into Yeshua's arms, José and Luke stepped back to regain their composure. Seeing Makeen in Yeshua's arms, José's emotions again overwhelmed him and his weeping became sobs. He quickly covered his face with his hands. It was several minutes before Makeen would ease his powerful embrace and raise his face to look at Yeshua. "My heart is shattering. I cannot imagine you can forgive me for the many lifetimes I have forgotten who I was or the horrible deeds I have done."

"It is not I who needs to forgive you. I have no judgment, nor does God." Yeshua lovingly assured him as he took Makeen's face in his hands, looked into his dark eyes weighted with grief, and spoke: "It is you who must forgive yourself to live the life you seek."

Makeen's hard exterior melted. Luke noted how soft his face appeared, as if the hard edge and weight of the world instantly vanished. "This is the definition of grace," Luke whispered to José.

"Come now, let's sit and nourish ourselves, and we will talk after." Yeshua swept his arm towards a wooden table filled with food. Suddenly they were all aware of how hungry they were. None had eaten since morning. Anxiety and questions had filled their stomachs but not nourishment.

José was still stunned, Luke was waiting to wake up from what had to be a dream, and Makeen looked radiant with hope.

They sat in silence as they ate, each processing their thoughts. Luke's prayer silently thanked God for more than bread, salt, and water.

When the meal was complete, Yeshua began to speak. "Now for the 'Why?' What I will share with you is of the utmost importance. Clarification is needed. The record needs to be set straight.

"This world is on the cusp of collapse. Many of my teachings were distorted or fictitious, the worst being the denial of my beloved wife and the mother of my children, by Peter's deliberate censoring of the gospels that were, unfortunately, adopted by the Christian religions because of their obsession for me to be above human desire and the only son of God. This is not only far from the truth—it is an outright falsehood.

"I could not have been fully human nor have been complete as a man had I not been wed. Of course, I was not the only son of God. Everyone is a son or daughter of the Creator. Nor was my dear mother a virgin after she left the temple. She had been a temple priestess and called a virgin, as they all were, until the age of fourteen, when the threat of her menses starting arose. It was then that she was betrothed to my father."

José stammered, "Lord, what are you saying? How could you have been married?" He could not comprehend his misgivings.

"Why are people surprised? Marriage and children were expected of a Jewish man. Mary the Magdalene was my wife and bore me two sons and a daughter. She was a Galilean Phoenician priestess who abandoned her life of wealth after meeting and falling in love with me. She was my wife and a partner in redemption. She stood beside me, embroiled in the politics of the time. We had thirteen profoundly beautiful years together before my crucifixion. She was my rock."

"How was this kept from us?" José was still shocked.

Yeshua answered, "Paul worked the gospels to suit his beliefs born from his roots. He was against anything to do with my family life and attempted to hide and exclude those teachings and texts. He was hostile against Mary the Magdalene as well and my brother James, who took over the leadership after the crucifixion. The authentic gospels were hidden, so as not to be burned and to protect the lives of those who held them for safekeeping.

"Most were encoded with hidden meaning, even the Old Testament. They had to be protected and could only be decoded by those who understood the original language and definitions of the codes. Many have been found that survived the burnings but remain hidden by those who do not want their empires threatened."

Yeshua could see how distressed José was. "Brother, you could not have known, with the life you chose to live. Even the passages that were correctly stated were translated from one language to another, leaving considerable room for error—let alone the meanings inserted or removed by priests and scholars who knew the truth but were forbidden to reveal it to protect those in power.

"Greed is one of the seven deadly sins, and the one humanity struggles with the most profoundly. It is the male energy that has not transcended to higher realms of intuition, inclusiveness, divine wisdom, and inner knowing."

Makeen was about to speak but sat back when he realized he had nothing of value to say—only that his whole world was plummeting and something within him was relieved as though he had waited for this day his entire life.

Yeshua continued, "You must understand this is the reason I have called the three of you together before we meet the others." Yeshua put up his hand to stop the questions he could see arising on their faces. "Each of you chose a life without marriage, based on inaccuracies. The balance of the masculine and feminine within is what creates the divine or fully divine human, and these lessons are easiest to master with a partner who expresses and embodies their partners unawakened aspects of self.

"It was Mary the Magdalene who gave me many essential gifts so that I might fulfill my mission of becoming fully human and divine. She taught me to love unconditionally with no judgment. She understood the wisdom of being in silence to hear and seek union with the divine.

"She embodied what she heard and therefore could understand beyond human knowing, and that is why many of my teachings were given to her and not shared with you. Her wisdom came from her focus on the inner worlds of initiation and direct knowing. She carried sensitivity and the energy of the feeling world, finding divinity in the senses. Hers was the path of the sacred marriage accomplished within, through inner reflection and transformation."

Luke timidly raised his hand from the table to seek understanding.

"Yes, Luke?" Yeshua allowed the question.

"Are you saying we need a woman to become fully human? Or is it the sacred marriage within that needs to be accomplished?"

"What I am saying is that having an intimate relationship with a woman can shorten your time needed to fully awaken and bring you the many gifts that reside dormant within you if you do not resist them. But you must embrace and learn from the sensitivities and intuition of a woman instead of only the force and logic of a man. This doesn't mean that a woman or man will or can save you. It means they can share their unique perspective to awaken yours within."

"Thank you, I now understand." Luke nodded.

Yeshua continued, "I gave her my gift as a healer, although she was also a priestess and healer herself and trained with sacred oils and herbs. I was able to easily clear her seven chakras, or energy centers, as she had already done much inner work. These centers are creation itself but also represent the seven deadly sins or seven demons, if not filled with light. They are mankind's addictions—sloth, anger, judgment, greed, lust, pride, and envy.

"My beloved Mary was cleansed of all human traits that are viewed as sins, and only because she was already consciously purifying herself. She was free of all transgressions, and it was evident that the seven virtues or angels of light resided within her. She was one of the rare ones who have achieved this."

This time, it was José who questioned, "Then why, after the resurrection, did you say, 'Stay away from me, you soiled woman'?"

"I never did. Most ears cannot hear, and therefore my words were more harmful than good. That would have meant I was not a healer. For how could she have sins or be soiled if I had purified her?"

All three men opened their mouths in realization. José spoke again. "Please, tell us, what did you say?"

"I said, 'Do not cling to me because I have not fully ascended to the Father.' She was the one person who could have kept me on the earth plane. I loved her that dearly. I was between worlds, attached to the earth, and still had time to choose to come back or not. You now call this a near-death experience. It was her strength and love for me that caused her to pull her hand away so I could move into the other world. But unbeknownst to her at the time, there was more to that story. That is for another time.

"It tore apart her heart, but she knew she must carry on my teaching and raise our sons and daughter. I informed her to go to my brethren and tell them I ascended to my Father, and your Father, my God, and your God, for each of us are sons and daughters of the one Creator.

"She did as I requested and was rejected, for they did not have the ears to hear. She wept but did not get angry when Peter and the others accused her of lying when she spoke my words after the resurrection. Mary did not judge those of you there, nor speak harshly. She wept at your inability to know that from her words came truth—the teaching I had delivered to her to share with you."

There was silence for reflection before Yeshua began again. "She could read the Tora, integrate her wisdom with the logic of the masculine, and understand the power she held within, so as not to need to rely on a man. She became fully integrated, but the church painted my beloved as a whore so as to not acknowledge the power and importance of the divine feminine."

"Yeshua, the church must be corrected. Her statues still have the inscription beneath her feet. She must not continue to be shamed and deemed as unworthy," José stated passionately.

"Jose, did they not share with you as monks that the Catholic Church in 1969 finally acknowledged that Mary Magdalene was not a prostitute?"

"No. This information was not brought to our attention, nor did our church correct the inscription on Mary's statue in our sanctuary, beneath her feet." José was mortified that he had lived a life shrouded by the well-kept secrets of the Church.

"You would have known this if the church did not bury the information. Instead of removing all passages expressing this grievous mistruth, they left them, as it is not convenient for them to reveal the truth. They contained the information and made it obscure, so as not to have to admit their errors and challenge the teachings that they claimed were infallible. They are not," Yeshua exclaimed.

Makeen spoke quietly. "They spoke of oils Mary anointed you with, in the tomb. I always questioned how a woman who was not one's wife could do this. So it was true. She could because she was your wife?"

Again, José was startled. Why hadn't he ever realized this? It was still true to this day.

"Yes, after the crucifixion, as the gospels agree, it was Mary the Magdalene who went early Sunday morning to wash and anoint my crucified body as the gospel of Mark did state. Not just anyone could anoint another. No woman would wash the blood and sweat off a man unless she were his wife. Mary the Magdalene was my wife, and she did go to the tomb and prepare my body for burial."

"It still mystifies me why Pontius Pilate would consent to crucify you." Luke's sigh was weighted with sadness.

"It is a miracle that I was not killed long before, as I had many enemies who wanted me dead. My messages were not just religious but radical, political, and threatening to authority. I was carefully watched. Although it was Paul's altered accounts from which the greatest damage arose because they are where Christian churches have their roots."

Luke said, "Now I see my error. Instead of shunning all religion, because I knew within that they spoke falsely, and turning to the stars, I should have searched for the ancient texts and those having the wisdom to properly transcribe those scrolls that proved what in my heart I knew."

"We must not grieve for what cannot be changed. We shall move forward," Yeshua assured him.

Tears covered the faces of the men before him. They could see their error of not questioning the teachings long ago. All three knew deep within that Mary the Magdalene was wrongly accused, and none had spoken out on her behalf. José was ashamed that he had allowed others to overshadow what he knew in his heart as truth.

Suddenly a scene unfolded before him. He saw his life in Assisi, Italy, 1,200 years ago, with his beloved Clare and how he had pushed her away and chose to live separate lives with the other monks. His heart ached for that loss of her kindness, compassion, and wisdom.

Knowing the cause of José's grief, Yeshua looked at him and said, "Yes, you were St. Francis, and Clare was your beloved as Mary the Magdalene was mine. It is not time to grieve. It is time to rejoice for what can be achieved before it is too late."

José sighed. "You are right, I have wasted enough time in despair over right or wrong."

"I have done the same," Makeen confessed. "It is time to move forward."

"Speaking of time," Yeshua said, "it's been a long day. Shall we go to the chapel, meditate together, and then retire? There is plenty of time for discussion tomorrow."

"That would be an honor," Luke expressed sincerely.

The others nodded their heads in acknowledgment.

After meditation, the men parted ways to return to their rooms. Luke's and Jose's rooms were close to each other, so they silently walked together. After a few moments, Luke said to José in wonder, "Nothing could have prepared me for the events of the last twenty-four hours. Nothing."

"Nor I," José confirmed.

CHAPTER 71

Leaning against a massive Roman column in St. Peter's Square, Ben wondered, as the morning turned to afternoon, how they would find the Indian man they had both seen in their dreams the night he was with Tony in Mexico. All they knew was that he would be somewhere close to the three-tiered fountain and would have on a saffron shirt. The clock began to chime. 12:15.

"There are a lot more people here than I expected for a winter day. Do you think we should walk around and see if we recognize anyone?" Ben asked Tony.

"December is Christmastime, so I think the crowds have more to do with that than the weather. Let's head back to the fountain and see if anyone resembling this man has arrived," Tony offered.

The group of a dozen tourists standing in front of the fountain as they listened to their guide parted and moved towards St. Peter's Basilica. Suddenly Ben yelled, "That can't be, can it?"

"What?" Tony asked before looking where Ben was pointing. "Is that Professor Reynolds? Impossible! But he certainly resembles him."

Ben began to run. "Come on!"

As they got closer to the fountain, they realized it *was* Jake. Tony paused and held his arm out to stop Ben. "Wait, he is with someone."

"Yeah, he's with the guy I saw in my dream!" Ben exclaimed.

They both began to walk swiftly towards the two men and were only steps away when Jake looked up and shook his head in astonishment, saying, "Ben? Tony? What are you doing here?"

"Meeting you, apparently, as well as this gentleman," Tony said as he extended his hand towards Akbar. "You're the man I saw in my vision. You are who we came looking for. And we had no idea we would also find you, Professor Reynolds!"

Akbar stepped forward. "Yes, I know you also, Peter. My brother Peter, we meet again!" Akbar exclaimed, reaching out towards Tony.

Tony's face turned ashen, and then tears burst like a flooded dam giving way. Visions of his life with Yeshua, Judas, John the Beloved, and the rest of the disciples sprang into existence. Putting his face in his hands and crouching to the ground, he cried out, "My god, John the Beloved, and of course, Judas. Lisa was Junia! How I mistreated the women. Mary the Magdalene, all of them, how will I ever make amends?"

"My brother," Akbar reached down and put his hand on Tony's shoulder, "the Lord would not have called you if you were not worthy! You have repented for lifetimes and even came as a woman on several occasions to understand your error. Stand and embrace those who love you," Akbar commanded.

Ben noted that Professor Reynolds was still in shock and without words, so he inquired, "Tony, who was John the Beloved?" Jake thought he made up his comment to the Vatican thugs, and although he suspected it might be true, this was the first time all the pieces began to fall into place.

Wiping his face with the sleeves of his jacket, Tony looked directly at Jake. "Professor Reynolds, you were John the Beloved, and Tyler was—"

"Judas, Tyler was Judas!" Ben's mind cleared, and he saw the veils rapidly evaporating. "A true and powerful beloved of Yeshua for agreeing to such a difficult assignment."

"Absolutely! Tyler was Judas, and I saw his wife in a dream. She will join us also," Akbar affirmed.

"She is already here. Her name in this life is Veronica," Jake replied as he reached for Tony and embraced him, saying, "Call me Jake, my brother!"

Finally, Ben hesitantly spoke. "Was I not one of the disciples? Do any of you have a remembrance of me?"

All eyes were upon him. No one answered. After several moments, Tony said, "Ben, soon enough, all will be clear."

The silence broke when Aaron yelled out Akbar's name. Turning, they could see him approaching with two women following closely behind. It was then that Aaron felt a powerful blast of energy from the guy standing near Akbar. He momentarily halted and watched a scene of a life lived hundreds of years ago. There stood the man he had accompanied in Assisi, Italy, eight hundred years before, and Aaron began to run.

When he stood in front of Ben, Aaron threw out his arms and exclaimed, laughing, "It *is* you! Brother Ruffino, my beloved friend!"

Ben embraced Aaron. "Brother Leo, how can this be?"

Now it was Ben who could not contain his emotions. His life of hardship, devotion, and being with St. Francis and Brother Leo revealed itself. Brother Leo, who was one of St. Francis's most loyal disciples and secretary until his death, stood before him.

"Well, I guess that answers Ben's question," Tony whispered to Akbar.

At last, the two men turned towards the rest yet kept their arms around each other's shoulders. Aaron spoke first. "No wonder I was waylaid and ended up in Assisi instead of heading directly to India! I told Britt that I felt like I was home, and if I hadn't had an urgency to head to India, I would have stayed." Aaron turned. "This is my mother, Ruth, who I had no idea would be here until I saw her rushing by the café I was sitting at, and this is Br—" Aaron stopped, again hit by a realization. "Why didn't I see it before? Britt, as in St. Clare's younger sister?"

"Yes," Ben removed his arm from Aaron and stepped forward to put his hands, as in prayer, around the hands of St. Agnes of Assisi. "Sister, it is indeed you."

Britt, looking into Ben's eyes, heard and felt the accuracy of his words and knew them to be correct but was too astonished to speak.

Akbar stepped forth. "But, Aaron, I knew you only as the brother of Moses and the transcriber of the texts. How can this be that I did not realize until now that you have had many lives?"

Aaron laughed. "My brother, can you know everything?"

Akbar began to laugh also. "You are right!"

The laughter was a relief and broke the intensity of the situation.

The focus turned to Ruth. She began to speak as she studied Jake's eyes. "John the Beloved, do you not remember me?"

Realization hit. "Yes, yes! Ruth, younger sister of Yeshua," Jake said, shaking his head and exhaling as if he had been holding his breath. Stepping towards her, Jake put his arms around her, holding her close like a precious child.

She looked up at him and said, "You took me away at the request of my mother to leave the foot of the cross. I knew you did not want to leave my brother, but for the sake of my mother and me, you did. Thank you." Tears ran down Ruth's face. "Until recently, I did not understand my wounds of staying stuck in betrayal, as I thought my brother had betrayed me."

"This is beyond anything I could have ever dreamed up, so I know I am awake, but I need to take some time to wrap my head around all this. Would it be agreeable to gather where it is more private to continue our conversation?" Jake requested, intensely exhaling.

"Agreed! By the way, where are Lisa, Veronica, and Tyler?" Tony inquired.

"They are waiting at our hotel a short distance from here. If you all don't mind, let's get them before continuing," Jake requested.

"I don't think we need to." Ben pointed and began waving.

Lisa, Tyler, and Veronica decided it was too nerve-wracking to wait for Jake to come back. They left him a note with Veronica's Italian phone number, in case they missed him, saying they were heading to St. Peter's Square.

"Is that Ben waving?" a surprised Veronica asked.

Both Lisa and Tyler blurted out, "It is!"

"This is getting wilder each moment!" Tyler pointed out as the three began to run.

For the next twenty minutes, everyone talked at once, sharing stories primarily muted from onlookers by the splashing of the fountains. Lisa was overwhelmed by the remembrance of Tony as Peter and Ruth as Yeshua's young sister Ruth. She turned to Jake and, holding her hand to his heart, pronounced, "I knew in my gut that you were John the Beloved."

"And after two thousand years, you still leave me breathless," Jake said as he took Lisa's hand in his and kissed her lips.

It was Veronica who suggested they head back to their hotel, which happened to be where they all had mysteriously booked rooms. "Bizarre" was all Tyler could say.

Not wanting to be overheard, they headed to Lisa and Jake's suite. Jake stopped at the front desk and asked if water, teas, coffee, juice, and pastries could be sent up.

As they entered the suite, Ben stated, "Always knew there was something up with the two of you." He looked at Jake and Lisa with a nod and a smile.

"Yep," said Tony, "but it did become especially evident the last few months."

Lisa blushed. "That obvious?"

"Anyone who had eyes or sensitivity could see there was something between you two, and most likely before either of you acknowledged it!" Ben affirmed.

"Great" was all Jake said, and then he laughed. "I guess you can't fool a group of intuitive spiritualists!"

"No kidding," Veronica said as she winked at Lisa, "but then again, this romance began over two thousand years ago!"

"True, true," Ruth said. "Even back then, you two were traveling and living together in Nazareth and Bethlehem, and you two thought you were hiding your affection. Perhaps this lifetime, you should just openly embrace your love! I am glad you found each other *again*."

"Thank you," responded Lisa, looking up at Jake as they wrapped their arms around each other. "We intend to."

Veronica cleared her throat and held up the papyrus Lisa had handed her. "Time to get down to business, the whys of why we are here." Shaking the papyrus, she inquired, "Does anyone else have pieces of the scroll with information about this mysterious meeting place where we are supposed to gather?"

"Yes," came multiple responses.

"Akbar was sharing his and Aaron's with me when Ben and Tony found us," Jake answered.

"Let's compare them and see if we can figure out our next destination," Veronica stated. "Lisa's and my scroll was discovered beneath the foot of an angel in Verona. It reads 'at the <u>actual</u> place.' That's all."

Akbar turned and nodded to Aaron, requesting that he read the scroll. "Ours was discovered in a bird's nest atop a marble canopy at Gurdwara Damdama Sahib in India and says '*The eight of you will travel together. We will meet*'—as you can guess, it was making us nuts trying to figure out who the other six were, and we prayed the bird who was harboring it didn't have anything to do with the missing meeting place."

Britt stood up and said, "Ruth found ours in the Porziuncola, inside the Basilica of Santa Maria degli Angeli." Britt then looked at Ruth and inquired, "I never asked, where did you find it?"

"Do you remember the seat you took, vacated by the German man?" Ruth asked.

"Of course," Britt nodded.

"When he came in, he leaned down beside me and picked something up from under the bench I was kneeling at and said, 'Did you drop this?' I recognized it as the papyrus I had seen in my dreams and quickly took it from him and thanked him. Please read it, Britt," Ruth requested.

Britt unrolled it and read, "*on the December solstice.*"

"Tony and Ben, you're last. I do hope we have more clarity after." Jake vocalized what was on everyone's mind.

Tony read the last scroll. *"Of my birth."*

After they read off the pieces of papyrus, Ben announced, "This reminds me of the first day in your class, Professor Reynolds, when you sent the pieces of the jigsaw puzzle flying across the room and told us the importance of every single piece to create the whole."

"Something none of us will forget," Veronica affirmed and added, "Let's put the other fragments on the desk and let Lisa piece it together."

Matching the pieces of the scrolls by the torn edges, Lisa read aloud, *"The eight of you will travel together. We will meet at the actual place of my birth on the December solstice."* Lisa paused and added, "The word *actual* is underlined."

Everyone gathered around and looked down at the papyrus pieces that had previously made no sense.

The eight of you will travel together. We will meet at the actual place of my birth on the December solstice.

"Nazareth," Jake, Tony, and Ruth said in unison.

"Yes, Nazareth was the actual place of birth, not Bethlehem like most Christians believed," Lisa affirmed, adding, "My dreams showed me those same images."

"That doesn't give us a lot of time to make arrangements," Britt said, still in awe of the events that had so swiftly unfolded.

"No, it doesn't," Jake affirmed, pulling Lisa close to him. "Why don't we all get some lunch and relax a bit before arranging travel. It has been quite a day for all of us!"

"That's an understatement," Lisa sighed, happy to be in the comfort of Jake's arms.

"Sounds great. I have been so anxious about all the events that I haven't been able to eat a thing since yesterday," Ben admitted.

"Hear, hear," Lisa agreed.

"I've got the perfect place." Veronica sounded like herself for the first time since hugging Tony and Ben when they arrived. "And I know the owner. He will give us a private room so we can talk."

"Of course she does." Tyler smiled as he pulled her more tightly to him and kissed her cheek. "She knows all the best shop and restaurant owners in Italy!"

Lisa pulled Jake close and whispered, "You do realize it is a bit humorous that the Vatican police are looking for you in the United States, and you are right under their noses."

"Yes." Jake squeezed her. "Believe me, I wasn't only looking out for Akbar as I stood waiting in the square. I was scanning for any thugs."

CHAPTER 72

Meg barely raised an eyebrow when she saw Jazz and Andrew walk in together. Jasmine was a lovely woman, and if dinner turned to overnight, it was finally with a woman who matched his strength and intelligence instead of one of those ditzy airheads he often invited for social events.

"Good morning, Meg," Andrew said as he approached her desk, "any calls regarding our inquiries of yesterday?"

"Good morning, Mr. Turner and Ms. O'Sullivan." Suddenly Meg could not conceal her surprise and blurted out, "Sir, can I get a fresh suit for you?"

Andrew looked down at his rumpled Armani. "Ha-ha," he laughed lightly, "Ms. O'Sullivan is a wild one! She did this in the elevator coming up!"

Jazz was taken aback but quickly recovered. "Yes, I was checking to see if his suit was made from an organic fiber and was also fair trade. I had to wrestle him to the ground. It was really difficult to find the tags," she said with a grin.

"Oh, of course, but isn't that the suit you wore yesterday? Oh dear, oh dear, I can't believe I said that out loud. I am so sorry, sir!" Meg stuttered as her cheeks turned bright red.

"Meg, it's OK. In fact, it is the same one. Perhaps a fresh suit would be a good idea. Now about the calls?" Andrew inquired.

"Yes, sir, on your desk." Meg was still about ten shades of red. "A suit will be brought to your office in five minutes."

"Thank you, Meg." Andrew smiled.

As they walked next door to Andrew's office, Jazz whispered, "Yep, twenty shades of red." She laughed. "I didn't have the heart to ask Meg my question from this morning. And by the way, five minutes? What, you have a closet here?"

"Of course," Andrew said, "you never know when an event is coming up and one needs a change of clothes, or when a fiery redhead lures you into bed."

"Ha, not true, now let's get down to business!" Jazz glared at him as she squinted her eyes and shook her head.

"Let's! Lots to do," Andrew agreed.

Meg timidly knocked on his office door. "Sir, I have your suit."

"Come in, and thank you," Andrew said as he stood transfixed by the message he was reading on his desk. "Meg, who delivered this letter?"

"Oh, that one, yes, it was a bit odd. I had to go down to the lobby to receive it. The young man wouldn't come up. Security called and said that he wanted to hand it to either you or me personally. The odd thing was, he seemed to know who I was. And he also didn't ask me to sign anything."

"You have never seen him before?" Andrew inquired.

"No, never. But I thought perhaps it was sent from one of the scientists who had been an informer, and when I did question, the young man quickly rode off on a bike."

Meg and Jazz both stared at Andrew, waiting for a reaction.

"Thanks, Meg, that will be all," Andrew said as he turned to Jazz.

Meg closed the door behind her, and Jazz asked, "What is it?"

Andrew handed the letter to Jazz. "What do you make of it?"

The envelope was a modern-day manila envelope, but the contents were some species of parchment. "Is it papyrus?" Jazz inquired, not waiting for an answer, and began reading the words: *"Are you ready to remember? Time has run out. The place and time are when you two first met two thousand years ago."*

Jazz was confused. "It's torn. Something is missing."

"What does that mean?" Andrew questioned. His face was pale. "When we met? Ireland?"

Jazz examined the manila envelope and pulled out a smaller piece of parchment, reading it aloud, *"Martha of Bethany, sister of Lazarus of Bethany. Remember."*

With those words, the room morphed, transforming before their eyes to an ancient time when Lazarus was dying and Yeshua came to Martha's home. It had been the first time Andrew noticed Martha of Bethany. As quickly as the room had transformed, the images disappeared.

Andrew and Jazz made no sound, nor moved. Time felt suspended. They looked at each other, and Jazz had tears in her eyes. "I was there also. As a disciple, that is. I was in Bethany, and I remember. But how did someone know I would be here with you in this room when you opened the envelope?"

Suddenly she couldn't breathe, and Andrew rushed beside her and put his arms around her. "Breathe. Just breathe. Sit, my dear, I will call for water," Andrew said as he guided her to his sofa. "Meg, please bring in some water, and no need to knock," Andrew instructed, still dazed.

When Meg entered the room, she quickly closed the door behind her when she saw Jazz's pale face. It had already been pale, but now it was sheet white.

"Sir, may I help? You know I have the utmost discretion," Meg offered.

"Yes, please. I am going to need tickets to Jerusalem for Jasmine and myself. I don't want to take my plane."

"British Airways, first-class direct. I am on it, sir," Meg responded.

"I will also need clothing for Ms. O'Sullivan, suitable for winter," Andrew added.

"Right away." Meg looked at Jazz and spoke softly. "Ms. O'Sullivan, just nod if you are a UK size ten, which is small to medium-small."

Jazz nodded, and Meg quickly departed. Although, Meg realized Jasmine would probably have agreed to whatever she said.

"Jazz, darling, are you better?" Andrew was beside her, offering her a glass of water, which Jazz gratefully accepted. He was baffled as to where the "darling" came from. He had never called anyone darling.

"Yes." Jazz finally spoke and again began to tear up. She shook her head and pressed her lips together to contain her emotions. "One day I am being thrown out of your office, and then I am in bed with you, and now I discover I have known you for over two millennia, and soon, something big is going to turn our lives upside down."

"Whatever it is, we will be together, and we both know this is something we have to do. It is not optional for either of us."

"You are right, I can feel it in every cell of my being," Jazz confessed.

"As do I." Andrew nodded in agreement.

CHAPTER 73

The next morning, the church bells rang before any light penetrated Luke's small cell in the monastery, which consisted of a wooden chair, a small window, a modest dresser, an oil lamp, a box of matches, and a single bed with woolen blankets pushed up against a stone wall. He reluctantly opened his eyes, still exhausted from the events of the last several days, but knowing José was used to getting up in the early hours and would most likely already be at the chapel.

Suddenly Luke bolted from his bed, realizing that Yeshua's appearance had not been a dream. Now he was wide awake and began to wash quickly using the porcelain basin and pitcher of water on top of his dresser. He didn't want to waste any opportunity for discourse with Yeshua. Luke put on his clothes, carefully tucking in his shirt and combing his hair out of respect instead of running his fingers through as he normally did.

As Luke opened his door, he could see José in the hall. "José, I thought you would already be in the chapel."

"Buenos dias, I would have been if I could have found my way in the dark. I already got lost going through some little doors and long stairways. I was lucky to find my way back without my lantern going out," José confessed. "I was afraid I would awaken the dead with my banging into things."

"My good fortune," Luke smiled. "With both our lanterns, it will be light enough to find our way."

"How did you sleep?" José inquired.

"Oddly, I awoke several times with a strange sense that these walls are haunted by those murdered in the past. And Mark Twain's voice saying, 'In all that dreary time they have not heard the laughter of a child or the blessed voice of a woman. They have seen no human tears, no human smiles. They have known no human joys, no wholesome human sorrows.' Besides that, I slept pretty well, although the name Bethany came to mind several times. How about you?" Luke inquired.

"That's a bit depressing," José divulged, "although I do want you to know that even though I lived in a monastery, I never felt that way."

"But you did hear a woman's voice or children laughing, correct?" Luke retorted.

"Yes, but not often. I have never read Mark Twain. It seems I have missed a man with a great talent for words," José confessed. "As far as sleep, I don't believe I rested well, too much excitement and endless questions. Although, I also dreamt of Bethany and Lazarus."

"Of course!" Luke exclaimed. "I thought the name belonged to a woman we would meet. Do you suppose we are to journey there next?"

"I thought Yeshua said Nazareth? But I don't pretend to know anything anymore," José confessed.

"Nor do I," Luke responded. "We will know soon enough."

Again, the bells chimed three times, and they quickened their pace. "Good morning, my brothers," came the soft, distinguished voice of Yeshua. José and Luke jumped, not seeing him standing next to an arched stone wall.

"Good morning, Yeshua," both said in unison in an equally quiet voice as they reached out to embrace him. Luke stood shaking his head, not saying a word; he was still pinching himself. As the dreams of the last several months had been so convincing, he was still waiting to wake up. There was no need for words as they walked to the chapel.

When they arrived, several other monks were already there in prayer, including Makeen. No sooner had they sat down and closed their eyes than their minds went blank. A veil parted, and the events of their lifetimes began playing out in fast forward, going from each man's first meeting with Yeshua to the present day. Although it was happening in their minds, it was as though it was occurring outside of themselves.

Luke snapped back into his body and gasped for breath, followed by José. Luke and José looked at each other and then at Makeen's dark questioning eyes staring back at them. Makeen was sitting several benches in front of them, and by the look on Makeen's face, it was apparent that he had not been spared.

The brother beside Makeen gave him a startled look raising his thick furrowed brows, and returned to his prayer. Yeshua remained in what appeared to be a state of bliss as though nothing had taken place. Luke tried to close his eyes again, but regardless of whether they were open or closed, all he witnessed were opportunities in his lives that he had passed by, making one excuse after another.

He was devastated. How many lifetimes had he wasted because of his fear of the unknown? José must have felt the same, for he reached his hand over and rested it on Luke's. Although Makeen was again facing front, both Luke and José could see that Makeen was covering his face with both his hands. Fear had directed their lives, and it could be no more.

An hour later, the bells rang again and the chapel emptied except for the four of them. At length, Yeshua stood and motioned for them to follow him across the cool stone floor to the front, where they sat together as Yeshua spoke.

"What I will tell you will remain secret. It is not to be written, nor repeated. When you leave the sacredness of this space, all remorse will be eradicated. Every belief of sin or karma will vanish. Your lives now begin anew, and you shall do great things as promised.

"Say no more. Do not discuss among yourselves, for it is done. Stand beside me as my brothers, and give all you can without forcing your beliefs upon your sleeping or hungry brothers and sisters. Await their inquiry, for when they are ready, they will have ears to hear. You are the examples of ones who live without fear and embody God's love. Your purpose is to serve.

"Those who are ready to choose a life from the guidance of their hearts and cast aside their greed, anger, control, remorse, and laziness have the opportunity to transition into the new world that awaits. They will exchange their faults for the remembrance of their true self and will be attracted to you.

"These remaining years are few, but there is still time for souls to gather and remember. Each of you will know the love of a woman who will become your partner to fulfill your role as a fully integrated human being. You will know sacred love in human form."

With that, Yeshua began to walk towards the door. "Tomorrow morning, we will head to Jerusalem and make a stop in Bethany. Today is for silence and conversation in the sacredness of your being. We will eat in silence and spend the day in reflection and meditation. You may rejoin me in the chapel if you choose."

The three men nodded and spoke no words.

Just before Yeshua reached the doorway, he turned. "By the way, Luke, Mark Twain missed the rich inner world of the monks he met, which was beyond comparison to Mark Twain's world of laughter and human smiles."

CHAPTER 74

"Were you able to get reservations for all of us on the same flight to Tel Aviv?" Britt inquired hopefully.

"Yes. I had to book us into two sections, business and economy. I hope that is OK?" Jake informed the entire group gathered for breakfast at a pleasant restaurant Veronica had recommended. Tyler was correct: Veronica really did know all the best places, and their owners also.

"I hope you booked Tony and me in economy," Ben announced, smiling. "Easier on the pocketbook!"

"Actually, I did. I thought you might appreciate that," Jake declared with a grin. "But here is the catch, and I hope it was all right that I took the liberty to go ahead and book it—the flight is at 8:00 a.m. tomorrow, and there is one stopover in London. The layover is almost eleven hours, leaving at 20:35 from Heathrow, so we can take in a few sights and grab a couple of meals. It's a four-hour-and-forty-five-minute flight to Tel Aviv. Therefore, we arrive at 3:20 in the morning, so I booked a hotel for all of us. We can get a little sleep before heading to Nazareth."

Everyone nodded in agreement, with Ruth adding, "Cutting it a little close to our arrival in Nazareth. Although, since everything has been falling into a divine order, I am sure it will be perfect."

"Definitely, it's been unreal," Aaron said, shaking his head in awe, "to meet up with my mom in Rome when neither of us had any idea where the other was, or the fact that I had met Britt unexpectedly in Assisi and then my mom showed up with her here. It is all too extreme to digest. So trusting every event as it unfolds is the only option."

"Amen to that," Akbar and Tyler said at the same moment.

"Just saying yes to what unfolds is the only thing I can wrap my head around the last few months!" Tyler said, shaking his head in amazement.

"This is great. We can all spend today together, visiting some museums or sites. I am sure Veronica will be happy to be a tour guide." Tyler smiled, winking at Veronica, and quickly added, "Although, some may want to do their own thing and we can meet up later."

"Sure, I would be happy to," Veronica responded. "I will make some suggestions, and people can decide whether they want to be a part of it or not."

The consensus was that they would all stay together. No one wanted to be left behind; a remarkable, energetic connection had formed in such a short time. Then again, each knew that bond began lifetimes ago.

Upon arriving in London, they grabbed a shuttle to downtown, trusting the café they had researched would be as good as it looked. Windsor Castle was only eight miles from Heathrow, and the restaurant was within minutes. It was humorous, having just come from Italy, but they all finally agreed on an Italian restaurant called Sebastian's Italian.

They had intended to experience the local cuisine, but the thought of mash, fish and chips, scones, battered onion rings, and other strangely mushed-up menu items, such as Cornish pasty, mushy peas, and gravy, sounded much too heavy, and no one felt their stomachs could handle it.

As they walked into the restaurant, passing a table for two near the window, Veronica whispered to Lisa as she motioned her head towards an attractive couple, "Wow, new love and a power couple on top of it. Romance must be in the air! Isn't it wonderful to observe body language?"

"Looks like you and Tyler, and Jake and me," Lisa responded with a knowing giggle.

"No kidding!" Veronica agreed.

Everyone ordered something different, and only in an Italian restaurant could one get away with passing bites across the table and sampling each other's meal. The consensus was, the crab linguine was very good, the classic Mediterranean salad was great, the ricotta stuffed with butter and sage was loved, the calzone was delicious, and the service was superb—all set on the stage of a busy and fun atmosphere.

The conversations were wild as they got to know more about each other, and everyone appreciated the chance to kick back and laugh after all the intensity of the last several months.

Lisa whispered to Veronica as she pointed discreetly to the new-love power couple, "Don't look, but they may be the only Londonites in here who seem to be amused by our enjoyment."

"I think the word is *Londoners*," Veronica politely corrected as she scanned the room. "And I believe you are bloody well correct! Although, the woman doesn't quite fit the English model. Perhaps she is just visiting her English lover," she added with a wink.

When the group finally left the restaurant, the couple was still in their window seat and smiled and waved good day. "Enjoy your day," the woman said, with her refined Irish accent, one of a professional woman. The gentleman just nodded and smiled.

"Nice folks," Ben said as he tipped his finger on the tip of his imaginary cap, wishing them a good day also.

"Agreed, they've got good vibes," Tony declared.

Britt was cold. The temperature at Windsor Castle was approximately forty-two degrees, not much different from the cold they had just left in Italy, but it was damper, more chilling to her bones, and she was glad she dressed warmly. The castle was massive, beautiful, and quite grand, as would be expected, but not Britt's cup of tea—much too formal and stodgy. She felt she should be curtsying or doing something "royal."

Lisa, Veronica, and she had voted for the Stonehenge Inner Circle Access trip. Britt and Jake had voted for the British Museum. But both groups were outnumbered by the guys, who wanted to see the castle. Ruth was neutral. Jake was concerned about getting back in time and suggested that Stonehenge was a trip for when they could spend several days in London and also enjoy the museum, perhaps on the way back.

Granted, the camaraderie of the group made the visit quite enjoyable, with much laughter and role-playing, including Ben and Tony as British guards and the terrible attempt at an English woman's accent by Tyler playacting a distressed senior woman with guards refusing to speak.

"Give it up, Tyler! This is sad indeed!" Veronica laughed as Ben and Tony did an excellent impersonation of undaunted guards as Tyler played the role of a fainting woman lying before them, clutching at Tony's leg.

Each enjoyed the horsing around, knowing well that what lay ahead for them was anything but play.

CHAPTER 75

After lunch, Andrew and Jazz enjoyed a trip to the British Museum. They discovered that they shared similar tastes in art, small antiquities, sculpture, and architecture.

"A match made in heaven." Andrew smiled, and he playfully nudged her with his shoulder.

"Seriously, I believe it was," Jazz said as she returned Andrew's smile and elbowed him back.

Andrew was delighted to see her grinning again. It had been a rough morning. Looking into her gorgeous eyes, he couldn't resist this beauty standing next to him. Impulsively, he grabbed her hand and pulled her behind a collection of upright Egyptian mummies. Usually this room was well occupied, but not today.

Cupping Jazz's face in his hands, he kissed her lips passionately. Jazz eagerly returned his affection. Finally pulling away, Jazz spoke softly. "Thank you for erasing some of the confusion. You are the one thing that makes sense in my life."

"Dearest, I feel the same," Andrew assured her as he kissed her again.

After a few moments, a man loudly cleared his throat.

"Enjoying the exhibit, folks?" the security guard asked with his arms crossed over his chest and his legs spread just enough to demonstrate a power stance.

"Why yes, thank you. The lady was commenting on the decoration used to illustrate and commemorate the person in the coffin." Andrew nodded his head sincerely, taking Jazz's hand and kissing the top of her wrist.

"Indeed, I was admiring a fantastically beautiful example of power and assuredness," Jazz added as she glanced from the guard to Andrew, smiling as she scanned him up and down.

The guard, looking a bit confused about what to do next, uttered, "Carry on, and enjoy the rest of your visit."

"Cheers, we shall," Andrew assured him.

As Andrew and Jazz walked away, Andrew said with a smile, "You're a naughty one. And by the way, he did say carry on, correct?"

"He certainly did," Jazz said, laughing, "but perhaps we better head to another floor!"

Having returned to Jasmine's hotel room to pack what she needed for their trip to Bethany, Andrew inquired as he ran his hand across Jazz's shoulders, rubbing her long, responsive neck, "Hey, gorgeous, are you ready to get going to the airport?"

She pushed her head deeper into his hands and nodded yes without speaking.

"Everything all right, mate?" Andrew asked, concerned.

"Yes, love, just so much to take in the last few days," Jazz confessed.

"I admit, I was gobsmacked when Meg told me the story about the mysterious delivery fellow, and it just grew from there," Andrew said as he began to gently massage Jazz's scalp.

"It is all still unbelievable. I can't wrap my mind around all the events that have transpired. Who would have thought that one 'Hello?' when I decided to accept Meg's call just as I was leaving the hotel would change my life so dramatically?" Releasing a deep sigh,

Jazz turned and looked into Andrew's eyes, searching for answers that couldn't possibly be there.

Andrew took her face in his hands and kissed every inch of it. "Remember, we are in this together. Whatever transpires, we both know we longed for the answers to lifetimes of events, so there is no escaping whatever awaits us," Andrew reasoned.

"True, true, that's the crux of it," Jazz admitted.

Andrew notified the front desk to send Jasmine's remaining bag to his office, to Meg's attention.

"Very well, sir," the assistant manager answered, needing no further directions, "it will be taken care of right away. Although, your driver is outside. Would you prefer that I leave it with him?"

"Thank you. Yes, that will be fine." Andrew marveled, looking at Jazz's questioning eyes, and said, "Meg. It had to be Meg's doing. She knew what time we needed to leave for the airport. I never appreciated or paid attention to how loyal and efficient she was, nor how she seemed to know what I needed before I did. I am fortunate, although surprised, that she tolerated my bad behavior for so long."

"I have a feeling that Meg was one of the few who could see past your faults and into the potential of your soul," Jazz replied. "I sure didn't!" she added with a laugh, which lightened their spirits.

"Come on, you, we better get going," Andrew declared, escorting Jazz out of the room as he grabbed her suitcase.

"Blimey! Look at that," Andrew exclaimed as he saw Lisa passing his seat as she walked up the aisle. "Can you believe it? It's the same young woman we saw in the café."

"It is. What are the chances of her being on the same flight as we are?" Jazz asked, just as amazed.

"Her mate, although a good deal older than she, seemed like a good match and a respectable bloke, at least from what I overheard," Andrew replied. "I did enjoy hearing their lively conversation. Quite a delightful group of friends."

"Granted, he was older, and I also agree, they seemed to suit each other quite well," Jazz affirmed. "Their energy together was magical."

"What does that mean?" Andrew asked, puzzled.

"A bit like ours," Jazz offered with a mischievous smile.

"Hello, my dear, do you remember us from the restaurant?" Jazz questioned with a smile as she addressed Lisa, who was now walking back down the aisle towards business class.

"Oh my gosh, yes, of course!" Lisa exclaimed, just as surprised. "It is lovely to see the both of you again. I do hope we weren't so loud as to disrupt your meal?"

"No, not at all, it was good to see people enjoying themselves," Jazz assured Lisa.

"Are you all on holiday together?" Andrew probed.

Lisa didn't know how to answer, so she said the first thing that came to mind. "Holiday pilgrimage. We felt Christmas was a good time to do this." *Well, it's the truth*, Lisa assured herself, not being one who liked to fib.

"Delightful, perfect time of year, not too hot," Jazz assured Lisa.

"What about you two," Lisa inquired, "are you on business or pleasure?"

There was an awkward silence, and then their words tumbled over each other. Jazz put her hand up to signify to Andrew that she would answer. "Both business and pleasure."

Lisa could see by the looks in their eyes that something else was going on, but it wasn't her business, so she added, "Great, it's always nice to mix the two. Well, I guess I better get back to stretching my legs."

"Cheers, for now," Andrew replied.

"Ciao," Lisa said, waving without thinking, having recently been enmeshed in the energy of Italy.

Returning to her seat, as the lights began to dim so passengers could attempt to sleep Lisa casually whispered to Jake, Tyler, and Veronica, "You will never believe who I ran into!"

"Who?" all three questioned.

"Remember that enchanting couple we saw in London in the café, the redhead and the distinguished gentleman?" Lisa casually asked.

"Yeah, what about them?" Veronica inquired.

"I just saw them in first class, and we had a curious chat," Lisa said, looking at Veronica.

"Curious how?" Veronica pushed.

"I can't quite figure it out. They asked me a lot of questions but were secretive and vague when I questioned them. My intuition says they are hiding something," Lisa said, raising a brow.

"You do realize we are secretive and vague also," Jake responded with a low chuckle.

"Touché," Lisa said with a laugh.

"Now come here, you. Let's try to get some rest, if that is possible!" Jake suggested.

"At least our seats are wider, with more legroom than the guys in coach. We can be thankful for that," Veronica noted.

"Amen to that," Tyler said as he turned on his side and shoved the mini pillow under his head and closed his eyes.

The next thing they heard was the sound of a woman's voice announcing they would be landing in Tel Aviv in thirty minutes.

"What time is it?" Lisa asked.

"The local time is 3:00 a.m.," Jake responded.

Veronica opened her eyes and proclaimed, "I feel like I was hit by a train. I probably shouldn't have fallen asleep. I don't do well with naps."

"Come on, Veronica, this is an adventure of a lifetime!" Ben said, playfully rubbing the top of her head as he stood in the aisle.

Veronica groaned.

"Hey, guys, how are you both doing?" Lisa asked, seeing Tony standing behind him.

"A bit cramped back there, but it wasn't that long a flight. We ended up talking most of the trip," Tony replied, "and don't let Ben's casual voice and actions fool you. He is a bit nervous about what comes next."

"Hear, hear!" Tyler said, in Ben's support.

"I think we are all doing a great job at trusting, but honestly, it is knotting my stomach up," Lisa confessed.

"Agreed," Veronica added, "I am looking forward to this mystery revealing itself, because I am not sleeping well. Too many dreams are still filling my mind."

Just then, the steward pushed back the drapes that had been separating them from first class. A man was standing in the aisle, stretching. "Hey, isn't that the guy we saw in the restaurant yesterday?" Ben inquired.

"Yep, we will tell you later, but they, too, are a mystery," Lisa remarked.

CHAPTER 76

Waiting to pass through customs, too tired for much dialogue, Aaron pointed to the mystery couple in line, about a dozen people ahead of them.

"I met them on the plane, although they never told me their names. But then, neither did I," Lisa confessed.

As the line crisscrossed around, Ben whispered to Aaron and Lisa, "They're back!"

Separated only by the black retractable belt, Ben addressed the couple. "What are the chances of you being on our same flight from London? Interesting coincidence. Lovely to bump into you again. By the way, I'm Ben, and I believe you already met Lisa."

"This is a coincidence. That is, if we English believed in such things. Nice to meet you, Ben," Andrew said as he shook Ben's outstretched hand. "And nice to formally meet you, Lisa. I'm Andrew, and this is Jasmine." Within moments, everyone had introduced themselves, and this time, Lisa didn't ask where they were going. She assumed that if they wanted to share that information, they would.

Without prompting, Jazz added, "Andrew and I are heading to Bethany to visit old family friends. How about you? And don't tell me you are all going there also!" she added with a laugh.

Jazz gravitated to this group's energy, as did Andrew. "There is just something likable about them," he had expressed to Jazz when they first spotted the eight of them in the customs line.

"No, we are off to visit a few holy sites, including Nazareth, with a million others, I suppose," Tony said in despair, not liking crowds.

"Come on, Tony, it's going to be a captivating journey," Britt assured him.

"Hmm, we'll see," Tony remarked skeptically as Veronica nudged him and said, "It's going to be great, I promise."

The line began to move again, and they all said goodbye to their new acquaintances. "Perhaps we shall meet you on the return flight." Jazz's smile almost convinced them of the possibility.

"Perhaps," several replied.

"At this point, I wouldn't be surprised if it was sooner rather than later," Jake said to Lisa, pulling her close and tucking his chin over the top of her head as it rested on his chest.

"Nor would I," Lisa whispered, "nor would I."

CHAPTER 77

The streets were lively. People of all nationalities were in Jerusalem for the holiday season. Some were solemn, some were hopeful as though expecting a heavenly encounter, and others were just there for the experience. Holiday decorations and lights surpassed those Luke had experienced in the States, which surprised him. He didn't know why, but he wasn't expecting this.

A man wore a Santa Claus costume as he walked atop a wall, and there was even a camel near a flocked Christmas tree filled with stars. He couldn't complain about the weather. It was pleasant, but somehow none of it seemed authentic nor even suitable.

Yeshua, Luke, José, and Makeen had arrived in Jerusalem and only stayed long enough to eat at a local café before traveling to Bethany. Throughout the hours since leaving the monastery, silence prevailed; the presence and energetic profundity of the man called Yeshua needed no words. Finally, when they finished their meal and headed to the street to flag a taxi, Luke looked at Yeshua and inquired, "Is someone meeting us in Bethany?"

"Yes, they just don't know it yet," Yeshua answered as he turned to a taxi driver who had rolled down his window before giving him directions to their destination. "Jump in, gentlemen," Yeshua said as he opened both the front and passenger doors. "Makeen, why don't you ride in front?" Makeen was reluctant until Yeshua insisted. Yeshua was well aware that

Makeen often got carsick. Makeen felt more exposed in a land where he didn't belong but reassured himself that as long as he was in the company of Yeshua, he could withstand any unpleasant events.

Upon their arrival, Luke presented the money to the driver as they pulled up to what appeared to be ancient ruins and a stairway with broken walls on both sides. The driver looked at Luke, gesturing with his hand and waving it back and forth, speaking in Hebrew, of which Luke didn't understand a word—but he did recognize the hand gesture and the admiration in the driver's eyes. "There is no charge. A holy man has honored me," the driver said as he bowed his head towards Yeshua.

Yeshua returned his nod and spoke to the man in his native language. The man's eyes teared, and he got out of his taxi to embrace Yeshua. Releasing the driver, Yeshua again spoke in Hebrew, kissed his forehead, and placed his right hand upon his head before turning away.

José closed his eyes and, putting his finger to his forehead, made the sign of the cross. *Old habits are hard to break*, José thought with a sigh.

Yeshua, reading his mind, responded with a smile. "To bless yourself or another is a habit worth keeping."

Without further explanation, Yeshua turned and walked down the uneven and time-worn rock stairs, through a canopy of vines, and into a courtyard. Makeen noted that the driver stood at the top of the stairs, sobbing until they were out of sight.

There were palm trees and some haphazardly potted plants sitting on tumbled pieces of stone blocks, most obstructed from the sunlight by the high walls. A few long rays of light crossed the ground before them as Yeshua sat on one of the green iron benches. "We will wait here. It will not be long," he announced.

Without a word, José, Makeen, and Luke sat beside him. Silence remained until Luke's curiosity got the best of him. "Master, what do we wait for?"

"Breathe. Be at peace," Yeshua said through closed eyes.

The silence broke again, but this time by the laughter of a woman followed by inaudible words uttered from the man accompanying her. Luke again opened his eyes to witness the couple emerging from a grove of trees. He was about to close his eyes again but noticed the man, having caught sight of them, put his arm out to stop the woman.

Perhaps they don't want to disturb our meditation, Luke thought, until he realized the man was not staring at them, but at Yeshua, with opened mouth. Luke heard the woman answer, "What?" and the man stammer the response, "It just can't be." Pointing to Yeshua, the man continued, "That is the man who was in the vision I had the day my old world fell apart at my lake property!"

By this time, all eyes were open except Yeshua's. The man and woman walked closer and stood before him.

Yeshua opened his eyes and spoke, "Ah, you have arrived."

CHAPTER 78

As the group gathered on the street and waited for a taxi, Aaron announced, "You know, I have always wanted to visit the tomb of Lazarus and check out the energy. In the lifetime when I was with St. Francis, he was a brother also. Do you mind if I meet up with you guys later?"

"I wouldn't mind going either. May I join you, Aaron?" Britt asked.

"Absolutely," Aaron responded.

Within moments, the entire group decided to head to Bethany since they didn't need to leave Jerusalem until evening.

"Al-Eizariya," Aaron informed the two taxi drivers, who were necessary for the group, "tomb of Lazarus."

After they all piled out of the cabs, they followed Aaron down a walkway, down a dozen stone stairs, and into an ancient stone courtyard. Veronica didn't exactly find any of it beautiful or terribly exciting, but she enjoyed Aaron's enthusiasm. Looking up at Tyler, she realized he also seemed equally interested, so it was cool.

"This way," Aaron said optimistically, pointing to a small open doorway made of ancient blocks of stone. "I believe that is the entrance," he exclaimed, motioning to the group to hurry up.

"Look, can you believe it?" Ben asked in amazement. "You were right, Jake, sooner rather than later! And in my gut, I knew it also!" he said as he pointed to Andrew and Jasmine.

"OMG," Veronica exclaimed, looking at Lisa, "what are the chances of that?"

Lisa shook her head. "Somehow the moment Jake said he wouldn't be surprised if it was sooner rather than later at the airport, I knew it to be true."

There stood Andrew and Jasmine in the courtyard, appearing as though they'd seen a ghost, as they spoke to four gentlemen sitting on a bench.

"Perhaps we should see if they are in trouble," Veronica suggested.

"They are going to think we are stalking them," Akbar answered, amused by how bold Americans were.

"We can casually walk by, and if it looks like they are in trouble, we can stop and chat," Tony suggested.

As they changed direction, the group made small talk to appear nonchalant as they approached Jasmine and Andrew. Suddenly Britt noticed that Ruth also turned white as chalk as she called out, "Brother?" pointed towards the group, and then fainted.

Confusion silenced the group. All movement froze. Sound ceased. Lisa felt as though she was spinning backward in time. Jake grabbed her arm to steady her trembling body, and if he hadn't been focusing on her, he knew he would be the one watching time evaporate in front of him.

"Ah, a day early, in an undesignated city," said the commanding presence of a man, with an amused chuckle, as he came forward and gently gathered Ruth off the ground, holding her close to his chest, and said, "Sister, wake up."

CHAPTER 79

Beyond exhaustion, with the last clue held firmly to her breast, Angelina ran, blinded by her tears. People stopped to watch her, but she was not aware, nor would she have cared. There was no need to look again at the papyrus paper clutched in her hand, which contained the map and the last of the puzzling metaphors that posed as clues telling her where she was going.

Angelina knew the place like the back of her hand, although it had been over two millennia since she had last been there. Things had dramatically changed, but her night dreams had prepared her.

Since arriving in Egypt, and now Nazareth, Angelina had been overwhelmed by the memories playing out in her mind as if they had recently occurred, everything from her life in the Temple of Isis to the final dwelling that was not far away—of this she was positive. Her entire body began vibrating as if plugged into a hundred volts of energy.

She began seeing visions, just like she had before approaching every accurate location. The closer she got, the clearer the images became. The woman she saw was dressed in a long white dress, wearing woven sandals. Her dark hair was veiled in soft woven gauze, and her cape was the color of sapphire blue. Although her appearance was different, she knew that the woman she was seeing was herself.

Shocked, Angelina stopped, for she was witnessing herself standing before the man she had so dearly loved, with tears streaming down her face in that same sapphire-blue cape, just like the dream she had written down. She could feel her heart shattering just as it had two thousand years ago as he gently held her hands, trying to explain something that she refused to listen to.

Of course, she should have known that Nazareth would be the chosen meeting place, the actual birthplace of her beloved, and in every cell of her being, she had always known this regardless of what the church claimed. It was not Bethlehem. Yeshua was born in Nazareth. Why hadn't she figured this out long before? It was fitting, a new beginning, a new birth, and the opportunity for the world to discover the great cover-up and to open their hearts and allow their true divinity to empower them.

This was a chance to reveal the authentic life and teachings of Yeshua, her beloved, this great, radical heretic who came to tear apart old structures, all while embodying unconditional love, compassion, equality, and his ultimate gift to the world: salvation through the depths of love and forgiveness.

She took a deep breath and began running again. This gathering was what she had been waiting for her entire life, as well as so many prior lifetimes.

Upon her arrival, Angelina was directed to a long hallway that opened into a large courtyard, and just beyond was the meeting room. Suddenly through blinding tears, she caught sight of him. Although, it was his energy—a pure, divine radiance that she could see emanating from him—that alerted her. It was a presence so unique in its frequency that it extended well beyond the aura of his body. All exhaustion left her as she continued to run.

There was no mistaking it, despite the fact that his physical appearance was completely different—it was undeniably her Beloved. He stood when he saw Angelina running towards him. As he reached out to her, she stumbled on a corner of the stone-tiled floor and almost fell as her knees gave way, but his powerful arms caught and steadied her. She began sobbing like a lost child who had been found.

Yeshua wiped the tears from her eyes and embraced her firmly. "My dearest Mary of Magdalene, my cherished, faithful wife, confidante, and companion, you have come." He validated the name and title she believed she had once held. It explained why she had so fiercely defended Mary Magdalene throughout her life; she knew within every molecule of her being that what the church had said about this woman was a lie, and it was why she could never fully open her heart to her husband James, as it already belonged to another.

Stroking Angelina's hair as he held her close, Yeshua acknowledged her presence in a low, soft voice. "I am so joyous that you have come," he repeated once again as he kissed her forehead.

Angelina stopped sobbing and wiped her eyes with the backs of her hands. "Was there ever any question, my Beloved Lord?"

"No. Never. I am infinitely grateful that all those called were able to join us, although it disheartens me that James was not able to reunite with us this lifetime."

"Us? James, my James?" Angelina was stunned.

"Yes, James has trials to work through, but do not trouble yourself. He will find his way."

Was that my attraction to him in this lifetime? Angelina wondered, trying to wrap her mind around her initial attraction to James.

Without needing her to voice the question, Yeshua answered her thoughts. "Yes, that was your attraction to him in this life. It was divinely orchestrated in hopes of James remembering his divine self, remembering what was important, and not choosing the path of object-oriented systems that the dark forces have successfully put in place. Much of the planet is under the same spell."

"Was it my fault? Could I have done more?" Angelina was alarmed by this new possibility.

"No, you acted as his perfect match, and every soul is responsible for their choices. Each person must understand the immense evolutionary transformation we are in, the opportunity to balance the darkness and the light through compassion. It is a very bleak time on the planet for those who choose to ignore the most profound experience the soul has to offer—the birthing of a new world within them.

"Those in this room accepted the challenge, the trials to overcome fear, blame, anger, and greed. Each of you trusted the voice of your soul to the core of your being. James is the only one who can save himself."

Angelina pulled her head back from Yeshua's chest, wiping the remaining tears from her eyes, and looked around the room. It was only then that she noticed the others. She could see that they were as speechless and awestruck as she. Her eyes locked on Lisa's. Angelina felt she had once known this woman intimately, and then she saw the spark of recognition on Lisa's astonished face.

Angelina burst out, "Junia! It's you, my beloved friend, dearer to me than any sister."

"Yes, Mary of Magdalene, blessed one, it is I."

Lisa and Mary were rushing towards one another with open arms and uncontrollable tears of delight. As they embraced, each broke down and sobbed. It had been so long ago that they were together, and the recollection of their love for each other could barely be contained in their joy. They had no words, yet they recollected every experience they had shared.

Finally, Lisa turned her gaze towards Jake and Rose. Both came forward with broad and loving smiles and outstretched arms, and again Angelina's eyes flooded with tears. "Oh, my dear friend John, the beloved one, dear Mother Mary, you too are here."

"Yes, precious one," Rose answered, "we are all here. And what a relief that we have recaptured the memories we had forgotten! Even I allowed this one aspect of my multi-selves to cease remembering my divine connection in order to play my part this lifetime."

"Yes, yes. It is true!" Angelina instantaneously remembered every event that played out in her dreams—the veil had lifted. She sighed, releasing years of anxiety. This was the first time she didn't feel alone in the world. Drying her eyes once again, Angelina scanned the room, recognizing each person's essence from so long ago.

She started to laugh, and again her arms stretched out as each person eagerly came forward as she called them by name. "Judas, my dear friend, what a role you agreed to take on. My heart has ached for you and repeatedly prayed that you would remember the profundity of the part you played for all of humanity. Only one who loved our Lord so completely could have agreed to such a difficult assignment!"

Tyler began to sob as he cupped his face with his hands. Both Angelina and Yeshua wrapped their arms around him. "If only I had remembered instead of believing what was written," Tyler managed to express between sobs, "and spoken about me. In my heart, I always knew I loved you so much, Yeshua, and could not imagine that I could bring harm to you for any amount, especially for only a few pieces of silver."

"I never left you, dear friend, even in your darkest hours. I was your breath when you couldn't go on. I carried you when you couldn't get up."

Finally, Tony came forward, uncertain about how Angelina would receive him, so he did not outstretch his arms.

Angelina put her arms out to receive him. She could see the pain in his eyes. "Dear Peter, you were forgiven long ago, for how could I not love you regardless of how you treated me? It would be my Lord who would suffer."

"Mary Magdalene, or shall I address you as Angelina?" he questioned.

"Angelina is less confusing," she smiled. "And shall I call you Tony?"

"That would be great. I realize jealously did not become me. We knew our Master loved you more, but it was beyond that. Most of us recognized that you understood what we as men could not. You had come more fully onto the path to become wholly human, the perfected integration of feminine, masculine, light, love, and darkness. Please forgive me."

"I did not see from the eyes of the mind. It was through the eyes that looked between the soul and the spirit that I saw the visions and heard the words of Yeshua. I knew my ears would deceive me. Worry not, two thousand years is far too long to hold a belief that I should not love you regardless!" Angelina reassured Tony and embraced him tightly. She was stunned by her ability to step out of the mind of Angelina and into the knowledge of Mary of Magdalene.

Pleased, Yeshua spoke. "It is the divine heart of God that makes us see, and the light within brings us clarity." Then, turning to Angelina, Yeshua spoke again. "There is one more who has joined us but isn't here. He will be back briefly, as he is on an errand for Mother Mary. She requested something she thought may be of interest to you. It is your friend Luke. He followed the stars," Yeshua said with a laugh.

"How delightful!" Angelina exclaimed with a smile. "He always did look to the heavens."

Yeshua put his arm around Angelina and held her close. Witnessing the precious beings who stood before him, he spoke. "All of us have traveled great distances to be here, so for now, let us put all our concerns aside and rejoice at this reunion. A great feast awaits us in an adjoining room. Let us share our journeys and the joy of being together.

"Tomorrow we will make our plans and create a strategy to ascertain how many are willing to make the changes needed and be saved from the endless repetition of fear, chaos, and uncertainty that plagues humanity."

Night had fallen. They walked into the great hall, yet this time, unlike the Last Supper, the table was round and set with dozens of candles flickering off the stone walls. Garlands made of olive branches decorated it, and the fragrance of exotic flowers filled the air.

CHAPTER 80

Jazz and Andrew met up with Lisa and Jake even though it was late, knowing it would be impossible to sleep. The four of them bonded immediately. It was evident through their conversations that they had shared many mutual lives together. A local resident had given them the location of a bar close by that stayed open until the early morning. Andrew grabbed a corner table hoping to be out of earshot of the somewhat rowdy patrons out on the town enjoying the beautiful night.

"This OK?" Andrew asked, looking at the others as he pulled the chair out for Jazz.

"Great," Jake said, looking at Lisa, who nodded her head in approval.

"I suppose we should order so we are not bothered for a while," Jazz suggested when she saw the cocktail server approaching.

As they waited for their drinks, Andrew turned to Jazz and said, "I'll be right back. I want to change my order."

Her eyes followed him, and she thought about their all-nighter in London. *What was that term the English women used? Oh yes, "Now that's a hot butter biscuit!"* She watched his athletic and handsome body move across the floor and quickly felt ashamed of the desire engulfing her. She told her body and mind to stop. Deeply inhaling, she realized that to lust after a man in this way was beyond her comfort zone. She had never done that. *Oh, maybe once*, she thought, *but I was seventeen, so that didn't count.*

As Andrew returned, Jazz noticed she wasn't the only woman enamored by him. Several women were unabashedly giving him the eye. Jazz shook her head in disbelief. It was as though they were undressing him right before her eyes. Jazz looked away and down at her hands, realizing that he possessed a confidence that knew he could catch any woman he desired. She quickly pushed the thought away. What was happening to her? And now, of all times, for God's sake.

She acknowledged that this hardcore self-centered man had resurrected as a kind and loving gentleman, and she wondered if he was "her" man. She felt like a starstruck teenager and shook her head to clear the thoughts.

When she looked up, she caught Andrew's dark eyes intently penetrating her. Nonverbal communication passed between them, of romance and lust equal to her own. Jazz blushed and turned her gaze to Lisa.

"OMG, I am so sorry! I don't know what has gotten into me." Jazz's face now matched the color of her fiery red hair.

Lisa laughed. "You are among friends! Believe me, I understand what you are feeling."

"Really?" Jake shot back in amusement and pulled Lisa closer. "Is there something I should know?"

Lisa threw her head back and laughed. "Ignore us women. We seem to be in our own world."

"And what world is that?" Andrew asked.

"Women wonder if it is love or just a passing romance. They hope it is real and forever because what they feel their man represents is everything they were missing in their lives, which they didn't even realize until they had it," Jazz answered, speaking for the two of them.

Andrew and Jake looked at Lisa, who quickly answered, "What she said." She tilted her head towards Jazz. "You do realize that regardless of who we have been, we are still human!"

They all laughed in agreement.

The rest of the evening was spent sharing about their lives. And as the veils fell away one by one, they shared those incredible stories of lives previously forgotten.

Hearing a *bing*, Andrew looked down at his phone and scanned a text he had received. "Sorry, I thought my phone was on mute. I'll have to read you what a colleague sent. It's an Instagram post that a woman wrote. 'Let's be clear, there is a new-age narcissistic corporate greed that is masked as spirituality.' Nothing like calling a spade a spade! I can't tell you how many of these corporate chaps I have run into."

Jazz shook her head. "Not just corporate, but personal greed. How many people do you know running around saying the words, wearing the clothes, chanting the mantras, throwing out phrases, and it's all empty? Why would I trust anyone hiding behind a word or belief?"

"Good thing you fancied me and gave me another chance!" Andrew said, laughing as he kissed her cheek.

"You just got lucky!" Jazz responded with a wink and a quick kiss.

"Well with that, we better get back," Jake finally said, noting that the night would break into daylight in a couple of hours.

"I suppose romance missed its opportunity." Andrew winked at Jazz.

"Yep, seems so. Hopefully you won't be just a fleeting memory of the one who got away," Jazz said with a laugh.

"I am guessing not," Jake assured her. "I see how Andrew looks at you when you aren't aware!"

"Hey, we chaps are supposed to protect each other," Andrew shot back.

"That's exactly what I am doing, my friend, that's what I am doing," Jake assured him good-naturedly.

As they exited the bar, a young woman in a lightweight, cream linen garment with a matching scarf wrapped around her head and neck walked up to them, slightly dazed, repeating the name of a location several times.

"That is where we are heading. Would you like to walk with us?" Jake offered.

The woman paused and stared blankly before responding. "*Oui,*" she answered, revealing a strong French accent.

"Tell us your name," Lisa sweetly asked, noting the disorientation of the beautiful, almost angelic young woman.

"*Mon nom est* Sarah."

"Lovely to meet you, Sarah. I'm Lisa, and this is Jake, Andrew, and Jazz," Lisa said as she pointed to each person. Sarah nodded at each introduction, saying nothing.

After walking in silence for several minutes, Jazz spoke. "Sarah, are you on holiday?"

"*Non, je suis là parce que mon père m'a convoqué. Désolé, comment dire en anglais?*" Sarah inquired.

"*C'est bien,*" Andrew responded, "*je parle Français.*" Turning to the group, Andrew repeated Sarah's response. "Sarah said, 'No, I am here because my father summoned me.'"

Jazz inquired in English, "Who is your father?" and then switched to French, "*Qui est votre père?*" She found it odd that this beautiful young woman was on the streets alone at this hour of the early morning, lightly dressed, and wearing a pair of sandals in the winter.

Sarah looked at each one, utterly baffled. "Yeshua, *mon père est* Yeshua."

CHAPTER 81

When they reached the hotel, the group knew it was essential to reach Yeshua even though it was before daybreak.

"You call," Andrew said, looking dismayed as he passed the lobby phone to Jake. "You might be able to explain this better than I."

"I am having a hard time wrapping my head around it myself," Jake confessed as he watched Lisa and Jazz sitting down with Sarah in the main lobby, "but I'll give it a go."

"*Est-ce que Je suis en train de rêver?*" Sarah said to Jazz, wondering if a dream would reveal itself as real or not.

"She is asking if she is dreaming," Jazz said to Lisa, perplexed on how to answer. Turning to Sarah, she spoke softly, "*Non, vous ne rêvez pas, vous êtes à* Nazareth."

Frightened, Sarah cried out, "*Non, non, papa a dit de ne jamais revenir en Israël!*"

"It's all right. You're with us. Yeshua will come soon," Jazz responded, quickly changing to French. "*C'est bon, vous êtes avec nous. Yeshua viendra bientôt.*"

Andrew, observing Sarah's fear, motioned to Lisa, who excused herself for a moment. "What just happened?" he asked Lisa.

"She asked if she was dreaming, and when Jazz told her no, that she was in Nazareth, she panicked. Something about her dad telling her never to return to Israel. She is disoriented, and I am beginning to feel like I am dreaming this whole event myself!"

Jake, having put down the phone and looking as though he saw an apparition, overheard Lisa's response to Andrew. "Yeshua will be down shortly and asked us to keep her close."

"Is that all he said?" Lisa inquired.

"No, I am not sure if I heard him correctly, but something about a tear in the space-time continuum and white holes. And that it was not intended for Sarah to be here. He was unclear how she believed herself to be summoned, but perhaps it was a summons from thousands of years ago."

"Oh my god, this is unbelievable," Lisa said as she put one hand over her heart and the other across her mouth, "just when I thought nothing else would surprise me. How did we not know he had a child? I know it was rumored, but why have none of us seen this in our dreams?"

Lisa turned to look at Jazz and Sarah. Jazz was holding Sarah's hands gently in her own, and she mouthed to Lisa, "What is going on?"

Moments later, Yeshua entered the lobby and rushed towards Sarah. He hadn't bothered to comb his hair or tuck in his shirt. The moment Sarah saw him, she began to cry and ran into his arms, speaking in ancient Aramaic. Yeshua tucked her head against his chest, embracing her in his arms as he whispered to her. Jazz had stepped away and joined Jake, Andrew, and Lisa to give them some privacy.

"Perhaps we should suggest that we move to Yeshua's room, or just allow them time to be alone to sort this out," Jake said, feeling uncomfortable with the scrutinizing stares from the front desk.

"I agree, even though we all want to know what is going on, the two of them should head to the privacy of Yeshua's room." Jazz affirmed what they were all thinking. "I will let him know our thoughts."

A few moments later, Yeshua, holding Sarah's hand, approached them. "Yes, as Jazz mentioned, we will go to my room, and I will see all of you in the morning. Thank you, my friends, for bringing my daughter to me."

"No problem, we will see you at 9:30. I am guessing that is still the plan?" Andrew stuttered, hoping for an explanation.

"Yes," Yeshua affirmed, putting his hand on Andrew's shoulder and nodding.

As he began walking away, he turned back and spoke to the four of them in English. "It appears that her desire to be with her mother and me in France two thousand years ago created a white hole, a tear in the space-time fabric between dimensions. Sarah's future lives and her ability to even be here now can alter if anything happens to her while she is here." Yeshua offered an explanation that left them more mystified and with even more questions.

They nodded their heads as though they understood what a tear in the space-time fabric meant and allowed Yeshua and Sarah to pass.

Once they were out of range, they all spoke at once. "One at a time," Lisa suggested, looking at Jake. "Yeshua never died on the cross? They all went to France?"

"So the stories are true?" Jazz blurted out. "I always questioned his death. Both Mary Magdalene and Mother Mary were trained in essential oils and the healing arts, and Yeshua knew how to enter states of breathlessness. I felt both were possibilities."

Lisa looked up at Jake. "I need a few hours of sleep. My body, as well as my brain, is fried."

"We all do," Andrew spoke softly, having no energy to spare.

Still unsettled, they watched the elevator doors open, and Yeshua stuck his head out and said, "Would you be so kind as to ring Mary of Magdalene and ask her to come to my room? But please, so she isn't completely caught off guard, tell her what has occurred. And if you cannot reach her, please leave her a message to contact me."

What was witnessed by the inquisitive night manager at the front desk were two women and two men nodding their heads and looking like deer caught in headlights. He shook his head and picked up the ringing phone.

CHAPTER 82

By the time Yeshua arrived for the morning gathering, the group was passionately engaged in conversation—at least everyone aside from Jake, Lisa, Andrew, and Jazz, who remained silent. They were uncertain of what they could say or do since they had not located Angelina.

Veronica, puzzled by Lisa's aloofness, questioned her. "What's up? Why the silence?"

Lisa only shook her head and mouthed, "Later." Seeing the hurt on Veronica's face, Lisa added, "I promise."

Yeshua had arrived alone, without Sarah, which meant they were still sworn to silence. Lisa noted that although he was alert and focused, he also appeared as tired as she felt with so little sleep after all the events of last night—or more accurately, early this morning.

Minutes later, Angelina rushed in expressing her apologizes for her late arrival. Lisa shot a wide-eyed glance at Jake, Jazz, and Andrew, who all wore the same perplexed expression.

Yeshua called to her, "Angelina, may I speak to you for a moment?"

"Of course, I apologize again for my tardiness. I had some urgent business last night and only now returned," Angelina informed Yeshua as she approached.

They could not hear his request as he wrapped his arm around her head and looked into her eyes, but only Angelina's soft response: "Yes, absolutely." She sounded as bewildered as the four of them.

Yeshua raised his hand to address the group, who once again had returned to their conversations. "Dear ones, we will have time for a conversation shortly, but for now, let me explain why you were all called to be here." Angelina looked up at Yeshua with misty and questioning eyes. She knew the seriousness of his tone. She also knew that regardless of what role she would play, she was "home," and Angelina could feel her heart leap with joy.

Yeshua closed his eyes and began breathing slowly and rhythmically. As he stood in silence, Lisa could see the light pulsing from his aura. Sitting cross-legged on her meditation blanket, she duplicated his breathing and merged with the light she felt emanating from him. This energetic light was bliss. This energy was grace.

When he opened his eyes, a golden-diamond-white light permeated the room. Yeshua lovingly focused on one person at a time, warmly acknowledging their presence before he began to speak.

"We are in the final chapter of these times. I came into the world two thousand years ago so the blind could see and the deaf could hear, to reveal to humanity that only love, self-governance, and equality could be the authentic rulers of this world.

"The distortions of the fundamental teachings hindered that original design—that all humanity could live in peace, love, honor, abundance, integrity, and joy. Now again, I am summoned by humanity's prayers for salvation. It is my final attempt to assist in undoing some of the damage that religious orders and corporate greed have brought about upon this earth. Humankind has run out of time, and as they so fondly put it, this is humanity's 'last curtain call.'"

Angelina guessed what was coming next, and questions filled her mind. *How many will commit to the dedication it would require to take the leap into the new world?*

"Disaster is threatening the planet. Every system is breaking down, as secular values have overridden spiritual values. Humans are connected, yet sovereign beings designed with everything they need, including the wisdom and ability to self-heal and know truth from deceit. Their instructions reside within and will connect them on a path of peace and harmony as long as they do not fall prey to those that don't have their best interests in mind. Dark forces, summoned by every selfish desire for personal gain over the good of the whole, continue to cause the planet to tremble. Humanity has forgotten its origins, its oneness. Each person is a wave supported by the whole of the ocean, and without each other, the dream of Maya could not exist. Dark times are upon this beautiful earth, my beloveds, and I must warn you, much of humanity will not align with the energy necessary to enter the new world. The new world I speak of encompasses other realms of existence, as well as staying on planet earth resonating at a higher frequency allowing the individual to experience a different reality from the masses."

All eyes remained transfixed on Yeshua. Unnoticed were the sounds of the birds singing in nearby trees and the footsteps of hotel staff walking across an outdoor gravel path.

The birthing of the new world, and access to it, is not an easy road for those still stuck in materialism, hatred, blame, false spirituality, and greed. Recently, the darkness has tipped the scales and gained excessive power. Many of Mother Earth's treasures will perish. She will survive, as she has in the past, but most of her creatures will not. All souls have the opportunity to be redeemed if they act quickly and, most importantly, if they are willing to heed the call to do what it takes to realign with the light of their original design. It is important to keep company with those holding the same high ideals and vibrations."

Jake, who was sitting next to Lisa, took her hand in his as he studied the troubled expression on her face. He gently reached out and rubbed her hand and kissed it. Lisa smiled in gratitude for his presence.

Yeshua continued, "All of you, along with twenty-seven others, have been with me in various lives as the loyal and loving holders of truth who stood beside me and defended my family and my teachings. As you have noted, not all of those the Bible speaks of are here. Before me are the men and the women who never forgot nor altered the authentic teachings. And for that, I treasure you dearly and have stood unseen next to you during every moment of questioning and despair.

"Many of you endured much hardship, even torture, during the darkest times of the church. Some of you were men and came back more than once as women because your souls encouraged you to work through your prejudice and beliefs that men were superior. What you discovered was the gift of intuitiveness, wisdom, and the sensitivity of the feminine.

"You succeeded. It brought balance into your lives and fullness to your hearts. I commend you, as you endured much injustice and discrimination in those lives. Most people in the world today still do not see the importance of equality of all of the Creator's children. Each being is a beautiful facet of Divinity. Even when you went astray, you soon returned to the consciousness of love, empathy, unity, and equality for all."

Yeshua paused. His eyes smiled and were tenderly penetrating each of their hearts. "And now, my beloveds, we are all together once again."

A long silence filled the room.

"Where are the other twenty-seven, and why are they not here?" Ben inquired softly, realizing he was breaking the silence. "And is Anandamayi Ma one of them?"

"Yes, Ben, she is. This new world we speak of is infused with love. Anandamayi Ma is the embodiment of divine love and bliss, and she is an integral part of the preparation of the new world. Many of these twenty-seven beings are working on various planes. Each one has an important function to fulfill, and they cannot be interrupted." Yeshua stopped and explained no further.

Lisa wiped her eyes. Just the mention of Ma's name filled Lisa's heart with a profound longing. She noticed Jazz and Veronica doing the same. Lisa still couldn't grasp that she was sitting among a group of beings whom she had spent at least one genuinely profound life with—and with others, multiple lifetimes together. She prayed she wouldn't wake up and realize it was all just another night vision.

Breathing slowly and deeply, Yeshua continued, "Once again, you will have direct access and clarity to my original teachings without the distortions and fabrications provided by the church. Sadly, many were executed in ignorance or the quest for power, control, and financial gain. You no longer need to question your beliefs—that knowing that tugged at your heart and soul that what the church and state declared was incorrect. You have always known what the truth was in your divine hearts, and what was pure fabrication. Although, now there will be no questions."

A tangible sigh of relief resonated from all present. Joyful chatter filled the room. The weight of this burden of truth that each of them had carried for lifetimes fell away.

Finally, the room became silent. Angelina, sitting next to Jazz, removed her hand from Jazz's before asking the question looming in everyone's mind. "Beloved Teacher, we are all aware of the insatiable hunger of those who profit from the endless wars, their struggle for power and control, and their astonishing greed.

"We are aware of these tragedies taking place. The false flags to redirect humanity's attention, the disclosures that are thirty, forty, and fifty-years old that will be presented as recent discoveries to manipulate humanity, and that much of society has chosen to be influenced by the power of mind manipulation directed by a few families, including the Church that control the media, Hollywood, governments, science, medicine, and religious orders instead of trusting their inner guidance, making them easy prey. We are aware of those who desire to control the masses and how they create fear to keep the majority of humankind in line."

Angelina paused long enough to take a slow, deep breath before continuing as though she was uncertain whether she honestly wanted to know the answer to the question she was proposing. Visions of the final days of Atlantis and its destruction had filled her dreams for the last two nights, which was the reason for her absence the night before. Luke had brought her the proof she had searched for: a star map of the heavens and the seas. The charts confirmed that the images in her visions were accurate.

"We know that all the power, or financial wealth possible will never be enough to satisfy their thirst, as what they search for to fill the hunger within themselves cannot be found in domination or external acquisitions. So my question is, will humanity survive, or will the dark forces win upon our planet as many of us witnessed with the fall of Atlantis?"

Yeshua raised both hands. The room mutated into energy, and suddenly each of them witnessed a vision revealing the fate of humanity. A perfect hologram was playing out each of the impending events that were rapidly approaching. In unison, many cried out and gasped in horror.

Veronica, Tyler, Jake, and Lisa grabbed hands while keeping their gaze transfixed on the visions that were unfolding before them. Several of the group cried openly, others silently, and the rest sat quietly shaking their heads in disbelief.

As every segment completed, they were stunned by the unconsciousness of humanity's actions for each event: the poisoned plants, the contaminated soil, the polluted oceans pounding the earth, the slaughtered animals, the darkened skies, and the sickening sound of the cracking of the fault lines abolishing everything within their paths for endless miles. They witnessed billions of humans crying out, many on their knees, begging God to be merciful. With the opportunities to change repeatedly ignored, time had run out—it was too late.

Finally, even Mother Earth cried tears of sorrow as torrential rains hammered the globe, sweeping away almost everything that was left.

Abruptly, the screams, prayers, crashing, explosions, begging, and sobbing stopped. The earth was silent. The sky cleared. The oceans settled.

The earth had survived, but little else.

Divine Mother Earth wept and dried her tears. Her light once again kissed the mountaintops, the oceans, the forests, her plants and animals, and every living thing that had survived. *"Good luck, my children, good luck."* Finally, she whispered to the creatures of the land and sea that survived, *"I love you, dear ones. Know this—it was not your fault."*

For several minutes, the room was silent as each person dealt with their grief. Veronica and Lisa grabbed each other, hearts shattered, and wept.

CHAPTER 83

This time, it was Jake who interrupted. "Yeshua, please, we must not forget those of profound goodness, those who have lived lives of service to man and beast, striving for authentic spiritual growth, taking radical action to integrate the light and the dark and to love unconditionally and compassionately. And those who dedicated their lives to preserving nature, the animals, and the beauty of this planet."

Yeshua spoke with great sincerity and compassion. "Each person will have the option of tasting their divinity. How that plays out is determined by the energetic frequencies they align with. That is why it is important to choose those who are uplifting and loving to occupy your inner circle. As my dear friend and the master teacher Paramahansa Yogananda once said, 'Environment is stronger than will.' Know his message to be the truth.

"Those who shift their energy through internal inquiry will align with higher realms of consciousness and have the opportunity to move into exalted states of awareness. They hold the key to their pure essence without contrast, choosing to reside in physical or non-physical form.

On this earth plane, you needed to discover what you didn't want in order to know what you did want. This duality will no longer be necessary. You will be realized and evolve without contrast. The high frequency of love through the spiritual heart will be your guide."

Again, Yeshua raised his hands, and the hologram showed a new world being born: pristine waterfalls, rich dark earth, light shining across unpolluted waters, and a rich spectrum of brilliant colors far more intense than Mother Earth. The sky showed planets closer than ever seen before, and plant life looked alive as it vibrated and shimmered with light. Animals of every kind had also made the evolutionary journey.

The holograms revealed the story of the arrival of those who had transitioned. It appeared to be a funnel of light, a birth canal that their experiences with the dark night of the soul had readied them for, to be birthed into this profoundly wondrous world. Luminous beings stood in harmony, in a realm of peace, beauty, and joy, as the new co-creators for this chapter of humanity's story. Others agreed to stay on the earth plane resonating at higher vibrational golden frequencies to assist those remaining.

As the hologram dissipated, the cries were no longer of sorrow but of joy. All those in the room started talking at once, and several started chanting. Soon, all the rest joined in.

"Brother," Ruth questioned with concern, "how many will take this leap of faith seriously and transition into the new world?"

"In humanity's present state, only eighteen percent," Yeshua answered, with great sadness filling his eyes.

"How many are possible?" Ruth pushed further, with new hope. José, sitting next to her, nodded in agreement, as he was about to ask the same question.

"If consciousness radically changes immediately, and love, empathy, generosity, gratitude, prayer, and meditation become the predominant factors in people's lives, forty-four percent will make the transition. The process will not be simple, as humanity tends to wait until it is too late for change. Each person must understand that heaven resides within their divine hearts and souls, and they must let go of any religious or social beliefs that have kept them separate from their brothers and sisters of all walks of life.

"It is their false belief of separateness that has bound them to the limitations and control of the mind. The egocentric mind is the false god, and believing in their thoughts instead of heart guidance is what will cause their destruction. The hierarchy of the world churches and governments that have kept humankind intentionally in the dark will not make the transition. It is their fate to experience what is out of their control, as they have imprisoned hundreds of millions for thousands of years and are the root of the destruction of this world. If they think they will escape in their secret underground shelters, or on a flight to Mars, or any other planet through quantum white wells, they are wrong."

Aaron whispered to Ben, "It's coming up again, the quantum white wells we have both dreamt of."

Ben turned to Aaron and nodded. "Yeah, I caught that too."

"How do we start bringing awareness and the urgency of the situation to those who will listen?" Luke probed.

"Humanity must rediscover the traditional wisdom found in all ancient knowledge. Know this, the rulers of darkness will not allow this to happen without a fierce struggle. They know they will perish, so their motive is to take as many as possible with them. No man or woman can stand on the sidelines and remain neutral. The question will be, will they rise to the enormous challenges of our time with the collective shadow of the dark ego pushing back before the planet undergoes this apocalyptic destruction?"

Aaron stood. "Lord, how can we assist people to awaken?"

"People don't awaken," Yeshua replied. "Consciousness sprouts from the remembrance of one's original self. That is what awakens. Awakening is a by-product of the diminishing ego. It is a falling away of the controlling aspects of the mind—either through spiritual practices, profound suffering, or a combination of the two—that weakens the egocentric mind. Consciousness happens through you. It is not something that happens to you, or by you."

The question lingered on the mind of each of them. How many would step up to a new way of being? How many would heed the call of this last opportunity seriously enough to make the drastic changes needed to transition into the new world? They did not have the answer, but each knew they would do their best to assist as many as possible.

With that, Yeshua paused and offered one more ray of hope. "We may be in a global dark night, but I will share a secret. It's a simple one but often overlooked—the power and high resonance of gratitude, joy and a smile. Each one is humble yet the most profound energies, as they align with that of God. The Buddha always had a smile on his face because his out-breath in meditation was a smile. I suggest you remain here as a group and try it."

He then turned to Angelina and, taking her hand, led her away.

CHAPTER 84

As Angelina walked through the stone entry to a living room adjoined to Yeshua's suite, the color drained from her face. She caught her breath, and rushing forward, she reached her arms out to embrace Sarah. "*Ma fille bien-aimée!*" Speaking in French, Angelina continued, "I wore you as I did your father and brothers, like a garment upon my soul. I have never left you, even though this life was one of forgetting the past to fulfill a prophecy. There were dreams of faces I did not know and flashes that tugged at my heart I did not understand until now."

Beside herself with happiness, Angelina said, "In a vision, I saw you looking at me with questioning eyes many years ago as I sat peering into my pond, and once again not long ago. But you did not recognize me, nor I you. Nevertheless, I knew you were important to me."

Angelina's speech reflected how overwhelmed she was by the mystery of how it was possible that she was holding Sarah in her arms. Her tears ran freely down her face, blurring her vision, but all she could feel was the profound love that filled her heart.

When Yeshua first walked through the door holding Angelina's hand, Sarah had let out a gasp and covered her hands to her mouth before Yeshua could speak a word.

Although Sarah acknowledged that her mother looked different than she had but days before, or more accurately, two thousand years ago, before she had parted the veil and stepped through time, Sarah recognized this woman called mother the moment she set eyes on her, even without Angelina adorned in her favorite sapphire-blue cloak.

Sarah was still confused and perplexed at the unplanned events that she knew were a part of the divine play. She did not understand the hows of transcending time, even though her father tried to explain it to her the evening before. All she knew was that she was in a strange land with the two people she loved and trusted above all others.

Her heart grieved after hearing the events transpiring on the planet that her father spoke of a night past. Two thousand years may have ensued, but it was still a world where its desire for power through greed and dishonesty had not subsided. How could humanity have learned so little from past mistakes and horrors, about the importance of loving each other as themselves? Did they not understand how they and all of humankind benefits from kindness and equality? Were her father's teachings and his life, as well as all the great prophets of the past, pointless? So many opportunities to make the right choices were missed each day.

Sarah had questioned her father with sorrow until the morning sun shone brightly through the windows and it was time for Yeshua to meet his guests.

Speaking French, Sarah released herself from her mother's hold and took Yeshua's hand, holding it to her heart. "Father, the world is in a grave state, but my being here is a miracle. I need to believe anything is possible. I will not question the workings of God, but I want to hold on to the possibility that the people on this planet still have time to change before the upcoming shifts upon the earth."

Yeshua looked deeply into her eyes and saw the goodness of her soul. He spoke in a hushed voice. "Then you shall stay to assist us. Perhaps it was God who sent you through a white portal, and it was not solely your will. Being that you can discern the difference between those who will never be satisfied and have no desire to hear, and those who are truthful seekers, you will know who not to waste your precious breath on."

Taking her face in his hands and looking into Sarah's eyes, Yeshua spoke again. "You see what others cannot and listen with ears that know the authentic truth. Your love for humanity and your nonattachment to personal gain guides you. Therefore, you are capable of understanding a person driven by wrongful beliefs that possessions or power will bring them love and happiness. For never will they know true joy and the power of this moment."

Silence hung between them, each left to their emotions of the approaching world events. Finally, Sarah picked up the thread from where Yeshua left off. "Yes, father, I understand. They cannot see the gift of this moment, nor the abundance of wisdom that each shadow within their being also carries the light, as they are too busy looking and chasing illusions yonder. They know not that they are already the light of God, like a wave looking to the sandy shore or the jagged rocks wondering where the ocean is."

Gazing sorrowfully back into her father's eyes, Sarah proclaimed, "But, my dear father, I must try."

As Yeshua rested his hand upon her forehead, he spoke the words, "Your heart is pure. Henceforth, you shall speak in tongues to ease your journey."

Angelina stepped forward and embraced Sarah. She began stroking her daughter's long, dark hair. "You must remember, darling Sarah, that there will be many who dispute what you share, and also those claiming to be channeling God's voice who are only attuning to the astral world.

Most are beings who are stuck between worlds and never ascended. They are of limited understanding coming from the filters of the channelers' flawed beliefs. Many will try to claim you wrong or false—be not discouraged, pay them no mind. Bless them and move on."

"Thank you, beloved mother. Although I wish to travel with you or father, I will travel alone if it is the most effective way to reach more souls." Sarah spoke with the strength and assuredness of a person who had absolute trust in life, humanity, and her connection to the infinite.

"Guidance will reveal that soon enough, Sarah, but for now, come to meet those you have not. It is they who have stood by your mother and me for over two thousand years," Yeshua said, catching Angelina's look of curiosity that flashed across her face.

"Yes, Angelina, our friends are already wondering, '*What will transpire next?*'" Yeshua answered her unspoken thoughts as he gently kissed her forehead with a mischievous grin and flashes of light emanating from his eyes. "It's time for them to meet the elementals—devas, nature spirits, fairies, flower spirits, and more. For they have much they would like to share. Perhaps Jake can assist," Yeshua said with a wink, "as he has a stolen manuscript from the Vatican that speaks of the angels of air, water, fire, earth, and aether or void, which they would like back. This event is the battle for survival for every living thing upon this planet, seen and unseen."

Seeing the look of disbelief on Angelina's face, Yeshua's laughter echoed off the stone walls. "Aw, did you think the stories were only fairy tales consisting of imaginary beings? And the powerful gods and goddesses of mythology were created only through pure imagination?"

Angelina opened her mouth to speak, but her voice produced no sound.

"Why, was it not you who trained in the arts of the revered and guarded mystical teachings of the priestess in ancient Egypt?" Yeshua asked, looking directly into Angelina's eyes.

With Yeshua's last remark, the final veils fell away. Angelina watched in astonishment and reverence as her life as a temple priestess, going through the rigorous preparation of initiation, was presented to her.

Reaching out his hand, Yeshua lovingly stated, "Angelina, come, it is time for us to join the others. My time is falling short."

Angelina swallowed hard and barely held back her tears. She took Sarah's hand firmly in hers as they walked through the stone arches, knowing there was no turning back for any of them.

"Yeshua," Angelina, still puzzled, inquired.

"Yes, my love?"

"Why does Jake have a stolen copy of a manuscript from the Vatican?"

"Why shouldn't he? He wrote it. It may have been two thousand years ago, but his ownership shouldn't expire because of time," Yeshua said with a smile. "Besides, he is not happy that his great work was suppressed from humanity."

CHAPTER 85

As Yeshua, Angelina, and Sarah entered the hall, Yeshua raised his hand to silence the room. It was unnecessary. The moment Sarah was spotted, several mouths fell open. She was the spitting image of Yeshua—the Yeshua who was their teacher two thousand years prior.

"My beloved friends, this is Angelina's and my daughter, Sarah. She has joined us from France," Yeshua announced as he put his arm around her. "She traveled from the past through a time portal early this morning and was brought to me by Andrew, Jazz, Lisa, and Jake, for which I am immensely grateful." Yeshua nodded to them before continuing, "The particulars are not something I will go into detail about, but I want to clarify that she is not savvy to the twenty-first century. She has come to assist with the awakening of humanity. Please, look out for her on my behalf."

"Without question," Jake spoke for the group.

Sarah walked up to José, who had tears streaming down his face. She crouched down to where he was sitting on a meditation bench and put her hand on his face. "Sweet Balthazar, I would remember you regardless of your form. You were an astronomer and one of the three magi who followed the stars to celebrate my father's birth. You came to France as an old man when I was a young child. When you departed, I was heartbroken."

José reached out and hugged her as though she were his lost daughter. "I didn't believe my heart could be any fuller, but now I see that is untrue."

Luke stammered, "What? An astronomer? No wonder we instantly connected."

Yeshua reached his arms out to Rose, his earth mother. "Come, your grandmother is with us."

Sarah rushed to her and wrapped her arms around her grandmother as she spoke. "I knew you heard my prayers and were watching me, blessed *grand-mère*. I felt your pink light surrounding me last night."

"Yes, my darling," Rose affirmed. "I heard your prayers asking for protection."

Rose returned Sarah's embrace and kissed her repeatedly. "The color of my skin didn't fool you even for a moment, did it, my precious granddaughter?"

"No, as with you, we are all equal and the same in the eyes of our Creator. It is the soul alone that speaks. That is all I felt and saw," Sarah responded with great love.

"My god, this is mind-bending," Veronica stammered.

"I have no other word," Aaron seconded.

The moment Yeshua left with Angelina, Lisa explained to Veronica and Tyler the events that had transpired since meeting Sarah early in the morning. But even she would never have guessed José had also been Balthazar. *But then, why would I? I never met him in that lifetime.*

When the room settled, Yeshua nodded to Lisa and Veronica.

Both stood up to collect a tray of holy oils and herbs. Now all eyes were on Lisa and Veronica as they approached Angelina and Rose, offering them the elegant golden alabaster tray holding the vessels of holy oils.

Angelina looked questioningly at both ladies and then turned her gaze towards Yeshua.

Yeshua smiled. "I requested the sacred oils that you and mother used to anoint me twenty centuries ago in Bethany. It appears Veronica's family still has access to the rarest and purest sources."

Rose smiled and stepped aside to allow Angelina to perform the sacred ritual she had used two millennia ago on Yeshua, but this time for each of those in attendance.

Angelina's hands covered her face. She was too moved to say anything but shed silent tears.

Yeshua took her face in his and kissed both eyes. "I know how painful the church's exclusion and distortion of your wisdom, purity, and love was for you. And through it all, I held you in the vast sacred space within my heart. It was you who taught me the power of profound human and divine love. And without your presence in my life, I would never have achieved the transformation through the divine union of masculine and feminine power within myself. I needed John the Baptist for his fierce strength, but you taught me how to love without restrictions, and through it, I discovered profound peace. Your dedication to me was unceasing, even throughout all the heartbreak. I am eternally grateful."

Lisa embraced Angelina, "Come, my dear friend, it is time to let the past go and create the world we were meant to embody."

Angelina wiped her tears and reached for the tray that Veronica was now presenting to her, to anoint Yeshua once again.

"Rest them there," Yeshua said as he pointed to the end of the bench.

Angelina set them down and motioned for Yeshua to sit beside them. Instead, he gently guided her to sit next to the oils. "It is I who now wishes to anoint you, my beloved. Far too long has your importance been ignored."

Lisa's and Veronica's eyes glistened as they beamed at each other and then, catching Angelina's eyes, nodded their heads in approval.

With that began a sacred ritual of loving tenderness. Yeshua recited prayers from ancient times—some in Sanskrit, some in ancient Aramaic, and others in Coptic and ancient Greek.

It was exalted poetry. The room began to vibrate with a mystifying and profoundly enchanting resonance that resembled the heavenly choir. No one moved, nor wanted it to stop. But finally, there was silence, a soundless void like no other, where all worlds and all things meshed.

Yeshua then motioned to all those present in the hall to come forth one by one. He anointed each one of them with such gentleness and love. When the ritual was complete, a silence encased them in bliss for hours.

The remainder of the day transpired with both sober and gratifying sharing—brainstorming strategies and deciding on partnerships and who would be playing each role. Finally, evening found them exhausted, and little had been eaten from the grand dining table laden with food. Knowing their time together was growing short, they retired for the night, for what they desired most was to rest before their final time together as a group concluded.

CHAPTER 86

That evening, once Jazz and Andrew had returned to their room, all Jazz could think about was getting some sleep and the profundity of the events that had taken place in a matter of weeks.

Dropping their clothes in a heap on the floor, they both climbed into bed.

With Jazz snug in his arms, Andrew whispered, "Hey, beautiful, I know that this has been an intense time, but I wouldn't mind getting some lessons in the 'divine lovemaking and its true glory' that you mentioned at dinner the night we were in London."

"Seriously! That is what you are thinking about as the world is on the brink of destruction?" Jazz exclaimed sternly as she lifted her body off of Andrew's chest.

Startled, Andrew replied in defense, "You're asking a guy that question?" Then he saw the smile on her lips and knew, once again, she had him pegged. "Just because I am English doesn't mean I take everything seriously! You just caught me off guard. You're a rat!"

"Okay, lesson one . . ." Jazz's voice trailed off as they overheard groans and rhythmic tapping against their adjoining wall.

Andrew stopped to listen. "You have got to be kidding, what a buzzkill! That's Jake and Lisa's room. What are these walls made of, cardboard?"

Jazz started laughing. "Revision to lesson one, begin this practice of sacred lovemaking at home!"

They both laughed so hard that the tapping stopped and they heard a knock on the wall.

Jazz shouted out, still giggling, "Yes, we can hear you."

In response, they could hear the laughter from Jake and Lisa through the walls.

Moments later, there was a knock on Andrew and Jazz's door. When Andrew opened it, Jake stood there smiling. "Well it is obvious that we are all awake and need to move some energy, so let's go out on the town since lovemaking is out of the question. Oh, and the laughter, thanks for wrecking a romantic moment with a goddess of the forest."

"Pleasure," Andrew replied, smiling.

Just then, Lisa walked up behind Jake and added with a shy grin, "Yeah, we are not really into group sex. So let's hit the town and pretend that didn't happen."

Now in a robe and sticking her head out from under Andrew's arm that was holding the door open, Jazz chuckled. "That would explain the rose petals in Lisa's hair."

"Oh, how embarrassing," Lisa replied, turning pink and brushing the top of her head with her hand as rose petals floated to the floor.

The door across the hall cracked open, and Tyler stuck his head out. "Hey, we can't sleep either. Can we come?"

"My word," Jazz said, "I'm sure glad we could hear Lisa and Jake or the whole floor might have been up taking notes on the fine points of sacred lovemaking that Andrew was inquiring about."

The night was beautiful, the air fresh and the mood uplifting. The six of them strolled down the street and spotted Akbar, Aaron, Tony, and Ben, who were about to walk into a local restaurant and bar. "Looks like we aren't the only ones who can't sleep," Jake called out as he lifted his arm to wave.

"Hey, you guys, want to join us?" Aaron answered back.

Jake looked to the group and noted they were all nodding yes. "That would be great," he called out.

Veronica let out a sigh of relief.

"What was that about?" Tyler inquired.

"I am happy to see them. They will keep things light," Veronica replied, "and right now, I feel we could all use a bit of playfulness!"

CHAPTER 87

As Angelina's hand moved to clutch her chest, the ring Yeshua had given her caught the early morning's light and shot beams towards Jake, yet none spoke. Jake could see that all six women were also profoundly moved by Yeshua's words describing the potential of the new world they would assist in creating. He wished more of humankind could be saved and still clung to the possibility of Yeshua revealing his true self to the world. Jake inwardly sighed, feeling a bit disappointed that he hadn't been as trusting of Source as they had proven.

Breathing deeply, Yeshua hesitated a moment, closing his eyes and turning his head upward, allowing the sunlight to bathe his face.

Angelina couldn't help but think how strikingly beautiful he was. This was an inner beauty that surpassed anything humanly possible.

Jake knew what was coming soon, and he didn't know how to process the wave of despair that suddenly overtook him, which he could not suppress. He was trying to regain control and keep his mind clear. Now was not the time to lose himself in the emotions that were trying to choke his vision and his ability to speak. Pressing his fingers hard against the inner corners of his eyes, he thought, *No tears, not now.*

Lowering his voice, Jake looked down at his feet, avoiding the profoundly compassionate eyes staring directly at him, or more accurately, through him. "Please, Yeshua, my friend, for the love of God, don't leave us. Just perform a few miracles, and then people will realize who you are and make the necessary changes in their lives. Think of how many would be saved from this impending chaos. Mankind deserves another chance."

But in his heart, he felt humanity deserved nothing of the sort, as most had continued to live in anger, fear, greed, competitiveness, and hatred since his friend had left more than two thousand years before.

Jake steadied himself, softened his voice, and made one last plea: "Yeshua, I beg you, for the love of God . . ."

Yeshua spoke compassionately, in answer to Jake's plea. A deep sadness that Jake had never heard filled his friend's voice. "Jake, I have been doing miracles for thousands of years. It won't change anything. Miracles acted as a catalyst for me to attract people to come and listen, as it often seemed to be the only way to get humanity's attention. Not this time, my friend, as many have followed me for the wrong reasons. They wanted someone else to save them and weren't willing to do their part, nor understand that it is they who is their savior.

"They, too, were given the opportunity to become Christed, an anointed one, as I had." Yeshua looked sweetly at Angelina, Sarah, Rose, Ruth, Jazz, Veronica, and Lisa, all who were sitting closest to him on large boulders, before continuing. "They wanted me to perform miracles, instead of taking responsibility for their own thoughts and actions that originally brought about the cause of their unhappiness or illness. I gave them the tools to explore the reasons for their suffering, giving them the opportunity to choose differently."

Yeshua paused long enough to allow his words to penetrate before continuing. "I showed people by example what they were capable of doing, that they, too, could perform miracles. The message was clear. I was empowering them to take responsibility for their own lives and not to believe themselves to be victims of life but capable of living the life they longed to experience.

"I was not their savior—they were. I was their loving friend, brother, and guide. All they needed to do was take the time to silence their minds, go into the quietude of their eternal hearts, and realize they were not these bodies but so much greater. The divine soul is the gateway. It is the discovery of the Christos, the Christed self within their own heart of hearts, the sacred heart. The birth canal and gateway to Source."

As Yeshua continued, his voice softened. There was a mournfulness that took Jake by surprise, almost crushing him. "They came for a show, the show of magic and miracles, and I was the star of that show. That is not what I came to accomplish. Nor was it ever my wish that my words be distorted to enslave others instead of freeing them.

"I came to show the way, to save humanity not from others but from themselves. Every antidote resides within, yet most keep searching outside themselves for the answers. And I will say it again—it is no different than the wave looking to the shore for the ocean when, all along, it is one with it.

"Can you not present yourself as the long-awaited savior?" Luke optimistically inquired.

"I cannot be their savior, even if I wanted to, which I do not. I would rob each person of their divinity and the satisfaction in the gift of discovering their transcendent self. Although, if they are ready to claim their true God-given power through the understanding of their connection to the divine, they will find that the 'Second Coming' meant only one thing—the savior they wait for is themselves. The Christed within, the doorway to their Creator, is waiting patiently for them to open the inner chamber within their sacred hearts."

Yeshua gazed somewhere far in the distance as he continued. "Christians expect me to come back looking like their statues and holy pictures on a white cloud or rays of light. They expect me to behave as their Bible reads. They expect me to perform miracles, but this can't be.

"As I have mentioned before, many of my words were misconstrued and, even more, were purposely twisted to control others. Some were unintentional altered by unlearned men, others by the church deliberately removing or burning anything that suggested self-liberation to control humanity."

Tyler broke his silence, trying to keep the desperation and emotion out of his voice. "You could set people straight, assist in rewriting the Bible to contain what is true."

Yeshua's look told Tyler what he already knew. He was talking nonsense. He was trying to stall Yeshua's departure, but it was too late—time had run out.

There was a gentle stillness that only early morn could bring. Ordinarily, Jake loved these hours as the earth was awakening and everything was fresh with promise, but not today. Ever since Yeshua had informed the group that he would not be staying to assist in the transition between worlds, Jake felt he was internally choking from the pressure within his chest, and unable to stop it.

"I, along with many other awakened souls and prophets of all beliefs, have shared some simple yet profound truths. There is no point in giving humankind more. The messages from thousands of years ago still apply today—love, compassion, and forgiveness, and to see every person as oneself. Everything is a facet of God and not separate from that which created it.

"People do not understand that others are but a reflection of themselves, as there is nothing outside of themselves except the belief in the mirror of the mind. It is akin to cells within the body that are fighting with each other, believing they are separate, yet they are only killing themselves. People fighting among themselves is no different from destroying the body of God.

"To love thy neighbor as thyself, one must understand the deeper truth. That one cannot love another until they radically love themselves. Love thyself, as there is no 'other.' When one learns to deeply love, they discover who they are, and that is when they will embody non-duality.

"Love each person as God does, for you are the stars God pulled from her womb and cast upon this earth to glory in herself like a dance upon the heavens."

A far-off look preoccupied Yeshua for several minutes as though he was viewing the outcome of the future. He turned to Jake and posed a question. "Jake, if I stayed as you proposed, and I revealed myself to the people, to the church, it wouldn't be the Jews who would crucify me. It would be the Christians. They would call me blasphemous, the devil, the Antichrist, and I would be hunted like an animal. Every breath I took, and every word I spoke, would be challenged. It would be one more external distraction."

Angelina held Yeshua's hand tightly as he turned his gaze to her. "Krishna, Moses, Ramana Maharshi, Anandamayi Ma, Gandhi, Buddha, Pocahontas, and even Martin Luther King, who—unbeknown to most—was a holy man. Humanity has come to know these and many more as saints who battled these same demons to gain passage into their authentic selves. If humankind wants this knowing and inner peace, they must start looking inside themselves for the answers—it is time to address the world they have created from their thoughts and beliefs."

"You could compel them to see the truth—"

Before Ben's words finished, Yeshua's faraway look was replaced by his direct gaze, with one brow lifted. Yeshua repeated Ben's words. "Compel them to see? I would not, and could not, interfere with the laws of human free will. Not even our Creator will do that."

Jake knew what Yeshua said was valid. He had always known that, but he interjected, "Please, we beg you, don't leave, or at least promise to come back soon!"

"It would likely be too late. Regardless, do you think humanity would recognize me this time or anytime?" Yeshua's voice challenged Jake.

Yeshua removed his hand from Angelina's and placed it on Jake's shoulder. Looking directly into his eyes, Jake could see the expression he had come to love; a twinkle of amusement was emanating from his eyes.

"By the way, Jake, this wasn't the first time I came back. I have walked the earth hundreds of times since my crucifixion, and mankind has discovered hundreds of ways to kill me ever since."

Jake's mouth hung open.

"Listen carefully, my cherished friend, and all of you. I have been both male and female. I have been the beggar lying on the street, and the whore in the alley. I have been the minister's wife who was abused by the man who stood in front of others and called them sinners, a nun and a priest forced into silence, and the orphan child no one wanted.

"Those who have professed their love for me the most earnestly were often those who treated me the cruelest. To them, I have been a servant, or an abused employee. Or when I was lying on the streets, they often walked around me or even kicked me. Never did they look into my eyes with any love or kindness, including the life of being declared a witch. I was burned at the stake for miracles deemed the devil's magic by the church that supposedly represented me. That was the life I cured illness with the oils of flowers and herbs. Natural healing was far too threatening to the church. They wanted to be the healers by charging fees and forcing others to be subservient and repent."

Jake's shock took the wind out of him. Unable to speak, he just shook his head as the tears welled up.

CHAPTER 88

Yeshua had begun preparing for bed when he heard footsteps abruptly stop outside his door. Unhurriedly, he answered the aggressive knocking. It was too late for a social visit, and he already knew it wasn't one of his beloved and faithful friends.

"At some point this was inevitable, so there is no point putting it off," Yeshua said, speaking out loud to himself as he opened the door.

Staring kindly at the two stern faces scowling at him, Yeshua asked before they could speak, "Is there not already enough blood dripping from your hands and that of your church?"

"You can come quietly or forcefully, but either way, you will be coming with us," threatened the larger of the two.

"There is no need for force. I was expecting you. Let me grab my coat."

"No. No tricks, just come with us," snapped the snarling face. "And if you attempt anything, it will be your friends who pay."

Passing the hotel lobby, Yeshua whispered as he looked back, "Be well, my dear friends. I know you will take care of each other," before reluctantly stepping into the darkness of night, where a thug of a man dressed in dark clothes pushed him into the awaiting car before speeding off.

They drove for some time before arriving at an airport, where a private jet was waiting on the landing strip.

"Get out," the harsh voice commanded.

As Yeshua stepped onto the tarmac, his captor pushed him towards the steps of the jet. "Get on."

"I came without resistance. There is no need for you to act barbaric," Yeshua announced as he walked up the steps and into the plane.

When they landed in Rome, Yeshua was taken by car to their final destination. Heading through numerous gated entries, Yeshua ascertained that he would not be leaving alive. Otherwise, he would be blindfolded. "Has darkness also claimed your souls?" he asked his captors.

"Quiet," hissed the driver.

The car stopped in an alley, and the man beside him barked, "Get out!"

Escorted down a long passageway, Yeshua was shoved into a dark room lit only by the light of the quarter moon coming through the barred windows. He glanced out to see a stone wall just beyond. A loud click of the wooden door was followed by the sound of an iron bolt thrust into place behind him.

"God, is this necessary?" Yeshua questioned as he raised his arms and grasped the bars before him before lowering himself to sit on the stone floor. Crossing his legs and breathing deeply, he quickly went into a state of samadhi, where the veils between light and darkness vanished, and a great peace overcame him.

It was sometime later before he heard the iron bolt slide back and the door open. "Come with us without delay," the familiar harsh voice commanded.

His captor shoved him through the dimly lit hallway and into a stone passageway where the light shone brightly from the other side of the sizable paneled door sitting ajar. They stepped into an ostentatious gilded room filled with frescos of saints, and the leaders of the church were dressed in elegant finery as they blessed the poor in rags on the streets from the safety of their carriages or balconies.

Before Yeshua sat a council of twelve, equally elaborately dressed and jeweled as those of popes, cardinals, and archbishops, lining the walls.

"I see by the look in your eyes, you have already tried and convicted me," Yeshua said without malice or emotion.

For over an hour, the council ridiculed and taunted Yeshua. Retorted was every question he answered with allegations of him being an imposter or a conspirator working with Satan. The committee gave him the ultimatum of performing miracles to prove himself to be the savior, and his refusal furthered angered them.

"I never said I was your savior. It is you who are responsible for saving yourselves. And whether I performed miracles or not, which I won't, you would discredit them as Satan's work. You have refused me an audience with your pope. And we all know he is aware of my presence and the events that are taking place. Therefore, I see no point for further conversation." Yeshua spoke without contempt.

A cardinal sitting in the center of the twelve stood and warned Yeshua, "I advise you to remain silent until questioned!"

Yeshua disregarded the directive. "You have discredited and condemned me with this mock trial. An unappeasable hunger for power drives you and holds the reins that control the decisions that affected over a billion Catholics. And it is you before me who hold my life in your hands, as you have many times since my original crucifixion, so enough pretense."

The now red-faced cardinal bellowed, "Anyone who can speak in this imposter's favor, let him come forward and plead on his behalf."

But nothing was brought forward in his favor. No one else was present except two guards, who remained silent with eyes transfixed on opposite walls.

"Two thousand years ago, it was Pontius Pilate who decided on my trial and crucifixion. Like you, it was those who feared me in their lust and obsession for power who crucified me. Still, they killed me not. It was made to appear to them that way. Because of both Mary's mastery of herbs and sacred oils, and my training in breathless states, I was resurrected and taken to France. Now you discredit and condemn me after this mockery of a trial. You may kill me and stain your hands with my blood, as you have many times since your documented biblical text, but you cannot kill what is the Spirit of God."

They unanimously sentenced him to death, debating whether they should turn him over to religious extremists to wash their hands of his blood. A verdict was reached, and the guards were summoned to return Yeshua to his cell.

"How do they intend to dispose of me this time?" Yeshua inquired to the guards pushing him into the dark cell.

"If you were the true Jesus Christ, you would perform miracles to save yourself!" bellowed his captor. With that, a dagger appeared from under the guard's cloak.

Yeshua's final words reverberated throughout the Vatican: "I shall live again. You may kill my body, damn and release my soul, but you don't stand a chance against my love." *

Moments later, lightning flashed, thunder cracked and the earth rumbled and shook at the exact moment of Yeshua's death.

---

* inspired by Robbie Robertson: Ghost Dance "You may kill my body, damn my soul, but you don't stand a chance against my love."

CHAPTER 89

"For God's sake, give them their proof. Flatten them if you have to. Just get out of there!" Jake yelled into the dark room.

Startled awake, Lisa sat up and exclaimed, "Jake, what's wrong?"

Jake bolted out of bed. He began pounding his fist against the bathroom wall. "My god, why does this have to be so?"

Tears filled his eyes.

"It was just a nightmare, my love," Lisa reassuringly informed him as she slipped out of bed and came up behind him. Wrapping her arms around him, she rested her head on his back and felt the sweat covering his body as he cried out, "Oh god, oh god, he was right. Yeshua tried to warn me that it was pointless to reveal himself to humanity. I saw how they would kill him if he stayed."

Lisa held Jake tighter and let him cry, all the while holding back her tears. It was her turn to be strong for the man she loved.

Finally, Jake turned to face Lisa. He held her face in his hands and spoke softly and painfully, "He has to leave."

"I know," Lisa said, looking into his grief-stricken eyes as she stroked his face. Peering intensely into his eyes, she lovingly whispered, "Now come back to bed, my love. There is much to accomplish before Yeshua departs."

CHAPTER 90

Before first light, Yeshua joined the others in meditation. When the celestial music given to Akbar by a Buddhist monk came to an end, they opened their eyes. It was evident by the profound peace that permeated the room how powerful this group was.

Yeshua began sharing the news about the final steps to assist humanity through this global dark night of the soul. After two hours of discussion, he added, "It is important to protect yourselves and those who will listen with divine light, as you will be under attack from any negative or dark forces. The mantras and prayers you use are potent. They will be kept safe. Call on Divine Mother or me for our shields of light whenever needed.

"What I want to stress is not to interfere with a person's right to free will, nor share or create modalities that require the mind. Make it simple. The egocentric mind has taken over the spirit. I have outlined ideas that each of your consciousness surpasses in, and I will present those packets before I depart. Now is not the time. Most of this information you already know in every cell of your being, so no sense dwelling on the obvious.

"Remind humanity that it is the simplest modalities that connect them to the divine. Take them into the journey of joy—to express and be joyous is excellent protection from darkness and disease.

"Surrender to divine truth—to be in the space of complete surrender and trust is to allow God to intervene and guide on your behalf.

"Trust—you cannot know the larger picture, although God does. Follow the energy of sacred love.

"Remember, *love* is a verb—show and express it without manipulation or expectation. Otherwise, it holds no positivity. Pure loving energy releases toxins and raises one's energetic field. That is the reward. All forms of uplifting sacred dance and music also raise our frequencies. Forget the technique. Allow the natural rhythm of the divine self to tap into Source energy.

"Since the dawn of human civilization, dance has been an essential part of living. All movement that enhances spiritual experiences is what is urgently needed. Qigong, Tonglen, Tai chi, Native American Ghost Dance, whirling dervishes, ecstatic dance, Indian dance, and so forth are all forms of movement that is inspirational.

"Address the crisis we are facing in this evolutionary cycle and the fact that there is no time left to wait another moment. Humanity's energy is scattered because each person has too many choices and focuses on the next new modality looking for the ultimate solution or fix instead of the inner stillness without mind. They are deeply asleep bound in the lie of a monetary system that reduces them to numbered slaves. Humanity is designed under a Universal system with internal instructions where everything needed comes effortlessly. Sadly, most of humanity bought into the fear games of the those desiring power and control. Maximum trust in one's own Being overcomes all challenges.

"For those who are ready to hear, I encourage them to seek that which is lasting and not what is temporal, which will quickly fade. Offer, to those who are capable of understanding, the significance of becoming the witness to who is speaking within themselves—is it the person, the mind, or the absolute? To establish one's focus on the 'I Am' without history is to know the peaceful and gracious unfolding of life.

"It is the attachment to being right, or a belief in the past or future, instead of the most direct solution, which is to know the self without a story, that keeps humanity stuck. Catch the mind each time it engages in its narrative of excuses, projections, or beliefs. Ignore what is being spoken about, and instead ask the question, 'Who is speaking?' The 'I' was the firstborn and over time became comfortable believing itself to be the person. This misnomer must evaporate to remember one's original purpose of creation.

"Those who are searching for sensationalism and mystical experiences are often looking for validation from themselves or others and missing the mark. Sensational experiences are the reward of the mind, and how it maintains control. When the person becomes the peaceful observer, they settle into their true 'I Am' self, and life unfolds effortlessly without drama. They no longer search for spiritual experiences, nor try to fix or change anything. Instead, they pay attention to the moment and allow whatever is occurring to come into natural alignment. Observe the sense of divine presence unfolding without the urge to attempt to describe this wordless state of creation."

Angelina was aware of the challenges before them. But glancing around the room at this incredible group of sages and ancient souls, she knew it was possible.

"Meditation, open heart, and mindfulness are the most powerful tools to teach. It allows humanity to connect with their divine self and stay centered regardless of the chaos occurring around them or in their lives. Avoid fancy or complex meditations. That only give the mind a chance to interfere, create lists, and criticize. This core peace within is the natural state of our being. Teach people how to breathe fully into the stillness of their essence to assist with mindfulness, and how to remain centered through the little upsets in life. Soon they will find that centered peacefulness even when their life in the outer world seems to be falling apart."

Yeshua paused to reflect and then continued. "Remember, contrast is what allows humanity to see their light. Light cannot exist without darkness. Fearlessly go into the shadows within, for that is where the most significant gifts hide. There is also an entire angelic realm waiting to be of service to humanity, but one must ask for help and then be willing to surrender to the outcome. One doesn't need to know how to help themselves. They only need to be respectful to the invisible ones who are there to serve. Talk to them as a loving friend, and allow them to do their job. Please include nature when at all possible. Her beauty creates a high resonance that raises consciousness. She opens her heart and heals without one's asking.

"Surrender to your highest aspect of divine self, and trust the answers that come from your sacred heart. These are the most powerful avenues to experience a life of high-frequency spiritual awareness—and the most difficult. Trust, and know you are loved beyond your imagination. This planet is filled with countless miracles that go unnoticed each day. When I have parted, I want all of you to share stories of seemingly impossible situations that resolved themselves effortlessly once you fully surrendered and turned the situation over to God."

Every head nodded in agreement.

"Accuse no one. What humanity blames another for is a shadow within themselves. Teach my beloveds to pause before the desire to project outwardly robs them of the internal reflection begging to be healed.

"Aaron," Yeshua said, glancing in his direction, "I would like you to start collecting these stories. Humanity forgets so easily even when the miraculous happens to them. Start with your experiences, which include the angel of light in Ruth's bedroom, saying '777,' or your fall from the fifty-foot cliff and the angels who spoke to you on the way down, before you hit the sand."

"Oh yeah! Mind twisting!" Aaron replied. "How seconds become lifetimes!"

"Ask Lisa about the heavenly choir. Ben, the condo in Mexico. Veronica, the nature spirits. Sarah's arrival through the tear in time,

Britt having only thirty-six dollars to her name and the results from fully letting go, Angelina's two near-death experiences on freeways, and so on.

"Remind humanity they are not alone, and to discover the joy waiting in each moment! Dance, chant, play, write poetry, sing, smell a flower, hug a tree, love an animal, be childlike by not being concerned about what you look like to others. Watch how desperate the mind becomes when it realizes you are the light in this dark world. These dark forces will not be satisfied with fifty-six percent of the population. They want to drag everyone into the darkness of forgetting the authentic self, which includes the forty-four percent of humanity who have an opportunity for transformation and entry into the new world."

Yeshua fell silent. After some moments, he looked towards Rose and nodded for her to speak.

In her soft, sweet voice, Rose addressed the group as a loving mother. "The glowing pink light, as well as the golden-white light of the divine, will provide humanity with a safeguard as they open their sacred hearts to their eternal wisdom and grace to transition into the new world. It is also advised to share the information on the quantum scalar technology that Angelina has access to."

Angelina interjected, "And please remember the importance of two or more coming together to multiply the energy field."

"Yes, this will strengthen you," Rose affirmed. "And, dear ones, please assure all my beloved children that I am omnipresent and that the moment I am called upon, if the requester is sincere and rests in the silence of the breath, they will feel a wave of peace throughout their being. It will grow and be more tangible as they deepen their practice and expand their energy body. The light shield will be a safeguard as they open their hearts to their divine wisdom to transition into the new world even through the difficult times when they are not sure if they can go on."

Angelina spoke after Rose stepped back. "I want to stress the importance of meeting in groups to meditate together. If possible, use the powerful waves of the quantum scalar to continue to neutralize and remove dark energies, as well as heal recent and ancient wounds. The program for the pineal wave will also provide clarity to those who are frightened and struggling by providing more clairaudience. I will make sure each of you is familiar with this technology before we go our separate ways."

"Jake," Yeshua raised his eyebrow, "in your possession is the Gospel of John you wrote over two thousand years ago that the Vatican suppressed. Teach the world about the angels, the elements, and how the life force heals and provides youthfulness and clarity. My missing years are not important at this juncture of humanity's survival. What is important to remember is that each person's vibration is what will govern their personal experience. Humanity is calibrated to the Universal flow upgrading their body each moment they choose Universal principles over fear, and if they detach from the old system they are protected and safe."

"I will. I promise," Jake said, bowing his head. *Nothing gets past Yeshua, not even the manuscript that I hid beneath my floorboards. And after the profundity and horror of my dream of Yeshua's murder, I no longer have any desire to convince him to stay a moment longer than necessary*!

Looking at the group around him, Jake winked and whispered, "We got this, right?"

"Yes," Andrew replied, "we have each other's back, and the entire angelic realm is behind us as well."

The mood lightened. But each person present knew that their time together as a group was short, and that weighed heavily on their hearts.

CHAPTER 91

"Good morning, Jake, I know it's early, but Jazz is in the shower and I need to come over and speak with you and Lisa if that's all right?" Andrew's tone was low and mysterious.

"Sure, sure. Everything okay?" Jake asked, shooting a questioning glance towards Lisa. She was sitting in the bed next to him. "Come on over," he remarked. "We were getting up anyway."

Jake jumped out of bed and threw Lisa her robe. "Andrew is on his way over. He wants to talk to us about something. Sounds mysterious." Jake answered the door just as Andrew was about to knock. "Hey, what's going on?" Jake asked with concern.

"I need both your help and discretion," Andrew stated.

"Sure, anything," Lisa and Jake responded simultaneously.

"I'm going to ask Jazz to marry me," Andrew said nervously. "Yeshua has already agreed to perform the ceremony, but I need your help pulling it together."

"That's fantastic, Andrew!" Lisa piped in.

"Thanks, Lisa. I honestly never thought I would be one to tie the knot."

"You better ask her first," Jake advised with a wink as he reached his hand out to congratulate Andrew.

"I called my secretary, Meg, yesterday. She is sending my grandmother's wedding and engagement rings by express delivery. They will be here today before noon. I will need help with flowers and whatever is needed. Lisa, I wondered if you and Veronica could help me with that? God, I hope she says yes," Andrew said, looking a bit concerned.

"Of course Jazz will! And we would love to help! How exciting. I will get on it with Veronica this morning after the group meets. We will be discreet. And don't worry, she will say yes!" Lisa assured him, joyfully smiling as she gave him a big hug.

Jake laughed. "Calm down, Lisa, or Jazz will be suspicious immediately."

"I know, I know. It's just so exciting and romantic and auspicious with Yeshua performing the ceremony! OMG, what about a dress?"

"Handled. My secretary is on it. She is a miracle worker. She knows Jasmine's size and style. She pulled together Jazz's wardrobe for this trip within hours. Besides, Jazz looks stunning in everything," Andrew replied with a twist of his mouth and a delighted smile.

Andrew's hand paused on the door handle. Suddenly his face went blank. "Lord, I hope she says yes."

When the door closed, Jake took Lisa in his arms and laughed. "Never thought I'd see that man jumping out of his skin. I must say, it's entertaining to watch."

"A marriage proposal from a sworn bachelor and playboy will do that!" Lisa chuckled. "Now, it's time for me to get ahold of Veronica and immerse ourselves in wedding plans. You and Tyler, make sure you are there to help Andrew keep his wits together."

"Veronica, it's Lisa. Andrew has a mission for us. It's all very hush and exciting." Lisa laughed but then was serious. "You and I are in charge of flowers and decorating for Jazz and Andrew's wedding. The catch is, Jazz doesn't know about it yet. Andrew is going to propose as soon as his grandmother's engagement and wedding rings arrive from England this afternoon."

"Holy crap, Lisa! That's delicious!"

Lisa could plainly see Veronica jumping up and down in excitement. And she was equally sure her free arm was waving around. It made Lisa smile. "Hey, you could get just a little excited," she teased.

Finding flowers was much easier than Lisa imagined. Winter in Israel was the best time for flowers and no-frizz hair days with zero humidity. Who would have guessed winter was the ideal time? With such a fantastic abundance to choose from, Veronica and Lisa were spinning in circles at first. Then they found the happiest, free-spirited flowers—pale shades of ruffled pink peonies. The florist was in the midst of making a bouquet for another wedding party when they spotted them. It was perfect. Simple and elegant—and a bit wild like Jazz.

They hurried back to the hotel to share their news with Andrew. The florist was holding three dozen peonies for two hours. "Veronica, look," Lisa said, pointing to the front desk. "Andrew is signing for a package. I bet it's the dress and ring for Jazz."

"Yes, let's tell him we found the most delicious fluffy pink peonies!" Veronica said with satisfaction. "I suppose we don't need to tell him about binding the stems with satin ribbon!"

"Too much info for a guy. But let's wait until we make sure the dress will match. What if Andrew's assistant sent an odd color? Let's ask." Lisa hid the fact that she would be so disappointed if Meg sent one of the ghastly dresses she had seen many of the Royals wear.

In the garden, Andrew got down on one knee to a surprised Jazz. His eyes were pleading. "Jasmine O'Sullivan, marry me. Marry me. I love you more than any heart could express. I want you forever by my side."

Jazz was stone silent. She obviously was not expecting Andrew's proposal. "Oh god, please say something," Andrew begged.

"From the first moment I set eyes on you, I knew some part of me loved you. I just didn't realize how much until now," Jazz spoke in an intimate whisper.

"Is that a yes?"

"Yes. Yes! Of course, yes! A hundred times, yes." Jazz overcame her shock and jumped into Andrew's arms.

"How could I have known that this fiery redhead I threw out of my office would turn my life upside down?" Andrew answered with a relieved laugh.

As Jazz extended her finger, Andrew spoke with such love and gentleness. "How is it possible that I could be so in love with who you are, and who I am with you?"

Lisa found it interesting to watch as Andrew slipped the ring on Jazz's finger. Her long, narrow fingers make the diamond look even more substantial. "I can see by the look in his eyes that he is concerned that it may be a bit much for Jazz. I have to smile because I can see she's beaming from the inside out. "Could this have happened to a more amazing couple?" Lisa asked Veronica, standing next to her.

"You mean, besides the two of us?" Veronica sassed back.

"Of course," she laughed softly. What else could Lisa say? "I'm just relieved the dress is ivory and very sophisticated."

Tyler whispered with admiration to Veronica, louder than he had intended. "You know Jazz could take half of someone's face off with that rock."

Jazz held out her fingers and gazed down at the six-carat diamond ring that had once belonged to Andrew's grandmother. "A bit much?"

"Heck no. It's perfect for you. Anyway, the good thing is, it's so big most people will assume it's fake." Tyler grinned.

"Jazz, hurry. You're going to be late for your own wedding." Lisa smiled as she handed Jazz her pink and green-stemmed flowers wrapped tightly with a wide white-satin ribbon. Her eyes followed Jazz's every move to make sure she would get to the altar without mishap. God, she looked nervous. "Are you getting cold feet? You don't look well." Lisa dreaded asking but felt she owed her that even though she didn't want an unfavorable answer.

"No cold feet, not at all. And I am not ill," Jazz said, still holding Lisa's gaze. "I just didn't think I could love someone so quickly, and so completely. I suppose I am waiting for the other shoe to drop."

"Believe me, I know exactly how you feel. But these amazing men are our soul mates, and they came into our lives for a reason. We belong together, and we both know we deserve the vastness of this love. I promise you, Andrew adores you, and I know you are equally devoted to him." As Lisa spoke those words to Jazz, she realized they were also for her to hear.

"You're right, Lisa. It happened so fast. It's all a bit overwhelming. My fears are unfounded and foolish. It's just hard to break old beliefs of unworthiness because of past failed relationships."

Lisa couldn't believe this wild redhead was now in an elegant, ivory-satin, slim sheath of a dress that fit like a glove, simplistic and beautiful beyond words, with pearls running up the center back. A transparent plain veil fell to the floor, held by a delicate row of faux diamonds to Jazz's swept-back and piled-up hair. A few long and loosely curled strands cascaded down the right side of her face. "Just wow, lady, just wow!" Lisa shook her head, beaming at Jazz.

Hearing the tapping on the door, Lisa knew it was time for the ceremony to begin. "He awaits you. You look incredible! Just keep your eyes on Andrew. No one else matters. Now go!"

Looking exceptionally handsome, Andrew stood outside the door. He reached out his hand and said, "Stunning."

Feeling the anxiety in her stomach, Jazz whispered to the incredible man in front of her, "Not getting cold feet? Your hand is shaking."

"Never. Just nerves. I only want to make you happy and never let you down. I hope I can do that."

Lisa loved being the fly on the wall, watching from right inside the door. *I knew it. He adores her.* It made Lisa smile from here to forever.

Jazz held him close and then released him as she looked into his eyes. "I don't expect you to make me happy. That's my inside job. Just be there for me. Love me the best you know how."

"You leave me breathless. I will never get enough of you." Andrew held up her chin with two fingers and ran his other hand gently down her face.

Lisa swore he had tears in his eyes. "Jake will never believe this," she whispered louder than she thought and caught Jazz's glance towards her with sparks of light flickering from her eyes. *Crap, I think I am going to ruin my makeup!*

Andrew put out his arm, and Jazz gratefully clutched it.

The chapel was intimate and held a magical glow. White and pink blossoms filled the simple altar as well as the four benches, two on each side. Hundreds of tiny white lights lit the rafters, appearing as stars in the night sky. Delighted, Veronica grabbed Lisa's hand as she passed through the arched doors and headed to their seats. "We did good," she whispered.

"Sure did," Lisa confirmed, not taking her eyes off Jazz and Andrew as they walked down the short aisle towards Yeshua and Jake. Andrew's hand was holding Jazz's, and every so often, he lifted her hand to kiss it. Jazz had requested to walk up the aisle with him. She said she had waited hundreds of years for this moment and wanted him beside her. Lisa spotted a face that wasn't familiar. "Veronica, who is that?"

"Oh, that's Andrew's assistant, Meg," Veronica whispered. "Seems she couldn't believe her boss was getting married. Anyway, she found the perfect veil, as we can see. Bringing it herself was the surest way to get it here on time. She is super sweet and said she fell in love with Jazz the first day she met her—the day Andrew threw her out of his office and told her never to come back. Ha-ha! Guess that wasn't in the cards."

"She's got a good eye. And she sure has Jazz's style and size down. Fits like she was sewn into the dress."

Yeshua reached his arms out to greet the couple and his beloved friends. He placed one hand of each upon the others. His words were a blur because Lisa couldn't hear or see anything except the expressions and tenderness between Jazz and Andrew. A few times, Lisa honestly thought she would lose it and not be able to stop crying. Jazz kept it together until she spoke her vows. They came from her heart. Nothing was written or rehearsed. Her words were as real and raw as love could be expressed. Lisa wasn't sure if Jazz even realized she was crying until Andrew pulled out his hankie and lovingly wiped her eyes.

Yeshua finished and, without delay, announced, "You are now one in the eyes of God. Love and be loved."

Andrew grabbed Jazz by the waist and kissed her now-smiling lips. Everyone stood and clapped, with a few howls thrown in. Lisa was in tears and noticed Meg was also. *Hmm, I heard he was a jerk before his awakening. I wonder how she could have stood by him all those years.*

CHAPTER 92

When morning light pierced the dark sky and the sound of birds singing filled the air, Yeshua paused and spoke with a firm voice. "Come, it is time. I know we all had a late night celebrating the union of Andrew and Jazz, but it is time to gather your coats and follow me."

The disciples followed without discussion, feeling their connectedness to each other and the energetic pulse of the universe. Their eyes now saw through the eyes of God and the glory of all creation. The air was gloriously sweet, and the quiet of the morn was welcomed.

The group had only been hiking for about twenty minutes before they found a beautiful ridge and made themselves comfortable, zipping up their jackets or wrapping their shawls around themselves to shield them from the chill of the morning air.

Yeshua had taken Jake aside the night before and shared volumes of ancient teachings, mind-twisting events and affairs taking place for eons regarding extraterrestrials, as well as the names and locations of those masters and saints on the planet who would help him organize and execute his wishes, as well as advising him on the distribution of the rare manuscript Jake held in his possession.

Yeshua knelt in front of Angelina, whose eyes had been closed to suppress the emotions she was struggling to process. He took her hands tenderly in his and said, "Beloved, I am saddened by your pain, as I dearly love you."

Angelina acknowledged the depth of his love and touched his face tenderly and nodded. "It is my love of you that rejoices for you," she whispered, "as I know you are always with me. It is humanity I grieve for."

"I know this well," Yeshua answered, "and that is why, in your room, I have left clear instructions on the power of joy and how its vibration aligns and creates a direct connection to God-Goddess. This understanding alone will save hundreds of thousands. I have also included information containing the covert operations your scientists, governments, and NASA have kept from the human race. They direct humanity's attention to government-created catastrophes, so humanity is ignorant of what they are trying to hide.

"Science points to the black holes as they explore the white wells of energy. Not only do they know how to tap into their power to travel instantly, but they know they can heal and rejuvenate the body, as well as the soil and water upon this earth. Travel to Mars decades ago was accomplished by tapping into these energy sources. What I share is but a brief overview. I would like you to include Luke, Aaron, José, Akbar, and Jake in the initial conversations before sharing with the rest of the group. Makeen, if you are willing, I would like you also to join the group, as you have extensive knowledge of warfare. I know it is not a life you want to remember, but you will be alerted to situations the others would not."

"If that is your wish, Master, it will be my honor," Makeen assured Yeshua.

"Thank you, my friend." Yeshua bowed his head to Makeen. "When you have concluded, a group decision will be made on which individuals and organizations to share this information with."

Luke stood, and Yeshua nodded at him, knowing he had a question. "Yeshua, do these white wells of energy have anything to do with using scalar waves to attract and assist movement within realms and planets?"

"Partially, Luke, and that is why I want you and José to be a part of the initial discussion once you analyze the information. Thank you for bringing Angelina the proof she had searched for, confirming that her visions of Atlantis were accurate. Both Angelina and Lisa are recalling more information about their lives in Atlantis and about its rise, its annihilation, and how they escaped."

Lisa's and Angelina's eyes locked. Their eyes filled with tears at the remembrance of the horrors and final days of the ancient city.

Yeshua reached out to his loyal friend Jake, grabbed him in his arms, and then looked him in the eyes. "You realize that every vision you have experienced regarding the past came to be true."

"Yes," Jake affirmed.

"Then know," Yeshua continued, "your dream of my future if I stayed is what would transpire."

Jake clenched his lips together and nodded as he held back his tears. The two men silently held each other tightly before pulling away.

Tyler, Veronica, Andrew, Jazz, and Lisa rose to embrace Yeshua before stepping aside for Angelina, knowing her heart must be breaking.

Angelina stood slowly, and Yeshua held her lovingly in his arms and kissed her face, her hands, and her lips. As much as she wanted to, Angelina would not allow herself to kiss his lips back; it would just make it infinitely more painful. Instead, she stroked his face, kissed his cheek, and brushed back his hair before stepping back. "I love you. Always have, and always will," she said, gazing into his eyes.

"As do I, throughout eternity," Yeshua acknowledged. "You were not only my wife, the mother of my children, and my confidante, but it was you who was intended to take my place when I needed to leave. This time, those here will not allow you to be silenced, undermined, or devalued, or to have your name slandered."

He reached out for Sarah, and both Angelina and Yeshua embraced her tightly. Yeshua kissed her forehead and said, "I will be with you always, my beloved child."

Yeshua turned his attention to Rose. He put both his hands out, and Rose took them in hers. They did not speak, but their eyes said everything. Rose kissed both of his hands, and after several moments, he took her in his arms and embraced her tenderly.

Yeshua approached Aaron and Akbar, embracing each. "My dear and trusted travel companions in so many lives, now we again must part. I entrust my beloved Mary in your care, and the other women who will need your support and strength as they step into their leadership roles to guide humanity. Love everything so profoundly that all else buckles beneath its strength. Remind those who are ready to grasp and embody this level of awareness, that out of the 'I Am,' the whole world is born."

"And I will always remember your words," Aaron added. "Loving does not mean condoning bad behavior."

"Correct," Yeshua responded, "and use caution not to judge."

"Fear not, Master," Akbar assured Yeshua, "we will do as you request."

Turning to the others, Yeshua spoke softly. "José, Tony, Ben, Luke, Makeen, Britt, and my dear sister Ruth, come, all of you, let me kiss and embrace my beloved friends."

Each, struck by the deep love they felt for Yeshua and the complex mission ahead of them, welcomed his adoring embrace. An ecstatic joy and strength filled each of them. Light illumined their minds, and their hearts filled with the grace of his love. As they were released, new awareness permeated their being.

"You have a lot of work ahead of you. The next time I see you, it will be right before the final days. As for now, you are ready. All of you are exalted beings able to step into your divinity," Yeshua declared as he gazed lovingly at each devotee. "And now, my time is up. It is time for me to leave."

It was done. Yeshua raised his arms to the heavens and bowed his head. "So be it."

Jake could not allow himself to think that in a moment, their beloved friend would be gone. He swallowed back his tears and yelled to the disappearing figure of Yeshua, "I promise, if there is a next time, the human race will recognize you!"

"Really?"

"Yes!"

"Even as a woman? A child born through the womb of a black woman?" Yeshua inquired with smiling eyes.

Jake smiled back as his friend's final words echoed through the canyon.

Yeshua was gone before Jake's panicked response slipped into the new light of day. "WAIT! How will I recognize you?"

In the stillness, as the pristine air filled Jake's lungs and the pinks and oranges of morning's sky collided with the bright orb of the sun, Jake had not expected an answer, yet it hit him as though someone stood in front of him and suddenly pushed him.

One word rang through the valley. Jake froze, standing as still as the statues lining the cliffs of Easter Island, listening until the canyon walls swallowed the final vibrations of the great man's echo, and then jumping with arms thrust overhead in triumph, he yelled, "Oh My God, That's Brilliant!" He shook his head and laughed as he hollered across the still-vibrating canyon. "Too bad the rest of the world didn't get to experience your humor!"

At that moment, each heavy heart turned to joy. The final gift bestowed on each of them was the blessing of pure awareness—"to be divinely human, fully realized" as Yeshua had promised. But this time, they would never go back to sleep. What remained was the imperishable self. No story, just timeless, pure awareness. Great peace and joy filled their hearts.

Lisa jumped up into Jake's arms, hugging him as he shook his head. "I like seeing you smile again," Lisa proclaimed.

"Even I surprise myself sometimes," Jake answered with a broad smile.

Looking at those who made up this remarkable community, committed one last time to assist those sincerely willing to change their lives to access the new world, Jake proclaimed, "Now we must disperse throughout the world and bring as many of the forty-four percent of the population as possible through the white wells in order to spare them from the upcoming apocalypse. No time to stand around. There's work to do!"

With one final glance towards the cliffs, Jake smiled and bowed his head to the man who was no longer there but always with them.

The women stood and joined hands, claiming their divine feminine power. Light enveloped them and filled every cell of their beings. They nodded in awe and acceptance of the role they came to play, and through a mist of tears, they turned towards a disbelieving but desperately hungry world.

Suddenly, a loud boom shook the rock beneath their feet, and a luminous, golden, diamond-white light pierced the morning sky. Before them stood a young man appearing to be in his mid-to-late twenties. He blinked his eyes and shook his head before exclaiming, "Mother, Grandmother, Sarah, where is father?"

ABOUT THE AUTHOR

Angelica Christi, is a transformational teacher, interior & landscape designer and mentor. Her focus is the liberation of all beings through the process of deep inquiry. She has never been interested in doing something for herself that she could not teach to the masses. She lives and works from the hologram and has a memory of circular reality, which is very distinct to her and very unusual for the human species. She uses innate wisdom and the insight acquired on her life and inner journey as a catalyst to serve humanity.

Her passion is guiding people along the path of personal awareness and transformation as well as assisting them to heal through beauty. "I believe the high vibrational energy of beauty holds a quality of light that opens and expands our souls."

Angelica was born with the ability to feel the pulse of creation and read the energy of people and the planet. At six years of age, she started creating remedies from nature to heal insects and animals. She also used the vibrational frequency emanating from her hands and energy field. When she was seven, Angelica realized not everyone could do what she did, so she suppressed her abilities to fit into her family and her world. When she was seventeen years old, others began recognizing her abilities; thus, she began a journey of remembering.

She is a lover of art, interior and landscape design, architecture, nature, photography, poetry, and the healing arts, and is passionate about traveling the world.

Angelica has lived in Hawaii, Mexico, Northern and Southern California, Oregon, and Washington.

ADDITIONAL TEACHING BY THE AUTHOR

Journey beyond the book with additional teaching by Angelica Christi. Connect with Angelica at http://www.angelicachristidesign.com

"Human life on our planet is on the cusp of evolutionary destruction. If we do not see ourselves as one people, one consciousness; a reflection of all of creation and align with Source energy we will cease to exist."

– Angelica Christi 2018